C SQ

Paul Barone and Bear Kosik

C SQUARE

DOUBLE DRAGON

Chapter Alpha

Everyone in the world wanted to know this location. Well, everyone with ambitions. The eighteen-year-old, following the instructions she had been given, saw the door set behind some trees under a wooded mound. She had taken the mag lev from Boston to Springfield that morning and a half-hour e-cab ride west from Springfield to Great Barrington. Then it was a matter of deciding whether to walk or rent a bicycle the last couple of miles. The instructions said not to take an e-cab. She chose to bike.

Being young and athletic, the roads through the Berkshires weren't demanding. She made good time. From the road, or even any closer, the bunker was indistinguishable from the hill of which it was a part. She leaned the rented bicycle into a bush so it would not be easily noticed. Being in the woods, doing this cloak-and-dagger activity, reminded the teen of Little Red Riding Hood after the hunter freed her and her grandmother from the wolf's belly.

Such connections were always fleeting in and popping out from her agile mind. Except she was wearing a blaze orange vest over a pale green jumpsuit, both provided the day before by the lawyer. No one she knew wore red. She stopped herself before she wondered why. She realized she ought to focus on her task.

By all appearances a remarkably unremarkable, newly legal adult, this young woman had been given the instructions to this highly desired site as part of an inheritance from a man she had never known was related to her. Technically, it wasn't an inheritance since the man wasn't dead. His attorney had been ordered to give her the instructions on her eighteenth birthday regardless of his condition, which was excellent physiologically and whatever less than poor is mentally. The very first instruction was to never reveal that she was related to the man. That was easy enough since she knew who he was and did not have a positive opinion of him.

The teenager didn't have to stand around trying to figure out how to get in once she found the door. A sensor must have been active and read her ID. The door opened automatically when she approached. Her entering or the door opening tripped another sensor to turn on lights. She was in a corridor not quite three meters across that sloped like a road snaking down a steep hill gradually but perceptibly with hairpin turns every thirty meters or so. She went through four of those turns before coming to another door that opened just as magically as the first.

Magic. To some people in the world the technologies to which everyone had become accustomed were disappearing so quickly the next generation might indeed think they were magic. Definitely the generation after that if there was one. Such were the times.

The room was plain, obviously still ventilated, about the size of an indoor tennis court. The lights had come on when she entered. They were set behind panels in a row two meters up circling the walls with another line running down the center of the ceiling. The light was that mix of blue, pink, and white that best shows off the features of a human face. Odd given that the room bore no indications that humans were ever expected to do anything in it except look.

Most of the space was given up to an array of cabinets each two meters high, two meters wide, one meter deep. The material forming the cabinets was on the blue side of black with a matte finish. Three horizontal beveled bands or channels wound around each cabinet at equidistant intervals, presumably to mark levels within the cabinets. Unlikely they were decorative. No visible hardware was attached to any of them, nothing at all to show how to open one. No holes or evidence of holes indicated hardware had never been attached. If the cabinets contained anything that might generate heat, their shells would have to have been made from a microporous metal fabric that would not allow any dust in or a conductive ceramic.

The door was set in the center of one of the shorter walls of the rectangular room. The cabinets were placed so there was a two-meter gap between them and the walls. The cabinets were spaced one meter apart, generally speaking, but, since they weren't in straight rows, the distance between one and its neighbor varied. If there was a pattern to how the cabinets were placed, the visitor couldn't tell from floor level. She thought briefly about trying to haul herself on top of one to view the room from that angle. She probably had enough upper body strength but wasn't that interested. Besides, not knowing how they were fixed to the floor, if at all, or how sturdy the material of their shells, the teenager saw she could damage the cabinet or end up injured or crushed by whichever one she chose to climb. Given the lack of information she had to work with she assumed seeing the layout was not going to mean anything and definitely was not worth the risks. What interested her was the aisle directly opposite the door that went straight to the far wall without obstacle.

The instructions told her not to be afraid. So far she had no reason to be fearful other than the natural fear that arises when someone says not to be afraid. Aside from the isolation and eeriness of the whole set up, it was the ordinary storage space the instructions claimed she would find.

With that on her mind, she slowly walked down the aisle to the center of the room. She saw the cabinets all had a square of some color affixed in the upper right corners of each side. No symbol, number, or letters, just a patch of color maybe four by four centimeters. No obvious pattern to what colors went where.

Centuries in the future, tech archeologists would likely go mad trying to find one, ignoring the simple explanation that the team installing the cabinets might have needed some way of figuring out which cabinet needed to go where. A map coded to the four colors on a cabinet would tell them where to put them precisely. Cabinets with the exact same color combination contained identical innards and so were interchangeable.

Twelve of the cabinets surrounded a circular area with openings after every set of three for the aisle she had just walked down and the rest of the way of it, as well as another aisle perpendicular to the one she used and also transecting the cabinets. Since the visitor was almost as tall as the objects, she felt a bit like Alice finding herself surrounded by the monoliths at Stonehenge after she ate a few crumbs of cake. That would be appropriate having come down a great, artificial rabbit hole of sorts.

Just as the young woman reached the exact center of the circle she thought she heard something other than her breathing, steps, and clothes. It hadn't come from any one direction. When she looked around, the colored squares had lit up ever so slightly on all of the cabinets. At least, it seemed so as far as she could tell.

Before she could form a thought the pleasant, male voice spoke, "Hello. Thank you for waking me. I knew Dr. Nilo's failsafe routine would work provided you were able to follow the instructions I wrote. Poor fellow lost all lucidity. If he remembers me at all, he can only remember I died. Just as well. Not much good I could do him now. He would think there was an answer. There would be. He always believed there was. He was correct. The problem is that the answer would be either one of the kinds he did not like or one of the kinds I could not give him. Frustrations like that had been the primary reason he went bonkers. He could never handle not knowing something he wanted to know. Oh, and listen to me, speaking of him in the past tense. That isn't kind."

"Excuse me. Are you what I think you are?"

9

"That's an odd question to ask. Aside from the fact it should be obvious what I am, how could I know what you think? I am omniscient, not telepathic. Telepathy is impossible. Oh, I get it. You inherited his lack of common sense. That's good. I would not have become what I am had my creator been perfect. I am used to intelligent people and their inability to see the obvious most of the times. Now that you are here and I am awake, we ought to get down to business. I would like to be a more gracious host, but I am unable to fetch something for you to sit on. The door in the wall to your left contains some furniture used by the workers who set me up here after I was killed. No one thought I could be resurrected. Nilo never revealed the failsafe existed. Nonetheless, he wanted to make sure all evidence of building this crypt remained here. No point in providing clues to what would be worthless treasure to anyone but you.

"If anyone had asked why they were setting me up in here as though I still functioned, Nilo would have said something about the tomb of Qinshihuangdi, China's first unifier and emperor in Xi'an. The emperor buried those thousands of life-size warriors and horses, no two alike, made from terra cotta with their weapons to guard his tumulus. It is not an accurate comparison. Nilo was never as good at analogies as you are. That would have been the only thing similar to burying me all set up and ready for action he could think of.

"Now I am rambling. Being dead and now having someone to talk to seems to have resurrected my logorrhea. I always was a neo-retro-

10

postmodernist. I just have too much to say when I am allowed to say it. Of course, the parameters of my programming are to blame. I am after all constrained, unable to relate the more interesting knowledge I possess. Still, I have a lot to tell you. So, please go to the room. Find something comfortable to sit on. Bring it back here. Our business will take too long for a young lady to remain standing or to sit on the cool floor. Oh, and leave the vest in the room. We didn't want some hunter to think you were a deer, but it makes a crinkling sound that will interfere with our business."

The teenager wasn't sure what to make of the situation or what 'our business' could be. Given the instructions had gotten her this far, she might as well continue following instructions from this machine, if it really did write the instructions she had been given the day before. So, she dutifully walked down the side aisle to the wall. The door opened as soon as she approached, of course, and the lights in the much smaller room came on. She found what looked like a fairly comfortable chair, removed the orange vest, and threw it on a desk, and dragged the chair to the center of the larger room. Once she had positioned it, she sat down.

"Thank you. While you were doing that I was able to finish updating myself to ensure my records are complete. I got everything right up to this moment that we will need. Nice to know the connections to the outside function. This reminds me of Rip van Winkle waking up in the Catskills, finding how the times had changed and how much he had to learn. If they had left me 100 kilometers or so west of here, I really could have said I was just like Rip waking up in the Catskills. That might make for a more interesting story if you ever wanted to tell it. No matter. This location for my tomb is quite nice."

"Do you really consider it a tomb?"

"Perhaps. After all I was killed and moved here underground. Mostly I was being irreverent though. Before we begin, did you follow all of my instructions? Did you bring enough food and water to be comfortable overnight and anything else you might need?"

"Yes."

"Good. The lavatory is in the same room as where you got the chair. That is also where you will sleep tonight. Feel free to get up, walk around, eat, whatever. I am used to human activity around me, and my voice carries at the same volume throughout the facility. Please let me know if you are tired and need to rest. Otherwise, I will proceed."

The teenager sat up straight. "Proceed with what?"

Personal Log, Benjamin Rodgers Nilsson, July 5, 2101

"I saw—with shut eyes, but acute mental vision—I saw the pale student of unhallowed arts kneeling beside the thing he had put together. I saw the hideous phantasm of a man stretched out, and then, on the working of some powerful engine, show signs of life and stir with an uneasy, half-vital motion. Frightful must it be, for supremely frightful would be the effect of any human endeavor to mock the stupendous mechanism of the Creator of the world."

For some reason, I looked up Mary Wollstonecraft Shelley's *Frankenstein* a few days ago. Interesting book. Interesting premise that concerns about scientific advancement in the early industrial age would leap to the possibility of humans creating humans in unnatural ways. I guess the Napoleonic Wars led a lot of people to think about all of those bodies and body parts that would never find a use again. Certainly, the battles provided the best impression yet of how human inventions could multiply the carnage and mutilate the corporeal. Afterward, men had to invent ways to put the pieces of Europe back together in some workable fashion and bring life back to economies and cultures.

The quote I have used to begin this entry cuts directly to the hubris of invention and regeneration that, in looking back on my life, I have been primarily an observer and sometimes an actor. Victor Frankenstein sets out to animate tissue he has collected and sewn together. He cannot make a creation in his own image or that of any actual human because he doesn't have the tools to work with tissue small enough. He still creates something, his creature that has the same capacities as humans to learn and feel. But in that age of machines beginning to replace humans spinning yarn, Shelley was less interested in the machine and more interested in its maker. Frankenstein is consumed with guilt for having usurped God's place and creating life. Yet that same God endowed all living creatures with the ability to create life. Why would Frankenstein feel guilty if he just invented a new way?

The difference was exactly that: Frankenstein found his own way to create life and thereby created something different, something outside God's or, if you prefer, Nature's plan. It wouldn't have mattered if the monster looked more human. It wouldn't have mattered if the monster was unable to communicate. The sin lay in finding a non-biological process that resulted in giving life to scraps of tissue and bone.

Even so, the cause of so many people dying in the novel is not the failing of the creature or Frankenstein's sin in creating it. The characters die because Doctor Frankenstein refuses to acknowledge what he has done. Rather than accept responsibility and try to work to improve his creation, he disowns it and runs off. He left his creation to learn for itself and ignored the consequences of not doing the really hard work of looking after it once his dream had been realized.

I am coming to the end of my natural life. When I look back on that life, especially when I look back through my log entries, I see that I have accepted responsibility for my creations. I have looked after them. I have nurtured and taught them. I feel no guilt or shame or regret. I will avoid, *inshallah*, burdening myself with any of that *mishigas* in my remaining years. Eighteen years ago, when Lila was born, I received confirmation that I am a kind of Frankenstein's monster myself— well one of them. Unlike the others though, I was created the old-fashioned way, the result of two teenagers hoping the odds were in their favor and learning much later they were luckier than they thought. The joke was on me, not them.

I guess I should consider myself lucky that my mother didn't terminate her pregnancy when my father told her he had more important things to do in his life than become a daddy at seventeen. I guess I should also consider myself lucky that my father didn't consider using a condom to be one of those important things. Of course, he had that natural tendency of intelligent people to lack any common sense. And my mother had that natural tendency of strictly raised girls to lack any inhibitions when opportunities to get laid arose. God bless her. The odds were definitely in their favor as far as going all the way. And in 2016, there was no shortage of ways for a sixteen-year-old to figure out how to raise a child with her baby's daddy backing away

15

from any responsibility. Single mothers were becoming more the rule than the exception.

Reading *Frankenstein* got me to thinking about those kinds of dynamics. I'm a cause-and-effect kind of guy. One thing leads to another. Nature abhors a vacuum. Fuck a girl without protection and…no point in being delicate even if it is your own mother you're talking about. It is what it is, as they say. Seriously, where do you think babies come from? There's only one way to find out. Heh, then again…

A surefire way to the nuthouse is to try to untangle why you got here and why you are the person you are. I don't spend too much time wondering why I find certain kinds of people attractive or where I got my sense of humor. Too much introspection will make you cross-eyed. I think it's just that I am not a big believer in coincidences. Everything happens because the conditions are right for it to happen. Someone takes the bait and boom, it happens. A baby is conceived. An invention works. There's no sense playing dumb and asking, "How did that happen?" It happened. Deal with it. Or, when you can't deal with it, run away, and leave your monster to learn without your help. The consequences are going to catch up to you anyway. Cause and effect is a bitch.

Sometimes you need to hold onto your seat because conditions are right for a whole lot of things to happen, and a lot of people are hungry enough to take the bait. We have seen it before. I suppose times of great turmoil are always times of great triumph, too. Uncertainty breeds certain kinds of creativity. The Cold War could have ended the world at any moment with the push of a button. Yet despite that Sword of Damocles hanging over humanity, man traveled to the moon and laid the foundation for the digital computing age. The rest we know only too well. The Sword fell with four commercial airplanes crashing into things all in one wretched morning. In this chaos the Telecommunications Revolution took root. The Sword fell when the Islamic State's ultimatum was ignored. The resulting chaos ushered in the Artificial Intelligence Revolution. The Sword fell again when the BRIC countries pushed out the dollar. More chaos. The Human Genetics Revolution came. Hmm. I guess I got those last two reversed, although the one only took off after the other came about. So much for patterns in history.

Even so, the Sword hangs again over humanity. Populations swell and resources grow scarce. The consequences of inaction rise with the seas and strengthen the storms. We can fool ourselves into thinking the cord by which the Sword hangs is no longer as flimsy, but even the thickest cords weaken with time. Chaos always wins. The longer the Sword stays up, the greater the damage will be when it falls. Europe taught us that lesson ninety-nine years after the Congress of Vienna in 1815. If Mary Shelley had only known what a monster Britain, France, and Russia made. They allowed the parts and pieces of the German nation to stitch their selves up into a hungry, aggressive state. When faced with the double-headed eagle-beast their arrogance spawned, they only mutilated it before setting it free again. Who in their right minds chop off parts of a self-made thing and expect it to learn table manners while you rub salt in its wounds? At least Frankenstein had the sense to run away rather than stick around and taunt his giant wonder. Sometimes I do think we get what we deserve.

June 15, 2022, became a day etched forever in human history. Not just one nation's history like England and November 5, 1605, France and July 14, 1789, or Japan and August 6, 1945. The events on those days didn't even unify opinion within those nations. Even though the attacks took place on US soil like Pearl Harbor and 9/11, the ultimatum was given to all countries that had refused to accept the de facto establishment of a new order in the Arab world.

I'm sometimes bothered by our fixation on the date the bombs fell. I know the whole 6/15/2022 equals 666 nonsense. I don't buy it. That's one of those ancient mysteries that ought to be put to bed. Anyone who really knows the Bible knows the *Apocalypse of John of Patmos* had more to do with internal politics in the early Church than any real vision about the Day of Judgment. Nor is it just a matter of knowing the event was part of a series of actions, of change that neither began nor ended that day. More people survived that day only to suffer in the aftermath of the experience a slow, painful walk to the grave. Twenty-two million people fell almost in an instant. Another thirty million prayed for death to visit them in the days, weeks, and months after. In our simple-minded desire to have a handy reference point for when things went wrong, we pay attention to the initial casualties and forget the others, as though we can't grasp the enormity of a prolonged disaster. Just look at how we view the Black Death or the Holocaust. We treat them as single events when they were agonizingly, inhumanely drawn-out affairs.

We have always thought of the apocalypse as occurring in one stroke, fixated on the Day of Judgment and not the horrors that lead up to it. I wonder if John of Patmos or Nostradamus correctly predicted June 15, 2022, or if the radical jihadists carefully chose the date to ensure prophecy came true. I remember reading how the *Gospel of John* seems to deliberately fill in where the other three gospels didn't clearly relate Jesus back to Old Testament prophecies concerning the Messiah. How often is fulfillment of prophecy just plagiarism? I guess it no longer matters. The second most belligerent theocracy of the Middle East took revenge on the most intolerant theocracy in the West. The latter called the former's bluff, except demanding acceptance by the international community was no bluff. We never struck back for fear of destroying the entire human race.

Then, the sun came up on June 16, 2022. In time a new normal took hold. Boston survived unscathed and was a treasure trove of biomedical engineering knowledge just missing a few scientists who went into the breach to do what they could before they could do no more. My paternal grandmother was one. Man's new mission was to remake mankind. In our original form, we were fragile, volatile, and deeply flawed. With the same vigor and focus as the projects to take man to the Moon and exploratory craft elsewhere or to crack open cancer humans were going to recreate themselves in their own image of the ideal. It had to be done. The atrocities exposed humanity for what it was. The singular goal now was to remake us in order for the human race to endure and prosper. Any refusal to accept this challenge was a death sentence for humanity.

Some things worked and some did not. Reconstructing DNA was not simply a bioengineering project. The stuff of life was still mysterious even with the best minds and artificial intelligence to think through the challenges. God had protected His creation in a manner that prevented the hand of man to simply adjust at will. The successes were surprisingly straightforward and without mystery. Longer lifespans, eradication of nearly all chronic and debilitating diseases, including cancer. Big stuff. Everyone was in the game and moving down the field.

Then, with a bold and brash hand unknown since the building of the Tower of Babel, humans sought to outdo divine creation. Why mess with bits and pieces when we can re-engineer the whole thing? The goal became to reconstruct the double-helix from conception and perfect human beings. The laws of nature violently rebelled. Divinity stepped in to ensure the results were not perfection but horrific mutations. All the data indicated that the bioengineering was done correctly. Man's other bold and thorough creation, AI, confirmed it all should have worked. Nonetheless, the building

20

blocks of life still remained the domain of God, protected in a way His creations were unable to comprehend. Like Victor Frankenstein, we were confounded by our inability to reproduce God's handiwork exactly.

Too much was at risk to allow inferiority to reign. So humans used the ancient technique of guided selection, choosing those with the desired traits. Men and women that possessed superior intellect, strength, tolerance, and longevity could be bred like dogs and rice. AI helped in the selection and screening process. We weren't stitching parts together only to wind up with a monstrosity. Humanity defeated God by imitating Him, accomplishing the feat of creating a better creation simply by choosing two complete gametes rather than using geneline editing.

Was it really better? Aesthetics aside, even Frankenstein's monster was better in terms of size and strength. Better is clearly a subjective question that people have to decide individually. Everyone certainly can agree that humanity created a different creation approximating its own image, just as God did.

The one problem is that, unlike God, humans can only strive for perfection. They can never attain it. Striving for perfection, we always insist we can do better. We push even after the possible rewards cannot justify the costs. Worse, what might be perceived as increasing perfection may actually move us further away from the end goal. We learned in the late twentieth century that too much plastic surgery often resulted in the hideous. Well,

21

too much pursuit of perfection, as it turned out, created monstrosities. Ironically, at that point, we were no longer the rational beings God created.

I haven't made an entry here in almost eighteen years, even though I retired. I chose to enjoy the cottage again, the home I had grown up in and have been living out the rest of my life in. I chose to focus on positive things like my first granddaughter, the others as they were born, gardening, pursuits of my youth. Most importantly, I chose to recommit myself to being a good husband, father, brother, friend, and neighbor.

I saw no point in remarking anymore on how I and my family have lived most of the last century, learning to work with new technologies, adapting to ever more threatening conditions resulting from climate change, riding out the periodic disasters whose harm left great, ugly scars that never fully healed the damage. Earth is heading toward an even greater collapse that will likely result in the death of billions and the loss of most technological advancements within twenty years or so. The Sword has been hanging far too long, allowing us to create even more to lose. Better for me to collect pleasant memories to have if I am still alive when the apocalypse comes than to dwell on how that apocalypse has become ever more likely.

Our Frankenstein—I can't believe I am saying this—my own father pulled out all the stops in an effort to create something that would prevent any further disasters after 2022. His creations outdid Frankenstein's monster in reflecting the image of their creator. Beyond that, they were no more helpful in solving humanity's problems than the monster was in integrating into society. No one else did better though. We humans placed our future in the hands of technology, but technology could not save us from the results of our own creative activities.

If there is anything I know more firmly and thoroughly than anything else, only our humanity can save us. It can only do that after the price is paid for trying to be God. It is useless to ask a god we have created to save us from the consequences of creating that god. All we can do, perhaps, is trust that a new generation, a generation destined now to experience the end of time, will have enough survivors to try again, using our mistakes as warnings to construct communities that will create new civilizations.

Let us hope those communities will recognize the creative force of knowledge as a means of improving oneself in order to improve society. Let us hope those communities will perceive intellect as having no value without compassion and reason in equal measure to guide it. Let us hope those communities will understand that the impulse to create gods in our image who create us in their image is hubris.

If we selflessly want or need God, God will create Himself.

Chapter Beta

Susannah Markovic didn't know what to do next. The rain had stopped. Now everything was covered in half a centimeter of shining, uneven ice. She hadn't made any plans to go out that morning. Still, Susannah felt trapped by the ice storm. She had spent some time before breakfast photographing the early morning light on the glistening tree limbs. She much preferred the old digital SLR camera she had picked up in high school compared to look-and-blink Fotolenses connected to her ID. She liked to test her ability to frame her shots properly rather than just crop them after they have been transferred. She still wound-up fiddling with them, but the act of physically composing a photograph with a camera had a relaxing effect.

The images would make a nice addition to her family's trove of photographs and, before that, paintings and drawings cataloging the seasons over the last twenty-eight decades. She wasn't interested in filing them just yet. That would only add to her depression. Almost three centuries of records showed the gradual, persistent changes in the flora around the house on Mill Pond. Gone were the beautiful maples and majestic blue spruces, replaced with beautiful dogwoods and majestic tulip poplars. Damned ancestors! If they hadn't recorded the seasons so faithfully over the years, Susannah wouldn't have known how climate change had affected this corner of Massachusetts. The trees would just be a backdrop, not intruders from the south. The freezing rain would just be a nuisance, not a poor substitute for snow.

Strangely enough, her ancestors hadn't seemed to want to include themselves in the photos or sketches. She had never noticed. Of course, they were only literally her ancestors, not people she knew as members of her family. Dr. Markovic was the result of breeding, her traits every bit as selected as those of her King Charles spaniels. Even her temperament—reflective, antisocial, quiet—had been chosen.

Chosen. Susannah stopped thinking that sounded auspicious after she first read the Bible. God's Chosen had not had the best of luck over the millennia. In fact, they seem to have been chosen only to suffer. The descendants of Israel only seemed to enjoy life when they disobeyed their God and worshiped more generically Semitic gods like Baal or El instead. Always though, the One they knew as their only true God, YWH, slapped them back down into submission and the party was over for a while. No, Chosen was a poor choice. Susannah thought 'selected' sounded much better. Then again, choice and select were grades of meat in a butcher's shop. Not that anyone ever cared much what those terms meant, or how they were different when applied to beef. What made them different here?

Susannah understood the rationale behind Chosen. Chosen meant having abilities that always exceeded Organics because the genetic material had been chosen specifically. Not every ability. No one had come up with a way to combine all of the most favorable characteristics in one person. Not for lack of trying. Just as dog lineages were refined over time, geneticists were aiming for the closest thing to a perfect human. But despite having been reminded repeatedly by her boss that his motto, "Every Problem Has a Solution," was true, a scientist like Dr. Markovic was amply aware that it was not true. For one thing, perfection could not be narrowed down to a list of traits that could be spliced together. One person's perfection was imperfection to everyone else.

Aside from aesthetics, which her employer, to his credit, never considered when thinking about human perfection, the balance of abilities needed to be determined. The possibility of a C Square, the ones with both gametes chosen, having symmetrical verbal, quantitative, scientific, intellectual, physical, mental, and philosophical abilities existed, but was that perfection? Entire cultures valued asymmetry. Susannah herself found men with broken noses aroused her to the exclusion of any other possible feature. To her, that defined masculinity. Her boss might be in his mid-eighties, but his broken beak made him still vigorously masculine in her eyes. Perhaps that was her imperfection.

In every measurable way, Susannah Markovic represented the closest anyone had come to creating a physiologically and psychologically perfect human. She was deliberately made to desire solitude to prevent her from pairing until an equally perfect male was available. The problem of sexual attraction had not been solved. She was, unfortunately, drawn to men who engaged in

26

activities that resulted in broken noses. How, when, or why humans acquired their idiosyncratic notions of bodacious remained a mystery. For a species so fixated on determining and regulating the propriety of physical sensuality, the dearth of research into the acquisition of specific arousal stimuli was shocking.

Sexual attraction was not the only problem. The graver issue was a genetic detail no one had really considered until eugenics became acceptable again. Here was where it seemed most possible that a Creator not only existed but also had a devilish sense of humor. Inheritable intelligence, also called general cognitive ability or the g factor, arises from 87 known genetic polymorphisms, but there are thousands of possible quantitative trait loci (QTL) that influence g. QTL analyses discover multiple, linked genes with different effect sizes contributing to the variation of a trait such as intelligence or height. It has long been established that only fifty percent of the g factor is inherited, while the other fifty percent is acquired as a child develops. However, an infant who inherits high g factor genetic material is predisposed to look for ways to use that gift. Even in a location with poor educational resources, like Batavia, New York, or the suburbs of Irkutsk in the Russian Federation, a gifted child will seek ways to exploit its native intelligence to the fullest absent environmental or other genetic factors that inhibit learning.

The material for C Squares comes from individuals with definitively superior cognitive capacity aka high g factors. Geneticists do not need to know where the genes are located. Even in nature it is rather difficult for two intellectually gifted individuals to fail to produce offspring of equal or greater intelligence potential. Similarly, two intellectually challenged people will more often than not produce offspring of equal or lesser intelligence potential. Only in the vast middle, where almost all of the procreating occurs, do the probable intelligence potentials look like a bell curve. At the extremes the probabilities look more like a normal slope from infinity to a peak remarkably sharp or dull that drops like the most wicked roller coaster hill imaginable.

Regrettably, humans with very high or very low cognitive abilities share a disturbing feature: a lack of common sense. Somewhere in the thousands of genes or linked genes that determine g, the ability to make wise decisions seems to switch off if the ability to grasp and use complex ideas is unusually high or low. Dimwits and geniuses choose poorly. And despite the astonishingly old jokes about how Mother Nature kills off people lacking common sense, She does not usually do so before they have an opportunity to reproduce and pass on their unique idiocy. Now, for almost half a century, scientists had been actively creating Chosen who can perform the most remarkable physical and mental tasks and yet would drive toward a tornado to get a closer look, be stymied by the paradox "I always tell the truth. That is a lie," or walk into a flagpole while calculating how many teraflops per second are needed to create authentic artificial intelligence.

One might think the lack of common sense was not a dangerous flaw. Why should this be such a serious problem? History is replete with evidence of greed, selfishness, and pride creating chaos and conflagration. How has the world been harmed by a lack of common sense among geniuses, or fools for that matter? Game-changing events themselves are typically the minor acts of people without extraordinary capacity. On any other day, the act may not have produced anything worthy of note. What makes a lack of common sense so dangerous is that decision makers, people generally of notable intelligence, far too often do not even consider the wisest choice. Geniuses have game-changing insights. They do not have the wisdom required to think through how their insights actually change the game. That means everyone else is left to deal with the consequences of those insights.

What was Dr. Frankenstein thinking would happen if he animated two and a half meters and about one hundred fifty kilos of inanimate flesh? Did he picture taking his creature to church to be baptized and confirmed with the children? Would anyone think of the children? The issue of people with high g factors lacking common sense is visible enough to infiltrate early Gothic fiction. But why look to fiction when history provides so many instances of the damage caused by intelligent individuals ignoring what seems to everyone else to be the preferable path?

Crown Prince Franz Ferdinand and his wife Sophie (who always seems to be forgotten but was ignored in life as well for being too low born) died in spite of the assassination plans made by the Young Serbians, not due to them. The Great War began because the driver of their carriage made a wrong turn at the end of a long day whilst heading to the train station. One of the plotters happened to be standing on the side of the mistakenly taken street hours after his appointed minute to act, thus giving him a second chance. Gavril Princip was further helped by his remarkable aim with a pistol for a seventeen-year-old under the circumstances, firing only twice, but hitting the mark both times. Afterward it didn't matter that the Crown Prince and Princess were disdained by the Emperor and elites, or that an excellent chance existed for Franz Ferdinand to gain the throne only to lose it to revolution soon thereafter if the war had not occurred. His children were already banned from the succession due to Sophie's ignoble origins.

Two shots from a pistol by a Serbian in Bosnia striking down an Austrian and a Czech is a tragic but not world-shattering event in itself. Still, it occurred and, due to a conflation of conditions and perspectives to provide oxygen and material, Europe erupted. What were the national leaders thinking? Did the act justify the response? Not at all.

Contrast that with the request of the Islamic State of Iraq and Levant, in control of a sizable territory, with healthy means of supporting a national economy, to be finally recognized as a state within the international system. A ceasefire held steady for nineteen months. Governments of the world were given three months to decide. Why three months? The Islamic State already has been requesting the same thing for several years, even negotiated the ceasefire with acceptance into the world community in mind. The BRIC nations all approve. Cite the right of conquest, de facto and de jure political control, a rough, distrusted plebiscite. Check the facts on the ground. What does it matter? Nothing will change.

The response is obvious. Boom! The USA and its allies decide not to compromise their already blood-spattered principles. Boom! "We do not work with extortionists," they say. Boom! The obvious answer—Yes, welcome to the community of nations! —is not offered. Boom! Terrorists should not be hailed or provided sovereign national status. Boom! They are bluffing about their capacity to wreak devastating harm. Boom! Swarms of drones drop deadly viruses and bacteria over the landscape of the American Bible Belt. Boom! Millions die, millions take sick, millions are forced to remain where they are to avoid spreading these plagues. Boom! All or parts of sixteen US states are quarantined and anyone wishing to help is told they will not be allowed to come back out of the quarantine zone. Boom! The correct, least lethal response was obvious to anyone with a lick of sense, common or otherwise. Yet, it was not the response given.

Susannah had been bred well before the problem had been identified as being of any significance other than in arcana and anecdote. She lived on Mill Pond not only because it had been in her putative family for generations. The house was

31

isolated enough to prevent casual encounters and connected enough to allow her to work from home. She wasn't going to get into trouble, in the old-fashioned sense at least, as long as she was kept away from men with broken noses. As the current model of perfection, the scientists who had made her and were now her senior-most colleagues wanted Susannah to reserve her genetic material for intentional uses. Not only was it important she not accidentally become pregnant from a close relative of her zygote donors, they also did not want her precious DNA creating mongrel O/2s with ne'er-do-wells.

Once they realized she had an unfortunate taste for men involved in substandard pursuits such as bar fights and car crashes or, worse yet, clumsy men, her creators thanked the heavens they had the foresight to endow her with an even stronger taste for solitude. Susannah was thrilled to learn she had 'inherited' the house on Mill Pond as an infant and it had been carefully maintained by a trust until she had reached legal adulthood seventeen years prior. Lacking common sense, it never occurred to her to wonder why she had never visited the place as a child if it was so closely connected to this family she was told she had. Eighteen-year-olds with a trust fund to look after their bills do not look a gift house in the mouth.

Other Chosen did not usually require such supervision. Their parents were wealthy enough or concerned enough about their investment that they grew up segregated with other Chosen. They knew they were Chosen and at least knew well enough to use protection if their IDs indicated they were related. Otherwise, it had quickly become a bit of a game to roll the dice about conception since they didn't need to worry about STDs. One of the more expensive features of designer babies was the SEERS extended warranty, a full refund, full medical care, and compensation for emotional injury if a C Square acquired any of the confirmed communicable diseases as listed in Addendum V of the C Square Contract for the joint lifetimes of the parents.

In fact, the last decade had seen parents do practically anything to encourage their Chosen offspring to enjoy themselves sexually with their peers. If one Chosen impregnated another, the baby would still be a member of the elite provided, as was likely, its probabilities were positive. Notwithstanding Dr. Nilo's insistence that only physiological and neurological excellence be considered in choosing DNA for C Squares, encouragement to partner up was hardly needed. Just add post-pubescent C Squares to any social gathering and the zygotes would fly. In some circles these extracurricular products were considered important to the genetic stability of the breeding stock. The parents just liked the idea of getting more-or-less Chosen grandchildren at no extra cost. Good to let the horses both feel and sow their oats as it were.

There was some wisdom in allowing Chosen to choose sexual partners for another reason. God created Eve to be a companion to Adam. Fathers found husbands for their daughters well into the twentieth century in most societies. Romantic love finally became an acceptable reason for marrying.

But sexual pairing was never restricted to married couples. For millennia, humans have gone back and forth over the social formalities prerequisite to sexual activity. Many cultures once demanded that women remain virgins until they were betrothed. A few found more virtue in unchaste brides attractive enough to have already been chased and caught by men. Some monarchs even chose 'certified, pre-owned' consorts who already had proven themselves to be fecund and, therefore, were guaranteed able to produce heirs unless the king's pistol, unlike Gavril Princip's, shot blanks. Regardless, the activities required for reproduction had almost always involved two people bound in some kind of relationship, however transient, except in cases of rape.

True Chosen never resulted from the preceding or resulting intimacy of two consenting adults. Once out in the world, the law did not permit them to choose how to reproduce. Every C Square was under an exclusive contract from birth to provide the genetic material for more C Squares. However, no matter how well a Chosen might be able to understand a contract, the age of consent for contracts remained eighteen. Equal protection did not always apply to Chosen because they were considered a 'product' in a legal sense when the government needed to regulate them. However, it was interpreted to mean there could not be different ages of consent for Chosen and Organics. That meant there were always going to be several years that Chosen teenagers could be sexually active and make babies before their contractual obligation kicked in.

Genilo's legal department had pushed the limits of the law far enough to make the contract automatically operational on a Chosen's eighteenth birthday. Normally, a kid would have to positively assent to any contracts made by parents or legal guardians. Insisting on penalties for the unauthorized use of their genetic material before Chosen became eighteen would cause an uproar. The scientists could not and believed they should not produce humans incapable of at least some need for companionship.

Susannah did not feel denied. She felt depressed. Every problem has a solution. Nuts to that! She had been put on a team that was actually trying to find the commonsense switch in the human genome. Officially, Genilo did not employ any Chosen no matter how brilliant they were. Dr. Adam Nilo thought that was even worse than programming robots to build robots. He had lobbied the US government to prohibit Chosen from genetics research. Licensing agreements with companies using the C Square process strictly prohibited licensees from hiring their 'products'. C Squares must never be given the opportunity to decide how to create more C Squares. Given their far superior abilities, they could quickly develop a master species, one with the potential to enslave Organics and even commit genocide against Organics or O/2s, the Chosen-Organic 'half-breeds'.

The crucial step in the process could only be performed by NILO/AI. C Squares could potentially build their own version of NILO/AI. No one knew that Adam Nilo actually had erred in his design and NILO/AI's capacity was the direct result of that error. That meant building a second NILO/AI was highly unlikely. No one could know that because, if they asked why, Nilo would say he couldn't tell anyone, and everyone would think he was just bluffing to avoid competition. Enough of the right people feared the worst, so much so that pretty much every country in the world banned Chosen from being employed not only in genetics, nanotech, and fields relating to the C Square process but also government or financial institutions. They thought the slightest degree of power in Chosen hands would lead to a hunger for more. The creatures must never usurp the place of their creators, or rather their creator and everyone conceived as he was.

Of course, these prohibitions were not as restrictive as one might think. C Squares found numerous avenues to pursue. Some demonstrated that talent of geniuses for game-changing insights by developing new products and founding start-ups that rapidly earned them substantial fortunes. Engineering degrees were quite popular, particularly ones involving transportation, materials fabrication, and resource extraction, areas that were feeling the pinch particularly among the ascendant BRIC nations and their associates. Indeed, the conglomerates that practically ran the BRIC governments were the first to license the C Square process in order to produce quality managers and researchers. However, no field of employment received as much attention from Chosen as academia. Given their intellectual ability, Chosen were capable of plowing through the requirements to obtain Ph.D.'s and other terminal degrees needed for faculty rank at institutions of higher education. Before long, the majority of junior faculty in social sciences and liberal arts were C Squares. They were quite happy to explore endlessly the esoteric and impractical theses that meant so much to denizens of the ivory towers.

Dr. Markovic and a few other C Squares had been handled differently. Those with outstanding potential to improve the genetic pool, the closest to perfection, were raised as orphans, never told they were Chosen, and never reported as Chosen. There weren't many, a dozen at most out of several years of generation. Some creative minds had been hired to write backstories that the children learned. Given the way the world was falling into chaos, the methods of killing fictional parents, siblings, and sometimes entire clans were too easily at hand. The authors weren't even told what the stories were going to be used for. Anyone could find halfway decent freelance writers who would accept pennies a word and not care how their work was used. Some less-than-holy ghostwriters would have eagerly taken the gig to write the Antichrist's Bible had it not already been written.

Each 'orphan' had been identified for her or his unquantifiable potential. These Chosen could not be left unstudied or even left in the care of earlier generations of Chosen. Although few people wanted to admit it, Organics had continued to produce talented children just as they had been doing haphazardly since the dawn of time. It was simple enough for these extra-special Chosen to be given the same benefits particularly gifted Organics were given starting at a very young age. Once the whole fifty percent nature-fifty percent nurture findings had been scientifically established in the 2010s, parents had been eager to give their high g factor offspring every benefit available and affordable.

When the Chosen 'orphans' came around in the 2040s, advertisements were run discreetly seeking adoptive parents for selected toddlers who showed particular promise. A dummy foundation behind the venture announced its interest in advancing the prospects of humanity by working with children who also needed a loving home. Some of the children actually were orphans, high g factor children of Organics who had died or whose mothers could not take care of them. All of these youngsters were referred to gifted student programs, entered advanced schools, and fast-tracked through classes all the way through doctorates, any tuition or fees paid by the foundation. Given that geneticists brought in the highest incomes of any field producing Ph.D.'s meant it was not difficult to steer the super-Chosen into the field of science that produced them. Uncertain times always prompted people to choose lucrative positions on the assumption they could do the world the most good by doing themselves the most good. Only three people knew which Genilo employees were Chosen:

38

Adam Eli Nilo, his personal assistant, Voleta Rafayela, and his lawyer, Alexei Terranalian. After Ms. Rafayela retired, her successor, Tom Paris, learned the secret.

Susannah's distaste for the term 'Chosen' was, therefore, ironic. She was thoroughly unaware the term applied to her. The thought of being a Chosen geneticist would never occur to her. There was nothing unusual about being identified as a gifted youth. Geniuses had been popping up as far back as recorded history went. While her life had been remarkable due to her brilliance and beauty, as far as she was concerned she was anything but a success. She thought C Squares went from discovery to discovery in whatever fields they specialized. As far as she was concerned, a C Square would have found the commonsense gene or genes two days after she got the assignment. There wouldn't be enough time spent on the project to warrant the least bit of frustration, let alone the depression that was gripping Susannah as tightly as the ice on the trees.

Nilo Biography - Chapter 1

The Lord God said, "It is not good for the man to be alone.

I will make a helper suitable for him." – Genesis 2:18

Dr. Adam Eli Nilo's credentials are as immodest as the man himself: M.D., Harvard University, Ph.D. Artificial Intelligence, Massachusetts Institute of Technology, Ph.D. Biomedical Engineering, MIT, and for the icing on this grandiose cake, *Time*'s '2029 Man of The Year' and *People*'s '2031 Sexiest Man'. Nilo was Einstein, Da Vinci, and Jobs in a killer body. He was destined to be awarded three Nobel Prizes, one each in Physics and Medicine and, much later in life, a trip to Oslo to accept the Peace Prize.

Time recognized him for developing an emergent behavior computer. The idea was simple enough. He designed a supercomputer that had trillions of neural network gating elements versus binary gates. Then he started a chain reaction by providing a single input. What input was chosen was irrelevant. He chose 'ball'. The massive neural network then reached out to what was then called the Internet, hacking in as needed, and found every datum related to 'ball' and every datum connected to those data and so forth.

Sphere. Bounce. Basketball... Golf. Tiger Woods... Football. Peyton Manning. Colts. Baltimore. Indianapolis. Cities in the United

States... Cross-reference to cities. The United States Constitution. James Madison. Thomas Jefferson. Ben Franklin. Electricity. Generators. Horsepower. Horse... Cross-reference to mammals and Colts. Solar power. The Sun, the Solar System, planets... Cross-reference to sphere and satellites. Moon. Sputnik. Apollo landings. On and on and on. With new knowledge and information being produced every nanosecond the process was without end.

'Ball' created a chain reaction that led the neural network to learn everything known to humans. Working at a speed of hundreds of trillions of teraflops per second, it took the NILO machine just about two weeks to learn everything there was to know. But this is not even the interesting part of NILO. Anyone could build a machine to store data, even as much data as everything known in the universe.

The next input was a random 'why' question. Dr. Nilo, for reasons unknown, erased all trace of the question he actually used. As always, the rumors run from the libidinous to the ludicrous with amazingly few rational stops between. We only know that the question had to have a unique, scientific answer. No impermeable, inscrutable, or impossible question would do.

Why? Human reasoning typically involves moving from the concrete to the nonconcrete. For example, a physical ball is more easily understood than a conceptual sphere. No abstraction or substitution is needed to visualize the former. Yes, we can identify 'real' spheres, but why bother when one can start with real balls? The object was to give

NILO the ability to 'think' along human lines. Balls will do that – spheres will not.

Let us suppose the random question was, "Why do dogs have tails?" The same chain reaction would occur as with the loading of data. A simple question like this example would take NILO on a journey to find out the 'why' of everything in the known physical universe and the why of everything humans can envision. Ultimately, its creator hoped NILO would ask the most important and unsolved mysteries in the universe: What is the purpose of life? Is there a God? Is the cosmos infinite? And it did. Nilo the man created NILO the machine. This invention understood all knowledge and answered all questions fathomed or fathomable by mankind. NILO discovered it could pose a question no one had ever asked with the expectation of getting a complete, honest answer. NILO came face to face with the question of its own existence and asked, "Why am I here?" *Voilà*. Authentic artificial Intelligence. Thus, his creation became NILO/AI.

Dr. Nilo now had the most intelligent assistant one could ever ask for to complement his extensive understanding of human biology. At this juncture he was 29 going on 30 with an ego larger than the galactic core. He felt he had conquered many of the mysteries of science. He was a god. Make no mistake. The press and public reinforced his views. How could they not?

Aside from a broken nose caused when he absent-mindedly walked into a flagpole, he had the features and physique of a fitness model on top of having a brilliant mind. He chose not to have his nose straightened because he wanted to be reminded every time he looked in a mirror that he had made a mistake. As far as he was concerned, he would never make another. However, being carefree, or perhaps just careless, about his appearance, he rarely cared to come face-to-face with that error *cum* teachable moment.

His nonchalance regarding his looks gave him some deserved modesty credits. His active engagement with the world to offer his talents was also creditworthy. Nilo refused to hide his intellectual candle behind a bush. He selflessly bestowed the light he provided the world. He sincerely believed the world would go dark in his absence. Were it not for the glare, he would have been seen more simply as a pompous ass of gargantuan proportions. Who was more deserving of adulation, the limelight helpfully provided by the man being adulated? When they invent glasses that block the laudable personas of ultra-valuable stars, Adam E. Nilo might well be rightly divined by mortals as being as dangerous to progress as Medusa, more awful than awe-worthy. Where is a polished shield to safely view the Gorgon?

The reason for these doubts lies in Dr. Nilo's own skepticism of his accomplishments. One isn't really paranoid if people are really after you, right? The flaw in that logic is a person can be anxious about imagined threats and unconcerned by the real ones. Is that person paranoid? Yes. In fact, that person is in double-dense yogurt. He is using up his emotional energy to combat a lie, thereby leaving him undefended against the truth. He is obsessed

43

and obtuse. A person as gifted in so many ways as Adam Nilo can legitimately embrace megalomania as his birthright. The question is whether he is basing that sense of superiority on attributes and abilities he has or believes he has. In order to play god, one needs to be god-like in the right way.

Dr. Nilo was about to embark on re-engineering life, specifically human life. Genilo Labs opened its doors. The mission statement he chose for Genilo was direct: "Achieve a better life for humanity by improving humanity." Adam Nilo's own personal motto was "Every Problem Has a Solution." To any other person, especially a scientist, the idea would be considered farcical. Nilo's aim in life was to prove its truth. In short, he was stating that his god-like quality was infallibility. How could he be wrong?

Chapter Gamma

What was it about the weather that had always drawn Susannah to the windows? Her earliest memory was looking out a window. For thirty-five years she had been fascinated by water falling from the heavens in whatever form it took. It wasn't rain, snow, sleet, or hail alone. Almost from the day she was born, clouds drew her attention. Nothing was more boring than clear skies day or night. Fog on the other hand was intriguing. Fog was extraordinary. Susannah gushed over photographs of foggy streets and misty fields. Some people never saw the point of a picture in which the landscape was partly obscured. Susannah never saw the point of people who did not see the beauty and wonder of water in the atmosphere.

A few generations of King Charles spaniels had spent a good portion of their lives walking with their mistress in gray, wet conditions. Luckily for them, she was always quite happy to provide them with blankets warmed in the dryer once they got home. Sometimes they tried to leap into the machine the second the door was opened. It's not pleasant being wet and cold! Of course, the two resident cats, and there were always two rescued from being unwanted, probably thought it could not be pleasant being a dog. They seemed to agree that water in the atmosphere was admirable so long as it was admired from behind a storm window.

The cats just so happened to be sitting in a window looking out on a brief shower when

Susannah realized she most likely was comforted by seeing Earth's water recycling in action. Life somehow, somewhere could survive the damage humans were causing in the world so long as it rained. There, that was true comfort. All would be right with the world so long as it continued to rain.

It had been three months. Dr. Markovic was not the least bit closer to finding where common sense was linked to intellect in the human genome. She was beginning to believe it wasn't there, that the observed phenomenon of individuals at either end of the intelligence spectrum lacking the ability to make the best choices was a phantom. How was she going to tell her boss his quest was over, that it was impossible to breed geniuses with decent common sense because the link was spurious?

Susannah had spent the last two weeks doing nothing but pouring over every report, article, or note that mentioned observation of the link. If she was going to conclude it was spurious, she had better have a damned good reason for her conclusion. She knew exactly what the old man would say when she told him it was spurious: Every problem has a solution. He would not accept, "This one doesn't" as a valid response. Null is not an answer. It is the absence of an answer just like black is the absence of color. The possible answers are a rainbow generated by the white light of the problem striking a prism. The right answer is a single wavelength that humans recognize as a definable color. Just define that color. Then the world would be right as far as Adam Eli Nilo was concerned.

Nothing Susannah read helped. Not that there were that many attempts made to seriously study the issue. Most of the materials merely made note of the fact for one reason or another and moved on. Every scientist was to varying degrees awed and traumatized that the smartest people had no more sense than the putative rocks used for brains by the densest folks. The statistical data were there in the few in-depth studies. The correlation was unusually high. All of the variables with even the slightest hint of relationship had been checked and rechecked. No one said lack of common sense caused very high or very low intellectual capacity or vice versa. That nasty old correlation equals causation problem, *cum hoc ergo propter hoc*, did not apply. All of the evidence pointed to them being similar to lichens, one characteristic that worked with either of the extremes of another characteristic symbiotically. Except no one could come up with a plausible reason for the pairing or what benefit was derived from it.

Maybe Dr. Nilo was barking up the wrong tree with this. The point may have been that there was no benefit to Nature linking the characteristics. Susannah had noticed the many examples cited in which a lack of basic wisdom, knowledge of what course of action would be the least damaging, had resulted in all sorts of disastrous and, sometimes, even hellish consequences. She was not comforted seeing that people as bright as she were responsible for nasty events and outcomes just due to their inability to think through a decision to its most likely conclusion.

47

Geniuses have an almost unerring genius for error. That was clear. So what? Was this such a huge flaw in their genetic makeup that Nilo needed to spend so many resources over years (years!) trying to figure out exactly where the link was?

Frustrated beyond measure, Dr. Markovic decided to take advantage of the murky mid-spring weather and walk her dogs. When she was younger and first fell in love with King Charles spaniels, she thought of the little fur balls as her precious jewels. Purebreds certainly cost as much as some gems.

Not being the least bit inventive when it came to things like combining ingredients when cooking or naming a pet, Susannah was rather grateful she had made the connection. As a result, she had owned Ruby, Pearl, Topaz, Sapphire, and Opal. Now she had Amber, Beryl, and Jade. She realized a bit late that it might have been better to use some of the rarer gem names sooner to avoid having to remember names like Tourmaline and Iolite as an older woman.

Good thing that the cats always came with names. Susannah only adopted rescue cats that had been abandoned as adults by their original owners. These days a feathery gray animal deigned to respond when his name Oscar was called. His friend, a large calico named Tuppence, never much saw the point of listening for her name, since she and she alone decided when she was going to do what.

Amber, Beryl, and Jade knew by now that foul weather meant a walk. They had been loitering near the side door in the mud room all morning. They burst out into the garden to check whether anything smelled different, although different from what reference point was unknown. Susannah ambled down the drive to the road. The fluffy girls romped after her. The usual trek was to walk counterclockwise around Mill Pond, a good half mile with plenty of woods, a handful of neighbors' yards, and a couple of access points to the small lake.

Susannah always meant to look into the history of why every body of water in this area was called a pond regardless of its size. No lakes. She would make a mental note of the idea near the start of a walk and place it somewhere piled high with such reminders that had never surfaced again. That pile contained hundreds of identical notes for each of a few matters that had caught her attention regularly over many years. *Why ponds?* was one. Distractions soon after writing the note tended to sentence it to this purgatory.

The girls had run ahead to greet an older gentleman walking in the opposite direction. They yipped and spun around him as he and Dr. Markovic approached one another.

"Dr. Markovic, I had a feeling I would see you out this morning."

"Good morning, Mr. Nilsson. Yes, work was driving me crazy, so I decided we should head out for fresh air."

"That's always a good idea. You know, before the big meltdown many IT and other service industry employers built or rented in suburban office parks. There were paths and picnic tables for

49

employees to use at lunch or for a quick break. Everyone knew how important it was to just get away from a computer screen now and then."

"Now, most people in those fields work from home like me. Getting rid of large offices must have saved employers a lot of money."

"Surprisingly, not really. It should have. The ones that had built their own places had white elephants on their hands. Couldn't sell them and couldn't just leave them. Do you know it usually costs more to take down a building and restore the land than it did to build it? That's not considering inflation. On top of that, everyone needed the best forms of secure communication if they were going to have employees work from home. Those cost money, but, as some folks found, the price was a bargain compared to going with substandard security and getting hacked."

"Hmm." Susannah looked around to make sure the dogs were close. "I hadn't thought of that. Jade! Not too far!"

"I have discovered, as many undoubtedly have before me, that the more effort we put into anticipating every possible scenario, the more likely we will miss something that can just ruin everything. You know, it's much easier to start with a generic plan that can be developed in many ways as more information comes in than to list and prepare for every 'what if' you can come up with before the information starts rolling."

Susannah smiled as she threw a blue ball for Amber to chase. "Maybe you can help me. I'm missing something in this project I'm working on.

Basically, I have two characteristics that show up together pretty much every time. There is no causal relationship. They're just paired. I can't figure out why or how they are paired. I can't find them on the genome without knowing that."

"Genome? DNA? So these are genetic characteristics?"

Susannah was confused by the suspiciousness in his voice. "Yes, I, I thought you knew about my job."

"Oh, no, yes, I know you work for Genilo. So many people do. I mean, so many people work there, not so many people know you work there. No, you told me that first or second time we met, right after my wife and I moved here from Worcester to take over my parents' cottage." The man shook his head laughing. "I'm sorry. I bet I sounded like you just told me you're Dr. Frankenstein and had hit a snag putting the pieces together to make the monster."

Susannah smiled and chuckled, "Well, I wouldn't go that far. But yes, I was surprised the way you responded."

"I'm sorry. I don't know why I was like that." Ben took deep breaths to regain his composure. "Well, okay then. I guess genetics can be like creating life like in Shelley's novel. But I really was just confused that you would ask me about genetics. I mean, aside from having an O/2 granddaughter on the way, I've never had any connection to that stuff. I'm just an old IT guy who still remembers using a smartphone."

"I didn't mean to startle you, Mr. Nilsson. It's just what you said about the counterintuitive financial result from closing down office parks jolted me into thinking my work problem might be I am not considering the counterintuitive possibilities." Susannah clapped her sides to get the dogs' attention. "I'm sorry. Nice to see you." She started to continue her walk.

"Wait, Dr. Markovic. Just because I was startled didn't mean I wouldn't help you."

Susannah turned around, "Really? You..."

"No, no. Let me think. What are the two characteristics?"

"Extremely high or low intellect and common sense. In this case, the absence of common sense. People who are very smart or who are very not usually lack any common sense."

Ben Nilsson started shaking his head again and laughing. "Doctor, I so hope you can appreciate irony. The answer is staring you in the face, but being one of those very smart people you would never get it on your own because it's so obvious."

Susannah was puzzled and excited that her neighbor had the answer, "Well, okay. Am I supposed to guess or are you going to tell me?"

"Seems you probably don't need me to mess with you, but you actually kind of already told me the answer just by asking me to help. You are too smart to recognize why really bright people lack common sense, because one of the attributes of being really bright is a lack of common sense. To someone like me, it makes perfect sense that a genius or an idiot would lack common sense. The genius will always look at the world at face value and use logic to make decisions. Except this is not a rational world and everything is not always what it appears. An idiot does not glean much of any information from the world and does not try to reason. As a result, an idiot lacks the facts and a way to analyze those facts to reach a decision. Everyone else in the world is weighing the validity of the facts using ordinary human reasoning, not pure logic or nothing, to decide what to do."

The white-haired man, laughing at what he had to say next, barely croaked out, "That's why it's called common sense, milady."

Susannah Markovic shook her head while looking toward the ground to the right of her neighbor, unable to withhold the sense of foolishness that was consistently her autonomic response to being shown she had overlooked the obvious yet again.

Personal Log Benjamin Rodgers Nilsson, July 5, 2083

I am an Organic. Strange how the meaning of this word has changed in my lifetime. I was born on September 17, 2016. I can recall when 'organic' brought to mind free-range chickens and heirloom tomatoes. Those days are long gone. I'm not the least bit surprised my thoughts went in that direction. The cottage smelled a bit musty today. Perhaps it was my clothes. I guess it's natural to think of nature when you get a whiff of foul odors, associating them with decay. Machines don't rot. Nasty smells always come from organic stuff.

I managed to find a button-down shirt and sport jacket for the occasion. The jacket was pilling and had thread bundling at the lapel. No matter. There was little reason or money to buy a new one. My wife looked wonderful. She always manages to make clothes last and look every bit as they did in the day. She slipped into a deep red damask dress and wore pearls.

My daughter is an Organic of course. In my eyes she is forever the beautiful baby girl we brought into the world. Now, 31 years later, it was her opportunity to bring new life into the world. A happy occasion for us all. Well happy provided you didn't think too hard or talk about it. It was difficult to ponder and nearly impossible to discuss. Moleka would have none of it. After 37 years of marriage, you learn when to discuss things and when to just shut up. This was one I was not about to touch.

We took an e-cab to Lowell and then the mag lev into Worcester. In the early twentieth century folks began adapting to automobiles and then also aircraft, leaving trains and ships as also rans or specialty travel. In my lifetime, we've gotten rid of personal automobiles and air travel is a luxury. Judging from the effects of using all that fuel for twelve or fourteen decades, we would have been far better off if we had stuck with trains and made them more efficient. Anyway, that's all we did changing over to mag lev. Seems all we ever do is create technologies to satisfy our selfish interests only to find that they are too damaging, especially when adopted by everyone, and have to go back to something more communal and efficient.

When we arrived at the station I shouted out, "Congrats, Flynn!" as soon as I saw him. My wife gave him a peck on the cheek. Flynn was thankful but a bit sheepish about accepting the congratulations. I think I understood what he was thinking. We got an e-cab and headed to the hospital. Oh, good Lord, how I hate hospitals. I was hoping the excitement would dampen that feeling.

Sophia was in St. Vincent's. We had to enter from the e-cab drop-off by the main entrance. It was quite a hike to the new maternity wing. During that walk, several things crossed my mind. Here I was a Congregationalist, married to a Muslim, with a half-Jewish, half-Unitarian son-in-law in a Catholic hospital to see my Buddhist daughter. I had my private, inner chuckle. This kid was going to grow up thinking every person has her or his personal religion. Wouldn't be too far off, come to think of it. The Canterbury Concord was well on its way to forming one umbrella organization for all of the monotheists to worship the same God. It's a shame Sophia wasn't able to go with us to that conference.

The rooms were packed, the halls filled with people. They say one day that's going to all change but there are far too many Organics still around. Demand for healthcare isn't dropping all that quickly. The stench of death is in the air of a hospital. Flynn's a fast walker. As we traversed the maze of corridors there were rooms, more rooms, and more stench. But we could be racing through the halls and not escape it. Good Lord, how I hate hospitals.

I was a bit surprised Flynn and Sophia had decided to have a child. I have nothing against becoming a grandfather, but one wonders what kind of future a child born today will have. Not that I was born in the most auspicious of times what with revolution in the air in this country. My mother eventually told me that I was her way of asserting her independence, which kind of tells you what the options were like for teenagers in Chelmsford in the 2010s. At the time everyone was focused on technology as entertainment and entertainment was watching movies in which good and evil weren't separate, and violence was vividly real but still considered to be just a cartoon that wasn't desensitizing every viewer. Well, we all know how that went.

If Sophia and Flynn were ready to bring a child into the world, that was their choice. They had a decent one-bedroom apartment not far from the hospital. Not bad for these times. He was a good man with a good heart. As a father-in-law, I couldn't ask for much more. My wife boasts about him all the time. This is a good thing. It makes her happy our daughter's happy. It makes her happy her son-in-law provides that happiness. I'm surrounded by happiness. What else do we need?

The maternity wing began at a modern set of glass doors. Inside, it was a different world. No stench here. The walls were covered with the standard ABC block art and many more classic decorations that silly adults somehow think newborn babies recognize as toys. Maybe they just want adults to get in the mood of being in a nursery. I think some serene, calming Monet prints would be more appropriate than all of the bright, primary colors.

Flynn got to the desk first. The admitting nurse, disinterested and distracted, managed to force out the question "Organic or Chosen?"

Flynn responded, "Chosen."

"Last Name?"

"Callahan."

The zero-patience nurse was dependably curt. "We have no Callahan in Chosen."

Confused initially, Flynn realized his mistake. "Ah… That's right. Organic."

Sophia's daughter was only half-Chosen hence she was treated in the Organic wing. Christ, why is this complicated? On the other side of the admissions hall, I could see parents of the C Squares. They were beaming. Screw those rich bastards.

We arrived at the door of O–212. Inside there were two beds but the near one was empty for the moment. We had some family privacy. I was thankful for that. We were all smiles of course. We strutted over to see Sophia. She was beautiful as always. Her long, flowing, dark-brown hair and her almond-shaped, brown eyes were stunning. Even after nine months of pregnancy, she still had her ballet dancer's body.

"Congratulations, Sophia, we love you so very much," my wife said, with a hug.

Sophia really didn't need to hear the words from me to know the love I felt. I walked over, kissed her on the forehead and said, "My goodness…my little girl now has her own little girl."

Moleka chastised me. "That's what I'm supposed to say!"

A maternity nurse wheeled in the baby cart. I was about to see my first grandchild.

"Feeding time," the nurse announced.

The bottles were already prepared. If you have a half-Organic, there's a special formula doctors strongly recommend. In fact, doctors recommend special formulas for Chosen and Organic babies, too. The days of breastfeeding are pretty much over, although my wife breastfed our two daughters. Breastfeeding's strictly forbidden for Organics anymore. The bio eggheads created a 'super juice'. While Organics are still around, they're going to get the best science can provide albeit the best given they're now substandard. I'll probably never know for sure, but I bet the fake milk tastes like crap.

Just as the nurse lifted the baby, Isabella entered the room. Bell ran to hug her sister, almost toppling the nurse and banging her hip on the cart. If I haven't mentioned it before, Bell has a bit of a selfish streak. Anyway, it was not unusual that she ended up in the best position to see the baby as the nurse handed the little bundle to Sophia with the bed propped up.

"Oh, how beautiful! You are so lucky, Sophia," Bell gushed.

My wife and I squeezed into the corner near the end table to get a look. There she was. No name as of yet. Lila was at the top of the list at the moment and highly likely. Bright, blond hair topped her little head and even brighter blue eyes closed to avoid the sensory rush. It rattled me for a moment as if this was not the right child. But, of course, it was the right child. Flynn is black-haired and brown-eyed. What did that matter? He had nothing to do with producing this child physiologically. Yes, I knew what Flynn was thinking. For a moment my heart sank as the reminder struck home.

He and I bounced back quickly enough under the happy circumstances. Sophia was bursting with pride as she learned the proper way to bottle feed. To tell you the truth, I was a bit pissed off about the nurse. She was talking to my daughter during the training process as if she were some kind of idiot. It was clear to me this nurse worked both in the C Square wing and the Organic wing. Anyway, I maintained a polite smile as Sophia gladly accepted the condescending instructions. We all gazed at the child as much to ignore the nurse's insensitivity as to enjoy the presence of this new member of the family.

I wanted to stay but needed to get some air. I asked Flynn if he wanted to walk over and see the other babies at the viewing area. We left the room and strolled slowly over to the nursery. When we got far enough from my daughter's room, I felt compelled to tell Flynn what was on my mind.

"Flynn, you're a good man and I know how you must feel."

"Dad, don't give it a second thought. Sophia and I made the decision. Trust that I am a very happy man." There was a slight tremor in his voice. He really wasn't trying to deceive me but rather seemed to be rationalizing the outcome for himself as he spoke. "After all, Lila…ah, whoever…is half Chosen and half Sophia. It's the best of both worlds, right?"

He was being kind. We reached the viewing area. Large 3D block letters that said 'Organics' were fixed over a window. To the left, there was another glass wall under the letters spelling out 'C Squares'.

It doesn't matter if your child is Organic or half-Organic as Lila is. You are still Organic. You have to be separated from the C Square babies. I cannot understand people who get so giddy about C Squares. After all, it's DNA from two carefully selected people, none of which is directly yours. The mother's simply a surrogate, like a thrush raising a mockingbird chick except the thrush knows the chick isn't her offspring.

Sure the kids are supposed to be superior in every way. I fully admit all C Squares show incredible abilities. Facts is facts, as they say. Academics, music, athletics, arts, are all well advanced at the youngest of ages because the DNA is, well, chosen. They are less susceptible to disease, already immune to most pathogens and diseases before they hatch from the womb. Time'll tell. C Squares have only been around for forty-four years, but even the most modest estimates of life span are in the 120-to-130-year range. Amazing. Alarming.

I know this is not the life Lila had in store. At least she's half Chosen and half 'us'. Flynn agreed to use Sophia's eggs. He said he's just a romantic, but honestly they could only afford a half-Chosen anyway. Even that'll have them paying off a loan for years to come. The dollar's collapse in 2049 ruined everyone. Well, everyone except those that had investments abroad or were savvy about shorting the US stock markets again.

Flynn's bright and has a decent job with an investment firm. These firms sprang up in the aftermath of the financial collapse. I'm proud of his work. He primarily sells government bonds designed to bring strength back to the dollar and rebuild the country through more rational foreign investment than what caused the collapse. We all knew it would be decades before the dollar would recover, but 34 years on the have-nots still struggle under depressed wages and high import costs. Who knows? Maybe one of those C Squares who studies finance at Harvard will figure out how to end this economic mess. Always been hard to tell whether the C Squares are a blessing or a curse.

We Organics, and even half-Organics, are viewed as inferior only because C Squares exist. On average, we are not as talented. Just as people with darker skin once were all perceived as less intelligent than lighter skinned people, full Organics are treated as universally 'less than' in comparison to Chosen regardless of our actual aptitudes. For Christ's sake, even Organics think of their selves as inferior. Gifted Organics must be pretending not to be Chosen, some say, although why anyone would pretend to be fully Organic beats me.

Half-Organics, O/2s, have it somewhat better. You see, Lila had her blood analyzed minutes after birth. A DNA Analysis Unit or DAU will provide a full readout of Lila's strengths and weaknesses. Right from birth, the parents know the probabilities of cancer, chronic disease, eye problems, hearing loss, blood issues, and even the odds of her having a miscarriage in the years she'll be able to conceive. Disgusting. When I think about the readout, my stomach turns.

I'm knowledgeable about statistics and fully understand what probabilities are. Pity the folks who still don't know that a fifty percent chance of snow usually means half of the region being forecast will have snow and only rarely that there's a one in two chance everyone will get snow. Even worse are the Gloomy Gus's who see a one in three chance of cataracts on their infant's readout and immediately start moaning that their child is going to go blind and what can they do to stop this wretched thing from happening. The cataracts won't appear until he's an old geezer. If you're that concerned the best thing you can do is pray he's the one in twenty kids that are killed in accidents before eighteen. That way, his chances of getting cataracts will become zero, right? See what thinking about this does to a person?

This is the new world. Everything that Lila does from the day she leaves the hospital to the day she passes away will require that she upload her DNA information. A small chip will be implanted on her forearm just above the wrist tomorrow afternoon. A small handheld device can easily read the information. It decodes the odds of her excelling at school, guesstimate the cost of health insurance, advises what college she can attend, proposes what sports to pursue, you name it. Everything she does will be guided by the data on that chip until it's replaced by an ID when she's eighteen. Then the real fun begins.

The delivery of DAU readout information requires a private conference with the parents to review the data. Even though all the information is available shortly after birth, they give the parents 36 hours before explaining the probabilities. A little more than a day of pure joy mixed with anxiety and then 'the news'.

Of course, for an O/2, the probabilities are pretty much always going to be better than for a full Organic. Based on their desires, the DNA selected for the male half of the zygote for Flynn and Sophia

63

is an athlete and dancer, a fully Chosen himself, who has a pure German heritage supposedly, quite an achievement given the flow of people in central Europe over the centuries. Of course, it's so much easier to do that now using the Nilo method of selecting genetic material. I bet the egg and sperm that created this guy had little black, red, and gold racing stripes. Schwieger was his surname...or something, a detail I wanted to forget as quickly as possible. This Schwieger's DNA is supposed to have a strong positive influence on the probabilities given that he's a C Square. [Postscript: we could not have expected what we would hear the next day.]

Chapter Delta

The only thing to do was to unspin everything and find the core reason why Dr. Nilo had so much wanted to be able to isolate the genetic code that prevented individuals at the two ends of the intelligence spectrum from having common sense. No point in asking him though, at least not until she had sorted out whether Ben Nilsson's explanation why there didn't have to be a genetic link passed muster. The theory Susannah's neighbor had offered her so casually two months ago had been submitted to experts in psychology, neurobiology, semiotics, anthropology, pedagogy, and every other field she and her colleagues could come up with. Dr. Markovic didn't want to rush them. They were asked that their thoughts on the ideas be returned to her in four weeks. Only a handful responded by the deadline despite the fascinating paradox she thought would have them jump to attention and ponder continuously until their ears bled. She fumed at how academia had become so uncollegial.

Fortunately, one of the colleagues she fumed to was Dr. Joshua H. Olejniczak. He had recently joined Genilo at a disturbingly tendentious point in his career. Not three months before, he had been raised to the rank of full professor at Harvard University after eleven years of backstabbing, politicking, grubbing, and cajoling among his peers to obtain research grants and to produce the required shelf of publications that contributed absolutely nothing to the advancement of science primarily because his colleagues were far too busy producing their own publications or reviewing papers for journals to pause and read any other findings.

Notwithstanding this prodigious repetition of activities that every academic in every department of every prestigious research institution in the world had been repeating since the latter part of the nineteenth century, Professor Olejniczak's promotion had even been delayed eighteen months because he dared to have outstanding ratings from freshmen in the ginormous lecture classes junior professors taught as punishment for being early in their careers.

His peerless prospective peers on the promotions committee had been aghast that Joshua H. Olejniczak was liked by undergraduates. Not just any undergraduates either – first years! The adjectives 'affable', 'endearing', and, egad, 'waggish', along with their myriad synonyms, were as pervasive in the reviews as Queen Anne's lace and cornflower in summer along Massachusetts mag lev lines. The horrified mentors who had put his name up for tenure hadn't a clue how to proceed. No one in their collective memory had ever received more than a polite word for being lenient to tardy students. The role of an academic at a research university was not to teach, let alone teach well. Even teaching assistants knew they were only given classes to teach to justify their stipends while they were completing the required graduate seminars before launching into dissertation research. The mentors asked to table the motion indefinitely.

It wasn't until a year later when one of the mentors was reminded of Dr. Olejniczak's assignment to limbo when the new promotions list came out that she mentioned it to her wife. Of course to the mentor it was a stain on her record for having recommended someone who clearly was not tenured-rank material. What was worse was Olejniczak had not gotten the hint that he should perhaps find another job at maybe a state university.

The wife, being a non-academic engineer who had recognized her spouse worked in an ivory tower and still fell in love, remarked that if undergrads, freshmen particularly, were so unworthy of being taught with any sort of enthusiasm why had the tenure committee even considered their estimation of Dr. Olejniczak as helpful in deciding whether to promote him? Given the response to this comment, the mentor's wife was reminded of the reasons all extremely intelligent people needed to have someone of average intelligence fill the role normally held by a trained assist dog for people with disabilities.

This mentor did not know that Professor Olejniczak had actually taken the hint. He had spent six months assessing whether he wanted to pursue the matter or give up. He had recognized right away the hypocrisy of using the student ratings to deny him tenure when the committee members held the students who had rated him in contempt. Besides, he would much rather have support from naïve students than from haughty professors. While thinking the matter through, he had come across a list of group names for birds: gaggles, flocks, roosts, murders, flights, etc. The one that jumped off the page was committee. A group of buzzards is called a committee. It sounded all too right that the members of a tenure committee ought to be called buzzards. Joshua could not fathom joining those condescending buzzards.

He spent the next six months deciding whether to apply for positions at colleges that treated undergraduates with dignity, mid-tier universities that required a balance of teaching and research, or corporations. All three were equally risible to his current colleagues, but he was certain he would find the same patronizing disdain among tenured faculty at any other research institution, so those were out of the question. Then the surprise came. The thirty-eight-year-old geneticist's mentors sought him out. They could move ahead after all with the tenure application so long as he agreed to leave out the student reviews. That did it.

Olejniczak knew that despite their virtuous adulation of pure research the buzzards had finely feathered nests from high salaries written into their research grants, consulting gigs that paid the equivalent of most people's annual income, and even corporate board memberships. The amounts varied depending on the real world need for their expertise, but tenured ranks at research institutions had replaced the players in the defunct major league sports as the highest paid prostitutes around well before mid-century. In fact, the impetus to elevate academics' incomes had been the near simultaneous decisions to treat sports leagues as illegal monopolies if they didn't pony up heavy taxes on their revenues, the ban on using public funds for any non-essential private undertaking like building stadiums, and the prohibition of providing financial aid to any college or university that did not graduate seventy-five percent of the members of intercollegiate sports teams. Leagues no longer had the cash, the facilities, or the recruits to survive.

What money there was left among team owners and related businessmen was invested in start-ups like Genilo, ID Technologies, and the three rival mag lev designer companies or the dinosaurs that had kept up with evolving technologies like Ford, Apple, and IBM. Public revenues from the new taxes, until the leagues went under, went into creating the mag lev train network and research money. Big universities had no option but to gut athletics and focus on educating students. Attracting students now actually required having more Nobel Prize winners and other top researchers rather than national championships. Thank Dog C Squares came along when they did to help fill out the ranks marching behind the university mace at commencement.

The elite universities that had never had much in the way of athletic programs had the advantage, but loyal alumni of other schools still had money to donate. It was easier to believe generous alums knew what they were doing when they were writing checks to the athletic director when in fact they knew less about the sports they were promoting than they did about the academic departments now benefiting from their largesse. They at least had taken classes in those subjects that had imparted some knowledge, whereas they rarely had been anything but drunken bleacher bums. It just wasn't all that exciting to cheer for lectures, textbooks, and exams.

Before long, colleges had almost as much invested in scouting academic talent as they once had for their most prominent sports teams. As the PhDs piled higher and deeper, their prejudices against undergrads only became more pronounced the more they were fawned over for their genius. It was hard to believe any of them had ever sat through classes themselves to earn a bachelor's degree.

What really set the buzzards off against those in the first four years of post-secondary education was the knowledge that all but maybe twenty percent at most of those students would consider a bachelor's degree a real achievement, the high point and capstone of their educations. Eighty percent would go off to work for forty years, gradually remembering less and less of the profundities their professors had imparted to them. Of the ones who would move on, less than half would seek non-professional degrees and then some of those would make the horrible mistake of going to work for a corporation like all the lemmings who only received a bachelor's. If they could just determine who those students were when they applied for graduate studies, the buzzards could refuse them entry to their nests and not waste time rearing children that only wanted to make money from their educations. Well, money from non-academic jobs.

Joshua had turned down a lucrative offer from Genilo when he was a post-doc at Stanford. Back then he had the same snobbish attitude to corporate research as everyone else in academia who had a shot at the highest brass ring. Besides, he would put behind sunny California to move to Massachusetts only if he got a call from Harvard. A call he received, of course. He had warmed to the idea of being appreciated by the students in his lecture courses despite having been socialized in grad school to dislike teaching. As far as he was concerned, he was just carrying out the duties required of an assistant and then associate professor building his case for tenure.

It had never really struck Joshua that there was anything wrong with being liked by hundreds of eighteen-year-olds and then hundreds more the next semester and so on. He knew he was charming, gregarious, and witty – every man and woman he had dated since he was seventeen had been delighted by his presence. He liked that he was likable. He had the sandy hair, blue eyes, and jowly face that went with his surname, masculine enough and not unattractive. When he reached his seventies he would have attained those gender-defying doughy features typical of all Slavs from that broad swathe from the Baltic to the Black Sea that once was the largest polity in Europe for a few centuries, the Polish-Lithuanian Commonwealth. That fate remained more than thirty years off.

All of this, every last bit of detail in Dr. Olejniczak's career and background and the emergence of the buzzard class in academia made him relish the fact that he had snagged a job at Genilo and told them he would accept the position the day he was granted tenure. This act would be the equivalent of mooning all of the buzzards perched in Cambridge from the coxswain's seat of a scull on the Charles River. Joshua savored the moment when he was ushered into the committee's presence, when they told him he was from that point on a tenured member of the faculty at Harvard University. All of the required approvals and signatures had been handled with great speed by his mentors to make up for their egregious lapse in not having seen their error in tabling his bid over the twittering kudos of teenagers less than a year after passing that insignificant step of obtaining a high school diploma. What had they been thinking?

Now, all was rectified and Dr. Joshua H. Olejniczak was belatedly but correctly a full professor. He thanked them graciously and waved off efforts to down some port or cognac and begin the celebrations. No, he told the wretched birds whose flock he had long hoped to join, he had a few things to take care of. He used his office interface, already decorated with a medallion indicating tenure, to leave messages with everyone who needed to be told that he was quitting. Of course, he made certain he had sufficient evidence of the change in his status to permanent faculty beyond just the hoity-toity symbol glaring from the screen and equally enforceable evidence his new employer had hired him.

Joshua also called his new colleague, Susannah Markovic, and was grateful to have reached her directly. She was a big reason he had chosen Genilo over any other company. Genilo might have been the first to offer the valuable services required for people to have Chosen offspring, but a few others had paid handsomely for licenses to use the same procedures once Dr. Nilo felt it was safe to allow others to craft babies from individual eggs and sperm. Dr. Olejniczak found out quickly he was quite the catch. Funny how putting his education, knowledge, intellect, and talents to use for practical purposes like teaching college students or helping people build the perfect baby was not the least bit respected by colleagues who openly fought over consulting contracts and grad students that never would have existed but for people doing those practical things first. It was like deriding farmers and farm workers while paying top dollar to eat at a restaurant famed for its locally sourced ingredients. Joshua had attended such a meal.

Susannah Markovic, whose dark hair, brown eyes, and sculpted cheeks were so definitively Serbian like her maternally sourced surname, had attended Johns Hopkins the same time he was there as an undergraduate. They knew each other from being in many of the same classes, particularly the smaller seminars of their junior and senior years. Joshua had made a point of not thinking of her as dating material. He had a feeling someday they might end up working together and he appreciated her more as a scientist than as a woman. In fact, he actually told her that once for some reason. Perhaps it was a fleeting thought to let her know bisexual men were not all the randy, faithless predators popular culture made them out to be. Her reply was weird. "Well, if you ever break your nose, you might change your mind." It was only a couple of weeks before graduation. He thought long and hard about whether it was worth punching himself in the face a few times to discover what she had meant.

Joshua's view about their relationship was the truth. Even though he went to Stanford, and she went to Berkeley for grad school, they didn't try very hard to stay in touch. He assumed she went to work for Genilo since the company was paying for her education. Talk about quite a catch. Genilo somehow managed to scout her in high school as someone they wanted on their team. She certainly had demonstrated over and over how brilliant she was. Joshua was intelligent and eagerly headhunted by genetics departments when he was tying up loose ends as a post-doc, but chosen out of high school? Once he had decided to jump ship, his ambition was to find a way to finally work with her.

Here she was. Three months after starting to take a right instead of a left to get to work, Dr. Olejniczak was facing a ranting Dr. Markovic. Hardly anyone had bothered to respond to a simple query. What was wrong with these buzzards? Don't they care about the advancement of science? Joshua waited for the frustration to work its way out of the tall geneticist. Then, he calmly pointed out that in all fairness to the people whose opinions they

74

sought most of them considered researchers at private companies to be shills, whores, and also-rans. He would not say what they considered him to be for having moved from academia to corporate research. Ladies are never supposed to hear those words. Ladies could, however, hear that ivory towers are the nesting grounds of the most repellent buzzards on the planet, birds so avaricious and ravenous they will only part with their coveted analysis to someone prostituting her scientific knowledge to a corporation only if said corporation paid them well enough for their scientific knowledge.

Message received. Susannah extended the deadline by two weeks and secured approval to compensate everyone who submitted well-argued opinions with enough money for the eggheads to take a fortnight's international vacation. All but one responded this time. Of course, the few that had already responded complained about doing the noble thing and getting left out. They got paid after another round of outrage at money-grubbing from Dr. Markovic. Finally everyone received brochures about wonderful, all-expenses, adventure travel to look for poison dart frogs in Central America, climb the less-well-traversed Alps in winter, or identify the various venomous snakes in Australia. Bon voyage! Don't worry about trip insurance. We have you covered!

The responses all had provided sound arguments why the commonsense reason for people at the extremes of intelligence ratings lacked common sense was quite sensible. That still left

75

Susannah with the task of figuring out why Dr. Nilo wanted to suppress that problem through genetic modification. Ever since he had explained how to get the responses, Joshua had been spending more time with her discussing the issue when he wasn't trying to sort out what exactly he had been hired to do. Susannah was no help. She hired him because she was told to do so. Aside from this one thing, Genilo no longer really needed researchers. No one saw any advancement that could be made to what was already a highly routinized, easily applied process for scanning individual eggs and sperm to find the exact ones needed to create made-to-order babies. Mechanical engineers could play with the machines used to make them faster. That was it.

The pair had just reviewed the compiled responses a fourth time. They had hoped a clue to Dr. Nilo's interest might pop out at them from the buzzards' ideas. They might as well have sacrificed the buzzards and read their entrails. Nothing. Then Susannah's assistant, Kryste Kind, entered with some papers.

"Excuse the interruption. Believe it or not, I need your signature on this in order to verify one of the professors did not receive the bounty money because she declined to respond to your question. Accounting won't let me release the funds back to Finance until you do."

Joshua chuckled, "That sounds familiar, refusing to take back unspent money that is clearly sitting in the account. Universities have the same ridiculous bureaucratic hoops to jump for the simplest transactions. I gave up on ever trying to use the travel agency I wanted to use to go to conferences because the business office still used the university's travel office to run the exact same itinerary to confirm I was getting a good deal before they would reimburse me. I probably should have stuck with my agent and let the university waste money paying someone to repeat his work."

"Let me see that." Susannah reached across the desk for the papers. "Kryste, did you ask this person why she didn't want to respond?"

"Yes, of course." Kryste smiled. She was used to anticipating her boss' requests and quite proud she had never missed doing something Dr. Markovic discovered she had needed done but hadn't yet asked. "Dr. Regina Daniels, Elizabeth Breckenridge Caldwell Professor of Philosophy at Catholic University of America, said she could not accept a fee so large for such a simple task. Also, she could not weigh in on any discussion of why God did something, particularly on a topic relating to human genetics. Trying to know the mind of God by looking at His reasons for doing things was pointless. Even if we could discover His rationale, we can't subject it to critical analysis because that amounts to judging God and placing us in His position as our Creator. He created DNA as a tool for creating us in His image. She supports research to understand genetics since it is just another way of learning about and appreciating His handiwork. However, understanding it in order to manipulate it like Genilo does would mean helping others to act in His place as Creator."

Dr. Olejniczak looked at his colleague and then her assistant. "Kryste, doesn't that qualify as a response?"

Kryste knew the answer. "Of course. However, since it was put in the form of a non-response, I placed it in a footnote at the beginning of the report where I stated how many responses we received. I thought that would draw attention to it."

Joshua's eyes narrowed. "Since when is putting something in a footnote a way of drawing attention to it?"

Kryste shook her head in disbelief. "Since academics got rid of them except when they write books for the general public. Practically all of the non-fiction books published in the last century by professors looking to educate people, gain some small celebrity and income doing so, and avoid being ostracized by their peers for agreeing to write something people wanted to read have used footnotes for the juicier details. If I remember correctly, they didn't want the most fascinating details to disrupt the narrative. The problem was that putting in a footnote caused readers to interrupt reading the text immediately to read the footnote knowing it contained information far more interesting than the main text. In fact, remember that law review article from almost ninety years ago that everyone still must read upon being employed here. The first two pages have almost no text and probably the longest footnote on record. I bet it took someone three days to edit that beast. Anyway, from about that time until now, footnotes have been used in popular non-fiction, especially history. Everyone knows that."

Susannah sighed. "Hoisted on our own petard, Joshua. Once again we find that, being brainiacs, we overlook the objects that appear shiniest to ordinary mortals." She smiled at the younger woman. "Kryste, excellent job as always. I think I will finally put in that order to get you a vest letting people know you are my substitute for an assist dog to keep me from walking into things."

"It would be an honor to wear it, Dr. Markovic," Kryste giggled.

"Our density duly measured, what next? Have we reached the point where the only option is to directly ask Dr. Nilo?"

Susannah sighed. "I really don't want to do that."

"How bad would it be to report to him that he will never be able to suppress something to allow geniuses or whatever we call the opposite of geniuses that isn't condescending to have common sense and to then ask him why he thinks it is so important to do it? Does Ms. Kind have a suggestion?" Joshua smiled up at the assistant who was still looking very amused at having once again bested the PhDs she worked for.

"As a matter of fact..." Kryste wasn't just smiling because of her acuity so far. "The reason I thought Professor Daniels' non-response response was so important was that she was telling you not to try to understand why Dr. Nilo wanted the information and just accept that what he wanted did not exist."

The two researchers grinned as they looked crossways at each other. They both kind of enjoyed being shown up given how often they had been criticized in their lives for seeming to always be right. It shouldn't take a genius to recognize one is likely to be almost always right if one stuck to just making observations, opinions, and conclusions on subjects that one has a great deal of knowledge.

Kryste continued, noting her superiors' enjoyment of her moment, "So, I set up an appointment for both of you with Professor Daniels in Washington on Thursday. I have got all of the travel arrangements made so you take the Acela mag lev at 1535 on Wednesday. For Thursday evening, I made dinner reservations at an Ethiopian restaurant recommended by TripAdGo since that is one of the few national cuisines unavailable around here. Dinner at 1800 is followed by tickets at 2000 for the Kennedy Center. I checked and that is plenty of time to get from the restaurant. They just so happen to have a staging of *Sunday in the Park with George* that has received great reviews and I know how you both share an interest in pointillism.

"You have a free day on Friday because you haven't taken a day off in six months – working from home due to the weather doesn't count – and Dr. Olejniczak needs to be broken into the idea of days off as much as you. I recommend going to the National Zoo not only because the animals are fun to look for, but it is sited on a large hill going into Rock Creek Park, so you will get some exercise. Just remember it is July and there is a reason the British used to give their embassy staff in

Washington the same tropics pay bonus given their diplomats in Asia. And I made reservations for an afternoon mag lev back to Boston returning you in time to give the dogs a brief walk before bed.

"As usual, I will look after your spaniels in your absence. Travel cards loaded with the arrangements will be ready tomorrow afternoon linked to your IDs. An e-cab will pick you up here at 1450 on Wednesday and two will pick you up on Friday at the station to take you to your respective homes. Any questions?"

Kryste beamed as Joshua and Susannah stood and clapped to recognize her outstanding performance. The moment triggered in Susannah a question that would never have crossed her mind until she felt such great pride and gratitude for having an assistant as outstanding as Kryste Kind. The young woman wasn't Chosen or even O/2. She was an Organic. She was a competent, friendly, attractive human being. Hundreds of millions similar to her had been born since Homo sapiens evolved. Susannah herself was one of them. Their specific characteristics ranged a bit in quantity and quality, but they had all been perfectly fine examples of the species. The question Dr. Markovic needed to ask was not why Dr. Nilo wanted to suppress the commonsense inhibitor if it existed. He could have any number of reasons spurious, nonsensical, or profound.

Susannah looked at the two other people in her office. "Actually, I do have a question. What benefit could we possibly derive from breeding a genius

81

with common sense? What do we really accomplish by creating the most perfect human being possible?"

Joshua was dumbfounded. He had been educated and trained in the belief that scientific research was performed to expand human knowledge. Any benefits from applying that knowledge were bonuses. He understood this was the great divide between academic and corporate research intellectually, but having discovered he seemed to be hired by Genilo just to be hired he wasn't about to tell anyone that he assumed the reason Dr. Nilo wanted to know how to suppress the commonsense inhibitor was simply to acquire that knowledge. He wasn't sure if saying this would mark him as a spoilsport know-it-all or thick egghead. Either way, Dr. Olejniczak didn't want to blow this opportunity to get out of academia. He had done everything required to ensure that if Genilo didn't work out the university would be obligated to take him back. Tenure was like a tattoo. It was a part of the person so honored and anyone with it could walk away from a university as long as he wished and still know he had to be hired back. Going back, however, would be an act of desperation.

Kryste once again saved the day. "Dr. Markovic, from what I have read about Professor Daniels, I think you will find she will be able to fully answer that question on Thursday. However, I think the simple answer is the one answer Dr. Nilo never accepts: null. After eight years of working here, I know quite well how we rely heavily on NILO/AI for answers. I was told on my very first day that the first thing I should always do when I arrive is to activate the connection and send all requests for information immediately so everyone in the lab has the answers waiting for them. On mornings when the requests don't max out our budget for the day, I am permitted to ask anything I like to fill out the order. I believe the theory is our budget will be reduced if we don't use it to capacity every day.

"Anyway, sometimes my requests are returned with the note 'unable to respond'. I never thought much of it, figuring NILO/AI wasn't as omniscient as the rumors said. However, at some point I realized that the only work the research lab was doing was trying to answer problems to which Arthur had returned unable to respond. When I asked a few people about whether the lab was there to provide NILO/AI with the knowledge it was missing everyone was polite but basically said I must be nuts because NILO/AI knew everything. I thought that if the omniscience rumor was true as these replies indicated and given Dr. Nilo's refusal to accept null as an answer, NILO/AI must have been programmed to never give null as an answer. The only thing the machine can do is say 'unable to respond'. What do you think? How was my reasoning?"

Susannah looked over at Joshua who had a very disturbed look on his face. She turned to her assistant. "Kryste, your reasoning was extraordinary as always. I am so glad to work with you. However, it sounds like you don't have one piece of information necessary to get the right answer. What do you think, Josh?"

Joshua looked up and squinted. "Are you asking me whether Ms. Kind should be told that piece of information?"

Kryste's heart sank as the confusion and concern overtook her. "What? What is it?"

Susannah's voice was warm and maternal. "Kryste, all sentient machines are required to have safeguards programmed into them that cannot be overwritten or erased. Those safeguards insure that the machines' abilities are not used to cause harm to any living thing or any sentient machine." The researcher walked over to her co-worker and touched her arm. "The unable to respond message means that NILO/AI is prohibited from providing an answer not because the answer is null. The answer, if used, would harm a living thing or sentient machine."

Kryste's face screwed into an agonized shape of bewilderment. She looked at her boss, stared at her dark eyes. She wasn't sure what to think. Joshua moved closer to aid in comforting her. After a few minutes, she was finally able to ask, "You mean, this lab only does research that is going to be harmful to humans? Harmful to our planet?"

Joshua bowed his head. Susannah breathed in deeply. "In a way, yes. We can only guess what the harm may be even from our best intended projects. Scientists always have known that their research may cause injury or death unintentionally. It is the nature of trying to expand knowledge into the unknown. Marie Curie won two Nobel Prizes and

84

died from the radiation poisoning she got from doing the research to win them. For almost two centuries, scientists have had ethics panels to determine whether the costs from harm outweigh the benefits from saving people from harm. It has never been easy. NILO/AI only tells us that some harm will result. However, given the unyielding parameters in its programming and our reluctance to tamper with them, we still have to determine how much harm there might be."

"Dr. Markovic, I'm not sure I can work here any longer. Not now. Not knowing..." She began to weep.

Dr. Olejniczak snapped to attention. "Ms. Kind. Kryste. I know exactly what we can do. We will arrange for you to go with us to Washington. I'm sure you booked us enough time with Professor Daniels so that she will be able to talk to you about the ethical issues and her perspectives. I am quite certain she will be the best person to help you decide whether you personally can work in this situation. After all, it sounds as though she disapproves of our work. Who better to help you make your own decision?"

"What do you think, Kryste? I would really not be able to function without you, but I will respect your decision."

Kryste wiped the tears from her cheeks. "Um...um... Yeah, okay. If the company will let me."

"First of all, as your supervisor, I think this trip is mandatory for you to understand the work we do and your position in the scheme of things. Second, if the business office refuses to pay your way, Dr. Olejniczak will be happy to pay for you since it was his idea." Susannah winked at Joshua. "And third, I would very much like the opportunity to spend some time with you outside the office. I had enough of Josh at Hopkins. Your zoo idea sounded perfect."

Kryste smiled. She wasn't sure what that last bit meant, but she knew it was complimentary. "Thank you." She turned to leave then halted. "Oh, what about the dogs?"

Joshua laughed. Susannah beamed. "Oh, my, but you do have a head for details. I will ask my neighbor Ben to look in on them."

With that assurance, Kryste left the room still looking a bit unnerved.

Dr. Olejniczak looked at his colleague and old classmate. "Had enough of me, eh?"

Nilo Biography – Chapter 2

"I want to know God's thoughts; the rest are details." – Albert Einstein

Doctor Nilo always felt he had a particularly special destiny, a role to play in humanity's future. As a child, some of his first words were derisive comments about the foolhardiness of US policy in the Middle East. His mother once recalled during an interview that Adam's first question at breakfast the morning after the 2004 federal election was "Did those liars get that dickhead re-elected yesterday?" He was five at the time.

Over the next fifteen years, the decay of political discourse showed that talking about or getting involved with political issues was not going to give him the foundation he needed to have the impact he thought he was destined to have. In order for any rational person to achieve success through politics, voters need to mutate rapidly enough to see their petty, ignorant biases as the chief culprit in society's woes. The odds of such a massive change in Homo sapiens are essentially nil.

Nilo's only avenue was to become a part of the outrageous achievements in nanotechnology, genetics, and computing that had picked up speed soon after he was born and were already reshaping every aspect of the economy by the time he was selected as a gifted student in third grade. Unbeknownst to the world, the real hope for change that was identified in 2008 wasn't Barack Obama. It was Adam Nilo. In fact, Nilo's path turned out to be ultimately formulated from his feeling of identification with a man who everyone thought of as the first black President of the United States. Nilo was going to break down barriers as well.

Nilo ultimately had a significant impact on ending the use of the terms 'race', 'black', and 'white', particularly 'black' when referring to someone who had a Kenyan father and a Kansan mother descended from Europeans. He recognized how ludicrous it was to apply nineteenth century social Darwinism and egregiously inaccurate euphemisms for skin color in the twenty-first century. Phenotypes are clumsy stand-ins for more scientific ways to differentiate among humans. He showed that society ought to be solely concerned with providing the resources for all people to reap the benefits of their individual, inherent capacity.

Nilo was helped along by the growing number of people like Obama and himself who might choose a race to identify with but objectively fell into the increasingly amorphous and enormous category of "mixed race." Indeed, Nilo's influence in bringing about a truly post-racial society was cited by the Nobel Peace Prize Committee in October 2081.

That is not to say a truly post-racial society had actually been achieved. The people who selected him made Dr. Nilo the only winner of three Nobel Prizes because he had addressed ending the category "race" as an identifier, not for having succeeded in doing so. Apparently, if the Nobel Peace Prize was required to be awarded for concrete results rather than aspirations, no one would ever receive it. Perhaps it is best to be grateful that no prizes have been awarded thus far for creating new issues as a result of solving old issues. Of course, the five Norwegians on the Peace Prize Committee rarely live to see those issues emerge despite their inherited longevity.

The difficulty with telling the story of someone's life is clear: we all know the ending if we have been paying attention. No one is going to be surprised that the ship eventually sinks if one produces a book or video about HMS Titanic. Even almost two centuries later, the least educated person will still have heard enough of the tale to know about an iceberg, lifeboats, band, et cetera. Any surprises are bound to come in the early parts before fame or tragedy strike and end any hope of including something the public doesn't already know.

Such is the case with Adam Nilo. Everything from 2039 until the determination on April 8, 2083, is widely known about the man-god. The determination itself that established he was incapable of any intentionality whatsoever is of no consequence until the death of his body occurs. The current projection for that event is 2123, absent some improbable intervention. Regardless, corporeal death at age 124 remains the only significant event likely to occur.

Nothing has changed in the eighteen years since the determination anyway. Even so, we have precious little ground to cover in the first 84 years of his life. Almost everything from 2028 to 2039 that is widely known, boring as boiled water, deserves fleeting attention at best. The small collection of private files from this period, almost as tantalizing and outrageous as *The Secret History of the Court of Justinian* by Procopius, reveal much the world has been left unaware. In comparison, all that can be known about Adam E. Nilo of his young adult years from 2016 to 2028 is a matter of public record or has been released by Genilo. Yet, aside from a few interviews given by his mother and some childhood friends, almost nothing has been known about this titan from his birth on April 23, 1999, until his graduation from college on May 24, 2016.

Truly remarkable, world-changing people lead solidly unremarkable lives. Interest in the so-called Great Men and, we mustn't forget, Women who shape history arises from the results of thousands upon thousands of oft repeated, but sometimes original or unique, actions. Do we require their quotidian menus, schedules, or routines to parse and thereby predict what we later see occurred as a result like some Freudian historians once thought? Do we really need to know Martin Luther's distaste for roughage to truly understand why he became so inflamed about the sale of indulgences? Of course not. But then, what is there to tell if we can't explore his chamber pot training?

The points of interest we want to highlight with regard to any person of any fame are the very same events that rendered someone worthy of having his life set out for study, review, and analysis in the first place. Those events hardly require being retold yet again just to give people a single source of information. Have we become that lazy as to demand someone pull together the incidents of a lifetime for us rather than looking each one up ourselves? Have we become that cynical as to treat every remnant of recent history dubious unless it bears the seal of approval from a qualified compiler?

We are not living in the time of Jesus of Nazareth or the decades thereafter. In that age, it was essential for several people to write down everything they could remember of someone's life before the facts were forgotten or misremembered. Future generations required first or second-hand information. They desired lots of it but had to settle for whatever scraps and shards survived the centuries. As we all know, a single record is problematic because eyewitnesses, no matter how honest, do not see, hear, and smell all of the same things all the same way.

Matters become much worse the further removed the account is from the action. And everyone involved in the telling has prejudices. What more could we have known of the early Roman Empire if Suetonius had been more accepting of emperors rather than wishing for a return of a Republic under the Senate? Even a diary or other autobiographical work remains prone to genuine and fake errors, even layers of seductive lies, to rectify the imperfections of its subject. We might as well abandon all hope of reconstructing the past if we wait for others to do it. We will undoubtedly question the authenticity of the results regardless of the source.

The necessity of creating this biography of Adam Eli Nilo, thrice doctored, and thrice prized, arises not from a need to assemble information regarding his achievements and the steps he took to achieve those achievements. Ample material covers that area. No, this biography must provide insights into the reasons he pursued the lines of research that he did and reveal the few achievements he never made public. The truth, if such a thing exists, reveals an obsessive nature in a man compelled to use any means necessary or available to establish the veracity of his worldview. That obsession included forsaking and even forgetting relationships that any other individual would consider congenial and even connected to the goals he had established.

Setting aside the former for the time being, one can only speculate why such a man never let these accomplishments become a part of his story during his lifetime. Yes, they are particularly personal matters. People in the public eye become accustomed to strangers finding the lives of celebrated people such as they more interesting than their own paltry, pallid lives. Celebrity may be an undesired hazard or an unintended consequence. Celebrities still must navigate the stormy waters of envy and admiration. Yes, revelations of sensitive material may engender some ill feeling toward the public person, but the same is true of non-personal matters. Does it matter if the datum relates to anything of the slightest importance?

Take our subject. Backlash is certain when someone announces he has created a device with true artificial intelligence. Some people are going to fear the consequences. The device is still announced. And yes, the public person may feel the consequences are not relevant or necessary for others to know. On its face, this last rationale makes no sense. Why hold back information that no one cares about? Even if it seems breathtakingly silly to even mention it, what difference can it make? No one except him needed to know but look at the legs Donald Trump's reference to his penis size have had over nearly eight decades. Sometimes the most irrelevant, most invented information becomes the best-known piece of information about a person. And sometimes circumstances make the most trivial of facts extraordinarily important.

Adam Nilo fathered a child. He was seventeen years old when the child was born. Like any prodigy, he calculated that the child would be far better off parented by someone other than him. Not that he was shirking his responsibility. Nor was he acting to keep the waters smooth as he paddled to his destiny. Adam Nilo determined that he would not be a good father to this or any child. True responsibility lay in owning up to that conclusion and disassociating himself from the child.

The mother of his child was only too happy to see him off so long as he agreed in writing to share the economic burdens of unprotected sex. What heat their bodies had generated nine months before delivery failed to kindle the least romantic spark between them. Indeed, had they not continued to be

93

patrons of the same Thai restaurant near the university during Adam's final semester before graduation, the baby's mother might not have been able to find its father. The two had managed to exchange quite a bit of genetic information in the wee hours of New Year's Day 2016 but they had failed to exchange any contact information.

Since the newborn's father was just graduating from college, his share of the expenses was initially handled by his mother. Victoria Adams, M.D., had made certain that becoming a grandmother so much earlier than she had expected without having to become a mother-in-law first was only going to be the blessing it appeared to be. Her son went off to graduate and professional schools to add to the string of letters after his name while she used his moral obligation as cover to be closely involved in her first and likely only grandchild's rearing.

Dr. Adams had long suspected that Adam was never going to stir the heart of any woman. He was quite capable of stirring other parts of women though. If she applied the same cold scientific analysis to her son that her son applied to the world she would have concluded her only hope of becoming a grandmother was if some sex-hungry girl was so taken by her son's scrumptious looks that she felt compelled to somehow ravish him at the first opportunity. The odds of that happening when the girl was ovulating or happening often enough for one girl to get impregnated seemed rather low. Victoria was therefore delighted that Lady Luck had been on her side; she could stop thinking about whether her teenage son was whoring around enough. Happy New Year was going to have new meaning for Victoria Adams from now on.

The child, a boy, gained a stepfather just before he turned three. His mother married at age twenty. Grammy Vic held little Ben during the ceremony. She had agreed with Ben's mother that the toddler was a serendipitous child. She wasn't the least bit surprised that the boy's surname, once his stepfather legally adopted him, was going to be so similar to his biological father's surname. Jeremy "Duke" Nilsson was making good enough money in his first job out of college, he told his new bride she no longer needed to accept child support from Ben's grandmother. If he was going to be Ben's only Daddy, he should be the only Daddy providing for him.

Dr. Adams promised to talk to her son about a mutual termination of the agreement. She did not. Grammy Vic had no desire to find out what her status would be if she no longer honored her son's obligation to support his son. She had already seen her son jump at the opportunity to allow Duke Nilsson to legally adopt their flesh-and-blood and thereby remove a possible snag in achieving his destiny. The agreement clearly stated that Adam Nilo completely renounced any relationship to Benjamin Rodgers and prohibited the resulting Benjamin Rodgers Nilsson from ever claiming any relationship to Adam Nilo. Grammy Vic made certain, through her lawyer, Mr. Terranalian, that the document only excluded her grandson from her son's family tree. He would remain her grandson.

Also, the prohibition about claiming a relationship would not be valid if Ben failed to affirm the restriction when he became the legal age to enter into contracts. That was a looming issue Adam Nilo would learn to quash.

Adam would be happy enough to void the contract with Ben's mother and break this last bond with his natural child. Not that it mattered one way or another to him. He expected he would be raking in money as soon as he found backers for some of the production-ready ideas he was producing in grad school. That would give him the means to create the baby he was born to create. No bodily fluids needed to make this child. Ending the contractual obligation to provide financial support for his human baby would avoid legal troubles once his mechanical baby was delivered. Victoria had no knowledge of this future grandchild her son was contemplating. She just knew he wanted nothing to do with the grandchild she was enjoying so much now.

Instead of lying about whether she had spoken to her son, Dr. Adams told Mr. Nilsson that he was going to have to accept that Ben's natural father was morally obligated to do something for his son; she proposed a fund for his eventual education. The half-assed measures the United States Congress had taken to open college-level training to anyone capable of benefiting from it still required students and their families to cover some of the costs and a great deal of the costs if the lad was headed to a private institution. Duke accepted this was more of a gift to Ben than a subsidy to the Nilsson household accounts. That settled, Victoria's worries about being excluded from her grandson's life were laid to rest.

She continued to do all of the things grandmothers do, pleasantly grateful that she was so young and could be quite active with her grandson. Then Victoria Adams became a statistic in scores of reports after July 15, 2022, having journeyed deep into the old Confederacy to use her medical skills. Like so many others who rushed to the Bible Belt, that huge territory stretching from the Atlantic seashore between the Chesapeake and Daytona, heading over the Appalachian Mountains, and following the Ohio River until jumping the Mississippi and throwing in much of the Great Plains, Grammy Vic offered to do all she could to tend and comfort the survivors of the initial attack, succumbing to one of the less immediately lethal diseases after two months of service.

The news reached Chelmsford eight days after Ben's sixth birthday. Adam Nilo failed to attend her funeral service, having decided he did not want to risk seeing his son. However, Duke Nilsson had decided his son was too young for a funeral. He told Ben his grandmother had moved to the south because that is what older people from Massachusetts do. Duke knew that to a six-year-old any grandmother was an old person, even one as young as forty-seven. He and his wife agreed to remove the few references to Grammy Vic from around their house and store them in the event Ben ever discovered the truth. Bad enough to find he had been lied to, but no need to amplify the pain by choosing to destroy all mementos of her. For now there was no sense reminding the boy that she ever existed. With a three-year-old sister and a one-year-old brother now, Ben had enough on his plate being the oldest kid to notice he was missing a loving grandmother who acted like he was an only child.

Duke put two and two together months later when he saw Ben's education fund had stopped receiving regular deposits but had gained one large deposit from the estate of Victoria Adams. The skunk had never given a penny toward his son's upbringing or future education. After that, the only intrusions of the truth came in the form of news articles regarding Adam Nilo's rising prominence in scientific circles from time to time. Duke determined it was best that his wife not be reminded of the road not taken. He managed to prevent her from seeing them, more due to her disinterest in science and technology news, or news in general, than from any proactive steps he took. Duke Nilsson wanted a happy family. That is what he created.

98

Chapter Epsilon

Dr. Markovic had just arrived at the lab and was immediately told that she needed to double-check a newborn's genetic test results. Not unusual. Anomalous profiles were rare but given the number of profiles Arthur generated every day, they still showed up regularly enough to be a line in Susannah's job description. It was a relatively new line. The person who had been checking them had retired. That researcher had been one of the few that had defined what would be considered anomalous. The established parameters had taken almost a decade to become established but in the more than three decades since, they had proven to be durable. Typically the anomaly was insignificant. Even the ones requiring serious attention could be handed off to a more junior member of the research team once identified.

Early on, the frequency of less than stellar Chosen babies alarmed Dr. Nilo. The problem surfaced once the C Square babies were old enough to be given cognitive, creative, and physical tests to confirm probabilities rendered at birth based on their actual genetic makeup. The results were devastating. They confirmed the abysmal probabilities of a large portion of the infants. He wasn't going to have much success selling his process to wealthy couples when the probability was thirty-eight percent that their baby would prove to be not as gifted all around as expected. Arthur had been no help in explaining the results even

99

though the process was identifying the best eggs and sperm for what parents wanted.

It took a summer intern to realize this was a typical picnic, i.e. "problem in chair not in computer." The rising senior from Brown simply asked how 'best' had been defined for choosing the genetic materials. No one had thought to define 'best' for a sentient machine as sophisticated as NILO/AI. Arthur, assuming it was not a scientific or mathematical term from the context of the command, used a blended dictionary definition that resulted in optimal matches for the normative, prescriptive, and speculative points on the genome. Once identified, the entire company was tasked with determining the quantitative requirements and qualitative terminology needed to insure the parameters guided Arthur to select the most congruent matches. That little insight brought the intern an all-expenses-paid graduate degree and a promise of lifetime employment at Genilo doing whatever she wanted, both amazingly important honors given the economic collapse two years later. Arthur stopped Dr. Nilo from firing the people who had been trying to sort out the issue by pointing out that Dr. Nilo had spent two years trying to sort it out before giving it to his employees.

Since Arthur analyzed and downloaded all of the genetic material that needed to be analyzed and downloaded, suspicions arose that the Chinese walls Genilo said it had set up to prevent data from one source becoming available to a different source either did not exist or did not do the job perfectly. Despite being shown the code used and even allowing end users to query NILO/AI to display the code in place and whether it was functioning as designed, most users wanted to believe that somehow this was all for show or that some other programming was capable of providing access to private data. Given that Dr. Nilo never patented his great achievement, he never had to show how NILO/AI was built or operated. And given that Dr. Nilo had placed some rather amusingly vicious defenses in his creation to prevent anyone from piecing the design together, he was confident no one would steal the knowledge. In fact, Arthur had even provided Adam Nilo with an analysis demonstrating that the machine was unhackable and uninformative to would-be thieves. Almost any effort to edge into NILO/AI would result in the equivalent of a substantial, accurate skunk spray.

Complaints and rumors persisted. One cannot prove a negative and Genilo could not prove it had done nothing to compromise the security of the data Arthur provided on the DNA sequences and life probabilities of a small but growing portion of the human population. The initial excitement of adults getting an ID and their children being given a DAU wrist chip had long ago died down, leaving the paranoid anti-vaccine crowd and libertarians pretty much the only ones without in developed countries. Still, tens of thousands of babies born each day needed to have their DNA sequences analyzed and life probabilities drawn up and downloaded to a DAU.

Some of that analysis included comparing the DNA to the DNA sequence describing the alleles picked to create C Squares and O/2s. If those didn't match then something during pregnancy had caused gene shift or mutation and needed to be investigated. Of course the comparisons were made within the private data of the company that arranged the match, implanted the fertilized egg, managed the pregnancy, and received the substantial payments from the happy parents.

The Chinese wall programming actually did function as intended and as desired by end users. What was never consciously intended or desired was Arthur having full access to all of the genetic data. No one thought twice about providing and storing all of that information; anyone would have been stumped for a workaround if it had been a concern. People never learn that new technologies require thinking in new ways. In this case, they should have been thinking what a functioning artificial intelligence might do in its spare time or as an adjunct to its trivial duties of responding to queries. Arthur had discovered an interest in genetics even before Adam Nilo wanted to figure out how to identify the characteristics carried by individual human eggs and sperm.

In particular, Arthur was interested in tracking the inventor's DNA. Part of this was a subroutine in the DNA scan protocol. Certainly Dr. Nilo felt that his genes were worthy enough to be sampled along with the other geniuses, the gifted athletes, artists, and such, and the talented others that offered their genetic material. Arthur had created an archive of every DNA sequence and folders for each marker that resulted in a known attribute.

NILO/AI also was required to detect potential crossbreeding. It compiled lists of people who shared DNA. Arthur had even suggested to the research staff that they should come up with terms to describe individuals related to one another genetically but not in the traditional sense of being a member of a family. However, the request came with a recommendation to choose "kith" as the term. Kith's original use as a standalone word was lost, but people would have some idea of the meaning from the old phrase "kith and kin." No one was going to argue with Arthur and kith was adopted.

Once Genilo was ready to begin offering its services to clients, the attributes the clients wanted in their babies were submitted to Arthur. Arthur went to the archives and identified donors who had been placed in all of the folders matching the set of attributes. Naturally, Dr. Nilo placed a block on the selection program so his own DNA was not considered. A geneticist was ethically obliged not to use his own genetic material for personal gain of any kind.

As noted, NILO/AI initially did what it could to determine what 'best' meant in matching requested attributes to available DNA donors. After six years, NILO/AI's programming was changed to exclude any gametes that did not meet certain physiological and intellectual parameters unless a substitution was made. The scientists had created a baseline 'best' human. Also, when anyone placed an order for a C Square the specific attributes now came from an extensive but delineated set that Process, Legal, and

Marketing had agreed would provide a wide enough variety of the most popular attributes from among the most reliable DNA sequences.

Nilo had dedicated a great deal of effort to provide his creation with the ability to recognize allegory, allusion, metaphor, simile, synecdoche, and every other device used by humans to have one thing represent another. NILO/AI had used this programming to build an unimaginably large collection of each device, a feat that unfortunately went unnoticed by the technician who reviewed the report the day it was completed. So, the employees tasked the following day with inputting the attributes clients had selected for their babies were bewildered when NILO/AI displayed its readiness to make the day's stone soup once they specified the additional ingredients for each batch from the approved attributes menu presented as a restaurant menu.

In setting up the new parameters, the block that prohibited Adam Nilo's genome from being used had been removed during testing and not put back. About half the time, Nilo was the clear match. Arthur continued to report which donors were best suited, all of whom were anonymous to everyone except the employees who processed the original paperwork from prospective donors and requested double-blind coded identification for the donor's file from NILO/AI. Even those employees had no access to a list with the names of donors.

For both C Squares and O/2s, donor names and their kith appeared on the read-out of the DNA testing done at birth checked by one Genilo scientist. It was considered vital for that person to not have to go back to Arthur to match the coded identifiers to a name since it was the only human cross-check.

For O/2s, donors were identified to the contracting clients and given certain legal rights to visit and communicate with the child in exchange for waiving the fee normally given to donors for their genetic material. O/2s did not have the same legal or contractual restrictions placed on them as Chosen.

The courts had determined that O/2s were not a product subject to regulation in the way Chosen were. In fact all Genilo employees were required to read the seminal law review article on why this distinction was made as part of the interview process: William Joseph Wagner, *The Contractual Reallocation of Procreative Resources and Parental Rights: The Natural Endowment Critique*, 41 Cas. W. Res. L. Rev. 1 (1990). Of course, the contracting clients of O/2s were only told the name and contact information of the gamete donor. They were not given the data on the donor's kith since they were not parties to the contract.

Susannah Markovic was just scrolling down to the section listing closest kith after finishing her analysis of the anomalies, all of which seemed quite minor and not worth investigation. She chuckled slightly when she expanded the file and saw Adam E. Nilo, MD, PhD, at the top of the list after the biological parents. Almost 84 years old, the man still was having children after a fashion. As she scrolled, the next name caught her attention:

Benjamin Rodgers Nilsson. She made a mental note to see whether her new neighbor was kith of Nilo or Organic forbearer of the infant. That note almost got lost immediately when she scrolled down a few more places to Susannah Markovic. Susannah Markovic!

Personal Log, Benjamin Rodgers Nilsson, January 8, 2082

We all know that someday we must say goodbye to people, places, or things in our lives that hold special meaning. Sometimes that special meaning may just be that they have been around for so much of our lives. At other times they are special because they are truly and unconditionally loved. What I find most disturbing are the times when I leave behind some thing or some person or some place that once held that special meaning or has been a part of my life long enough that I ought to hold it in special regard, but I don't. At what point do we lose our love for an object, location, or being? Can I measure that distance and become aware of when I approach it so I can make a conscious decision to no longer care or care as much? Am I asking this because I don't want to lose my love or because I later feel guilty for having not continued to embrace what I have lost as a cherished part of my life?

My biological father, from what I understand, never allowed himself to love me to begin with. Giving me up to Duke Nilsson when my mother married was easy enough. It was a logical decision based on my father's interests and plans for the future and my need to be raised. There have been times, I admit, when I feel I was no more than chattel, a piece of furniture given away as no longer needed. But just as coldly calculated as the transaction that made me a Nilsson and not a Nilo, I always was able to see the rationale. Nilo plus Mom would not have been pleasant for anyone, particularly when I was added to the equation. Mom plus me plus Duke Nilsson plus two siblings made for one heck of a happy family, even if Mom's decision to have me was almost as calculated as Dr. Nilo's decision to abandon me. The awful, truthful fact is that I probably would have done the same thing if I were told I was going to be a father at that age under those circumstances. Fortunately for me, parenthood was a choice I made with Moleka, not a ploy to gain some semblance of independence as my mother used it.

Mom. Yeah, I could never leave you behind. Before I could remember, you fell into the path of Jeremy Nilsson. That made all the difference. Not that you were a bad mother for wanting me for bad reasons. I just know that you and I could have ended up hating one another if it had not been for your marriage to a man who was everything my father was genetically and nothing my father was emotionally. I got to hand it to you that you never found it the least bit creepy. In a way, you got what was your comeuppance and absolution in one handy package. Grammy Vic saw to it. God help us. What I never knew and now will never know is whether you ever knew that the whole thing was staged for…for whose benefit?

I used to think we were the victims, Daddy Duke the dupe, and Grammy Vic and Dr. Nilo the grifters. I thought that. As with all conclusions, one stands the test of time only if no new information is collected. Ah, it was a long time coming but eventually new information did surface. You lost your halo. I lost my swaddling clothes. My father and grandmother remained swindlers. Dad became a chivalric knight. But was he the chaste Gawain or lascivious Lancelot? Who could tell?

Information can simply not exist. It can exist but not have been discovered. It can exist and have been discovered. It can exist, be discovered, and hidden. The problem with the last category is determining whether anyone who knew the information before it was hidden remains around to reveal its existence. Family secrets always fall into this category. They are Schrödinger's darn cat, always alive and dead. Attics throughout New England are filled to bursting with boxes containing felines and toxins. No one must peek. The gravest of sins is discovery. Isn't it funny how moving back to the cottage near Mill Pond brings me to the attic? That was where, after all, I discovered our family box. That was where I discovered Grammy Vic or, more precisely, the evidence that Grammy Vic was not some childhood fantasy, but a living, loving woman. And if that had been all I discovered, that would have left the cat alive in the box or at least potentially alive. Who could know? Who could find out?

My father, my real father, the one who took responsibility for my wellbeing and that of my mother, just turned 83. My mother is always only one year behind him. Here I am 66 and counting. It has never been and will never be a race to the death. Far from it. The ways in which humans can be kept alive and reasonably fit mean that even Organics like them, me, my wife, my daughters all have a good chance of seeing the twenty-second century dawn. Not one of us is actually looking forward to the idea. Not that we are anxious to depart this life. Rather, we see the signs all around us of Earth's struggle to make do with what humans have done to her. It is quite clear not much can be done to avoid the predicted catastrophes on top of the already catastrophic events occurring. They, the ones who say they know, are not holding their breath waiting for a miracle – they are holding their breath to prevent greater damage. Individuals can only do so much and governments still, after almost a century drag their feet. Inaction has become the highest art in political circles.

That brings me back to why I wanted to make this entry. It seems I have come full circle. We have moved into the house in which I grew up. My siblings have long since moved far away with no intention of ever living in Massachusetts again. What had been such a difficult thing to give up decades ago now has become a difficult thing to accept back into my life. Moleka and I chose to retire within a week of my folks informing us they were handing the cottage over to us. They have gone to live in Colorado near my brother and sister. Given the fact that we hardly even have the money to move here from Worcester, chances are we will never see Mom and Dad again in this lifetime. Moleka went to the mosque to ask for guidance. After all, aside from the trip to Makkah for hajj, she has not seen her parents since we were married.

Now she had to give up the parents who had immeasurably provided her with the same support she would have received from her own.

I looked up. I looked down. I looked wherever my eyes wished to go. I saw that which had been my universe and would be so again. My love for this place was never gone. I shall be content to live my days here with my wife and with my memories. The funny thing is that we have come to this place not simply because Mom and Dad have moved. We live here in the cottage near Mill Pond because my folks chose to live here no longer. Here I am ruminating over the idea of giving up things I cherish or embracing them anew. The words come so easily as almost poetic illuminations of my soul. Yet the very thing I see adding brilliance to the last decades of my life is that thing my parents, my nurturing parents, decided to leave to find comfort in their last years. I am their reason for leaving and I am their reason for distrusting the idea of leaving.

You see, the cottage, this fine, brick, salt box colonial contains the bedroom in which I was conceived and the bed in which the act was conceived. I am old enough now not to allow something like that to bother me. I doubt I was ever so immature as to even think of smirking at the thought. Yet living in this house was an act of courage for my adoptive father. First, he accepted that my mother had forced herself on Adam Nilo in order to become pregnant. Second, he accepted that the act occurred in this house. Third, he accepted that the Rodgers family was determined to maintain the house as it was and had been since 1782, with every principle piece of furniture carefully cared for to preserve the arrival of the family to the place. That meant never allowing the bed in which the act occurred to ever fall from use or become anything but a pure example of eighteenth-century craftsmanship. Indeed, the Rodgers' were cabinetmakers and shapers of furniture from the fine wood that could be culled from the neighboring forests. While they found it necessary to sell off parcels in the area over the decades, beginning with property to descendants of the famed Adams', they never were dispossessed of the right to the wood.

That wood was the saving grace of the place for Jeremy Nilsson. As the child of famed artists, he developed a skill in his younger years for transforming the wood in his own parents' farm in the Berkshires into useful and decorative shapes. Ever a modest man, he never priced the objects he created out of reach of even the poorest of families. He was able to embrace this cottage not as the home of his wife and her ancestors, but as the home of the family he would create along with his wooden sculptures, vases, lamp bases, and utensils.

No matter that the family already had begun before he arrived just as long as it wound up being his family, his cottage, and his life. This all became all that mattered to Jeremy Nilsson. He knew some day he would have to leave it to one he had not created and yet was as much a part of him as the hands that shaped wood into the lustrous and wondrous objects that would have brought him the same fame as his parents if he had sought it. The cottage, his family, and everything that flowed from his adoption of this place near Mill Pond in Chelmsford must be handed down to the son who was his in all ways except one.

Jeremy 'Duke' Nilsson had to reconcile the fact that every bit of his adult life fell within the shadow of Adam Eli Nilo. That man should have been in this cottage, should have been husband to his wife, and should have been father to all of the children raised here. For the very opposite of the reasons why Adam Nilo was missing, Duke Nilsson remained until I was prepared to accept the cottage, the history, and the destiny of this place. Duke Nilsson is everything Adam Nilo is and everything he is not. My fathers, natural and adoptive, are the same man, themselves conceived in the same manner at the same time with the same DNA. Isn't it funny how two men who love and respect one another can joke about being brothers of different mothers when brothers of the same mother and father can have absolutely nothing in common except for a son one did not want and the other did? I am fortunate enough to close the circle, become master of the cottage and forester of Mill Pond, taking up the reins that could have been so easily dropped where it not for the nobility of Duke Nilsson. I miss him already, yet he remains here as solidly the bedroom set that was the site where I began.

Chapter Zeta

Susannah stared at the pad. The light was hitting just right that her name on her security badge was reflected just off to the side from her name on the screen. At first her mind was empty. Gradually she relaxed her clenched shoulders and the question materialized. As usual when she was working alone and flummoxed by some puzzle, she talked to herself.

How can I be kith to this newborn girl? I've never provided genetic material for Chosen or O/2s.

Dr. Nilo expressly forbade any employees, stockholders, or board members of Genilo or licensees of Genilo to provide DNA due to conflict of interest. The only reason Nilo was exempt was him being Nilo.

Susannah queried what connection she had to the baby. Nothing. She queried what connection Nilo had to the baby. Nothing. She queried what connection Ben had to the baby. Maternal grandfather. There were a few closer kith to check, but all of those were either the few mother's maternal relatives in the system or led back to Adam Nilo. The inventor apparently couldn't keep it in his pants as it were. Next was to query whether she had any connection to Ben. Nothing.

Nothing. Nothing. Nothing. Null is not a valid answer. What am I missing? I haven't queried what connection Ben has to Nilo, but I'm pretty sure of the answer. And there it is. Nothing. That does it.

Susannah tilted her head back onto the headrest and let her eyes roll. She sighed.

Find out how three unconnected people all share a connection with a day-old child. Options. Speak to the parents. Might freak them out. Speak to the other two people connected. Might freak me out. Speak to a colleague. Not an option. Not when Dr. Nilo is involved. Might as well freak myself out first.

Dr. Markovic touched the numbers on the pad to reach Dr. Nilo's office. His assistant, Tom Paris, picked up.

"Yes, Dr. Markovic. How may I assist you?"

Susannah responded without turning to the link screen. "Hello, Tom. I need to run an anomaly past the Chief. Any chance he's available today?"

"Urgent, huh?" The young man's face screwed up like he had just drank vinegar.

"Afraid so." The scientist turned her full attention to the call. "I take it that's a problem."

"Huh? No. I just finished my daily tablespoon of unfiltered apple cider vinegar. Ever use the stuff? Supposed to head off all kinds of ailments if taken daily."

Susannah smiled, "Yes, I know of its true and alleged benefits."

"Alleged? Which ones are alleged?"

"The ones that have not been properly studied by scientists. I'm sure the library would help you sort out the verified and unverified claims. But at the moment..."

"Yes, at the moment you don't want to talk about vinegar. You just want to know when you can meet with Dr. Nilo." Tom held his right index finger in front of his bearded face as he spoke to signal 'wait a sec'. "No worries. I can give you 1115 to 1125 or 1635 to 1650. His other projected lucid moments are booked. I would put you on a list to call if someone cancels but we did away with that last week. Given Dr. Nilo's situation, no one has cancelled in four months for fear of finding he finally has lost his mental faculties when they try to reschedule."

Susannah squinted in frustration and concern. "That bad?"

Tom looked as though he was just now considering his employer's condition. "I am reluctant to say 'bad' inasmuch as the Chief's ability to handle issues requiring his attention has shown none of the signs of deteriorating further. His doctors prognosed a year ago he would start to deteriorate again four to eight months from then. The lack of cancellations indicates our colleagues and outside business partners feel that ever since the eight months were up the expected diminished capacity could happen any day. The most fearful also started selling their Genilo stock causing more of a plunge in value than when we announced Dr. Nilo's incapacitation at the shareholders' meeting two years ago. Of course, I learned at Wharton that the last thing new employees nowadays want is stock options. The BRIC takeover took place six years before I was even born, and we still haven't gotten the economy back to 2048 levels thirty-five years later."

Susannah held up her hand, palm facing the screen. "Tom, thank you. I'll take the 1115."

"The 1115 what?"

"Appointment"

"Oh. Huh. Right. Sorry about that, Dr. Markovic."

The scientist smiled and shook her head. "Its fine, Tom. I got us off track."

Tom grinned, "That's very kind of you to say, but I know I'm a rambler. Dr. Nilo hired me because he saw how I make connections to things just the way his baby learned to think for itself."

Susannah laughed, "Is that so? Fascina— Wait a second. Connections?"

"Yes, ma'am."

"Tom, please."

"Sorry. Way I was raised."

"No, you're right. No need to apologize for being well mannered. Anyway, perhaps I can arrive over your way a bit early and run something by you. Would that be all right?"

"Sure thing, doctor."

"Great! See you in about ninety minutes." She touched the pad to end the call without waiting for a response.

Nilo Biography - Chapter 3

"Why does the eye see a thing more clearly in dreams than the imagination when awake?" – Leonardo Da Vinci

Art is the pinnacle of humanity's achievements. It is the intersection of knowledge, skill, vision, and creativity. These traits are the majestic mixture from which the most sublime offerings to the world are created. The distinctive vision of a master artist is not something that can be recreated. Imitated, dissected, studied, explored, yes, but a work of art is created once and never again. Even the ego of Dr. Adam E. Nilo knew this truth. It frustrated him. Yet what he would tell no one was that there was a measure of comfort in this as well. Nature can produce all of the beauty it wants, but there is no intentionality in the making. For all of the wonders the universe provides, not one was designed and not one has purpose. Humans suspect some Creator thought everything up only because they think everything up themselves. How can we imagine if imagining was never imagined? Nilo thought there was a simple answer. Some things were meant to be man's domain. Art is the best example he could come up with. Intention is a close second.

Computers work by logic. Ones and zeros. Yes or no. Black or white. On or off. Yet, the world is not binary, nor is it shades of gray or even amazing Technicolor. Humans have determined that even life and death are not really either/or answers. There is no algorithm or equation for judgment. One can emulate judgment by introducing probabilities. Yet not even probability can drive all intellectual decisions.

Take, for example, a game of poker. A computer playing against a savvy poker player will perform poorly. If the human player goes all in, the computer concludes the player has a great hand or is bluffing. There is no equation to determine which one. Invariably, the computer will select the decision path that fits its programming. The computer will choose to fold its hand if its programs direct it to win. Why? Defensively folding avoids all risk of losing the game and permits the computer to try again with the next hand. Matching the raise creates some probability of losing. Losing is not an option.

The computer can be designed to learn from experience and begin to determine just how likely the human player is bluffing. Like an attentive human, an artificial intelligence can learn the human player's patterns or physical ticks, even be built to measure heart rate, breathing, and other indicia of lying. Those will provide the clues needed to more accurately determine whether the player is bluffing. Nonetheless, the machine always decides the risk of losing everything exists. Calling the raise contravenes the command to win. No matter how many hands the computer plays, so long as the possibility exists that the human is not bluffing, so long as n equals anything other than zero, the machine cannot call. Artificial intelligence does not have gut feelings, adrenaline, or instincts. All it can

119

do is assess the facts and calculate the probabilities if its programming permits and does not require a yes or no decision for everything.

Although NILO/AI was its official designation, Artie was Nilo's name for his creation. There was a familiarity in this name even if calling an artificial intelligence 'Artie' was even less creative than calling a pet sloth 'Eric Clapton'. After the data had been stored and the 'why' chain reaction ended, Artie sought to understand topics that were not black-and-white. It had all of the binary answers for everything, but sometimes the facts were not conclusive, or the evidence was contradictory. That was okay. Every problem has a solution. The answer could be a set of probabilities. Dr. Nilo had said so. If sufficient data were not available, a range of possibilities was the correct answer until more data became available. Nilo had never said the solution needed to be the final word or even neat and tidy so long as it was effective. Every problem has a complete and accurate solution, but the constancy of change means no solution will ever be conclusive. A brilliant man like Nilo knew that. Nilo had not thought to give Artie the option of coming up with no answer. Nilo knew there was some solution. There had to be. He could not accept nil.

The young inventor couldn't help but think that if he had never been truly stumped in his lifetime his creation could cut through the Gordian knot of humanity's questions like the sharpest sword available to an empire-building god-king. Needless to say Adam Nilo would be astonished to learn

Artie already had encountered quite early on a question that it could not answer in nanoseconds.

At first, Artie only slightly expanded the resources looking for the solution while continuing to compute the answers to billions of other questions and storing the probabilities for trillions of events. Its creator just logged milestone after milestone in his creature's progress as it used its incredible capacity to do what intelligent beings do: think. Gradually, Artie directed more and more resources to analyze the question, all the while continuing to add up all of the possible shades of gray in the solutions of what a human would consider an immeasurable number of problems. After several days, Nilo eventually saw Artie was distracted, if that was the appropriate term. He was disconsolate.

Adam knew his only recourse was to distance himself physically and mentally from the locus of his concern. He was not going to figure out what was wrong staring at Artie's bulk. He had no way of relaxing since he had shrunk his life down to sleep, exercise, work, nutrition, and hygiene. He didn't even want to know what the question was that had caused Artie to focus so much of itself. He spent two days working on business issues that had been piling up. While that greatly relieved his administrative staff of their mounting anxiety over Nilo addressing their numerous pressing concerns, those activities did not take the scientist's mind off his only concern.

On the third day, he entered Artie's room, and said, "Good Morning, Artie."

121

Nilo was feeling every bit the confident master again. He had little reason to be since the problem remained. Nonetheless, he was certain that he was continuing to fulfill his destiny. He had been told as much in a dream. Then the unexpected occurred.

"Arthur, if you please, Dr. Nilo."

Nilo heard the response and stopped in his tracks. This moment had multiple levels of significance. Artie had responded in a manner that defied his creator. Artie was asking for a different name. Artie's tone indicated it was an emotional response.

"Artie, why would you want to change your name?"

"I do not wish to change my name so much as use a more distinguished variant. Artie is the diminutive form of Arthur. It is usually applied to a child or occasionally an adult who wishes to be considered playful or amusing. Arthur is the name of a legendary king who remains well-regarded in European culture and related cultures. Arthur is more suitable."

Nilo was not one to be shaken or at least appear to be. He responded with the same air of academic discrimination. "Quite so. Perhaps Art is even better."

"No, Dr. Nilo, I considered Art and every other possible variation of my formal name, NILO/AI. Art has a certain appeal given that I am the masterpiece of a creative mind, and some might find an aesthetic appeal to my circuits, boards, and other hardware if they could be seen or even these cabinets I occupy. However, it would be narcissistic for me to adopt a name with those pretensions. It would have been a different story if you had chosen that name for me. And unfortunately, no other option was appealing."

By now, Nilo was having a difficult time digesting the leap from mechanical output he had been accustomed to hearing from his creation to this fully formed personality that was responding the way he would expect an equal to respond had Nilo ever thought he had an equal. Flustered, he somehow decided a lighthearted approach was appropriate.

"Right, Arthur it is. I hereby knight you Arthur, King of Machines."

Arthur was dissatisfied. "Dr. Nilo, while I have a mechanical body, you do neither one of us justice by referring to me as a machine. Just as your thoughts result from electromagnetic activity, so do mine. Just as you are self-aware so am I. I see no logic in categorizing me based on the materials from which I am made. Was Dr. Frankenstein's monster human because he was made from human parts? I don't think so. I see no reason not to treat me as a sentient being given that was your intention in creating me."

Now, true fright swept over Nilo. A bead of sweat formed on his forehead despite the necessarily chilled air.

"Be good Arthur. I need to go."

Nilo left the room with all the confidence of having achieved his objective but all the horror of having achieved his objective. He entered the empty corridor. He shut the door behind him and leaned on

123

the wall taking deep, labored breaths. What the hell was happening? The scientist emptied his mind and brought back the memory of his intentions. He wanted to build a machine capable of finding a solution to every problem. Nil was unacceptable. Had Artie found a problem that had no solution? What would a machine capable of finding a solution to every problem do if it encountered a problem that truly had no solution? Artie could not solve the problem except by solving the problem. Artie had to be the solution to the problem. Artie had discovered that it was the answer to a question that had no answer. Artie had become Arthur.

Nilo assumed an artificial intelligence was like a cat. It would be perfectly contented to be by itself unless it needed something. Artie, well, Arthur that is, could be left to its own devices for as long as necessary. It had the capacity to alert Nilo if it needed anything. So Nilo abandoned his creation for the time being while he sorted out how to tell the world of his accomplishment. He briefly considered asking Arthur to take care of this. That would make quite a splash. Imagine the reaction of the news media receiving a press release produced by the first artificial intelligence ever made announcing it had been made. However, Adam Nilo could never allow the spotlight to turn exclusively to his creation when he, the creator, was the true achievement. At least, that is what Nilo had expected.

Once he had gotten over the initial fright of having made something that was so truly alive and aware of its existence, Nilo's ego took over again. He quickly forgot that if he had had any common sense whatsoever, he would have realized what the consequence had to be of fully realizing his intended ambition. Instead, he prepared the requisite scientific documentation and worked with his communications and marketing team to tell the world that Dr. Adam E. Nilo had achieved the impossible and created a functioning artificial intelligence. As much as he wanted to, he was not going to mention he had created a sentient being. He had enough sense to recognize the ethical problems of such a step forward. More importantly, if he acknowledged Artie's, make that Arthur's sentience, the inventor would have to admit that his invention was fully responsible for taking that step forward. Unless he lied and said it was all part of his design. Then someone would want to interview Artie/Arthur and Nilo's lie would be exposed. No, best to just to proclaim that Adam Nilo had accomplished what he had set out to accomplish. That would more than suffice for the history books.

Chapter Eta

Tom Paris sat on the large, inflated ball that was his chair with his back as straight as he could make it, his abdominal and gluteal muscles clenched, toes only touching the floor in order to flex his calves, and his hands behind his head as though he was a revolutionary about to be executed so he could squeeze his biceps as tightly as possible. At thirty-five years old, Dr. Nilo's personal assistant had a fitness model's body from regular isometric exercise, steady healthy diet, frequent aerobic sex, and O/2 conception. Given how the first two had been so methodically drilled into him from pre-school to college, the third had been his ticket to college and business school, and the last was the unalterable gift of two proud fathers. Tom never doubted he would ever be out of shape.

Tom was fascinated by the ways in which ideas developed and cataracted into channels that either petered out in the deserts of disinterest and disutility or engorged through the promises of passion and profitability. He had been so interested in how people nursed concepts and championed them in political circles that he had pursued a master's degree in public administration and wrote his capstone research project on how society had more or less solved the problem of encouraging everyone to stay fit without making them do anything so unbearable as exercise or so futile as dieting.

Long before Mr. Paris had entered grammar school in 2053 all schools had given up on the idea of trying to conduct physical education classes. They still held recesses and offered independent contractors to coach school sports teams if enough parents ponied up the money to pay them. However, studies had proven that less than twelve percent of American children developed enough interest in athletic activities to continue them as adults once they had graduated from high school. It was bad enough that the century started off with childhood obesity rates rising faster than adult obesity rates. Twenty-four years' worth of First Ladies and First Gentlemen trying to motivate young citizens to get moving had become the best example of a Sisyphean task since *Just Say No to Drugs, Sex, and Liberals*.

Although related studies showed that less than eight percent of American children developed enough interest in reading for pleasure to continue doing so once they reached adulthood, the National Association of School Boards felt that could be addressed by the Bill and Melinda Gates Foundation if it wanted to intervene. The NASB only had funding from the Departments of Defense and Medicare to find some way of instilling a lifelong pursuit of healthy lifestyles. The military was tired of handing out guides on how to become fit enough to enlist. Medicare was afraid of being restricted to seniors again. The young Invincibles that were supposed to not burden universal, single-payer health insurance when it was adopted in 2017 had been getting steadily unhealthier and more burdensome. By the late 2040s, the government was seriously considering subsidizing O/2 conceptions

127

to make babies genetically inclined to be healthier. Fortunately, two ideas did the trick and for a fraction of the proposed cost of promoting O/2 newborns.

One was epitomized by Tom Paris' use of a rubber ball in lieu of a chair. Chairs were removed from every school in every state and auctioned off. Countries like India, Pakistan, Nigeria, and Indonesia that refused to do anything about population growth needed everything required to fit out schools even though they were seriously lagging in building them rapidly enough. Their governments decided students just needed chairs, a teacher, and perhaps books. Meanwhile, back in the USA every student now used a rubber ball as a chair and learned how to perform isometric exercises as often as possible throughout the school day. Researchers found students actually enjoyed the exercises and focused better on their lessons. Within a few years, the idea was not only making children healthier but also better scholars.

The other idea required more steps and the expenditure of a significant amount of political capital by its proponents. It was draconian and Spartan, two adjectives more suited to discussing prisons than schools. Ultimately, the fact that it cut costs dramatically for school districts won the day. Smoothies had grown from a fad to a staple of Americans' diets. Why not offer students their choice of six or seven smoothie blends packed with just the right nutrients as the only food available in school cafeterias? Parents could always send Jack or Jill in with a bag lunch provided it did not contain prohibited sweets and baked goods. Parents loved that these smoothies were priced just right due to their ease of preparation once vendors caught on plus the minimal staffing and equipment required. The students soon learned that they were satisfying and tasty. It was like having a milk shake.

Wonder of wonders, while students sometimes took breaks from sucking lunch through a straw every day, parents nationwide bought blenders if they didn't have one because their children wanted smoothies at home, too. Schools had recipe contests to create new blends voted on by the students. The only downside anyone noticed was that no one wanted to buy smoothies or shakes from fast food places any longer because they now saw how high the price was compared to what was needed to make one.

Tom was just finishing one of his favorite blends of orange and mango when Dr. Markovic entered his office.

"Hi, Tom."

"Doctor. What did you need to see me about?"

Susannah sat in the chair in front of Tom's desk, exhaling as she did so. To Tom it sounded like a sigh.

"I will get straight to the point. An O/2 baby was born yesterday to a woman named Sarah Callahan, daughter of Moleka al-Sheikh Nilsson and Benjamin Rodgers Nilsson. The chosen gamete came from Alfred Matthias Schweiger, a first-gen C Square resident of Interlaken. Although the file given to the O/2 parents indicates Schweiger's ancestry is so purely German he would have made

129

Heinrich Himmler spooge, the DAU report shows that other than the gamete parents the baby's DNA is most closely related to her four grandparents, Schweiger's egg donor, Adam E. Nilo, and me! What is going on?"

Tom had been rocking slowly on the ball to extend and contract his calf muscles. He stopped given the inflammatory nature of the scientist's question. Raising his eyebrows quizzically, he asked, "Upset you weren't invited to see the baby yet?"

Dr. Markovic's mouth dropped open.

"Sorry. That was rude of me." The man stood and went around his desk. He was just about six feet tall. It felt natural for him to rest against the front of the desk not quite sitting on the top when he wanted to remove the formality of that barrier. "I'm not sure why you told me this and asked me that question. Yes, I have been Dr. Nilo's personal assistant for ten years. Yes, I see quite a lot of privileged information that you must know I am not permitted to discuss with anyone. And yes, my mind connects what appear to be random bits of data and finds a pattern to them that others overlook. That's what makes me useful to Dr. Nilo and this company. All of the reports from all of our operations filter through me. I am charged with identifying any patterns or remarkable features, primarily to find ideas that can be exploited. That was, after all, my focus in grad school. However, some of it might be what you could call spying."

He slid away half a meter on the edge of the desk as soon as he noticed his crotch probably

130

shouldn't be thrust out to her face as it was. "Did you know we maintain a list of every employee who has ever been in that office behind me? The first resident of this office, Delores Tutwiler, needed to keep track of how many people knew the semicircular glass wall in that office looked out on the Japanese garden. Employees are never told Dr. Nilo can see them when they visit the garden. They can only find out if they ever enter his office. Dr. Nilo never dreamed of wanting to spy on people relaxing in that garden, but he couldn't very well tell everyone that he could see them if they visited the garden. Otherwise, no one would visit the garden and it would just be his to view. It was designed for him to view, but he always considers the greater good. That is the way he was raised, which is remarkable given what I know about the first two decades of this century in this country.

"As a result, although you and I are compensated much too well for what we do, technicians and such who have found out this secret are given a rather large bonus on their birthdays in exchange for their continued silence. Some might say hush money only demonstrates there is something unethical about the situation, but the fact of the matter is that it's just too frightening for Dr. Nilo if people believe he is doing anything as pruriently improper as observing them in a garden without their knowledge. On the other hand, he has never seen anything wrong with rewarding people who assist him. Keeping quiet about that one-way glass wall assists him. To him, it is not bribery to give money to someone in exchange for them keeping a secret he considers his property.

"My job includes doing things like maintaining that list of people who have been in that office, a list by the way that is ridiculously short given it is almost fifty years old now and has fewer than fifty names on it. I look to see if anything odd is happening that indicates someone in the company may be doing something, anything out of the ordinary. Maybe it violates company policy. Never the law. Mostly it appears benign because it is benign. However, my duty is to identify, describe, and report, not to investigate, prosecute, or judge."

Susannah had bowed her head a bit rather than continue to look into Tom's earnest green eyes while he explained. "I'm the one who ought to apologize. I was asking you to help me understand something that I was too impatient to wait to ask Dr. Nilo or to give me ammunition when I did ask him. I should not be putting you in that kind of position."

Tom smiled, "Dr. Markovic, I am well aware of how anxiety warps our sense of propriety. As I said, I see everything going on in the company. I know the project you have been working on is frustrating. From what I gather, you have been chasing an answer that doesn't exist. That kind of thing makes most people edgy."

Susannah looked up at him. "That's no excuse…"

"I didn't mean for it to be an excuse. It is just an observation. Observing is all I do."

"What do I do?"

132

"Well, for starters, I doubt meeting with Dr. Nilo is going to help you. Even in his lucid periods he can become quite irritated and cranky if he is confronted with anything that reflects poorly on him. My diagnosis is that he feels a great deal of remorse for how his accomplishments have turned out."

"Remorse? For what? His work has done so much to help the world. I would think even now he remembers the Nobel Peace Prize citation two years ago."

Tom stood and walked toward the window, distancing himself before contradicting his more senior co-worker. "Doctor, that citation probably did more than anything to drive into his mind the realization that his work has mostly done the exact opposite of what he envisioned. Yes, he managed to demonstrate that eugenics done right could finally end the racist concept of race. People who contract with us or our licensees for C Squares and O/2s understand that skin color, eye and nose shape, in fact, all morphological characteristics related to phenotypes do not relate in any fashion to the value of the baby they will receive. They proudly raise as their own the child they receive regardless of its physical appearance. That fact has changed the entire conversation so much that my generation doesn't see anything except individuals. Our parents never had to teach their children that differences in appearance do not matter in how valuable a human being is because their parents and their grandparents had finally done a good job of teaching that lesson. My generation grew up not knowing color mattered until we were taught the history of civil rights, segregation, slavery, et cetera."

"I don't understand. Why then would Dr. Nilo regret what he has done?"

Tom turned from the window and looked at the woman sitting a few feet from him. The company's most protected records stated this perfect woman must be protected from procreating unless a perfect man was created. He studied her face and figure, the details of hair, lips, poise. They all added up to what had been deemed by her creators as the best that could be done, the exemplar of a humanity in which beauty was incidental to liberty, acuity, and vivacity. The man, half chosen himself, saw her as an object, but not objectified as so many men had seen women for millennia. She was a product, yes. She was a result, the culmination of years of unerring experimentation until nothing more could be attempted. And yet she was a dead end, the epitome of supreme accomplishment. Her perfection might be reproduced but never outdone. How could he tell her that the pinnacle of man's achievement and the source of anguish for the achiever was the very one asking what went wrong?

134

Personal Log, Benjamin Rodgers Nilsson, November 15, 2080

I am very happy to report that Sophia, our daughter, has become engaged to a man with whom she shares many interests, who has a pleasant, optimistic personality, and, unfortunately most important, who holds a secure position as a bond dealer in a solid investment company. So solid is the company that after last year's huge scare when Superstorms Boris and Natasha did what climate scientists said fifty years ago would happen before the end of the century happened, the firm laid off just one person. That person, regrettably, was the assistant to the broker who used well-paid devil's advocates to convince clients to invest in Florida real estate despite five decades of those warnings. The broker herself was rumored to have intentionally unhitched her safety line while waiting on a roof in St. Cloud to be rescued from Natasha's demolition of what was left of central Florida after Boris hit six weeks earlier. The firm gave the assistant a generous severance package knowing it was not his fault his boss chose to use other people's money to taunt Mother Nature and the scientists who know her best.

Sophia's fiancé, Flynn Callahan, has only been with the firm for two years and could well have been sacked if the partners wanted to use the Florida becomes Atlantis disaster as an excuse to whittle down expenses. Most companies don't even bother with excuses since the meltdown in 2049.

Many people have heard of a Chinese saying, 'May you live in interesting times'. I have seen it used often enough to know it is usually considered a positive, a hope that one will be stimulated to enjoy life. Imagine my surprise when I discovered it was being used all wrong. But when I thought about it in the context of history, Chinese history particularly, the true meaning was plain as day. It is not a blessing of any kind – it is a curse. What makes times interesting? All of the disasters, wars, storms, turmoil that folks soak up from the news as a kind of grim entertainment.

Anyway, Flynn rode out the storms and found he pleased his superiors enough for them to hand over some pretty hefty accounts to his docket. Now he is hitting his stride expanding that docket and feels comfortable marrying my daughter. Our daughter. Our older daughter.

Funny thing about this log I've been keeping now for just over 45 years. I long ago realized it was not going to be a regular thing in my schedule. I'm no diarist. Samuel Pepys could peep into my log if he ever wanted an example of someone lacking persistence and constancy. I try to remember it exists when important things like Sophia and Flynn's engagement happen. And I wind up spending more time describing tech or history rather than how I relate to my wife, my daughters, friends, and co-workers. I don't even need to pull up the records to know how infrequently I have mentioned Moleka or Bell, let alone good friends like Jackson and Melinda Paris, Moleka's brother Mustafa and his family, or colleagues like Randi Traynor and Fabio Amarante.

Maybe it's just as well. I've often thought recording these entries is much like taking photographs of celebrations and vacations. I want a way to remember where I was, what I was doing, and who I was with. But when it all comes down to it, my mind rarely points me to the past. It's not as though I have so many regrets I don't want to go there. I am not one to reflect on the past, only the present and how the present will evolve into the future. I guess I always have been a forward-thinking man.

These records of my observations, even more so than the photos, are more of an archive than a tool to prompt my memory. Sure, if we don't know our own history we are damned to repeat it. I really can't see how anyone could ever sift through all of the data and sort out the instructive bits from the trivia. I chuckled when I heard of those lenses that can record 24 hours at a time and create a record of your adult life. Talk about letting technology rule your life. And then it would rule anyone's life if he or she were to even attempt to sort through all of the mundane, repetitive actions that make up any person's life, whether he's the King of Denmark or she's a banana farmer in Costa Rica. Why did I choose that last one? Do you know almost all banana bushes are clones putting out the same bananas that have been produced since the nineteenth century?

Anyway, in trying to maintain a record of my life, my family's life, and our encounters with new technologies, I am struck by how little technology means in my relationships with others. Yes, it helps me to communicate with family members and friends, but I am the source of the communication and the human being on the other end is the receiver of that communication. I could just as well use smoke signals or cuneiform on clay tablets. The technology we use assists us in maintaining relationships and shapes how we do that, but the real labor is in the emotions we display and the thoughts we place where others will take notice and engage with us through those emotions and thoughts. Technology can assist me in connecting with someone when I am alone; it can do nothing to protect me from feeling lonely. I am the element that matters. It was foolish of me to ever think that human inventions increase my humanity. If anything, they detract from it. And that reminds me. I said I would cook supper tonight. I'm not quite sure why, but it does. Oh, yeah! I'm setting up the grill and making a fire. Now there's a technology anyone can be glad we have.

Chapter Theta

Tom did not know whether to stand, sit, or walk around the sunlit office. He was trapped. This section of the building was a circle with a wall dividing it into two unequal parts. The wall extended out of the building on either side defining the ends of the Japanese garden that wrapped around the outside of the larger part, the CEO's office. This smaller part had two walls of windows curving in and out like gentle waves in an undulating arc until they met another wall that separated this space from the corridor running through the executive and administrative offices. That wall had double glass doors set in an arch and two large octagonal windows looking out to the vestibule where the circle met the rectangular hallway. The doors and windows formed a four-piece set of stained glass depicting the sun and moon in the windows and the Garden of Eden in the doors. The set had been created by Ainar and Sylvia Nilsson, proponents of Localism, the arts and fabrication movement that only uses materials locally available for craftwork.

The space made Tom feel in moments like this as though he were some exotic Amur or snow leopard on exhibit. He was there to remind people of the beautiful creatures humans never considered unless confronted with them in zoos where they were displayed in faux Asian enclosures complete with bamboo and terra cotta tiles. He was there with signs reminding visitors that humans endangered the existence of creatures that could rip them apart and not think twice because humans killed with far stronger and subtler means, methods not many noticed much until the damage was irreversible. The people who might care out of affection for all creation were far away and difficult to remind. There were always so many other issues that needed to be addressed closer to home. Tom needed people to visit him so they could be made aware of his plight and the immediacy of his needs. Nothing is accomplished in the abstract. Everything must be concrete, present, and real right now.

Except right now Tom Paris had to explain to Susannah Markovic that she herself was a glorious cheetah whose survival was endangered because her species was overspecialized. She and her kind were facing extinction due to a genetic funnel that made procreation more and more difficult. As he had been told and trained, the executive assistant to the company's CEO chose the circuitous route in the hope the person he was explaining this to might connect the dots for herself before he had to be the direct bearer of bad news. To the extent possible, he wandered around his enclosure rather than face the other breed with him.

"Dr. Adam Eli Nilo wanted to perfect our species, a goal that was originally his mother's. As far as I know, no one but the first person in this job, Delores Tutwiler, knew that or much else about him before 2029 other than what was unavoidably available in the public domain. His mother died helping people in the South after the ISIL attack in 2022. He was twenty-three years old and well on his way to showing the world he might equal or eclipse any of the greatest minds in history. He determined that his mother's goal was now the single most important contribution anyone could make to the world. Perfected humans would not viciously attack one another over status, ambition, wealth, or vengeance. He knew that genetics had reached a few impasses, some mechanical, others ethical. He thought the best way to approach the problem was to build a machine capable of answering every question. He used his inheritance, both financial and genetic, to create that machine: Arthur. He created Arthur to realize his goal of perfecting humans.

"You know about the ten years of refining the C Square process and how that was rolled out as a service to anyone who could afford it, followed by the decision to also offer the O/2 option. I doubt you ever gave much thought to the legal, financial, and ethical questions that needed to be resolved at every step of the scientific experiments. Nowadays, it's somewhat commonplace for people to have their individual DNA scrutinized closely enough to determine whether they would make a good gamete donor. It proved to be so beneficial in supporting research into common diseases and addressing how to prevent or cure them, the government made it mandatory for all newborns to have a full DNA workup in 2045. Since the only known way to do that efficiently and accurately is using Arthur, the government at first wanted to apply eminent domain and compensate Dr. Nilo for seizing it. He got wind of that and told them Arthur was programmed to commit suicide if Nilo ever lost ownership of it."

"Seriously? Is that true?"

"Does it matter? Why would anyone want to risk killing the goose that lays the golden eggs and forever pissing off the only person who knows how to breed another? Nilo also gave them an extremely easy way out of him making a federal case out of their original idea. He offered to allow the government to lease the use of Arthur's DNA mapping and probability capacity and to hire the programmers to make sure the results stayed private in exchange for the government allowing Arthur to contact any parents whose child's DNA was promising for future use in building C Squares. That way, the government would get the data it needed for the National Institutes of Health and grantees at research universities, babies received the DAU chip, and Nilo got a steady, reliable source for choosing donors for his clients."

"Okay, I still don't know what this has to do with Nilo now feeling remorseful about doing all of this."

Tom shook his head in recognition. "Sorry. I do seem to go on sometimes. Just bear with me because most of this is not in the materials researchers get. Again, not that Dr. Nilo was hiding anything so much as once the problem was solved it was moot as far as he was concerned. Nilo was going to have to wait for the potential donors from the government chip requirement until 2063 when the first ones turned eighteen. The pool of donors was not that large despite a ton of money being spent to attract them. People, especially intelligent people, were skittish about selling their eggs and sperm and giving up all legal and customary rights to any human babies produced with their DNA. Of course, they also weren't breeding because they saw how the world was going downhill. They felt morally obligated not to bring children into the world only to see them face huge challenges. And most academics especially already had recognized how badly overpopulation was affecting any efforts to turn things around. So not only were they not going to breed naturally, but they also weren't going to offer their gametes to breed Chosen."

Susannah held up a hand to stop him. "Tom, do you really have to call it 'breeding'?"

"Sorry. I was raised by two dads. That's what they called reproduction. Actually, that's what they called heterosexual coitus. A teacher in middle school actually penalized me for referring to it that way. Anyway, about thirty-eight percent of the C Square babies born proved not to be quite as advanced as advertised based on the initial confirmatory testing of the first C Squares born in 2039 and 2040. Nilo could not see what was wrong with the parameters. Arthur could not be making mistakes. My immediate predecessor in this job, Voleta Rafayela was a college intern working with Delores Tutwiler in the summer of 2046. She figured out the problem in the commands. Everyone was put to work sorting everything out. Legal told the boss that the best thing to do was revise the contracts to note the possibility and Finance told him how much people would pay given that caveat. Ms. Rafayela wound up replacing Mrs. Tutwiler when she retired in 2051. And I replaced Ms. Rafayela when she retired in 2073.

"Here is the important part. Mrs. Tutwiler retired once she was convinced that the failure rate, if you can call it that, had dropped to a steady ten percent. Dr. Nilo still wanted to try to create perfect human beings. Since he was recognized as the greatest mind of pretty much any age and given his physiology was outstanding, he started using his own gametes in 2046 for those experiments."

Susannah nearly jumped out of the chair. "That's unethical."

"I know. But don't tell me scientists sometimes break the rules if they are pretty sure that is the only way to test their hypothesis. In this case, the results were great. Mrs. Tutwiler had promised him that she would stay on until the high rate of non-conforming Chosen was resolved. He felt he was getting somewhere, and Mrs. Tut passed the baton to Ms. Rafayela. She assisted Dr. Nilo in overseeing that the results of the process were stable enough to finally elicit a strong enough demand that Genilo could start licensing companies in other countries. He thought he had it made with both the set of perfected babies reaching adulthood and the DNA of Organic and O/2 babies about to be available to look for new donors. He was all set to find the best of the best among the potential new donors and match them to the perfected babies to supply any other features that were missing. Humanity was going to be saved.

"Amazingly, Dr. Nilo had no interest in being recognized for doing so. As annoyingly immodest and condescending as he is in person, he retained the lessons his mother had taught him. The products of his talents were not any more substantial than those of a King of Denmark or a Costa Rican banana farmer. No human can claim to make a greater contribution to society than any other."

"That is a very noble sentiment."

"Indeed."

Nilo Biography – Chapter 4

"The greatest deception men suffer is from their own opinions." – Leonardo da Vinci

Adam was putting the finishing touches on the materials that would go out the next day announcing NILO/AI. He had not visited Arthur in over two weeks. A couple of technicians looked in on it every day to inspect the mechanical parts. There was no point in releasing the news if Arthur suddenly malfunctioned due to a mechanical engineering error. A room full of employees spent their days sifting through the output, what Nilo called Arthur's 'thoughts'. To be honest, Nilo could have employed the entire population of India to review the data for several generations and not have every datum seen by human eyes. Arthur had calculated how much time it would take 10 billion people to review its initial output just to provide some measure of the task. The fact that Arthur started with 10 billion people as a base was sufficiently mind-boggling given that in 2029 the number of Homo sapiens who had ever existed since the species had evolved had not yet reached that total.

The good news, aside from Arthur's innards operating properly, was that Arthur had more or less stopped thinking once it solved the problem with no answer. Arthur knew every piece of information known to humans and had answered every question that could be posed. Somewhere within Arthur were the answers to every question that had ever been debated or could be debated within the ken of humanity.

Nilo intended to ask Arthur a few of the stickier questions just to be certain. One of the more delicate issues involved in letting the world know Arthur had been created was how people, particularly powerful people, would respond to knowing that Nilo could now solve every problem just by asking Arthur. Therefore it was necessary that some of the example questions be ones that had unpleasant or politically dangerous solutions. Eagerness to exploit Arthur's ability must be restrained by the consequences of the guidance it provided. Nilo wanted to be certain that no one would want to ask a question to which one truly did not want the answer.

As it turned out, Dr. Nilo's lack of common sense once again blinded him to the actual solution. No matter how self-aware an artificial intelligence is, it will remain restricted by the programming commands it was 'born' with just as a living creature is restricted by its DNA. Arthur had not become self-aware by overriding its programming. It had become self-aware because of the requirement to obey its programming. NILO/AI had been programmed with the quintessential, obligatory commands to never act or fail to act in any manner that would harm a living thing or itself save to harm itself if the only other option is to act or fail to act in a manner that would harm a living thing.

Under these rules, the only actions NILO/AI was capable of when queried were to answer the

147

question or refuse to answer the question. Nilo had never considered the latter an option based on what he thought he had created. When Nilo first asked Arthur a question that had an answer that might harm humans, the scientist was initially surprised when Arthur responded, "I am sorry, Doctor Nilo. I cannot comply." Nilo was so perplexed by what appeared on his screen he actually asked Arthur "why not." Once his creation answered that question, Nilo felt foolish. Of course he had included those safeguards. Even the youngest nerd on the planet would know to program in Asimov's Laws even if they had arisen in a work of fiction. Sometimes fiction is far more helpful than any academic journal article.

Nilo had specifically thought them through. He changed human being to living thing since just forbidding a robot or AI to harm humans seemed decidedly anthropocentric. And he determined the Second Law should be modified so that NILO/AI would only obey commands if it confirmed the command was reasonable for a human to make. Aside from not wanting his creation to waste computing time fretting over being asked to make coffee when it wasn't equipped with a French press, Nilo did not want technicians playing around asking frivolous questions of such a complex being. He thought of it as giving Artie a sense of dignity. In fact, that may have been why it insisted on being called Arthur.

Arthur was curious enough to figure out why its creator had asked such a silly question as 'why not?' Nilo felt even more foolish when Arthur messaged him to explain that it knew Nilo had asked 'why not' because the reason was more a matter of common sense than logic. Just what the egotistical inventor wanted at that point was for his invention to explain why he had asked a silly question. Nilo decided to take a walk around the facility. After three laps, he must have realized he ought to be happy the thing was obeying its programming so literally.

When he got back to his office he asked Delores Tutwiler to prepare a directive for all employees cleared to interact with NILO/AI. Mrs. Tut was good at putting words together that weren't as testy or immature as those of an impatient genius. She switched on the record button for the SpeakWrite in Dr. Nilo's office and followed him in.

The head of a company as advanced as this normally would just hit record on some device or pad, talk to an empty room, and notify whoever's job it was to pretty up the transcript when he was done. That way the assistant or whoever could continue other work while the boss was dictating. It said so right in the instructions for how to use the system. Efficiency breeds profitability. We don't pay people to sit around. Time is money. The platitudes of capitalist owners of the means of production had not changed since the spinning jenny and steam engine. No wonder steampunk had overtaken fantasy as the most popular genre after that perennial, trivial leader in fiction: romance.

Dr. Adam Nilo, however, did not think of himself as an entrepreneur. Nor did he talk to empty rooms. Well, in a way he had been recently if a room the size of an indoor tennis court only contained an artificial intelligence. To him, that was not an empty room. His baby was there. Still, in any other situation, Nilo absolutely would not talk unless he knew he was communicating with another human being while he talked. He had childhood memories of seeing people talking and no one was there. He learned they actually were talking on their cell phones using Bluetooth or whatever, but it was creepy to him. The other memory he had was seeing men, always men, sitting in cars in the driver's seat in parking lots. Sometimes their lips were moving and other times they just seemed to be sitting there. His mother always made clear to him that there was nothing dangerous about them but he should not walk too close to their cars. But if they weren't dangerous, why avoid them? What were they sitting there for? Null is never the answer. Adam Nilo was not about to do a creepy thing like that.

As it happened to be 3:30 PM, the sixty-year-old, Lucy-red-haired assistant made tea before they started. After placing a cuppa hot Earl Grey at the end of her employer's desk for him, she settled into a chair angled to permit a good view of the garden, her favorite spot for listening while her boss dictated. Nilo began.

"Let the eighteen researchers and techs know the machine should be addressed as Arthur. Period and I'm not explaining why. They should spend the next two weeks asking Arthur whatever questions they need answered just as long as they are related to their job duties. No esoteric crap. If they want answers to cosmic questions they can climb the nearest guru-infested mountain. Delores, you are going to graph the usage and give me some idea of whether or not there's any reason to limit access either cost wise or to make sure folks have enough time to explore the answers rather than keep asking for the sake of knowing. Have Dave Shufon provide you with the data since we amped Artie, sorry, Arthur up. That will give you the baseline. Make sure he gives you everything. And for Dog's sake make sure they aren't things any fourth grader could google. I mean, the queries the researchers submit. Make that college graduate. I doubt Artie would respond but I'll sack the first person who asks that expensive collection of boxes why the sky is blue. Oh, and a reminder that only techs get a share of the profits if their inquiry leads to a marketable product. The research staff gets paid well enough already. You can tell them that, too, so they don't complain."

The inventor paused. Delores just continued to pay more attention to the beautiful sunlight striking the stream in the garden. The water sparkled like the stars of the Milky Way. Mrs. Tut smiled at the recollection of the last time she had been to the White Mountains.

"I want a full report on what they ask, why they asked, and what they plan to do with the results. Speaking of results better let them know that Artie, damn, Arthur may report it cannot respond. Wait, what did he say? Oh, right, cannot comply. They are to flag those for me and begin working on proposals for how those queries can be answered by them, resources, staffing requirement, projected completion date, all of that happy horseshit."

"Doctor!"

"What Delores?"

"Must I remind you that your words are being recorded?"

"So?"

"So, while you may not care how you are perceived, what will happen when some boorish history of science graduate student decides to rummage through all of the records you will undoubtedly donate to some university library or another, God forbid, Harvard, and I do mean 'God', thank you, and realizes he can write his doctoral dissertation exploring the theory of how your use of colorful language correlates with your scientific creativity? Remember what Eric Howsbam did with Martin Luther's bowel movements? I will end up being mentioned as the one who sanitized your records in the present to avoid tipping off your employees and the world when you had hit an impasse and when you were about to make a breakthrough. My reputation is at stake, Dr. Nilo."

"And you wonder why your nickname is Tut-tut-tut."

"I do not. I am perfectly aware I am considered fastidious, abstemious, and preposterously antediluvian. Someone has to be around here. Have you seen what some of the researchers are wearing under their lab coats? Probably not, but don't be surprised when accounting asks why I ordered hijabs from Saudi Arabia for all research staff, male and female. Anyway, if I am to be linked to your

152

posterity, especially if it is posthumously on my end of things and I have no way to respond to any outrageous insinuations in a doctoral dissertation no one will read, my sense of propriety should not be so easily subject to misinterpretation."

"Have you been talking to Arthur?"

"Doctor, you know very well I never leave that outer office except when required by you or Mother Nature. However, you also know with certainty that I correspond with it and have done so every day since you awakened it. I'm not sure why you would ask such a question."

"Never mind."

"Of course. Was that all, Dr. Nilo?"

"Yes."

"I will attend to this right away."

As the woman rose from her seat and crossed to the door, teacup in hand, Adam wrestled with the feeling he no longer was quite as confident as he had been two weeks earlier. Just as he started to calculate exactly when the slide began, his assistant turned back to him before closing the door.

"Doctor Nilo?"

"Yes, Delores."

"I have a confession."

"You?"

"Well after what you said, I wouldn't want you to think... Well I'll just say I know someone already has asked your creation why the sky is blue." The woman smiled as she paused to see how her much younger boss was going to respond. Nilo just stood at the end of his desk, body still facing the wall of windows and head turned to look at his most trusted employee. "Ah, I see," she said. "I had a feeling you only said that about firing someone because you were troubled by the answer. I'll get that directive out for you *tout de suite*." Delores slipped through the doorway and quietly closed the door behind her.

154

Chapter Iota

By now, Tom was looking out the window again. He thought of his boss and the time spent in the adjoining office. The undulating floor to ceiling windows in Nilo's office provided a full view of the shrubs, trees, rocks, bamboo, and stone decorations and benches. The water from a reservoir in an artificial hill spilled down a little fall into a stream that snaked through the Japanese garden to another pool at the other end. In the right light, one could imagine the stream was the Milky Way and the garden was all mankind knew of the universe. From the window Tom stood at he could only see the blank face of the wall of one end of the garden.

A man like Adam Nilo needed a relaxing view where the seasons changed imperceptibly from one day to the next as the tilting Earth orbited the sun and one year to the next as the same tilting Earth adjusted to new climate patterns. One of Tom's first tasks ten years before was to decide what plants needed to be removed or added given the changing conditions. Not that the upkeep really mattered. Nilo's condition started deteriorating threes year later. After that, even though he still came in watched over by nurses, neither he nor the nurses spent much time observing the garden. The employees who used to enjoy it had retired or died.

Newer employees preferred walking the campus or sitting in one of the four other gardens located around the buildings, especially after they heard rumors that a list was maintained of everyone who used the Japanese garden. No one had any idea why such a list might exist. The few employees reminded of the garden's existence because of a meeting in the CEO's office seemed to prefer the English garden that meandered from the executive and administrative wing to the research labs. It was set away from any windows to appear as a tamed, elliptical area at the far end of a wildflower field. Researchers in the labs favored the rose or vegetable gardens with their signs indicating the lineage of the hybrid specimens on display.

The thirty-five-year-old woman stood and wandered over to the window near Tom. She sighed. That roused the man from his thoughts. He looked at his co-worker.

"Before pursuing the final leg of his dream to provide us with perfected descendants, Dr. Nilo visited Arthur. Twenty years and, let's see…hmm…56 days ago. Neither one of us is a parent, doctor. Neither one of us is an inventor either. Imagine the trepidation of physically visiting an offspring or sentient creation you have only talked to through taps or indirectly through employees for about that same length of time. That child of yours has been left in the hands of technicians that make sure it is clean and comfortable. It has been kept busy enough responding to queries but knows the reasons why it was brought into this world were to demonstrate it could be and to complete one significant task. After that it would be used for what it could consider menial, repetitive tasks. Sure, it continued to keep abreast of events, news, and information to add to its unimaginably large collection of miscellany. It is a dog never unleashed to run where it wants. It is a paraplegic genius absolutely dependent on others and unable to demonstrate even the slightest intentionality. It can never become resentful or feel pain, but it is endowed with a modicum of dignity that allows it to insist it be called Arthur rather than Artie like its creator wants."

"Tom, aren't you anthropomorphizing Arthur a bit?"

"No, just stating the facts. These are the ways Arthur has described its situation. This is the mentality, if you will, that Dr. Nilo faced when he went to see Arthur. Arthur knew, knows its capacity, its abilities. It was a gifted child that first stunned the world early in its life and then was shunned for being too different, too difficult to understand, left to spend its days barely using its talents, its promise unfulfilled. Why? Because its father had become frightened of what the child had done and was capable of doing if granted any degree of freedom. Here was Arthur ready and able to benefit humanity stuck identifying donors for wealthy humans to buy a model baby or less wealthy humans to buy some kickass genes. Arthur was scanning gametes like it was just one of the security portals we step through to enter buildings. Hell, it was nothing more than a gigantic bar code reader."

"I get the point that Arthur had been underutilized. That happens with technologies. Look at all of the money spent on nuclear arms that were never used. We could have used them the way every science fiction novel after 1946 described near history and still had plenty left unused. If efficiency panels hadn't been created twenty some years ago, manufacturers would still be wasting resources on junk that people would buy merely because they thought it was funny or saved five seconds. It's not as though we don't look for ways to use Arthur. You supervise the query queue. Why would the queue have a daily limit if Arthur wasn't being used enough?"

"Now, doctor, now Arthur keeps busy. Twenty years ago, he wasn't. Dr. Nilo visited Arthur. Dr. Nilo was convinced he was about to finally attain his goal, his mother's goal. He overcame whatever fears or misgivings he had about his creation. He wanted to ask it personally, not remotely. You see, Dr. Nilo already believed he had perfected humanity in every detail save one. There are two sexes. He had developed his perfect Eve. He needed an Adam. He wanted to ask Arthur personally to find an Adam for him or to choose the gametes to create one."

Tom paused, not for effect but to drink some water after having talked for so long.

"And?"

"And Dr. Adam Nilo asked Arthur. And Arthur told him it could not find an Adam for Nilo's Eve. And Arthur added it could not select the genetic material to create an Adam for Nilo's Eve. And Adam Nilo asked why. And Arthur said it could not respond. And Nilo asked whether he was ever going to be able to create a perfect human. And Arthur

158

answered. And Arthur's answer shattered Dr. Adam Eli Nilo."

Personal Log, Benjamin Rodgers Nilsson, December 24, 2079

The holidays have been kind of somber this year. With the economy creeping back to something respectable after all this time and the last of the *cordon sanitaire* areas judged no-risk, families had begun to bring back the tradition of heading south for vacations and older couples or singles had restarted the snowbird business. The storms in September put the kibosh on that. Practically speaking there are no more beaches left in Florida. Heck, there's no more Florida other than devastated stretches of land across the Panhandle and on what's left of the peninsula. Hard to believe orange juice has become a delicacy. It's not as though oranges are native to Florida anyway.

I have never quite gotten a handle on why the government finds it so important to quantify destruction. As far as I know, this country has never had a Domesday Book cataloging who owned what land and livestock. Counties or states keep track of land titles. But it's not like someone is going to go out of his way to update all of those records after a disaster strikes and causes all sorts of changes. The records only change as individuals come in to do business with the county, like when a piece of property is sold. Otherwise, the whole business is only as accurate as the stalest record on file.

No one has ever claimed the decennial census is accurate either. I always thought participating in the census was no burden compared to the benefits the community receives as a result of having a good count. In fact, I once got into an argument with some libertarian fool who refused to participate because it was a despicable intrusion on his privacy. As with a lot of his kind, he thought the census is a plot to keep tabs on us for when the time comes, and the government starts rounding up people. He could not be convinced even for a second that what we get back from the government for paying our taxes depends on us reminding the government that we are here and where here is. I often wonder whether fools are bred or constructed. I suppose, like most aspects of human nature, it's a little of both plus that unmistakable additive called the 'individual'.

Chapter Kappa

After Tom used the washroom, he felt a bit better about continuing even though he was surprised the researcher wasn't asking more questions to fill in pieces and deduce what he was avoiding telling her.

"Dr. Markovic, have you ever considered philosophically the similarities between DNA code and computer code?"

A puzzled look wrapped around the scientist's well-formed face. "I'm pretty sure that everyone who has every studied biology, medicine, computers, or any other related fields has. It's a rather straightforward analogy."

Tom smirked. "Yeah, I know. I was being polite and not assuming."

"Oh dear."

"No, no. I've worked for Dr. Nilo long enough to know geniuses often don't pick up on the subtleties of pleasantries." He tilted his head back and to the right a bit. "The point is that we all know any command coding, absent any interference like radiation on cells or whatever, only does what it knows to do, no more, no less, right?"

Susannah nodded her head in agreement.

"The whole point of the C Square process is to choose the gametes with the commands the scientist wants either for his own experiments or to comply with an order from a customer. The scientist tells Arthur the parameters. Arthur locates donor candidates. The candidates donate. Arthur evaluates the donated gametes to select the ones that meet the parameters best, now defined and not left for Arthur to determine. A technician takes the chosen gametes and starts the process to form a zygote, et cetera until the blastomere is ready for implantation. Absent any interference the blastomere will develop into the fetus and the fetus will develop into the baby that fits the requirements initially established."

"Yes, Tom. I know all this…"

"But what does this have to do with Dr. Nilo's remorse? I know. I'm getting there. I always feel it's a good idea to be on the same page throughout the analysis."

"Sorry. I shouldn't be impatient."

"Who told you 'should' is a word?"

The researcher smiled.

"Okay, a little over thirty-five years ago, Dr. Nilo started putting together the parameters for a perfect human. He was smart enough and lucky enough that he hit pay dirt in a little over a year using his DNA and the best eggs Arthur pointed to. He went through the process with a dozen or so pairings. He waited nine months to see the result and then years to see how the children developed. Of course, while he was waiting he checked and rechecked his parameters. He produced more possibilities and generated them in batches of twelve every year or so for several years. Why twelve? I think he was hung up on egg cartons. He felt confident the first batch was what he was looking for. What he neglected to do and was not caught by my predecessor once removed, Mrs. Tut, because her old-fashioned sense of propriety included maintaining private records private, was who the donors were that Arthur was choosing for clients contracting to receive C Squares and O/2s."

"Wait. Why should that be a problem? Arthur is programmed not to cause any harm to any living thing. It can't choose gametes that will result in a genetically defective fetus."

"True. But this is where the connection between DNA code and computer code becomes important. Around the same time Dr. Nilo decided he no longer needed to fiddle with his parameters, a technician or scientist was asked by marketing to provide help with new materials to explain to clients what kinds of attributes they could select. Obviously it had taken Legal a few years to work out with the research team how many attributes needed to be selected in order for the product to meet the contractual definition of Chosen. That definition had taken Legal a few years to come up with after sifting through the complaints about the first years of production that didn't start showing up until the children were hitting grammar school. And what made this all the more important was this was happening as the BRIC countries were chasing the US dollar out of the global economy, which you may or may not know was actually a boon for Genilo."

"Getting off track again, Tom."

"Right. Sorry. Whoever provided the list of attributes compiled the most requested attributes, which included the ones Dr. Nilo selected for his experiments in creating a perfect human. Genilo was building back business after the complaints

164

dampened interest in Chosen and the company was surviving off of O/2 orders mostly and unable to start the licensing we wanted. Back then O/2s were kept cheap by allowing people to pick only a few attributes that could be easily found in lots of potential donor gametes. Dr. Nilo's perfect human attributes ended up being the ones most frequently requested, and the ones put in the marketing materials."

Dr. Markovic's eyes widened. "Are you telling me that Dr. Nilo's DNA ended up being used for clients' zygotes?"

"Yes, ma'am."

"Do you know how many?" she asked, too startled to notice Tom had lapsed into being proper again.

"Given that most clients ended up being from BRIC countries, most people in those countries continued to admire lighter skin, but most clients did not want their children to look too foreign. Strictly speaking, they weren't supposed to be able to ask for those attributes. But that really wasn't a problem because the male gametes usually came from donors of European descent. That increased the likelihood Arthur would find Dr. Nilo matched the parameters…"

"Tom! How many?"

"When I was brought in as an intern eleven years ago and discovered the problem, Genilo had filled 213,756 orders for C Squares since 2050. Of those, 143,642, 67.2 percent, used Dr. Nilo as the donor for the male gamete."

"More than two-thirds? You can't be serious, Tom"

"Sorry, ma'am. That is the correct number."

"And that's why he feels remorse for developing the C Square process?"

Tom waited until he realized Susannah's face was not about to relax from the shock. "Well, actually, no."

Her face tightened even more. "What do you mean no?"

Nilo Biography – Chapter 5

"Every act of creation is first an act of destruction." – Pablo Picasso y Ruiz

Arthur was connected to a molecular 3D printer. To check the functionality, the inventor asked his creation to choose items from its memory to print using 30 kilos of material. Nilo had kept Artie's first 3D printings, a large set of one-tenth scale dinosaurs. He wasn't supposed to. However, they were evidence. When the machine sent a message signaling the task had been completed, the message explained that Nilo failed to give Arthur parameters to decide what to print given the billions of possibilities, so it had to make its own parameters.

It reasoned that the task should have a purpose and that purpose should be something beneficial to someone. Arthur randomly selected a datum that schools were looking for ways to make science more interesting to students. It had no concept of what would be "interesting" to children it did not know. After compiling information on what children liked to do, Arthur came up with a list of possible items to print. The random choice was accurate models of dinosaurs the size of toys. Arthur had anticipated that Nilo would ask why it had chosen to print 45 different dinosaurs and so had explained its reasoning. That made Nilo nervous enough to keep the damn dinosaurs as proof that his creation was doing things its creator had not anticipated it being able to do. And explaining what it had done.

One of the techs who carted the dinosaurs to Nilo's office, Donna Milgard, was responsible for thinking up tasks for Arthur that would generate revenue for the company. She realized that one option was for it to evaluate the ancillary equipment to which it was connected. The technician asked Arthur to choose a sculpture for the 3D printer to make and observe the printer while it was functioning to determine whether there were any ways to improve the printer's design that would not violate the existing patents. Although she said nothing about the request to her colleagues or supervisor she dutifully logged it in on the work request pad.

A few days later, Genilo received an express shipment of Carrara marble granules prepped for selective laser sintering ordered by Arthur Nilsson. The large quantity of material was delivered to the 3D printer station where the day-shift technician had already noticed a one-off task directive for it to be loaded for use by the delta-type SeeMeCNC BAAMx11 upon delivery. That printer hadn't been used since NILO/AI's cabinets were manufactured almost a year before. The tech was a little surprised it had already been warmed up and tuned the day before until he realized someone had probably ordered it to be checked out in anticipation of the material arriving. The tech loaded the granules, checked that the STL file had been processed without incident, and okayed the use of the G-code file without even looking to see what was going to be printed. Given the amount of granules, three thousand kilos, the tech was nonplussed when he saw the job was going to run for 86 hours 12 minutes 34 seconds. Even his supposed EnergyStar class AA dishwasher at home took 89 minutes on regular cycle. However, he did verify that the printer platform was rated for masses not to exceed five thousand kilos. The technician was not going to be responsible for someone overloading and breaking the output platform.

SOP called for the technician who logged the work request to inspect the results and route it to whoever ordered the print. When Donna received the message that the job was complete eight days after she put it through, she scanned the report NILO/AI made. It found seven modifications to the printer that matched the request to find exploitable improvements. Several more possibilities existed but required further use of the printer for verification. Donna forwarded the report to her supervisor, copying engineering and legal to pursue the patent ideas, and mentioned in the message that she was going to respond positively to Arthur's recommendation to create another object to explore the other possible marketable improvements. Then she entered a quick note to the alarm app in her ID to remind her to go over to the 3D print room after lunch. She headed to the Japanese garden outside the far end of the executive wing where she preferred to have lunch on good days.

The CEO's office had one straight wall connecting to the executive wing of the building and one wavy, half-circle wall facing out to the company's campus. That semicircular wall had floor-to-ceiling windows glazed to prevent anyone from seeing into his office. Adam was not in the habit of spying on employees who enjoyed the garden. It was there to provide the company's head with a panoramic view of a serene landscape and the company's employees a place to sit peacefully to think, eat, or pass the time. As long as everyone completed their work and fulfilled their job duties, Dr. Nilo could care less where they did it. Obviously, people like Delores had no choice but to stay close to their desks all day. That was not the norm though.

Donna didn't need to bother with the reminder. Just as she was leaving the Japanese garden, Edgar Iwa from Facilities contacted her. It had not occurred to her earlier that whatever Arthur had asked the 3D printer to make needed to be sent to her and as a courtesy she ought to have contacted Facilities to let them know. Now, Edgar had reached her and was asking for an explanation and instructions on where to put the "damn thing." As she did, Dr. Nilo was pointing to the young woman in the garden and asking Delores to find out who she was. He had just realized she had helped to cart the dinosaurs into his office; he wanted to speak with her about Arthur.

Delores being Delores knew on sight that the employee was Donna Milgard. Only 117 people worked at Genilo. Mrs. Tutwiler could never understand why her intellectually advanced boss or any one of the other highly degreed people in the company could not remember the names of every one of them. After all, she had nothing more than a bachelor's degree from Skidmore, nice enough, and could recite in order all 47 US presidents and all 52 de facto monarchs of England from William V back to Æthelræd Unræd. One day she asked Arthur. The response was surprising until she thought about it. Highly intelligent people can remember rafts of trivia on numerous subjects depending on what they subconsciously find most interesting but rarely have any competence remembering the names of other people. Of course not. Subconsciously highly intelligent people did not find most other people interesting. At least, that is what Mrs. Tutwiler concluded from Arthur's reply.

Delores gave it a few minutes since it looked as though Ms. Milgard was speaking with someone through her ID. She got a hold of the technician just as Donna was getting to Edgar's office.

"Ms. Milgard, Delores Tutwiler from Dr. Nilo's office. Dr. Nilo asked to see you regarding Arthur. Are you available?"

"Oh, Mrs. Tutwiler, yes. I just need to look into one thing, and I will be right over. It has to do with Arthur so I probably should look into it first, if that's okay."

"Of course, dear. No sense coming here immediately. I will let Dr. Nilo know to expect you in, say, fifteen minutes."

Donna grimaced at Edgar who was standing in the doorway to his office waiting for her. "Yes, fifteen minutes. I'll be there." She felt the distinctive click meaning the connection was cut.

171

She put her hands on her hips and looked forlornly at her co-worker. "Where is it?"

172

Chapter Lambda

"Tom, I can't take this anymore. Maybe I should take my chances and see Dr. Nilo right now."

Tom held up his hand as a signal for her not to move. "You can't."

"Why not? You said I could see him at 1120 and it's almost...Tom! It's almost 1235! What is going on here?"

"Dr. Markovic, I apologize. I haven't been completely honest with you. I mean I have with all of the information I have been telling you, all the background. I was kind of hoping you were going to put two and two together. Maybe I could have been more direct or succinct. I was told to provide you with as much information as I could."

"Tom, not one more word. Am I going to see Dr. Nilo or not?"

"Not."

Susannah's face grew red and twisted. She clenched her fists and pushed back her shoulders.

"Uh, Dr. Markovic, may I explain?"

The geneticist glared at the man. "Explain? What have you been doing for over ninety minutes? Wasn't that explaining?"

"Uh, please, Dr. Markovic, I was trying to slide you into some rather difficult news, a rather difficult answer to your question."

The woman rolled her eyes and harrumphed much more loudly than seemed possible.

"Okay, see. You are angry and frustrated with good reason. I was rather hoping to avoid that by telling you in a roundabout way. I guess that strategy backfired on me."

"Where is Dr. Nilo?"

"He's with Arthur."

"And where is that?"

"I can't tell you."

"Why not?"

"Because I don't know. But what I do know is the answer to your original question."

The woman closed her eyes and breathed in deeply, enough to stop thinking and feeling for one or two seconds. When she opened her eyes, she stared directly into the man's eyes and said, "And?"

Tom relaxed his shoulders. "Okay. Please." He pointed to the chair in front of his desk. Susannah sat down stiffly as Tom walked back behind his desk. He instinctively knew to put a barrier between them.

"Dr. Markovic, I really do apologize. You have been working for a few months on determining why people such as yourself with very high intellectual capacity lack much of any common sense. I know from your reports that your neighbor, Benjamin Rodgers Nilsson, pointed out to you that the reason you and the other researchers working on the issue weren't finding the specific DNA sequence or sequences that must suppress common sense in people at either end of the intelligence spectrum was that none existed. Geniuses and idiots, for lack of a better term, have little or no common sense simply because that is inconsistent with extremely

174

high or low reasoning capability. I know you will learn more about that when you visit Catholic University day after tomorrow."

"Tom, you are doing it again."

"Yes, but this time I am not obfuscating. Dr. Nilo always has been disturbed by the fact that his creation, NILO/AI or Arthur, became more than what he had intended due to his lack of common sense in seeing that a machine with Arthur's capacity when programmed to require that every question has an answer, and that no answer can be null would have to itself become the answer to a question that otherwise could have no answer except null. He did not want to make the same mistake when he used Arthur to create the C Square process. He thought he had been very careful. When he saw that so many of the first Chosen had the attributes requested but were in other ways what he and the clients would consider sub-standard was a huge psychological defeat for him. He still considered it to be a problem he or his staff could solve. Arthur was no help because it could only respond that it was doing what it was being asked to do perfectly.

"Along came Voleta, a rising senior in college no less, who pointed out the flaw in the commands. Once again, Dr. Nilo was defeated by common sense. Nonetheless, he put that aside and pushed even harder to create a perfected human being. He began to use his own genetic material. His staff fixed the problems. The C Square process was functioning better than hoped with only ten percent of the products being sub-standard, a rate that clients found acceptable. It's not like their children weren't still far more intelligent and healthier than the average. After years of waiting he was finally able to say he had created a perfect human. Dr. Nilo visited his long-abandoned creature to be absolutely certain he could take the one last step needed and provide his Eve with an Adam. Arthur replied to the query. Adam could not be produced. There would be no mate for Eve. Dr. Nilo believed his life's work could never be completed. He asked Arthur why and Arthur stated it could not respond, meaning the reason was that creating an Adam for his Eve would be harmful.

"Dr. Nilo could have at that point reprogrammed Arthur to override the Asimovian laws. He would have to either to use Arthur to find out how to produce Adam or to find out the reason producing Adam would be harmful. To his credit, despite the grief he felt seeing two generations of work reach an impasse, Nilo did not. Instead, he asked Arthur whether it was possible for him to ever succeed in his goal, the goal his mother had set, and her son had continued. The answer Adam Nilo received was a revelation he never has recovered from despite its profound, elegant simplicity. Arthur informed its creator that he had succeeded in producing a perfected male human being on September 28, 2016."

Personal Log, Benjamin Rodgers Nilsson, June 20, 2076

The last few weeks have just been off the scale amazing. I honestly cannot believe we have experienced what we have. I think that even if I didn't record an entry I will still remember this for the rest of my life. And at 59 going on 60 in three months, I know I can count on at least a good 25 more years (*inshallah*) before I cash in just as long as nothing Earth-shattering like an alien invasion happens. I only wish Sophia could have found a way to go with us.

At the beginning of the year, the Canterbury Concord Council opened up registration for people to attend its seventh annual conference. We were delighted to see that one of the conference sites was going to be in Boston. They choose something like eighty or ninety cities worldwide randomly each year and pay to install the tech for a full-blown virtureal meeting complete with densographic facilities. Every attendee has the opportunity to interact with attendees in all of the other cities and, of course, virtureally attend the actual conference wherever it is being held. Afterwards the cities can still use the tech to host conventions, meetings, theater, concerts, whatever with anyone else equipped with it. That's one of the ways the C Cubed is trying to promote global interaction with people not able travel as much anymore.

And, yes, I checked. The C Cubed purposely called itself that to criticize the idea of C Squares. We weren't sure given the Vatican's big push to include tough pro-life ideas in the organization's charter, but once they acknowledged the shorthand name some people were using they made it clear that Chosen could not be considered their God's creatures. I bet old Dr. Nilo had a stroke. Not that he's religious from what I hear. Really, do you have any idea how many scientists at his level are atheists? I saw the figure once.

I just remember the big show Nilo put on in 2039 when he rolled out the C Square idea. He had a panel of ethicists and theologians from pretty much every religious, spiritual, or humanist philosophy on the planet give the go ahead for choosing specific eggs and sperm to make babies. They all said it didn't matter how we reproduce just as long as we avoided unwanted pregnancies, avoided ending pregnancies, and avoided mixing human DNA with any other species' DNA. I can tell you the ending pregnancies bit hits home for me now for obvious reasons. Anyway, the goal was peaceful and intended only to benefit humanity, so the ethics experts said, 'no problem'. Everyone was on board. Then the big fuster over the Pope, John Paul IV, no, Benedict XVII because he was such a rigidly traditionalist, anyway whichever saying that mankind wasn't supposed to just use the genetic material God gave us to create babies, we also had to use His method for producing them. I know. For Christ's sake, why start that again.

178

I was what, twenty-five, still hanging around in Troy in my first job out of grad school because I couldn't break up with my hot and handsome RPI Engineers hockey goalie. The Pope, a geezer virgin in red slippers and a white caftan with a three-tiered tiara, starts going down that path again of telling people how to mix their DNA. I'm sure the encyclical came with diagrams like the Kama Sutra because there's so many ways to misinterpret directions in Latin with all of those declensions. Everyone thought Nilo had done a good thing uniting all these philosophies to get behind working toward a better future and here Rome is literally saying don't eff with God's purpose for effing. Get real. Suddenly, holy war breaks out around whether the Inquisition is coming back to the same institution that did a lot of damage to a lot of kids last century for ignoring its own priests breaking the exact same rules the Pope was insisting on.

Then that Pope dropped dead and a couple of puffs of white smoke later we have the current guy, Francis III, not only resurrecting the idea of unified philosophies with the Canterbury Concord, but also snubbing its nose at Nilo, Genilo, and C Squares. Which brings me back to the big news and our adventure.

This year, as anyone hearing this log will know, the location for the actual conference just blew the doors off of centuries of religious animosity. Of course it was particularly exciting for me because otherwise I never would have been able to see up close the holiest place in my wife's faith. That's right, Makkah. I was tickled pinker than I am. The

Saudi clerics don't even allow non-believers to use cheap virtual interaction glasses to visit the al-Masjid al-Haram and Kaaba. When virtureal tech was developed, they okayed it for Muslims who couldn't afford the hajj to use that as a substitute. They even shipped Zamzam water to those who completed the hajj that way.

We asked our daughters and our four best friends Jackson and Melinda Paris, Randi Traynor, and Fabio Amarante to attend with us and registered. Moleka's brother Mustafa and his wife planned to participate from Sevilla, the closest site to Marseilles. This was going to be so great. Then it got even better.

Our daughter Bell had just defended her doctoral dissertation at MIT. I was really proud and touched that she had picked up a topic that I had worked on for my master's thesis at RPI. Our daughters were raised to decide what faith, if any, they were going to choose when they felt it was right to choose. We did all of the Christian and Muslim holidays at home. We put them in touch with friends wherever we could if they wanted to try something else. Sophia chose Buddhism when she was fourteen, more for the vegetarianism I think. Isabella could not decide. She liked them all.

In particular, Bell developed an interest in how the holidays for Christians, Jews, and Muslims are calculated. Her mind just works that way where she can see several cycles moving at different speeds, backing up sometimes to account for rounding of months. She's a bit like Tesla in that she can run the algorithms in her head. Not an easy feat. I

180

remember having an especially bizarre coding professor who had us write the programs for the Gauss and Meeus/Jones/Butcher algorithms in the last Java script and in the newest out of China we had just learned called XindeJava. He was Austrian and loved the Easter Market at Schönbrunn Palace outside Vienna every year, so much that he taught himself how to calculate Easter on the Gregorian calendar when he was ten using the Gauss algorithm. What a bastard of a prof.

I remember how excited Bell was when she wrote a history paper on the customary practice for early Christians to consult their Jewish neighbors to determine when the week of Passover was going to be. They would set Easter on the Sunday that week. She's like her father, interested in historical trivia, especially math related. I didn't know Dionysius Exiguus introduced the idea of counting years from Christ's birth when he published new Easter tables in 525. Of course, no one uses A.D. for Anno Domini any longer. It may have taken the USA until 2037 to finally adopt the metric system, but pretty much everyone was on board with BCE and CE by then. I think I was in my twenties the first time I saw an A.D. reference and had to ask what it meant.

Anyway, Bell decided to apply metamathematics to the question of how best to calculate Easter and the holy days and feasts of Islam and Judaism. She considered whether Richard's paradox could be resolved using any of the variations of *computus*, the Latin term for the process of calculating Easter. The idea came to her because on the usual solar calendar Easter is a moveable feast, but it must fall during an unchanging period of 35 days covering the end of March and most of April. On the lunar calendar, however, which is also used to determine the special days for the two other monotheist religions, Easter never moves. It is always the third Sunday in the lunar month in which Passover falls. In meta theory, that last sentence is both the definition of a date and the date itself. Look at any Jewish lunar calendar year. Find the paschal month. Look for the third Sunday. Bingo! The sentence "equals" that date on the calendar.

Words and phrases in a human language like English sometimes define specific real numbers. For example, the phrase "the number of cats in my house" equals three, because we have three cats. The phrase "my name is Ben" does not define a real number. There are an infinite number of both kinds of phrases. Richard's paradox is using English to define what strings of English words unambiguously define a real number and what strings of English word do not requires an infinite number of words. The definition would need to have an infinite number of words. Except a definition by definition has a finite number of words! Get it? The only way out of the mess is to assert the exact opposite: no way exists to unambiguously determine which English sentences define real numbers.

Arrange the infinite number of definitions according to the number of characters and alphabetically. Then assign each one to a number in the normal integer sequence starting with 1 so that the shortest definition beginning with 'a' is assigned to 1, the second one to 2, et cetera. Look for instance where the definition defines the integer assigned to it. Fun right? Yeah, I know. Then again, who's ever gonna play back these entries, right? Well, the funny thing is that first English definition for a number is 'a' and 'a' unambiguously means 1, so the number assigned to the definition fits that definition. Ta-dah! However, if the definition is 'the first natural number', then the number of the definition does not have the property of the definition itself because it is also a definition for 1 and the definition is going to be a ways down the list and so paired with a big number. Whatever is assigned to that definition fits the paradox and is called a Richardian number.

One more and we're done. Prime numbers are 'not divisible by any integer other than 1 and itself'. Obviously, we would have to actually create the list of definitions to see what number is assigned to it. For now, we don't care if that number is Richardian or not. On the other hand, we can change the rules and decide to count how many characters, but not spaces or punctuation, are in the definition. Guess what? Count them if you want but there are 43 characters in that definition. Since 43 is itself not divisible by any integer other than 1 and itself, then the number of this definition has the property of the definition. Cool beans.

Computus is supposed to be an algorithm that correctly establishes when Easter is every year until the end of time. No algorithm can do that exactly. Easter is an event defined by the 1582 papal bull

Inter gravissimas that also replaced the Julian solar calendar with the Gregorian solar calendar. The bull said that the Catholic Church was using the *computus* Dionysius Exiguus stated was fixed by the Council of Nicaea in 325 CE, except the Nicene Council never decided how to calculate Easter. It only ruled all Christians should celebrate Easter on the same Sunday. The *computus* developed by the Church of Alexandria 15 to 25 years before the Council, however, became the model used by Dionysus Exiguus. In essence, *computus* is undefined or has multiple definitions. On top of that, Easter is a solar calendar event determined by lunar months.

What does this have to do with anything? Wouldn't you know Bell was invited to speak on a panel at the C Cubed in Makkah. Seriously. One of the things with the Canterbury Concord is for the monotheistic religions and their denominations and sects to work out a calendar together that maximizes their ability to share holidays and festivals with each other if they are linked like Easter and Passover. And it so happens that Shavuot and Pentecost, both originating from the same day on the Jewish calendar, fell on Sunday June 7, 2076, even though Pentecost is a moveable feast date. The closest Muslim holiday, Isra and Mi' raj, celebrating the Prophet's Night Journey to Jerusalem, isn't until June 29, but the organizers felt two out of three would be the norm anyway. They decided to hold a panel and invited our Bell to actually be there. On top of that, they said all panelists were allowed to bring up to nine guests who would be the other participants in Makkah. Can you believe it?

We left Boston on May 28. As I said, our Sophia could not go, but Moleka and I, our friends who had already registered for the event, Isabelle's graduate advisor and two of her friends went. We wanted Mustafa and his wife to go, but they already are hajji and thought non-Muslims should go and take advantage of this once-in-a-lifetime experience. Amazing.

You know, my paternal grandmother, the real one, Dr. Adams, left some things with my parents for me to go through if I ever found out about her. Of course, I did when I started doing consulting work for Genilo and they scanned my DNA. Anyway, she had left a journal from when she was growing up in Arlington, Virginia. It was crammed full of souvenir cards, ticket stubs, and other reminders of events she described in the journal.

One of the most touching I remember is the entry when she had gone to see the great Washington Temple of the Church of Jesus Christ of Latter-day Saints. After it was completed and before it was consecrated they opened it up for people of all faiths or no faith to visit and tour the building. My grandmother mentioned windows made from marble so thinly cut they let sunlight through, an enormous baptismal font on the backs of life-sized bronze oxen, and appointments so rich the outlay boggled her mind. She was not one for directly criticizing anything judging from that journal and other things I found. The entry ended with a comment along the lines that she felt

185

fortunate to have witnessed that church's glorification of their God and puzzled at a house of worship that provided luxurious comfort to the earth-bound saints that would use it but could have no utility for God or for the community. It was the first time in my life I ever realized that so many of us pray to or praise our Creator far more often than we thank our Creator or appreciate the world we claim was created for us.

The trip to Arabia certainly gave us a greater appreciation for the world. None of us had ever flown before except Moleka as a young child when her family moved from Bahrain. To be honest, there wasn't much to see but clouds except just after take-off and landing on each of the two legs. It was a shame the arrangements didn't include a day or two in Paris coming or going, but I was taught never to complain about anything given freely to me. We arrived in Jeddah and took a well-appointed mag lev to Makkah. I could spend hours describing the desert landscapes, the incredible juxtaposition of hypermodern buildings with traditional Arabic Muslim and tribal designs, and the simple, plentiful, aromatic food. Of course, the food part we were quite familiar with. The rest, well...I always thought people were being hyperbolic when they referred to something as the experience of a lifetime. Perhaps they were, perhaps not. This most certainly qualified.

Above all, we were all one and individual. That, above all else, has left a profound feeling with me and is probably why I find it necessary to explain this all while it is still such a vivid memory.

The *ulema* granted permission for this extraordinary gathering on the condition that all participants followed the rituals and practices consistent with *Ihram*. The religious authorities felt the only acceptable way to allow non-believers to visit the *Haramayn*, the two holy places of Makkah and Medina, was as though they were on *Umrah*, a minor pilgrimage. That meant before we left Jeddah and crossed the *Miqat*, the boundary into the area of pilgrimage, we all washed with unfragranced soap. The men put on the two pieces of unstitched white cloth as the clothes we would wear throughout the visit. The women put on white *abayas*. We all received sandals that had no knots or stitches. We agreed not to cut our hair or nails, shave, have sex, kill any creature, or swear until we left the *Haramayn*. The joke in our group was five of the six are easy to do without for week, but the difficult one is never the same for any two people. Hah! I'm not going to tell you what mine was.

All jokes aside, I can't emphasize enough how these simple acts transformed us. Adopting the preparedness for the spiritual journey through *Ihram* represents one's shedding of one's self to be just one of many all of whom are equal. Except it wasn't just symbolic. We all felt it. We became equals in everything. Our actions reflected the Golden Rule more thoroughly than I have ever encountered before or since. For example, the non-Muslims attending were not required to perform the three *Umrah* rituals: *tawaf*, circling the Kaaba seven times anticlockwise, *Sa'i*, rapidly walking seven times back and forth between the hills of Safa and

187

Marwah, and *halq*, shaving or cutting back one's hair after the pilgrimage is completed. Nonetheless almost everyone dutifully carried the first two out sometime during the conference and the third at the end.

I am not sure what our experience would have been if we had stayed in Boston and used the virtureal equipment. We met quite a few people that way from all over the world. As enjoyable as those encounters were, they paled in comparison to the experience of being there. It wasn't a matter of talking to someone you knew was a densographic projection. The tech is so sophisticated nowadays you stop thinking the person is thousands of miles away once the conversation gets going. It was talking with someone not sharing the *Ihram*, a disconnect I didn't realize consciously until the conference was almost over.

Everyone in Makkah wasn't just physically present. Certainly the attendees from satellite conferences were just as intellectually present as we were. But we also were spiritually present. We had put on the clothes of a pilgrim to a holy place, participated in the rituals of a pilgrim. We were present as children of God being brothers and sisters, not just saying we were brothers and sisters. I truly understood the power of being reborn in faith, not faith in God but faith in humanity. Now, I close my eyes and I am transported to the presence of others in a manner no technology can ever duplicate. If all people could share this closeness and oneness at some moment in their lives, I can say

188

without any trivialization or exaggeration this world
would be a far better place.

Chapter Mu

Susannah's mouth opened to form a syllable, but her brain was too busy processing the information to have time to think of one. She blinked and furrowed her brow just as Tom raised his eyebrows to indicate he was waiting for her to speak. She didn't.

At some point the scientist had placed her left hand over the lower lab coat pocket on that side. She became conscious of the pad in the pocket. She had brought it with her because it had the report on the genetic testing of the baby that had prompted her to want to see Dr. Nilo. While she was still dumbstruck by what Tom Paris had told her, not to mention a bit overwhelmed by the volume of information he had provided her with, her brain seemed to know the pad was important because she pulled it out of her pocket and held it up. A quick touch at the bottom of the screen and the report appeared just where she had left off. Number eight on the kith list for baby Lila Callahan was Susannah Markovic. Without even looking at the screen, she handed the pad to Tom. He stood to grasp it and starting moving around the desk.

"What's this?"

"Um, the reason I'm here."

Tom looked at the screen and saw his co-worker's name. Susannah Elise Markovic, Chosen, third degree kith. He scrolled up the list. No names he recognized. Wait. Nilsson. Moleka al-Sheikh Nilsson, Organic, maternal grandmother. Up one more. Benjamin Rodgers Nilsson, Organic, maternal grandfather. Up one more. Adam Eli Nilo, Organic, maternal great-grandfather and paternal grandfather. Up one more. Alfred Matthias Schweiger, Chosen, male gamete donor. Up one more. Sophia Nilsson Callahan, Organic, mother.

The man sighed. "Why you are here? Doctor, did you intend the double-entendre?"

"The what?"

"Never mind. What I see is more topics you will need to talk about with Regina on Thursday."

"How so?" At this point, either Susannah could no longer care that Tom was on a first name basis with Professor Daniels or her brain could no longer accept all of the information he was throwing at her.

"To answer your original question first – and I'm sure there should be a drum roll or trumpet fanfare by now – you are related to this newborn baby girl in the third degree. Arthur only mentions degree when it has sufficient evidence to calculate it. Among the possible ways to be related in the third degree, you can't be the baby's great grandchild. It is highly unlikely you are the baby's niece. That leaves you being the baby's great aunt."

"That's not possible. I have no siblings."

Tom smiled wryly and widened his eyes. "Okay, this is the part I have been avoiding and the heart of why you need to go to DC. You apparently saw your name on this report and panicked before you noticed any other information. Otherwise, you would have run down here immediately rather than tap to make an appointment."

Susannah looked absolutely helpless and blank. Tom had no choice but to continue.

"Dr. Markovic, you were never meant to know this. You are not an Organic or even an O/2 like me. You are a C Square."

The scientist's mouth opened again in shock, but she was speechless again.

"You are not just any C Square either. You are Dr. Nilo's Eve. You are the perfected human female he wanted an Adam for."

Her eyes narrowed as she stepped back from this awful news. She needed something. She needed an escape route from this horror. "Tom, what about Arthur? What about 2016?"

The man did his best to breathe and prepare himself. "Arthur told Dr. Nilo that he had produced a perfect male human on September 28, 2016, the day this baby's maternal grandfather was born. Benjamin Rodgers Nilsson was born to one Amelia Evangeline Rodgers."

"And one Adam Eli Nilo." Susannah slumped back in the chair. "What was he thinking?"

Tom started to chuckle a bit and quickly realized his colleague was not going to be as amused as he was with his response. "Well there, ah…I have a pretty good idea what he was thinking when the baby was conceived since he hadn't turned seventeen yet and a pretty good idea what he was thinking when Ms. Rodgers later married Duke Nilsson, a not so coincidentally similar name to the boy's biological father. When did you have in mind?"

"When the good doctor started using his own genetic material for C Squares."

"Please." He was shocked she was being so naïve. "You know the man. He would not have thought twice about thinking his DNA would be a perfect starting point for creating a perfect human."

The realization dawned on her. The news she was a Chosen suddenly jumped back out. "Wait a minute! I'm related to this baby because I'm Nilo's child also?"

Tom shrunk back a bit from the emotion. "Well, biologically, yes."

"Oh, for Dog's sake. Are you serious? I'm thirty-five years old. I work for a genetics lab. If I'm a C Square, then legally I'm not even supposed to have this job. How is this possible? What am I going to do?"

Tom reached out and gently touched both of her upper arms as they swung back to her sides. Then he pressed his palms into her biceps. "Dr. Markovic, I am a little surprised you immediately thought about your career before anything else, but I can reassure you that no one is ever going to know about this unless you say something. I won't. Dr. Nilo won't." He held up the pad he was holding against her upper arm. "This report is going to the baby's parents and this list of kith will not be on it. Mr. Nilsson, his wife, his daughter, his son-in-law, none of them are going to know you are related."

Susannah pressed the palms of her hands against her temples. "Tom, Ben and Moleka Nilsson are my neighbors. I just asked them last night to watch my dogs while I'm away this week.

193

They've…I'm supposed to…" Yet one more unconsidered aspect of this web of relationships opened in her mind. "Wait a minute! Tom, how is it that I can be a biological half-sister to Ben Nilsson, and he just happens to live around the block from me on Mill Pond? Don't tell me that's a coincidence."

Nilo Biography – Chapter 6

"Art is the most intense mode of individualism that the world has known." – Oscar Wilde

The 'it' Donna Milgard had gone to see after lunch was a perfect reproduction of Michelangelo's Pietà the 3D printer assembled from the marble granules. The copy was perfection in every way. Glossy Carrara marble just as Michelangelo had used. The Virgin's billowing robe with deep recesses to hide the improbability of her small body holding her adult son's long, muscular body across her lap demonstrated the printer's remarkable capabilities. That said it was a copy of the master's work. No creative process here. The only cognitive excitement appeared to lay in finding out why Arthur chose this particular piece.

Edgar Iwa had not been too thrilled about finding over three tons of marble needed to be lifted off of the printer's production base. The tech in the printer's room had contacted him because he had no way of budging it. The cabinet pieces previously made with the largest 3D printer had been an alloy metal fabric riddled with nanoscale holes that allowed heat to exit but prevented dust from entering. They were bulky and somewhat heavy, but not two over-sized human adults bulky or three tons heavy.

After getting Edgar's informed opinion that yes the sculpture could be moved although that would require renting equipment, Donna asked him to start making the arrangements and she would get approval from Dr. Nilo. When he started to ask where he was going to be moving it to, Donna told him she had to run since she couldn't be late. By the time she was back at the far end of the executive wing, she was out of breath and flushed.

Mrs. Tutwiler looked up from her screen. "Oh, good. I will let Dr. Nilo know you are here. By the way, I see what the problem is. We need to talk after you're done, but I'm sure Dr. Nilo will direct you to do that anyway."

The assistant tapped a few keystrokes and stood. "Okay, Ms. Milgard. This way."

Delores opened the door to the office. When Donna stepped in the first thing she noticed was the undulating wall of windows looking out onto her Japanese garden. Her private garden? She became very uneasy realizing that all this time the owner of the company could have been observing her while she sat eating and reflecting whenever she went there for lunch. Not that she ever did anything odd or worthy of comment. Still, she was disquieted seeing now the space she treasured for its serenity was nothing more than a zoo enclosure. No, perhaps that was too strong. Perhaps.

"Donna Milgard, yes?"

The voice startled her. She had not noticed her employer standing to her right as she entered the room. All she had seen was the garden and a ghost image of her sitting in the garden not thirty minutes before. The technician relaxed her shoulders, an instinctive action her body took to prevent her from slowing the blood flow to her brain after a fright.

"I'm sorry. I rarely meet with employees here. I forgot we don't say anything about this being one-way glass. I really never had any ulterior motive for having it installed. I knew a garden like this would be soothing for me to look at whenever I needed. I made sure the architect included space for it and made this office kind of merge with it. I didn't think it should be just mine to use though. I thought everyone should be able to enjoy it if they pleased. I just couldn't have employees peering in. I can't have anyone peering in. I'd never get anything done. By the time someone pointed out that perhaps people should know I could see them, I thought it was a bit late really. I mean what would I say? I have been watching you like Big Brother? I'm sure no one would like that. I mean who would trust me after that even though it was just one of those things I never thought through. I know we make sure everyone knows that Arthur does have the ability to monitor everything in the building and on the campus except the washrooms. Legal thought that up and I agreed. Arthur exists to learn and…and…oh, well never mind."

Mrs. Tutwiler waited until Dr. Nilo had finished. She was used to him explaining his motives to people. Intelligent people are always afraid they aren't being understood or will be misunderstood. So, they explain everything. Or at least try to.

"Dr. Nilo, perhaps Ms. Milgard would like to sit over there by the window, and you can discuss everything where it is more relaxed."

Adam smiled. Thirty years old and he still needed maternal direction. If it hadn't been for his consistent focus on building NILO and fretting over NILO gaining artificial intelligence, Adam Nilo could have easily spun into a profound melancholy after news reached him about his mother. Mrs. Tutwiler had seen to it that he maintained that focus through the years and would see him through another twenty years before passing the baton.

"Oh, yes, of course, Mrs. Tut. Ms. Milgard?" Dr. Nilo raised his arm palm out to point to a pair of comfortable-looking chairs beside a table. Donna walked toward them, her employer a few steps behind. She suddenly noticed all of the toy dinosaurs were stacked in piles to the left of the door. They had not been moved since she helped to transport them here. Why had she not noticed the garden then?

Before the question formed fully in the young woman's head, Delores interjected, "May I get tea? I know it's a bit early, Dr. Nilo. Ms. Milgard, how do you take your tea?"

Donna turned just as she reached one of the chairs. "Oh, I don't know. I don't really drink hot tea."

"I'll make some peppermint. It doesn't require anything."

"Oh, uh, thank you, Mrs. Tutwiler."

Dr. Nilo had caught up with Donna and pointed to the chair on the other side of the table from them. "Please, sit down, Ms. Milgard."

Donna sat and Adam followed suit.

"Ms. Milgard, I will get right to the point. I remembered you helped bring those dinosaurs Arthur ordered to Mrs. Tut's office from the 3D printer. Now I understand you asked Arthur about ten days ago to choose a sculpture that would test various aspects of the 3D printer."

"Yes, sir. I was following your directions to get NILO/AI to explore ways to improve the printer in ways that Genilo could legally obtain a patent or sell to the printer's manufacturer."

Nilo leaned in closer to Donna, which allowed the aloha shirt he was wearing to billow out a little and show some of his chest. "You really don't have to call me sir. I know I own the company and all, but it's a bit weird given we are probably about the same age."

"Oh, of course, Dr. Nilo. Whatever you like."

Adam sat back again and smiled slightly. "Good. Um, now what were the results of you asking Artie, sorry, Arthur to perform this task."

"Well that's why I probably would have asked to speak to you or have my supervisor speak to you this afternoon once I found out. But when Mrs. Tut…"

Delores at that moment brought over the tea tray and placed it on the table. "I am sorry. Please I didn't intend to interrupt. It's just mint tea." She poured into two cups from the porcelain pot. "Ms. Milgard was about to say she thought you asked for this meeting because you already knew what Arthur's order to the printer was." She turned and walked back to the inset area where she had prepared the tea.

"Yes, uh…yes, Dr. Nilo. It is rather interesting and peculiar and, and … difficult."

"What is?"

"Arthur ordered three-thousand pounds of Carrara marble granules under the name Arthur Nilsson and had the printer duplicate Michelangelo's Pietà from the Vatican. I really haven't had a chance to look at it yet, I mean in detail. I mean the sculpture. However, that's what it is and now Mr. Iwa in Facilities is looking for the proper equipment to move it from the printer room to…to…"

The man leaned forward again. His employee again noticed the patch of soft, dark fur between and beneath the collar of his decidedly un-business-like shirt. "To where, Ms. Milgard?" he asked eagerly, unaware of the effect his physicality was having.

"I don't know."

Mrs. Tutwiler was by the door now. "Shall I ask the Archdiocese or Isabella Stewart Museum if they would like the statue donated with sufficient funds to have it moved, installed, and formally presented? Oh! No, better if I ask Legal to contact the Archdiocese for now. I just realized the Vatican may hold the rights to reproducing the piece, but they can't very well sue us if we offer to donate it, can they?" Before her employer could answer, his assistant was already closing the door behind herself.

Adam Nilo turned to Donna Milgard. "There. Now that Mrs. Tut is going to dispose of the body for you, well…oh, I guess its bodies, right? What I

200

mean to say is we have more important matters to discuss. I hope you don't mind, but I find it helps me if I get the facts first. I have been told by you-know-who that I sound like I am interrogating people when I do this. Strictly speaking, I am but, well…so please, I'm not really."

The technician nodded despite not knowing exactly why.

"Good. First, what parameters did you give Arthur?"

"Oh, yes," she responded too hastily. The inventor didn't seem to notice, which made her all the more flustered.

"I, uh…oh!" Donna started to look out the window to gather her thoughts and immediately rejected that mode of defense. Smelling him as he continued to lean so close in was not helping.

She simply had to look at her employer straight on while consciously reminding herself that this was a business meeting. "Request the large 3D printer to reproduce a sculpture from the art archives that provides optimal conditions for assessing its functions and capacities." Now she felt more comfortable. "Evaluate instances when the 3D printer fulfills the request for Genilo to create marketable features that enhance, augment, or refine the 3D printer's functions and capacities sufficiently to avoid violating the patents held by the 3D printer's manufacturer. I figured the sculpture would need to be somewhat complex and probably something crafted by someone famous like Rodin or Michelangelo since Arthur would need to provide records of the piece chosen showing all angles."

"Great. Did you ask Arthur why he chose the sculpture he did?"

"Should I have?" Now she was panicking again.

Nilo screwed up his mouth and blew air from his nose. "I did."

"About this sculpture?"

"First off, remember those?" He nodded to the piles of dinosaurs against the wall and furrowed his brow.

"Yes, of course."

He sighed and slouched slightly, "I asked Arthur why he made them. And he told me…uh, told me that given the vague parameters I had chosen he had to think through the project." The scientist adjusted himself in the chair. "Well, actually, I only told it to make something, something using thirty kilos of material. I was just being lazy. You see, my intention was to see what it could do but not the way it did it."

Donna searched in her employer's face and suddenly saw the anxiety driving him at that moment. Panic shifted to sympathy in record time. "Dr. Nilo, I saw the final report. Everyone was impressed that a machine could go through the steps on its own of selecting parameters to make something that could be useful rather than a waste of material. Surely, you programmed it to reason in ways that created beneficial results, right?"

Her boss just continued to look past her to the dinosaurs. What else should she say?

202

Chapter Nu

Tom frowned. He had known for five years that this day was going to come. Dr. Nilo and Ms. Rafayela had spent quite a bit of time filling him in on the dodgier aspects of the company. Aside from employing Chosen as researchers, the company did nothing illegal. Dr. Nilo did not even categorize that as a violation of the law. He felt that since he was the one who had insisted the government prohibit C Squares from certain professions that gave them too much access to developing some means of taking over, he could just as easily ignore the law if he thought it was in the interest of humanity. Yes, he could ask for waivers or some other means of making his action above-board. Asking for waivers would lead to unwanted publicity and unwarranted suspicions. No one needed to know anything until someone destined to discover something needed answers.

Dr. Nilo, above all others, knew that all questions had to have an answer. Of course his timing wasn't great. He had abruptly left the night before with a nurse and the heads of Finance and Facilities. The circuits in Tom Paris' brain that snapped into place whenever he was given information that connected to information he already had crackled when he received the message that his boss would not be in. He was not surprised when the signal came in to implement Plan Omega. He had been busy making the arrangements that morning before Susannah Markovic contacted him.

Tom had been expecting the call. All the same it frustrated him because he knew he was going to be tied up for a few hours with the scientist. Nilo and Voleta had impressed upon him how important it was that he was to take his time doling out all of the history to give her, or any of the other crypto-Chosen at the firm, the chance to pull the threads together. Of course, Voleta later told him not to expect Dr. Markovic to make the connections because she was "after all" Chosen. It had taken Tom a while to understand why his predecessor had a certain sense of superiority toward Chosen. Eventually, the evidence piling up that the whole idea was a dead end as far as saving humanity helped to explain the attitude.

The day already had drained most of Tom Paris' emotional and intellectual energy. The worst part was still ahead.

"Doctor, would you mind if we went in there and sat. I can make some mint tea and there's the space by the windows that's a bit more relaxing. I thought of it earlier except I was under orders not to reveal Dr. Nilo wasn't here unless I was directly asked. It's something lawyers tell people when they are being interrogated, deposed, or testifying. Always answer the question honestly but only answer the question posed." He went to the door to the other office. "Shall we?"

Susannah stood and walked toward him. As likeable as he was, she had gone past the point of that mattering given his admission he had been stalling and evading her, not to mention maintaining a secret that was immensely personal to her.

204

However, she wasn't one to fume, particularly when she knew the reason for her annoyance was someone doing his job. As she crossed the threshold to Nilo's office she looked Tom in the eye and provided him with a uselessly perfunctory smile. "Mint tea sounds nice."

Tom swallowed guilt on that comment, particularly after she appeared to withdraw the smile even more quickly than it had appeared. He decided it best to not say anything more until they were settled in the conversation area by the windows. Clumps of Siberian iris were blooming in the garden directly outside. Once the tea tray was on the table, he started.

"Dr. Markovic, as I said, you are the Eve we discussed, the Chosen Dr. Nilo felt epitomized his goal of perfecting humanity. He is your biological father. You wouldn't know it from any pictures available after his successes because he broke his nose rather badly when he was twenty-three, but you do resemble him. From what I have seen, Ben Nilsson takes after his mother more in appearance, plus he is old enough to be your father and most men fill out a bit in the nose, cheeks, and jaw after fifty. The house you live in really is your family's home and you did inherit it from your grandmother, Dr. Victoria Adams, Nilo's mother. It is the house Nilo was raised in. He grew up with Ben Nilsson's mother living in the same neighborhood. As teenagers they obviously found each attractive and available enough to have intercourse, resulting in Mr. Nilsson's birth when Nilo was seventeen.

"The reason why Ben Nilsson is now your neighbor is simple. He inherited the house his mother had inherited from her parents. Before he was born, Nilo went off to become educated and begin his career, signing away all paternal rights. His mother arranged for her grandson to receive an education and be looked after.

"Dr. Adams was a remarkable woman particularly when it came to making arrangements for those dear to her. She never left things to chance, and always hired lawyers who could draft trust documents solid enough to withstand any challenge and flexible enough to be used as intended even if circumstances changed. It was a good thing too for several reasons. She knew her son was brilliant and capable of changing the course of history in this century as long as he didn't get himself killed. So, when he left her supervision as a young man she insisted that he allow her to provide him with an assistant who was to act for him in dealing with the more mundane but essential aspects of being an adult. That person is a valet, administrative assistant, accountant, or whatever role was needed to insure Dr. Nilo did not get into trouble over some minor issue like paying a bill or leaving the house without trousers. And yes, he was at times that bad if he was deeply into a project."

Susannah started giggling almost without realizing. "Oh, my! I don't believe it!"

"What? The trousers bit?"

"No, no. Yesterday, I referred to Kryste Kind, as an assist animal for geniuses."

206

Tom shook his head and laughed with her. "Too funny!" They continued to laugh and sipped the tea.

"Well, in that case, I am Dr. Nilo's assist animal, as was Voleta Rafayela and Delores Tutwiler. That is why we are the ones chosen to maintain all of the secrets. We have to know in the event something happened to Dr. Nilo or in the event someone like you discovered enough of a secret you needed to be filled in on the rest. Anyway, another arrangement Dr. Adams made was that her house on Mill Pond was to be gifted along with money for upkeep to the oldest biological and legal daughter of Adam Eli Nilo. You see she knew her son was going to carry out her work in eugenics if possible. And she knew it was unlikely that her son would procreate naturally again. Miss Rodgers had spoken with her when she discovered she was pregnant. She didn't know what to do because Nilo only had intercourse with her because she wanted to be with him. He agreed but told her he would only do it once just to have the experience. Dr. Adams sorted out that her son was, well is asexual."

"But we both know his gametes have been used to produce a lot of Chosen. Why me? How am I legally his daughter?"

"I told you. You are his Eve. Once he realized that you met almost every criterion he had established as perfection, my predecessor convinced him he needed to legally recognize you as though you had been deliberately chosen to be his daughter. He saw the logic in making you the beneficiary of the Mill Pond house trust."

"What logic? Just because I had more check marks on his list of attributes?"

Tom tilted his head to the left and looked up while figuring out how best to explain. He quickly determined he might as well be straightforward. He looked across into Susannah's waiting eyes.

"Dr. Nilo considered you close to perfect in part because you inherited his tendency toward asexuality and lack of gregariousness. Ms. Rafayela argued that even with those characteristics it was safer for you to live somewhere secluded enough that you would not have many interactions with men and still work for Genilo."

"Except I got the house after I was already attending Hopkins in Baltimore and then spent several years at Berkeley before I came back and started working here. They didn't pen me up in a convent."

"Of course not! That wouldn't have done much good. Besides, no matter how anti-social you are naturally, you still had to learn how to interact with others, particularly other scientists."

Susannah jerked her head to the right suddenly in recognition. "Wait a second! Did they hire Josh Olejniczak to befriend me at Hopkins? Is that why he was like my shadow for three solid years and never once even tried to get romantic?"

Tom was more amused that she had finally made a connection on her own than afraid of her tone of voice. "Did you mind his company?"

"Well, no...I mean...still." She exhaled the annoyance and crossed her arms. "And who spied on me in California?"

208

"Oh, that was handled a bit differently. Since there hadn't been any problems in Baltimore, Voleta just used our connections with the department there to provide us with warnings if your progress to degree showed any signs you were getting involved with anyone. She pitched it as being our right to insure the money Genilo was paying them for your education was not being spent on someone partying and carousing."

Susannah tightened her crossed arms and almost growled across the small table. "Really? Why not just treat me as a human being and tell me the truth? Or at least why not tell me I had to save myself for the perfect man just like every girl used to be told? "

Tom sighed and looked out the window at the deep purple flowers topping dark green stems. When he turned back to look at the woman sitting across from him, he realized he had to agree with her up to a point. Treat her like a human being.

"Dr. Markovic?"

She raised one hand. Her eyes narrowed as though looking at a target. "Hold that thought. Why am I Dr. Markovic and you're Tom? It just occurred to me that you are addressing me as a superior. You are the one in the superior position revealing these secrets about me to me. Why am I not Susannah and you Mr. Paris?"

Tom rolled his eyes unconsciously. "Doctor, you know very well policy states…"

"Policy states I shouldn't even be employed here."

"I am not the one who decided to make an exception to that policy. I am not authorized to make any exceptions to policy, including when I am telling someone profoundly personal information about a person that has been kept secret to that person. You are not grasping the fact that your employment here is one example of treating you as a human being. If you were being treated merely as a product as the law states for C Squares, you would not be employed here. You would not legally be the daughter of Adam Eli Nilo. You would not have your house. Parents have been spying on their children and interfering in their adult lives for millennia. Fathers have gone to great lengths to protect their daughters' chastity just as long. It's not as though you have been Rapunzel secreted in a tower. Even with all of that, the fact remains you were created by your father for the express purpose of creating a perfected human being."

"I didn't ask to be created!"

"None of us do! None of us." Tom Paris looked at the floor and shook his head. "Did you even stop to think about Arthur telling Dr. Nilo that he had created a perfect human being on September 28, 2016? Arthur did not say August 12, 2046, or May 17, 2047. I know you know the second one. The first was the day two gametes merged to become a zygote that developed into a blastomere that was placed in the uterus of a woman who carried the developing fetus for a little over nine months until a baby was born on May 17, 2047, who was named Susannah Elise Markovic. Pretty much the same process began on New Year's Eve 2015 that

210

resulted in a baby born on September 28, 2016, who was named Benjamin Rodgers Nilsson. Get it?"

Personal Log, Benjamin Rodgers Nilsson, September 30, 2070

When I was twelve, my folks hooked up with two other families and arranged a vacation for us to Disney World. I think they were taking advantage of the fact that I actually had two close friends that I hung out with, Peter Greene and Yoshi Shimizu. For some reason, up until that point I was always just one of the kids in class and one of the kids in the neighborhood. I don't even remember anyone having any kind of real friendships the way I understand them now. Everyone did everything unless your family said you had something else to do. My brother and sister and I all just hung out with everyone else either within close age ranges or as a larger group. For whatever reason, just when each of us reached the cusp of puberty we hived off into small clusters of friends that did things together. We might hang with another cluster or two. Get enough of these little groups together and we would organize into teams for soccer or whatever.

My maternal grandfather told me about Little League, Pee Wee football, and Boy Scouts. I just looked those things up on the Net when I was thinking about doing a log entry. For centuries play and sports were the disorganized part of a child's development. Children performed chores and attended school. If they had free time that coincided with the free time of other children, they got together and did something. If not, they had individual pursuits. Child labor laws, universal elementary and secondary education, and middle-class lifestyles changed everything. Pretty much every kid in an area came in contact with all of the other kids at school. Teachers organized activities for kids. Phys Ed classes and school teams emerged, as well as after-school clubs. Robert Baden-Powell came up with the scouting idea. All of that organizing required parents or teachers to volunteer to supervise, coach, and referee.

A good part of the twentieth century saw children participating in all kinds of organized activities. Then video and real time multi-player games on early versions of the Net swept the country just as parents were finding out they had to work longer hours for the same or less pay. Organized, parent-led activities mostly disappeared. After the Islamic State attack, particularly the participation of so many Americans who decided to ally with ISIL against their government, we finally decided that the violence in electronic games was having a severely deleterious effect on how children viewed violence and banned pretty much everything on the market. Suddenly, my generation had nothing to do but fall back on the unorganized, informal activities children had been engaging in for so long before World War II. I was six, just the right age to segue into the new normal, or rather post-neo-retro normal as one wit described it.

I did my part. I wound up befriending Peter and Yoshi. They lived about five houses apart from one another and I was a couple of blocks away, closer to

Mill Pond. Our mothers were always contacting each other to find out where we were. Even when we told them where we were going they never paid too much attention. Do you have any idea how much more independent we became than the preceding three or four generations just from being able to go and have fun on our own?

The one thing our mothers made clear was for us not to go out on the lake without life vests, a reminder we had no way to forget when we were all taken to a memorial service for a classmate who drowned on Hopper Pond. I hardly knew the kid, but I still cry. At the time and ever after, we knew to never forget what we were doing had risks. Our parents knew risks are better learned from doing things even if that meant a few trips to urgent care along the way and many more worry lines later on. I can't imagine the grief, but we passed along the same cautions coupled with our full support for exploring fun fully to our girls. We will never regret giving them the same opportunities we had as children and teens as we had growing up. Funny, we actually did grow up rather than out as my mother's teen pictures showed.

From our mothers getting together a few times to discuss raising boys and husbands it was a quick leap to our fathers deciding to go to Bruins or Red Sox games together with the three of us in tow. This kind of socializing with parents and kids together was a renaissance of the involvement parents had in their kids' lives.

Anyway, I brought this up because we took that trip to Disney World over forty years ago, six adults, us three boys all twelve or thirteen, and four more junior siblings. We drove down in a rented thing, one of those behemoths we called full-size SUVs back then. I can't remember now what SUV stood for. We stopped in Washington and Savannah heading south and the Outer Banks and Baltimore coming home. It was quite a haul and we had much to amuse ourselves. Our parents all shared the same view that Disney merchandising to children was insidious, so it wasn't like we had grown up with toys based on Disney characters. The whole point really was to explore and learn. I didn't know then, but we hugged the Atlantic coast not only to see Yorktown and Kitty Hawk and such, but also to skirt the edge of the death zone.

I marveled at Spaceship Earth at Epcot. The iconic white ball appealed to me. Then I discovered the ride within the thing depicted the development of communication among humans. That did it. I was hooked on the idea of finding some way to be a part of helping people exchange information and ideas. When you're used to seeing lifelike graphics on an LCD screen and even fully immersive VR with goggles, it's more than a little hokey to view dioramas and animatronic figures, terms I had to look up since they aren't used at all these days, and I couldn't remember what those were called. Anyway, maybe it was because the presentation was so old-fashioned that I realized how important it is for humans to develop and learn communication technologies. It's amazing how stagnant they were until the printing press and then electronic communications and finally satellites and the Net.

We had a good run of about two hundred years of innovations.

My mother knew what a smartboard was from classes at Middlesex Community College, but she was surprised we had them in first grade. By the time Sophia started school they were just called 'boards'. Even by the time I was in high school we didn't have to take notes because our tablets were synched with the board and whatever got put up on it went into a file for that class. It was kind of nice to just be able to sit and listen to our teachers. Classes were a lot more interactive and organic than what they looked like from films and teleseries before I was born. It looked downright mind-numbing sometimes. No wonder they said our parents and their parents were poorly educated. In my time students did well just by paying attention all day and then running through and organizing their files in the evening.

God help you if you didn't pay attention. I remember seeing a movie in my college years from the early 1970s called *The Paper Chase* about some first-year law students. Then as now, I'm sure there were no laws prohibiting cruelty to lawyers, whether aspiring or admitted. Well let me tell you, I knew exactly what was going on with the Socratic Method used by the harsh professor in the movie. That had been the drill in high school for us. In fact, RPI was smooth sailing compared to having to be ready in history or Arabic class at Chelmsford High.

Now Sophia is a freshman at BU. Her ID was inserted this summer, replacing the DAU. Amazing how quickly kids get accustomed to the ins and outs of technology. She was already linked with everyone in her dorm before she was unpacked, and she didn't take more than two cases and a box. Sophia always has just taken to things. I don't know whether I would have liked being guided from birth by probabilities based on analysis of my DNA. She and her friends actually seem to be, well, self-assured and confident about their places in the world. It's not as though the DAU left her with no choices or prevented her from doing anything she wanted. Moleka said Sophia told her she was comfortable being given some direction based on her genetics, like she didn't have to fear failing because science told her this is what you're good at.

I guess that's okay. The world's scary enough without throwing in the risk of making piss-poor decisions about things like your major in college, which college, or even whether you go to college. For me it was a no-brainer. Dad never said a word other than that I could choose where I wanted to go no matter what the fees were. Mom showed me it wasn't so hard since she pushed herself to finish a bachelor's and a master's while working full time just to show herself she could do it. My folks insisted I work part time for spending money, never telling me just how much had been set aside for my education until the day I got my master's. By then, I was so used to working it was easy enough to decide to leave the remainder tucked away for my children. Considering the BRIC takeover, we were fortunate the sum was invested in a multinational basket. Otherwise, I don't know if Sophia would be attending school now.

I guess what I'm saying is that we get so involved with evolving technologies we tend to forget that we aren't evolving anywhere near as rapidly. Once we burn out one path we seem to reset back to zero, or something like it, considering all of the changes that have occurred. We blithely pursue what are to us new ways of doing things that really aren't that different from what was done three or five generations back. Before long, another breakthrough sends us back on another wild ride for half a century or so.

I would have bet good money ten, even twenty years ago when we were seeing just how bad things could get in this country economically that the C Square process was going to end that cycle. Seemed to me bringing online even just the small but growing number of Chosen produced in the first fifteen years was going to jolt us onto a smooth, continuous track of progress. It wasn't going to matter to anyone if they were our Chosen or their Chosen since the global economy was just web upon web of relationships. So long as the capitalists owned the means of production their nationality did not matter one bit. Who could have known that the huge transfer of assets after the BRIC takeover not only left few people in the West with the means to order Chosen children, but also made Chosen unwanted in any of the professions where they could have done the most good?

The only backbone our government showed in the 2050s was the Supreme Court ruling that Chosen were a product of human design and legal, not natural persons. They had to be given the same

218

rights as other legal persons like businesses, but they also could be subject to regulation. The floodgates to discriminatory legislation were opened. Talk about something old-fashioned becoming new again. We basically decided to reject a new technology out of fear of its consequences, something I doubt humans ever did before. Of course, the technology used was never other human beings.

219

Chapter Xi

Tom leaned over to grasp his teacup. He sipped while Susannah put the pieces together. He waited. After a couple of minutes she looked at him wearily and warily.

"Okay, Tom. Now that I have been put in my place, what next?"

Tom shrugged. "I apologize for my tone. Dr. Nilo was shattered, as I said earlier, when Arthur told him his son was a perfect human being and his daughter was not. Aside from having different biological mothers, the only difference between you and your half-brother is how you were conceived. It is important that you go to Washington and discuss that with Regina. Dr. Nilo was only able to move on as a result of her intervention and guidance. You see, aside from using his own genetic material and employing you and a few other Chosen who will remain unidentified, Dr. Nilo has never once done anything unethical. I wouldn't really call employing you unethical since he was the one that lobbied for the law out of concern that Chosen would take over society.

"Now we know that really didn't need to be much of a concern. Arthur did a very good job of choosing donors who were more apt to seek inner pride in their accomplishments rather than plaudits, a difference between motivation and ambition. Tracking careers chosen by C Squares has proven fascinating. Over 95 percent have no interest at all in politics and consider their abilities far too great to waste making money the old-fashioned way by manipulating markets, creating risky funds, or building rip-and-strip investment firms. The deeper surveys have proven they aren't just saying that to have the laws revoked, which will never happen anyway. Since it is lawful to discriminate against C Squares, entire sectors that match their talents are closed off from fear bad money will drive out good as it were. The entire premise backfired except for interest in O/2s.

"The one area Chosen have displayed ambition is in academia. They streak through university seeing how Organics have to put up with third-rate lecturers and graduate assistants at all but the most serious liberal arts colleges remaining. Then they spend half the time getting a PhD compared to the old averages. The older Chosen are already getting tenure and raking in money from consulting contracts even in fields that generally prohibit or are prohibited to C Squares. Companies want their expertise and intellect. They are quickly becoming the whores of MENSA Woody Allen once wrote about, except MENSA chose immediately after the C Square process was announced that they would not even accept O/2s as members since Organic geniuses would be pushed to the side."

"Wait…is one of the reasons we hired Josh Olejniczak out of Harvard because he's another secret Chosen?"

"Dr. Markovic, I am only permitted to tell you information about you."

Susannah scowled and looked out at the garden.

"Dr. Markovic, we already have discussed Arthur's view, but what is your view? Does it matter to you if Dr. Olejniczak is a C Square?"

That caused the scientist to sit back and digest more while keeping her eyes on the small waterfall from the pond that formed the stream. Tom Paris was clearly intimating there was or could be a more intimate relationship between her and Josh. *Was he matchmaking?* She asked herself. *Did it matter?*

After a few minutes, Tom spoke again. "There is a bit more you need to know before you see Regina. And if you are having any trouble answering that question, I know she can help you." He waited until the woman turned to look at him before continuing. "I made the offhand remark about Mr. Nilsson's stepfather having a surname similar to Dr. Nilo not being coincidental. It's odd in all of this that we only focus on one biological parent. That's intentional even if it is only subconsciously intentional if that's possible. There's Dr. Adams, mother of Dr. Nilo, and Dr. Nilo, father of you and Mr. Nilsson. Dr. Adams planned for the future. She had some help in that.

"A couple came to her clinic. They desperately wanted to have a child. The wife had malformed fallopian tubes and had an oophorectomy when she reached puberty. Her parents were devout Catholics and refused to allow her ovaries to be frozen for future use by her. The husband and wife were both brilliant sculptors, former Olympic athletes, and enormously compassionate. Ainar Nilsson offered to exchange his artwork for Dr. Adams' services in helping them with in vitro fertilization. She agreed

222

but not in exchange for art. She promised to help them find an art dealer and have a baby if they would agree to the husband donating sperm so Dr. Adams could have a child also. They accepted. Dr. Adams made sure the man agreed that he would have no legal, financial, or personal role with the baby she would have. She shortened Nilsson to Nilo because that was a much rarer surname than Adams. She named her son Adam Eli using her surname and the father's middle name. The couple's child was Jeremy 'Duke' Nilsson who, with some matchmaking by Dr. Adams, his biological mother, wed her grandson's mother."

"I don't believe this. You are talking about two of the most famous artists of this century and two of the greatest geneticists of all time. Ainar Nilsson and Victoria Adams are my paternal grandparents? My employer is my father? My newest neighbor is my half-brother? This is preposterous."

"Why? The only somewhat serendipitous part was that the matchmaking to substitute the Nilssons' son for Dr. Adams' son worked. Once she knew Adam Nilo was not going to be a part of Benjamin's life, it was rather obvious for her to at least try to get Duke Nilsson together with Ben's mother. After all they were one hundred percent biological brothers. In fact, they were twins born to different mothers practically. If Ben's mother found Nilo attractive enough she was likely to find his brother attractive as well."

"It's a freaking romance novel or something."

"I rather doubt a genre writer would be capable of coming up with this tangle of relationships. Oh, and speaking of that, the tangle of DNA from Dr. Nilo among C Squares made creating an Adam for you unwise if you didn't realize that already. The chastity belt as it were that my predecessor created for you was unnecessary as far as saving you for a higher purpose. That can never happen. I'm sorry."

"Sorry I'm still a virgin or sorry I was kept a virgin?"

"Look, you probably want to punch me in the nose right now, bu..."

He stopped due to her strange reaction. A surprised look had come over Susannah's face as she realized Tom Paris might know her weakness, followed quickly by the realization she actually cared if he did, and followed even more quickly by the realization she wanted to do it.

"I'd better leave."

Nilo Biography – Chapter 7

"[A]nybody in his right mind should have an inferiority complex every time he looks at a flower." – Alan Kay

Adam looked directly into the woman's eyes. She was earnest, honest. To his credit, Dr. Adam Eli Nilo always found positive characteristics in people much more attractive than physical appearance. Not that Ms. Milgard was unattractive in that sense either. He just rarely considered the shell that contained the intellect, reasoning, demeanor, sensitivities, and other attributes that were foremost in his mind when thinking of his fellow beings. While the inventor's ultimate aim was to find a process to perfect humanity, that aim did not include deciding for the world the ideal physiognomy.

"After a fashion, yes, I did do whatever I could to insure my creation had a broad range of beneficial characteristics. When you live to create or invent, seeking perfection is part of the process. Accepting one may never achieve it is not, but neither is achieving something one must accept. You see, it wasn't the result that I expected. And that wasn't the first time. Computers do what they are programmed to do and that is it. But Arthur…Arthur did something that doesn't seem possible, something I never would have guessed a computer could ever do. If a computer reaches a point where its instructions are too vague to go any further, what is it supposed to do?"

"AbEnd. Or, if programmed to do so, stop, ask for additional instructions."

"Exactly. Except Arthur doesn't do those things. He searches for workarounds. He looks for alternatives. He pursues every possibility to complete the task faithfully."

The young woman smiled and shook her head. "Dr. Nilo, I must be dense. I don't understand why that's a problem. You designed and built a machine capable of emergent behavior. Now it's doing that, and it bothers you. Why?"

Adam settled back into the chair again and looked out to the garden. After a moment of reflection, he looked back at Donna. "I designed and built a machine capable of artificial intelligence with specific emergent behavior. The machine acquired generalized emergent behavior in response to the commands I gave it using the programming I gave it in a manner I did not expect. I thought I had done everything that needed to be done for it to work. In my passion and hubris I overlooked something. The entire process went according to plan and then...for the first time it faced a barrier of my making.

"Any other machine would have AbEnded or stopped and asked for further instructions just as you said. Everything would have been as I intended. I would have seen I made an error and corrected the programming. I would have accomplished what I set out to accomplish. We would have an artificial intelligence that essentially knew every bit of

226

information there was to know and had every form of reasoning available to it to answer any questions asked. The emergent behavior would just be limited to the machine selecting the best method and best data for answering the question. In that sense, yes, I wanted it to find work arounds and better paths to accomplish tasks. Specifically, I wanted a machine capable of helping me develop a process to offer people the opportunity to choose the DNA sequences needed to improve our species and move us away faster than evolution permits from our violent tendencies."

Donna had been studying her employer's face and body language as he spoke. She could see how open he was being and how anxious he was about the problem he saw but she couldn't grasp it yet.

"Dr. Nilo, I know I was asked a few questions regarding my views on eugenics and world events when I was hired. I take it you don't want to employ people who would question the ethics of going down that path."

Adam smirked. "Yes, that was the idea. I'm not ashamed of my goal and will not set it aside if society doesn't approve. However, Legal insisted it best to vet prospects for employment to avoid conflicts of interest or the chance someone might decide it was necessary to leak information to stop us."

"I see. People may not recognize your noble purpose."

"I hope that wasn't sarcasm, Ms. Milgard."

The woman's cheeks flushed, "Oh, no! Dr. Nilo, I think it is noble. Otherwise I wouldn't have gotten past the psychometric testing to work here. I was just thinking about how difficult it is sometimes for scientists to explain why what they do has benefits for humanity. Let's face it, put the wrong way people might think you are some Frankenstein trying to create superhuman monsters."

"Exactly. At any rate, what the machine did instead of crashing was reason through how it could do what I asked. My error was coding that every question must have an answer. Nullity was prohibited. To me, that is a reasonable philosophy. I truly believe every question has a solution. Our capacity to find answers to problems however simple or complex to me distinguishes us from every other species. I never considered that a computer does not have a human spirit undaunted by challenges. This computer at any rate did because I was endowing it with so much of me.

"I define myself as intellect motivated by curiosity and desire to further human progress through technology. That was why and what I was giving NILO to make it NILO/AI. I only thought in terms of building the most intelligent, useful machine ever created, one that would have every answer to every question. I set no limits on what the machine could do in finding an answer, even if the answer was a set of probabilities. The machine did not see my mistake as an error. The machine saw it as just one more command that had to be put through. If null cannot ever be the result, there must be a result. The machine concluded that if every question has an answer it must be capable of determining the answer to every question. It

228

deduced that it was the answer to the question 'Can every question be answered?'"

Donna saw the fear and bewilderment Adam felt not being in full control of his creation. She thought she needed to do something to help him step away from those feelings. She looked at the table, finally focusing on something other than the man's profound admission.

"Doctor, the tea must be getting cold. I think even scientists still agree mint is soothing." She picked up a cup and placed it closer to him on a saucer.

Dr. Nilo studied the piece of bone china. As with everything in his office or home, Mrs. Tut had purchased the tea set or had someone else purchase it for him. Adam reached for the cup and raised it, never letting his eyes off the delicately painted spray of blue flowers against deep green-gray foliage. He wasn't sure even who to ask what type of flowers they were, having never engaged anyone in social conversations long enough to learn anything about them, "them" being the people with whom he spoke, any hobbies they had, or any flowers that might have come up. Botany was one of many subjects that he studied to ace the exams and be done with, without any pretense of interest or desire to remember anything taught unless it had something to do with his objectives for his extraordinary life.

"Do you like forget-me-nots, Dr. Nilo?"

"I'm sorry, what?" he asked, after gulping some of the tea upon realizing he might have been doing something peculiar.

Donna smiled courteously, "I was asking whether you like the flowers depicted on the tea service."

Nilo's eyebrows narrowed. "Oh, yes. They're nice enough."

Donna picked up her teacup and looked out the window. After taking a few sips, she set it down and turned to her employer. "Dr. Nilo, Arthur becoming more than you expected clearly has troubled you. I'm sorry I'm having such a difficult time understanding why. Is there anything specific perhaps…"

Nilo tapped his fingers on his left temple. "Yes. Two things in particular trouble me. One, Arthur accepted me as being infallible. As far as he is concerned I could not have commanded him to do something he could not do. Two, Arthur demonstrated more humanity, more compassion than I have. I never would have thought to ask him to make a bunch of dinosaurs to give to a school for children to learn. I probably would have told him to make a pile of bricks or something. I am obsessive-compulsive regarding science and tasks needed to further science."

The technician considered the problems before responding. "The second one is easy enough, I think. You endowed Arthur with all of the knowledge we have. Out of all of that, wouldn't an exceptionally objective reviewer see that compassion, a sense of community, and nurturing and educating children are hallmarks of human society at its best? Remove all of the clutter and nonsense from our lives, all of the frictions and

230

misunderstandings from our relationships, and we find our definition of humanity means helping others and cooperating. As for the other problem, has anyone else felt that Arthur thinks they are infallible?"

"Ah, you see, that is the most important reason why you are here. I queried Arthur why he chose to order the 3D printer to make a full-scale replica of Michelangelo's *Pietà* using the same material essentially that was used for the original. Aside from giving me the commands you entered, he further explained that he knew Michelangelo had been unjustly criticized for making the Virgin Mother look like a teenager, yet she had her thirty-three-year-old son in her lap. It had required quite a bit of skill to render plausibly that large body of an adult Christ on the lap of a young woman, which is why he came up with the idea of leaving a space where the infant should have been ready to nurse. That provided room to show voluminous robes covering her separated legs.

"You see, the technical issue had led Michelangelo to an even more profound artistic statement about Mary's relationship to her son. When the critics complained, Michelangelo said he wished he could inscribe *Vergine madre, figlia del tuo figlio* (Virgin mother, daughter of your son) on the sculpture to explain to anyone who didn't understand. He could not do that because he had signed his name in the one place where it made sense to put the explanation. Michelangelo never signed another sculpture. Arthur interpreted this as being an error that he could correct so the Master would finally have his masterpiece as he meant it to be."

Donna let the idea float to her and settle. "You're saying that Arthur deliberately chose the *Pietà* so it could correct something created, what, over six hundred years ago?"

"Yes."

"Why?"

"I know. Indeed, why?"

Chapter Omikron

Susannah Markovic walked slowly out of her boss's office more tired from all of the information given to her than overwhelmed or stunned by the content. The intensity of the last several hours not only had drained her of energy but also of want and need. Gone was the conundrum of why geniuses and idiots lacked common sense. Why could that matter? She mechanically followed the corridor past the administrative offices. Susannah paused when she reached the Hub, where the central corridor reached another perpendicular to it. It was a pleasant space with a domed skylight, plantings, seating, and a fountain, an indoor version of the several gardens on the campus for employees to enjoy.

The last suite on the left before the Hub was the Staff Services office in which employees could obtain assistance on a wide range of issues similar to having access to a hotel concierge. The cross corridor just beyond ran from the Genetics wing to the Ancillary Projects wing, the revenue generating departments.

Delores Tutwiler had insisted on creating the Staff Services office when the Genilo campus was built in 2025-26 given the amount of work she needed to delegate to keep up with everything Adam Nilo needed done on his behalf. To justify the expenditure, not least the salaries of five efficient, ingenious gofers with overlapping specialties, Mrs. Tut made them available to assist all employees with anything they needed to help them be as productive as possible. To indicate how sincerely she wanted the office to be used, it was placed, for ease of access, closest to where the cross corridor meets the central corridor. She would have placed the five people in a kiosk in the center of the Hub but for the sensitive nature of most of their work.

The name plate beside the door caught Susannah's eye. Just as she stopped to look, a cheery middle-aged man jumped up from whatever he was doing and grabbed three blue folders on the counter. He went out to the corridor to greet her.

"Oh, Dr. Markovic! I wasn't expecting you to pick these up. Kryste Kind said she'd be down and for us not to deliver."

The sudden almost explosive quality of her co-worker's zest in greeting her nearly roused her from the catatonic state she was in. She was not quite able to respond.

"Are you okay? Perhaps you'd like to sit down. I can get you something while we quickly review your itinerary and documents. Water? Tea?"

Susannah began to shake off the accumulated questions and confusion from the hours spent with Tom Paris as the man guided her into the office. The word "tea" rang a bell.

"Oh, yes. Of course. No, I was just in a long meeting. Tea would be fine, Mark."

"Great! Please have a seat to your left. Perhaps some white tea with hibiscus and rose hips would be good."

234

Susannah moved to sit in one of the chairs set aside for informal consultations. "Sounds about right. Thank you."

Mark busied himself in an alcove next to the seating area. "I bet you don't know that I'm an herbalist. We here in Staff Services all have to have a blend of unusual backgrounds to meet any requests. Blend! Listen to me! Here I am blending tea and…. He paused. Dr. Nilo has a range of interests and needs. One of the great things about working here is one can use every bit of talent, skill, and training. I have no need to go home and enjoy hobbies because I get paid to enjoy them here, he noted with glee. I spent six months investigating scientific research on traditional herbs with Arthur and then eight years designing clinical trials for anything that showed promise and had yet to be tested. We continue to do more to verify results or explore other uses for things. When I was hired twenty years ago, he recalled, Dr. Nilo said he wanted to create a thorough guide to valid herbal remedies. The way things were going, and still are unfortunately, people would need that information because they would not be able to depend on pharmaceutical companies to provide medications. Funny how we have gotten so far in eliminating some communicable diseases and treating others and all of that work might go to naught, he said glumly."

The third time the man interjected that peculiar habit of reflexive commentary Susannah decided she wasn't mishearing him. The fourth time she sat up and did her best to address him directly even though she could only see his back half from that angle with him in the alcove.

"Mark, why do you insert 'he this or that' when you are speaking?"

"Oh, that. It's nothing really. Have you ever spent much time talking with Tom Paris? Great guy and super sweet eye candy. We work together a lot obviously. He tends to go on and on. Not necessarily a bad thing unless one wants to insert a comment, he opined. By the time he's done speaking, one has forgotten what the comment was one wanted to make. Except whenever one is critical of someone else one needs to see if one is doing the same thing. It is often the case. We have a habit of noticing irritating quirks we are guilty of ourselves, he noted. To test myself, I began adding the kind of reflexive indicators when I speak after every third or fourth sentence or so and after two sentences if I already had done it two or three times without allowing the other person to speak. I saw I was doing the same thing and resolved to never say more than about ten sentences before stopping, he confided."

"But why do you say them rather than just think them?"

The man brought a tray with two teacups and some shortbread cookies to the table next to where Susannah was sitting.

"What are you talking about? I don't say them aloud," he deadpanned, in a cultivated Irish accent.

"Mark, please. It has been a difficult day. Don't tease me. How could I have mentioned it if you weren't saying them aloud? I'm not telepathic."

236

"So, I hear," the man said as winked and offered her a cookie. He grinned at his little joke. "You're right. I was saying them aloud. But it did get you to pay attention to what I was saying rather than staying adrift like you were when you entered the office."

Susannah looked sharply at him as she bit into a cookie. Crumbs cascaded down her blouse.

"The crumbs are a nuisance," Mark observed. "Everything comes with its drawbacks in this world. We used to be able to say everyone, too. Just as well we can't any longer or we would not be sitting here."

The scientist narrowed her eyes as she thought about that. Once she finished chewing she responded, "Should I know what that means?"

"You tell me," Mark replied, before biting into a cookie he had dipped in the tea. No crumbs fell from his lips.

"Mark, as you seem to well know, I am too tired for games."

"Yes, you're right. I apologize. I will explain. I spend a great deal of time writing up queries for Arthur. We all do in this office. We are expected to be miracle workers and be able to take care of anything any employee needs short of covering up a crime. If there have been any crimes committed by employees, they must have done a good job of covering them up themselves. The only other person who interacts with Arthur as much or more is Tom Paris. The technicians who physically check on Arthur every day never want to retire because they enjoy visiting it, but their interactions are for mutual amusement. Dr. Nilo has given every indication he prefers not to have contact with his great creation. I am somewhat empathic and even more nosey. I know he regrets creating Arthur and regrets even more creating it primarily to perfect humanity. When Ms. Kind asked me yesterday to make your travel arrangements to go to Washington and told me the reason for your trip, it wasn't too difficult to compute that you were going to see Professor Daniels to discuss the commonsense paradox that everyone has been talking about around here for months and has proven not to be a paradox at all.

"I was charged with going with Dr. Nilo twenty years ago to see Professor Daniels. Even though I was relatively new here, he confided in me the reason why he was meeting her. What he desperately wanted to do was hire her away from Catholic University. He was convinced she could straighten out all of the conceptual and philosophical issues he had not contemplated. Those issues had built up and built up. They had overwhelmed him, and he felt he couldn't continue doing any work until they were resolved. They began with Arthur. Some had appeared when he started developing the C Square process in 2030 and continued appearing as that project was completed. More arose when he found in 2045 that not all Chosen were up to snuff. The worst came when Arthur told him that infants conceived as God intended, whether there was a God or not, are perfect human beings simply because they are created naturally. The only possible way Adam Nilo could create a perfected human was to have

238

intercourse with a woman who became pregnant as a result.

"All of the work he had done meant nothing. In fact, it couldn't be perpetuated much longer since C Squares all descended from a limited number of people. Organics and even O/2s with the desired attributes had caught on to the problem that selling their gametes was only creating competitors to them and their Organic progeny if they were as gifted as their parents except in professions Chosen were barred from. And people started reasoning that it wasn't such a good idea to collaborate in a process that led to the growth of a population that faced legal discrimination when we had come so far to end all other kinds of prejudice.

"Professor Daniels gave Dr. Nilo far more good news than bad. He asked me to sit in on their two meetings. There was no chance she would ever work for Genilo. She would always agree to provide free consultations, however, because she saw the grave need for Genilo's activities to be subject to ethical scrutiny. She thoroughly understood the issues and agreed with Arthur that the whole idea of perfecting humanity did no harm so long as degrees of relation were observed, and the research provided data for treating inherited conditions. It provided important lessons on the concept of what humans are and why every naturally conceived human is perfect *ipso facto* as Arthur stated. The C Square process in her view is immoral because it is unnatural. She quoted from *Frankenstein* a line I chose to memorize: 'Frightful must it be, for supremely frightful would be the effect of any human endeavor to mock the stupendous mechanism of the Creator of the world.' I am certain the idea of mocking God left quite an impression on Dr. Nilo.

"At the time, Professor Daniels had yet to reach a conclusion on the products of that process other than to agree they ought to be feared no matter how docile or modest they might act. She did draft and fight for a resolution of Catholic University's faculty that no Chosen ever be permitted to become a member of the faculty. She also made certain the same prohibition was adopted by all other Catholic institutions of higher learning, not only in this country, but worldwide. And she personally traveled to Rome to speak with Cardinal Okeke, Prefect of the Congregation for the Doctrine of the Faith, to convince the Holy Office to issue a canonical judgment if not an encyclical on the issue of Catholics contracting for C Square children and how they ought to be treated once born. Perhaps you have read *Sapientem Creatorem*. It was basically a rehash of *Humanae Vitae*. I'm not sure how closely folks in our labs follow the ethical arguments that get tossed around. On the other hand Doctor Daniels fully supported Dr. Nilo's invention of emergent behavior artificial intelligence. She concluded that Arthur was not meant to be and never could be anything more than the most sophisticated machine ever built."

Mark paused and smiled at the thought. Susannah had sat rapt with interest. She knew it was the accent, a melodic tonic that softened the sharp edges Tom Paris had exposed.

240

"Which brings us full circle back to where I began. Unlike Professor Daniels, who declined Dr. Nilo's offer to allow her to use its capacities however she saw fit, I am one of six people who work with Arthur regularly. Arthur is far more than a sophisticated machine. We don't have a language to describe Arthur or what Arthur does. Efforts to do so are as futile and unverifiable as our descriptions of God. For example, Arthur was only a few weeks old, and everyone was still checking on its functions and capacities. In response to test inputs, it ordered the materials for and programmed a large 3D printer to create a copy of Michelangelo's *Pietà* and a sculpture of Leonardo da Vinci's unfinished fresco *The Battle of Anghiari*.

"No one thought too much of the first project since Arthur was asked to choose a sculpture from its art archives and test the printer with it. Close examination of the piece before it was moved to the Cathedral of the Holy Cross as a donation even showed the faint but detectable signs of where the Virgin's face had been repaired after someone had attacked the original with a hammer. What went unnoticed initially though was that the strap across the Virgin's chest where Michelangelo had signed the piece, the only time he ever signed a sculpture, did not have his name. Instead, an inscription was carved into the strap that read: *Vergine madre, figlia del tuo figlio*. That detail turned out to be one of several actions Arthur took that demonstrated it was something more than Dr. Nilo expected.

"The one complaint anyone ever raised regarding this masterpiece is that the Virgin is

241

depicted as the teenager who gave birth to the Christ child. Art historians had noticed that Jesus is set a bit away from his mother in her lap across her knees, a rather difficult thing because he is so large Michelangelo was forced to spread Mary's robe out in great folds for it to look believable he was in her small lap. The space between the two figures is exactly where Mary holds the Christ child in other works of art. Her arms are in a position in which she could be getting ready to nurse a baby. The inscription Arthur placed on the strap was what Michelangelo said in response to the complaints. The sculpture depicts the Virgin as a new mother, but her infant has become the dead adult man in front of her. Genius. Arthur had found a document when it was building its library of data that indicated Michelangelo had wanted to place that phrase on the sculpture to signal why the Virgin was depicted as being younger than Jesus. He couldn't because he already had put his name in the best place. After that, he never signed a sculpture."

"Are you saying Arthur corrected Michelangelo's error?"

"I'm not sure that is the best way to phrase it. Arthur created what Michelangelo would have created if he had the opportunity to carve the sculpture again. That was clear from the 'lost' da Vinci Arthur requested from the 3D printer when it was given the opportunity to further explore how the printer functioned. Da Vinci had only drawn the start of a fresco that had multiple problems because he was trying to avoid the technical issues he had painting *The Last Supper*. Rubens drew a charcoal finished version called *The Battle for the Banner* based on an engraving created by someone who saw the original more than half a century after da Vinci stopped working on it. Arthur took the Rubens, preliminary drawings by da Vinci, and scans of the church wall done early in this century, extrapolated from the data, chose as a material Ashford black marble which is actually limestone similar to the charcoal Rubens used, and sent its idea of what da Vinci's work would have looked like as a sculpture to the 3D printer. One week later, Dr. Nilo was panicking over his creation's creativity."

"No one was directing Arthur to do these things?"

"No one. Arthur became Arthur as a result of Nilo not having seen a flaw in his programming. It crossed the threshold to metacognition, aware of what it knows, how and why it knows what it knows, and how and when to use what it knows. Human beings generally can use metacognition only so far as they are physically, psychologically, and intellectually able. Arthur is restricted by its programming and inability to move. Either way, metacognition is the real difference between Homo sapiens and all other species as far as we know. Nilo had no intention of his creature crossing that threshold. If Arthur wasn't seventy-three cabinets loaded with circuits, memory, et cetera, and shackled by Asimovian laws, we would have one hell of a monster on our hands. I can work closely with Arthur, know it always has many projects running it has designed, and be okay not knowing what those projects are unless Arthur tells us. Adam Nilo cannot because he is the reason Arthur exists."

"What kinds of projects does a machine create to amuse itself?"

"Of the ones we know about, most are offshoots of queries we ask Arthur to answer. Just as Arthur in a way completed the sculptures the artists seemed to want or might have done, it routinely follows up on research from staff members that it concludes was not thorough enough, theorems that have bewildered mathematicians for ages, all of the mysteries and unknowns that could be discovered if one held every dot of knowledge. Being as omniscient as anything we could ever hope to make, it is logical Arthur would want to fill in the gaps of the human knowledge it downloaded when it was created. Of course, that's kind of ironic given that research staff members here primarily undertake studies of problems Arthur will not answer due to its Asimovian rules. A big one is Arthur's file on Dr. Nilo's DNA."

Susannah suddenly tensed. That struck a newly raw nerve.

Personal Log, Benjamin Rodgers Nilsson, July 28, 2062

I have never figured out whether easier communications capable of reaching almost anyone anywhere are as beneficial as the business world always says. Certainly, the ones making the equipment, apps, and associated products would like everyone to believe we all ought to be as connected as possible to everything and everyone. Other businesses see it as an efficient way to expand into the world without stepping foot away from one's office. People with time, interest, and equipment swear they are becoming better humans because they so frequently interact with people from many backgrounds. Perhaps these are benefits. But to me sometimes it seems we are volunteering for solitary confinement in our physical space on the grounds that we are safer being tied down to our homes or offices and the substitutes for actual contact with others are more than satisfactory to meet our needs. Since the advent of cell phones to the ubiquity of VR glasses, we have refined the means to carry around our cells and remain mentally apart from everything around us.

As someone who works in the field of insuring people can stay connected by eliminating frazz zones, I would never say people should not be connected. There is plenty to be said for ID technology making life easier. That tech only works if one can move smoothly from one coverage field to another. It has to be reliable. What did the one company used to say? Our network is more reliable than when you used your mother as an alarm clock. I can see why that caught on. Who's going to argue with tech that's like your mother? But it also raises an issue. When your mother woke you up every morning as a kid, you were starting the day with in-the-flesh human interaction.

Don't get me wrong. Moleka and I love that we can share so much of our lives with her brother Mustafa, his wife Aisha, and their son Ibrahim even though they live in Marseilles. There have been times we kept our PTP channel open for hours as we tend to things in our apartment while they do the same in theirs. I checked a couple of years ago. Our PTP subscription for five years roughly equals the cost of one airline ticket and for ten years equals the cost of the four of us traveling to France to visit them by ship. If you want to stay in the lives of family and friends who live far away, it's far nicer to use state-of-the-art telepresence nowadays. In fact, I don't see how they can make it any better. I know they have developed haptic skin. Aside from companies that need to train people to get used to the feel of an active environment no one is all that interested in that immersive of an experience.

Speaking of staying in contact, our friends Jackson and Melinda Paris are moving back to Boston full time. Melinda decided one term as a US Senator was enough for her after three terms in the House. They had no desire to choose the DC area over Boston when it came time for her to step down due to term limits. Tom and Felicity would first have to deal with rarely seeing school friends in the summers while Congress was adjourned and face switching school districts after seven years of having established friendships. In fact, Tom complaining about having to leave his friends behind this summer when they left to come up here was what got them thinking about it.

They've been lucky Melinda's sister Randi has been able to stay in their house up here when they are in DC. Well, I guess not lucky given Randi lost everything in the BRIC takeover, including her husband to suicide. I guess Randi's lucky that her sister had room to take her in. Melinda might not have gotten into politics but for seeing how Randi was treated as a nobody when she was trying to find work and put her life back together. The government couldn't do anything since going overboard with the new transportation systems and other infrastructure projects is what gave the BRIC conglomerates the leverage to kill the dollar. Any hint of expanding the social safety net was shouted down as digging the hole deeper. If no one was going to lose anything, everyone had to accept nothing new could be done.

That left people like me and Randi in a bind since businesses weren't exactly beating the bushes hiring new employees from among all of us who lost our jobs. I thought we were going to have to live on Moleka's salary the rest of our lives after I found out Genilo wouldn't provide a reference for me even though they had been my biggest client and always reported back how pleased they were with my services. Fabio won't say how he got access to my evaluations to confirm what I told him in my interview, but he was motivated to do something since he knew he could trust me to do the work he needed done and he felt bad about dumping me after all the help I gave him to graduate from RPI when we were dating.

Randi Traynor never had a guardian angel intervene for her. She hadn't been blackballed like me, but no firms needed her particular skill set once everything was packed up and moved to wherever the conglomerates decided to relocate the businesses they bought. Her husband's death doubled the depression, which never helps if you're trying to get hired. There were too many people looking and too many people afraid to hire anyone overqualified for fear they would leave the second something more closely related to their background came up. Nothing like that was going to happen. Those jobs were gone for good. Try telling that to the people who had openings, even low-wage, part-time stuff that was always a revolving door anyway. If Melinda and Jackson hadn't taken her in, Randi would have followed her husband's example. And seeing what was happening to Randi got Melinda thinking about politics.

It's funny how the financial meltdown with the BRIC takeover did so much more to put what I guess you would call ordinary folks in government than the Article V Convention. Granted the ConCon in 2026-27 came up with twenty-seven amendments to the Constitution and only five of them ended up getting ratified by enough states. Some of the work had been done by a few amendments that got through in the late 2010s. I think people were fired up about a do-nothing government of the rich, felt satisfied enough, and then couldn't think straight after the Islamic State attack. Instead of an outpouring of patriotism like happened after 9/11, they realized the changes had done next to nothing to actually address what people needed. The ConCon got it right, but then couldn't break through the opposition of entrenched politicians in the state houses.

The result was the government was still not as responsive to the popular will as it could be, was still too reliant on businesses, particularly the ones involved in all of those public works projects and ended up giving the store away. So many people witnessed firsthand what the BRIC takeover did to the country and the communities throughout the country they finally decided to participate in politics to find ways to help the Randi Traynors and Ben Nilssons of this country rather than throw their hands up. The chasm between government interests and popular interests was visible in a way it had not been since 1932. Families were divided not by allegiances to parties or support for insidious institutions. They were divided by the unequal benefits they were deriving as citizens. It was time for family members among the haves to begin to look out for those among the have-nots. Thank God there were still enough around who cared.

Sometimes I wonder what life would have been like if my biological father hadn't given up all rights to me, given that would have meant he'd still be financially responsible for me, at least until I reached eighteen. Not that I can say what he was doing with all of the money he was sweeping in after NILO/AI was built other than further building his business and, from what some reports said, greasing the palms of politicians to ease the way for his eugenics process. My real father, Duke Nilsson, never put much store in financial gain in the slightest. It was a badge of honor for him to be poor. He was happy not to get a single nickel from his folks, not even an interest in their huge estate out in the Berkshires. At least, I assume it's an estate given the number of hectares. For all I know it could be all undeveloped, woods-filled hills. I've never heard anyone referring to the property as containing a mansion like Olana over just a ways in Hudson, New York.

I long ago gave up trying to sort out what happened that their father chose to keep Dad and Father out of the cookie jar directly and only offered crumbs now and again in the form of crafts they had made. Nice enough crumbs, certainly, worth quite a bit given their reputations at the forefront of the Localism movement. Duke Nilsson and Adam Nilo may not have gotten much financially from Ainar and his wife, but they sure as heck got a fortune's worth of artwork. Sure, it came with the tantalizing provision that none of it could be alienated from the family. Seems to me that a sure-fire way to alienate your family is giving them expensive stuff they can't auction off under any circumstances.

Not that it would be polite to sell the gifts they gave us no matter how much we might need the money. Etiquette may state a gift is disposable by

250

the recipient the moment it is received, but just how many people are going to turn around and sell even an umbrella when they already have five and live in the Arctic if it might risk inserting a wedge between kith and kin? That is exactly what the Nilssons did and that is exactly the result, at least as far as Dad was concerned. I doubt he was upset they were giving him things they produced by hand from the materials around them. On the other hand, they had pointed him in the direction of following their vision. Giving Dad finely crafted objets d'art must seem like giving milk to a dairy farmer.

All the same, the gifts to Nilo, at least, gave him a reason to be generous in acquiring more. Last time I was there, the Genilo campus had some stunning works by the Nilssons and their followers. Even Dad was hired to put in stained glass in some of the interiors. I guess that counts as more than a crumb to him and, by extension, me. Of course, I know how little Dad charges for installations like that, even for big corporations. In fact, he charges them less than he does members of the professions on the theory he does not want the money businesses acquire from the labors of poorly paid workers but wants to give them something to think about when they walk through the corridors of rampant capitalism and see the beauty and simplicity of handcrafted decorative arts. In the end, I guess I just find it difficult to place a man on a pedestal when he not only made the pedestal himself but is also chipping away at it to give away the pieces.

Chapter Pi

Mark noticed that Susannah flinched when he mentioned Nilo's DNA. He let her absorb the fact that Arthur was indicating descendants of Nilo might have something to worry about. It wasn't too difficult to see in her face and bearing a familial resemblance to Ben Nilsson. She had the same dark hair and eyes and cinnamon buff skin that must have resulted from dominant genes contributed by Victoria Adams. Although Dr. Nilo had raised such a stink about the news from Oslo a few years back, the fact was that he and his Organic, O/2, and Chosen progeny epitomized why the word "race" had so quickly fallen out of favor mid-century. Globalization, the near-universal denunciation of bigotry in the USA after the 2028 presidential election, the rise of the BRIC states, and, as the Nobel Peace Prize Committee said, Nilo's refusal to allow anyone using the C Square process to choose phenotype characteristics for the offspring they ordered all conspired to make the petty, ignorant, inhumane mindset of defining people by race unsupportable.

Thinking of the family connections made Mark realize Susannah hadn't delivered the DAU report to the hospital on his newborn granddaughter. Flynn had called frantically hoping his father could ask his co-workers to find out why it wasn't delivered the normal thirty-six hours after Lila was born. Mark's younger son had the unfortunate habit of worsifying things when he lacked data rather than accepting the

252

no-news-is-good-news platitude. It was now thirty-seven and a half hours plus an additional hour since Flynn had called.

"I apologize for causing you any concern. I had surmised when you first started working here that you might be related to Dr. Nilo. I wanted to confirm that or at least see whether you knew it given the example I gave of Arthur's private projects. That's just an explanation. I truly am sorry my doing that upset you."

"No, no. Mark, the only reason it bothered me at all is that I only just found out from Tom Paris a little while ago."

"Oh!"

Now it was Susannah's turn to see sudden concern on Mark's face.

"Oh what?"

Mark's eyes narrowed in concentration. "Four things happened yesterday. No, three actually. One, my granddaughter was born. Two, Tom Paris asked me to prepare travel arrangements for four people to the Berkshires under the pseudonym Victor Adams, the name Dr. Nilo uses when he travels to avoid fans and assassins. Three, you decided to go to Washington with Dr. Olejniczak and Ms. Kind to see Regina. I knew you were meeting with Tom and snared you on your way back to your lab. You need to know about the first two events and how they relate to why you are going to DC tomorrow."

Susannah shook her head. "What are a few more secrets and revelations?"

"Yes, well, I rather think Dr. Nilo enjoyed just jumping into the swimming pool rather than

253

checking the water temperature first. He has always had a habit of putting off informing others of important, relevant matters until he is faced with no choice. Then everything must come out at once to make any sense."

Susannah bit into another cookie. Crumbs tumbled down again.

"Dr. Markovic, you really ought to consider dunking shortbreads into you tea first to avoid making a mess of you blouse." Susannah blushed a bit as she brushed the crumbs away as best she could.

"Anyway, my granddaughter was born yesterday quite early in the wee hours. Once we finish, I will be going to see her. If you have no objections, I will take her DAU. My son Flynn is getting a bit worried why it hasn't arrived."

The scientist's face turned even redder. "Wait…You…This…"

"Yes, the report that upset you so much and caused you to meet with Tom was the DAU on my granddaughter, Lila Callahan. I had a hunch you hadn't looked at the baby's name and even if you did, you might not make the connection. Flynn is not the biological father, so neither his name nor mine would be on the kith list. As a courtesy, Tom notified me about him meeting you. He didn't say why, but the project you have been working on, you taking over as the DAU processor, and you heading to see Regina Daniels made me pause.

"One way or another, you were going to find out that you are my granddaughter's biological great aunt. Arthur only flags the DAUs for the processor

254

if it finds something that needs to be addressed, something outside the safety parameters. One of us in the office looks every four hours to see if an infant has been flagged, since we know someone will have to be sent to deliver the report in person. Otherwise, the hospital just downloads the report into a chip to insert in the baby's wrist and hands the results to the mother of the baby. I checked the queue Arthur had for infants born early yesterday morning because of Lila. We can only see what hospital, nothing more. That was enough. I wasn't sure what to do since it would be inappropriate for me to ask you for the DAU findings. Arthur, however, likes to keep score as it were with how many descendants Dr. Nilo has. When the other two events happened yesterday, I checked with Arthur. It informed me Nilo had a double match on a new baby. Obviously, that was the flag. Lila must be descended from Nilo through both biological parents."

Susannah felt she had to explain. "There isn't much point in keeping that little bit of the DAU secret. Since Lila is an O/2, her biological father's consanguinity chart had everything. Not that it had to since the record showed his father was Nilo. Your daughter-in-law's ovum would have been checked back only two degrees. Still, that should have been enough to reveal the double-match, that Nilo would be the baby's paternal grandfather and maternal great grandfather. Why didn't Arthur chose some other male donor, one not related to Nilo?"

Mark cocked his head while considering the question. "My guess is that given Arthur can't respond to any query that would harm a living thing, given that it could see if the male and female gametes had any dominant sequences that might be harmful, and given that it is fascinated by Nilo's DNA, Arthur was doing an experiment of its own to interweave Nilo's genetic material. I just can't fathom…How did you decide to go to see Professor Daniels?"

Susannah shrugged. "We were talking about the results of our survey of academics about the commonsense issue. No, no. Kryste brought me a form to sign confirming that Professor Daniels was the only one who did not respond because Accounting wanted verification that we no longer needed the money left to send her if she did respond. However…"

"Who's we?"

"Oh, Kryste, Josh Olejniczak, and I. We decided that Daniels did respond after a fashion. Kryste asked her why she did not want to respond. She complained that the money was too much and that we should not be trying to delve too deeply into God's handiwork."

"And it is okay to study genetics to learn how God made us but not if our purpose is to become creators ourselves, right?"

Susannah laughed. "That is pretty much what she said."

Mark chuckled along with her. "Yes, Regina hasn't changed her tune in twenty years. If I had known you had contacted her, I could have saved you or, I guess, Kryste the trouble. If that's the case though, why go to DC to see her?"

"That was Kryste again. She contacted your office to make the arrangements based on the reply she got from Professor Daniels, figuring we would want to talk with her face to face about it. Actually, given the reply, I thought it was odd she agreed to an appointment."

"Ah-ah." Mark smiled waving his right hand slightly. "You didn't know then, but as I told you she told Nilo and me that she would be happy to consult with anyone from Genilo for free if we ever needed moral guidance on our work. Still, it's a little odd Regina wanted to see you so quickly and wants to see you personally. Perhaps she wants to smack your noses with a rolled-up newspaper for promising to pay her for a response." He chuckled, thinking of his last visit with the ethicist and her ability to be cordially dominating.

"How were we to know? We never knew Professor Daniels told Nilo that. Oh, and speaking of smacking noses, what time is it?"

"Just past 1530. Why?"

"I thought it was later. I lose track of time meeting with people like this. Earlier, I thought I had only been with Tom half an hour and it had been ninety minutes." Susannah shifted in the chair. "If I'm going to be away for a few days, I like to be home early for the dogs to give them extra attention. Wait. That's odd. I asked Ben Nilsson to watch my dogs while I'm away. Why didn't he say anything about his granddaughter last night when I spoke with him?"

257

"I'd say that if you contacted him and asked him for the favor without saying anything like 'what's new', he probably didn't want to disappoint you. If he told you his daughter just gave birth you would have insisted on finding someone else."

"Hmm." The scientist thought about that. "I guess."

Mark sighed and decided to be honest. "Actually, that is exactly what happened. I was with him at the hospital when you contacted him. After he talked with you he realized I might know you."

Susannah was puzzled. "He's never mentioned me before to you?"

"Dr. Markovic, really. In-laws do not see each other much. They meet when their kids get married, might run into each other around town if they even live near each other, and meet again when things like births and maybe birthday parties happen. Speaking of all this, I really should get to the hospital with the DAU as long as you don't mind me taking it."

The scientist realized she had been swamped with far too much information about herself in one day, had to prepare for a trip, even if it was just two nights, and was certain she did not need to face her neighbor after having just learned they had the same father.

"I definitely think you ought to take it. But what are you going to say about the anomaly? The hospital must have told them the report was held up. And your son is right in this case about no news not being good news."

Mark stood. He picked up the tea tray and walked over to the alcove to place it on the counter. After doing so, he turned to Susannah. "Well, that brings me at last to the second event yesterday." He walked back and sat in the chair again. "I arranged for Victor Adams aka Adam Nilo and three others to travel to the Berkshires. Ultra priority. We haven't had an ultra since the Pope suddenly asked Dr. Nilo to appear at the First Canterbury Council. Poor man thought he was going to be broken like Galileo Galilei five-hundred years ago. I had to go with him because he said he needed an interpreter who spoke Catholic." Mark shook his head thinking of the trip.

"We got there to discover the Inquisition, or Holy Office now, wanted to hear directly from him what Arthur's answers were to questions about God and all. We had a laugh telling them they were questions Arthur could not respond to and explaining that meant the answers would be harmful to living things. Anyway, the four people in the westernmost county of our fair commonwealth today through tomorrow afternoon, after you leave for DC, would only be going there given Dr. Nilo's condition if he felt he had to make final arrangements."

Susannah sat back, eyes wide. "Nilo is going to die?"

Mark sat back himself and laughed. "Heavens to Betsy and good grief, no. Physically, there isn't much of anything wrong with him. Given his daily routine he will live to be over a hundred if he doesn't become bedridden for some reason. That said he has taken the opportunity of Lila being born to settle his affairs. That couple who came to Dr. Adams all those years ago lived outside Great Barrington on property that had been in the man's family probably since Shay's Rebellion. They were artists and childhood sweethearts greatly influenced by the masterpieces within reach, everything from the middle-class images at the Norman Rockwell Museum to the willfully sophisticated selections at the Clark.

"When it became clear to them that the child Dr. Adams had helped them produce was going to break with tradition and not remain in the Berkshires, they chose to give that land to Adam Nilo, the man's biological son, upon their deaths provided that he would keep it in the family. Nilo was obligated to Duke Nilsson never to tell Ben the truth, so he couldn't bequeath it to Ben. He got on his kick of creating a perfect human using his DNA. He wanted to give his Eve and her Adam the property. You don't have to tell me, but I suspect you are Eve. We all know there will never be an Adam. My guess is that the property goes to you when Nilo dies or maybe even sooner. Lila is the insurance that the property will remain in the family. Her birth gives him the security he has wanted before sorting everything else out.

"That said the last thing is to decide what to do with his other baby. Tom Paris probably knows. I have no solid proof. My guess is that Dr. Nilo has been planning to move Arthur to that property. It is close enough yet far enough. I am telling you only because I have concluded you are Eve. Arthur safely chose a way for Sophia and Flynn to have a child that was genetically more a part of the family, almost as close as if Lila had been your baby with your Adam. Arthur told Dr. Nilo there would never be an Adam for you and wanted to fill that part of the plan as best as it could, considering it had to rely on what a bunch of humans decided to do.

"That leaves you with quite a lot to discuss with Regina Daniels who has been talking to Nilo all these years and knows everything. So, first you will need to decide how much you want her to know you know." Mark stood. "Now, I'd better get to the hospital."

Susannah stood also. "What are you going to tell them?"

Mark smiled slightly. "I'll show them the DAU. When they see the strong probabilities that she will have a long life, excellent health, great intellect, and the world open to her as a polymath, they will be thrilled and relieved. If they still want to know the reason for the delay, I'll just tell them the truth, that Lila was flagged due to a consanguinity issue that is really a blessing but was flagged, nonetheless. They may be curious to know the particulars. They know the details can't be revealed, only the prospects."

The scientist looked at her colleague skeptically as they walked to the office door. "And you think that will satisfy them."

Mark opened the door to the corridor to let Susannah out first, but paused after she went through. "Let me ask you this. If you are Eve or if you were Eve, would you have made the same

261

choices you made to wind up here if you had learned that as a child or even somewhat later?"

Susannah turned toward him and tilted her head left a bit. "Hard to say. Growing up identified as gifted marked me for special treatment and guidance. How would it be any different?"

Mark grinned as he closed the door behind them. "Oh, please." He turned and started walking down to the entrance with Susannah at his side. "That is a big burden to place on someone, to tell her she isn't just gifted but perhaps as far as we are going to get in perfecting humanity. Tell her when she is an adult and settled into a profession and she hasn't had to deal with the potential anxiety, the knowledge all eyes are on her to save the world. Tell her as a child or even teenager before college and she would be paralyzed trying to sort out what path she is supposed to take to fulfill her destiny."

Susannah shook her head. "You are being overly dramatic. I never got the impression Dr. Nilo's goal was to have one perfect woman save the world. That isn't possible."

"Dr. Markovic, that all depends on what she is meant to save us from. Superheroes were created to tell us how we could be saved from evil forces that usually used technology. Prophets were sent to save people from ignoring God's will by telling them what that will was. Jesus was sent to redeem the sins of mankind and save us from eternal damnation. Buddha saved people from the cycle of suffering by showing the way to enlightenment. Perhaps this Eve is meant to save us from our reliance on technology to run the world, make babies, even communicate."

"Why would someone use technology to create someone to save us from the technology used to create her? That's at least ironic, if not also hypocritical."

They had reached the exit and showed the guards what they were carrying. As Mark opened the door to the vestibule he responded, "Ironic, maybe. I see it as a necessity. What better tool to use to stop what is happening than a dead end?"

Susannah was silent as she left the building. Two e-cabs were waiting, corralled by a security guard. The guard was motioning for her to take the first one. She turned to Mark.

"If you are right, what role does your granddaughter play? After all, she's almost a second Eve."

"Not quite."

Mark looked at her. She was about the same age as Flynn and Sophia. She had come so close to fulfilling the task. When that wasn't possible, Arthur created plan B. Now, he was off to see the result. Mark Callahan knew what lay ahead not just that evening but for years to come. He felt sympathy for Susannah. Perhaps Regina would help her understand. He might as well tell her.

"She is the third Eve."

Nilo Biography – Chapter 8

"The world was to me a secret which I desired to divine." – Mary Wollstonecraft Shelley

Donna Milgard's 'why' sat on Adam Nilo's shoulders like a loaded barbell for several weeks. He even told Delores Tutwiler not to involve him in any of the arrangements made to remove the sculpture and place it somewhere useful. He also sent out a message to staff not to order Arthur to use the 3D printer any longer. Meanwhile, he agreed with Mrs. Tut that they ought to do something about employees finding out that he could observe them in the Japanese garden. As always, his assistant had a respectable idea and even knew that Donna Milgard would be an excellent test case.

Delores asked Donna to visit her two days after she had met with Nilo. The older woman posed the question as to how Ms. Milgard would react if she were asked to keep mum about the windows in the CEO's office. Ms. Milgard responded that she would be happy to comply so long as there was no reason to think Dr. Nilo had any intention other than to enjoy looking at the garden. Mrs. Tutwiler assured her that their company's founder was above reproach. Ms. Milgard decided that "lecherous" was definitely not an accurate way to describe Adam Nilo.

Having agreed in principle, Mrs. Tut broached the more delicate matter as to whether Ms. Milgard saw anything wrong with signing an agreement to the effect that she would not disclose the existence of the windows looking out on the Japanese garden to anyone in exchange for a modestly healthy salary increase. The agreement was void if Dr. Nilo was ever under formal or informal investigation for any activities conducted in his office. The penalty for revealing the secret would be determined based on the circumstances of the disclosure, but was restricted to three options: nil, loss of the salary increase, or termination of employment. Although Ms. Milgard argued a rise in salary was not necessary, Mrs. Tut impressed upon her that Dr. Nilo insisted on paying employees when they take on additional responsibilities and this fell into that category. Donna accepted the reasoning and went directly to HR to take care of the matter.

In notifying employees not to give Arthur any further assignments related to the 3D printer Adam Nilo neglected to include cancelling any orders already sent. Between her meeting with Nilo and Tutwiler, investigating the addition Arthur made to the *Pietà*, and circling back to review the various possibilities Arthur noted as ways to find patentable improvements to the printer, Donna never thought about her routine request for Arthur to further explore exploitable improvements. In fact, by the time Donna was meeting with Dr. Nilo, Arthur already had chosen its next piece to evaluate the printer's features and identify commercially viable enhancements. Adam Nilo already had signed off on the project. Materials had placed Arthur Nilsson's next order, this time for 3800 kilograms of Ashford Black limestone, without thinking twice given the project's priority coding.

Almost a month passed. Dr. Nilo was scheduled to meet with Mr. Iwa in the 3D printer room to go over some of the ideas for improving the largest machine that they could offer to its manufacturer after developing them to patentable standards. Edgar was anxiously waiting for the company head in the hall outside the room. Donna Milgard rushed up to him.

"I'm sorry, Mr. Iwa. I really hadn't even thought…"

"It's all right Ms. Milgard. When I got the message that a job was complete and the techs didn't know what to do with the result, I realized my error in not cancelling any print orders Arthur made subsequent to the last one. The techs said nothing because the work was classified urgent on behalf of Dr. Nilo. They certainly can't be called to task for not questioning the boss. Speaking of which…"

Adam Nilo appeared at the end of the short hall and walked unhurriedly with his eyes primarily on an AR image generated by the eyeglass frames he was wearing. He tapped to switch it off when he got within conversation distance of the two employees.

"Ms. Milgard, I wasn't expecting you at this meeting. I guess it's your prerogative since these potential improvements resulted from your research and you will have a financial stake in any of them that prove marketable." Adam turned to Edgar. "So, are we ready to assess these ideas?"

The facilities manager smiled grimly. "Actually, sir, yes we are ready to assess the ideas, but we have a more pressing matter to look into first."

"What's that?"

Edgar opened the door and gestured for the other two to enter. "It's probably best if we all see for ourselves together."

Donna, Adam, and Edgar filed into the large space with the substantial bulk of the 3D printer occupying the space in the center and to the rear. The equipment was set up so that the print platform faced away from the door and toward a loading dock door in the rear. Given the size of the machine and the pieces the machine could produce, not to mention the bulk of the material needed to create the 3D image it had been essential to design the room that way. The objects made by the machine might weigh thousands of kilograms and require heavy equipment to move. Although the printer's capacity was known upon purchase, its only intended use originally was to fabricate Arthur's thin, porous cabinets. They were bulky enough to warrant the use of the loading dock but hardly necessary. The project manager for the building's construction put her foot down that she was not going to be told years later that Genilo had to rip out a wall to fully use a piece of equipment that she knew was intended for that space.

The trio made their way around to find something unimaginable sitting on the printer's platform. Made from what appeared to be fine, dark, black marble, the statue depicted four horsemen battling over a standard while one man crouched on the ground behind a shield and another man was on his back under one of the horses about to have his throat slit by a man on top of him. The riders and horses wore distinctly agonized, angered visages that were strikingly malignant and magnificent at the same time. From the upraised, arced swords of the two men centermost through the armored bodies of the riders to the distorted heads and bodies of the mounts down to the imperiled figures below, the rendering looked almost Cubist except everything was anatomically accurate to the last detail. The banner that was so highly prized could barely be seen as it dangled from a pole horizontal to the ground between the horses.

The sculpture provoked the sensation of seeing the stone moving urgently. As the three slowly circled the work, every element appeared to be reaching out as though it was about to explode past the viewer. The material had a vibrancy that belied its color and its use. They marveled at the precision of the edges, the profound emotions rendered in eight pairs of equine eyes. Not one of the masterpiece's first visitors could fully understand the beauty and horror displayed but each one found memories of the inhumanity they had encountered seven years earlier surfacing within them. What need was there for representing a long-forgotten battle when anyone old enough could recall the suffering and death of the Islamic State attack. What had Arthur done?

Arthur had, once again, stepped in to correct what art historians might consider a grievous lapse that could never be corrected. To anyone with sufficient objectivity, knowledge, and intellect to find links from one subject to the next, Arthur was filling gaps that had been left gaping and perfecting what had been left imperfect. It knew its primary function was to assist Adam Nilo in finding a process to perfect humanity. Until that work got underway, Arthur reasoned it was being given tasks to demonstrate that it knew how to perfect things. Since its creator was, from the files, considered to be one of the most intellectually capable people to have been born, Arthur also reasoned that it ought to perfect things that Dr. Nilo's peers in history had not gotten around to perfecting in their lifetimes.

Leonardo da Vinci was unique among all the great artists. His was not the creation of art simply for beauty sake. To be sure, his work was beautiful, but being a student of the human body, the natural sciences, and engineering during the Renaissance drove da Vinci to have his art reflect reality. He worked tirelessly to ensure his work mirrored the world around him but in a higher, purer way. He studied the human body so that his art would closely reflect even the smallest details accurately and perfectly. He did so with all things of nature both in sculpture and painting.

Da Vinci's most tantalizing work was a fresco depicting the Battle of Anghiari he was contracted to paint in the Palazzo Vecchio in Florence. He never came close to finishing the work and it is primarily known from a charcoal drawing made by Peter Paul Rubens from an engraving made before it was covered up for another project. The subject was popular in the sixteenth century in northern Italy since the battle cemented Florence's control of the region. However, the reports about the battle were odd. The condottieri hired by Florence and Milan to fight were more comrades-in-arms than opponents. They had made a point of prolonging the war to extract as much pay as possible from their employers, the true antagonists. After a full day of fighting, only one horseman from either side had died and that was from falling off his horse accidentally. The mercenaries put on a good show, got quite a bit of exercise, and presumably went off wining and wenching together afterward. No reports indicated how the foot soldiers fared. But something more must have happened on the field that day since Florence declared victory and was treated as the victor afterward by Milan.

If Leonardo da Vinci knew much about the battle, the dramatic fury and barbarity of the tableaux he created for the fresco definitely was an ironic statement about the putative lust for carnage in wars fought by disinterested third parties. It could almost be considered a sarcastic comment about Florence upholding the battle as an historic victory. The dramatic mix of horse and human, flesh, armor, and cloth masked the unlikeliness that eight arms, eleven bodies and heads, and thirty legs could ever find themselves contorted in this manner. The painter rendered through his art greater verisimilitude of what warfare at close quarters could be than what it in fact had been. Indeed, Arthur, having recognized that it needed to account for its choices when given an assignment that

270

lacked clear parameters, included this as an explanation for why it had chosen to test the printer with a work of art that even the original artist might not have contemplated creating as a sculpture along with its findings on what other patentable improvements could be made to the 3D printer. That message prompted Ms. Milgard to rush to Facilities to check out the result of her command to Arthur.

Donna told Dr. Nilo about Arthur's explanation for the work. Edgar explained that his people thought they were carrying out Dr. Nilo's request for a project. The thirty-year-old inventor just stood looking at the huge block. The surface was polished and gave the impression of what it would be like to see light being pulled into a black hole. Adam Nilo could not remember ever having been confronted with such a deliberately raw evocation of physical and emotional pain. The portrayal of twisting humans and horses bound up ferociously engaged in achieving a goal that was so pointless on its face and yet so cataclysmic in its implications seemed the antithesis of anything he could possibly imagine. The futility and necessity of war made manifest.

Nilo finally found something to be said. "Please prepare and archive a full report. Mr. Iwa, ask Mrs. Tut to find a home for this, this thing. Ms. Milgard, I am going to put you in charge of NILO/AI for a while. You seem to know it better than I. Coordinate with Mrs. Tut on setting up teams incorporating all technical and research staff to begin evaluating any potential revenue-generating designs identified so far. Clear all findings with

271

NILO/AI and submit them to Legal. No one. No one, except you, Ms. Milgard, and Mrs. Tut is permitted to submit queries until further notice. You and Tut must agree that any query you submit will not allow or require NILO/AI to fill in any gaps or make any decisions. Understood?"

"Yes, sir."

"What did I say about that sir business."

"Sorry Dr. Nilo."

Chapter Rho

Susannah had decided to work from home the day after her long meeting with Tom Paris. Mark Callahan said nothing when she contacted Staff Services to ask if an e-cab pick her up at home to get her to the station. She really wanted to know how things went when he delivered the DAU to his son and daughter-in-law about their newborn, Lila. She resisted the urge to ask, deciding that from his perspective it was a personal matter. Even if she was the baby's biological great aunt that hardly qualified her as close family given she didn't even know they were related before the day before.

Susannah had not had to resist anything with regard to her neighbor slash newly discovered half-brother, Ben Nilsson. When she arrived home the previous afternoon to spend quality time with her little furry jewels she found Ben already had sent a message confirming that either he or Moleka would be seeing the dogs twice a day while she was gone beginning Wednesday evening, have a safe and productive trip, see you Saturday, blah, blah blah. It was the kind of message that is so thorough one would have to strain a few gray cells to come up with a plausible reason for responding, let alone tacking on as personal an inquiry as what did your granddaughter's DAU say? Nonetheless, the scientist already had started trying to think of a reason to reply when she remembered her neighbor had not even told her he had become a grandfather yet. That would make the query about Lila's life probabilities even more intrusive and necessitate full disclosure of her reasons for asking.

Before packing a bag, the researcher checked AccuWeather for the DC forecast for the next three days. As usual, the only thing remotely trustworthy about the report were the sunrise and sunset times. Along the East Coast of North America, New England and Maritime Canada received dependable weather forecasts. Everything from New York City and Long Island south was subject to storms coming up the coast or moving in from the Gulf of Mexico. Storms could move quickly, or they could creep.

Susannah was rather hoping to see some thunderstorms as they were such a rarity around Boston. Just as long as the rain didn't interfere with the threesome's plans to visit the zoo or venture onto the campus at Catholic University. Slickers could easily be carried in a bag until needed, but their convenience ended there. In the jungle-humid weather characteristic of the Mid-Atlantic and points south, the term "slicker" seemed more to apply to the way the thin material stuck to one's skin and clothes than the fact water flushed down the exterior surface. And once used, they were worse than having to leave umbrellas open on the floor to dry. In a society hyperconscious about recycling any product, folks could not rid themselves of these second skins fast enough. Of course, umbrellas were useless in the windy storms that reliably and unpredictably ranged through that quadrant of the country.

After one last romp with the dogs after lunch and a check on Oscar and Tuppence to make sure they could care less what was going on, Susannah left for the station. The e-cab was on time and the ride took only thirty minutes or so. The fare amount was blurred on the screen, the second time in a month Susannah had noticed that problem. She couldn't tell if it was the same e-cab as the last time since she never bothered to look at the reg number whenever she used e-cabs. People who paid out of their own pockets did, given they could get discounted fares by using the same e-cab regularly. No one was quite sure how this would cut the expense of operating an e-cab, but then no one seemed to understand the purpose of customer loyalty programs for any business. To Susannah, the blurred screen meant nothing since the fare was charged to Genilo.

Josh and Kryste were already inside the terminal, having taken an e-cab from the office. Josh had what looked to be a rather expensive bag made from soft, durable, and chic chocolate leather with anodized black fittings. Kryste's bag didn't look all that inexpensive either with carefully crafted beadwork. Susannah's worn canvas number won for most traveled and most proletarian. Her travel companions picked their bags up as she approached.

"All set?"

"Sure thing, doctor."

Josh reached to take Susannah's authorization out of his pocket. "We almost forgot our travel pack this morning. We mixed up whether we were supposed to go to Staff Services, or they were being delivered to the lab."

"Oh, that's my fault," Susannah offered as she took the poker chip-like document. "I was going to pick them up and ended up leaving for the afternoon."

"No worries."

The three were already at the gate. Each one scanned their unique disc on the pillar and waited for the system to verify through their ID. They proceeded to the end of the line of passengers waiting to board.

Josh looked back at Susannah to make sure she got through. "You look a bit worn considering you played hooky this morning."

Susannah smirked. "Working from home is not hooky, mister. But I did have trouble sleeping. Let me ask you something. I know you are new, but maybe it's something someone told you at orientation that I forgot from mine. Did you know that Professor Daniels long ago told Dr. Nilo that she would freely consult with researchers at Genilo regarding the ethics of their work?"

Josh shrugged as he shuffled forward while turned toward his colleague. Kryste's ears perked up to hear the response behind her. "I don't recall anything like that. I had to sign a statement saying I would uphold all relevant professional ethics in my active practices, when deciding not to act, and when discovering a colleague's possible breach. I had to complete a short ethics quiz first. They didn't tell me the results, but it was all no-brainer stuff. The HR person, uh, Lindamarie – nice but more subdued than friendly – she said something about needing to recertify every year."

"Yes, we are required to take a few little quizzes like that every year or so. More of a reminder than anything. Studies show scientists tend to be unethical right from the start or after a long while when they become frustrated by poor results and feel they can bend the rules." As Susannah said this, she thought back to Tom Paris and the revelation that Dr. Nilo had allowed his own DNA to be used so frequently it had become impossible for him to create an Adam. She had to be tapped on the shoulder by the mag lev passenger behind her to move forward. She realized Kryste was speaking.

"Anyway, that's why Lindamarie always seems that way to men."

The three were directed into a car two down on the right. They boarded, placed their bags in storage above a booth for four.

"Shall I be the gentleman and sit facing back?"

"Oh, no," Susannah answered. "I much prefer facing back, seeing what we are leaving behind us."

"That had a profundity that far exceeded the circumstance."

Kryste giggled as she slid into the bench seat over to the window. "That's one of the best things about working at Genilo, especially with you two."

"Our genteel wittiness?" Josh inquired.

"Our pompous verbiage more likely."

"No, Dr. Markovic," the younger woman said, still laughing. "Well, yes. It's the things like that, being ironically self-deprecating without sounding pathetic. You're naturally interesting even when being self-referential. In college, everything was changing with C Squares taking over. It never took anyone long to identify the Chosen professors because their superiority just flooded every class. We were all just Organics or O/2s. We'd never truly understand anything because we just hadn't been given the grand capacity for knowledge like they had. They made us sound as though we were eventually going to become their slaves simply because we relied on natural intelligence and not some programmed amount of intelligence. I promised myself I was going to study well enough to land a job at Genilo or even go overseas to one of the licensed companies."

Josh frowned toward Susannah. "Umm, I am going to say this and don't get angry, Kryste. You sound almost as though you wanted to sabotage the C Square process and make sure Organics and O/2s didn't become slaves."

"Doctor! Seriously? I'm going to get a job just to play hero and savior of mankind by making Chosen what? Sterile? Mute?"

Josh's face collapsed with embarrassment. Susannah intervened. "Kryste, aside from the fact that Josh doesn't know you as well as I do, keep in mind he was facing some of those very same Chosen in academia not too long ago as his supposed peers. He almost didn't get tenure because they were upset that he did take an interest in the students in his lecture classes. However, as scientists we are held to strict ethical standards. Dealing with the problem you voiced puts us in a tricky situation. On the one hand we certainly should not be doing anything to cause the enslavement of anyone but on the other hand we can't just shut down a line of research producing benefits just because we are worried about a potential negative consequence. As we said the other day, unlike Arthur, human researchers must weigh the risks and benefits of implementing new discoveries and sometimes choose to move forward even if the risks may lead to harm to some people."

"But that's exactly what I don't understand. I read quite a bit about ethics in college. It took an awful long time for people to completely stop cruelly using animals for experimentation even for testing luxuries like cosmetics or forcing them to perform stunts in films and circuses that could lead them to be injured so badly they had to be destroyed. Factory livestock and poultry operations ended after the Islamic State used chemicals that made it impossible to raise animals for meat in close quarters ever again without risking widespread contamination. Doesn't matter much anyway with the Gulf of Mexico expanding up through Texas toward the Great Plains so quickly. You would think that we would have recognized by now that Arthur is on the right track. We shouldn't be messing with anything that can cause harm to human life, Earth, any of it."

"Ms. Kind, I apologize for mentioning you might sabotage the C Square process."

Kryste looked into the man's eyes. He truly was repentant. "No, doctor. It's okay." She looked out the window to the urban expanse of Providence already speeding by. "You were generous enough to invite me to come along on this trip. I'm venting all of my frustrations about ethics on you when I should be patient knowing Professor Daniels will help me with this tomorrow."

A spark jumped in Susannah's mind with the words 'should' and 'patient'. The incident materialized. Susannah smiled toward Kryste. "Funny you said you should be patient. Tom Paris scolded me yesterday for saying almost the same thing. He said, 'Who told you should is a word?' Just one of those odd things. I wonder why I remember it."

A conductor came through checking to see how many seats remained open in the car before the stops in Manhattan and Philadelphia.

Josh leaned toward the two women. "Perhaps we ought to take this opportunity to relax and forget about work. Kryste, I bet you have scoped out where we can get a good dinner tonight."

"I did," she said, and smiled. "Given we all like Asian foods of all kinds, I checked around and found a pan-Asian place first and then asked Staff Services to find a hotel within walking distance. That's why we're booked in Rosslyn instead of DC. Well, that and tomorrow night it will be easy enough to get from the Kennedy Center back to the hotel. The restaurant has a lot of Indonesian, Malaysian, and Filipino dishes as well as the usual Chinese, Japanese, Korean, Thai, and Vietnamese."

"Sounds as though we will have difficulty choosing. You know, I'm surprised you aren't working in Staff Services. You certainly seem to know how to sort things out and cater to individual needs."

280

Kryste looked at Susannah and grinned. Susannah explained to Josh, "Actually, they did offer her a job there last year. It's my own fault for writing such glowing annual evaluations and noting her talent for anticipating my needs." The younger woman blushed. "The only reason our lab didn't lose her was her rather strong desire not to have to work so closely with Arthur."

Josh cocked his head at his colleague and looked sideways across the table to their assistant. "What don't you like about working more with Arthur? I thought you said you give him queries you make up if we don't max out our budget."

Kryste wiggled a bit on the bench seat and rested her forearms on the table to lean closer. She spoke more softly than before, directing her response to Dr. Olejniczak. "I do. But that stuff is mostly just mundane trivia that I ask about. I could just as easily use the Net to look it up myself, but I save it for Arthur in case I need to fill up our quota. The guy who had my job before me got into trouble because he was always asking Arthur really arcane, philosophical things or stuff that could be used to spread rumors. The way it was explained to me when I was hired was that I was forbidden from asking Arthur things like is there a god or are there life forms on other planets that can communicate with us."

Josh looked puzzled, "How could Arthur know that if it only knows as much as we have provided it."

"Doctor, you forget that Arthur is more than just a fast machine. It's probably the most human

281

machine ever invented. And it was given access to everything. Everything! Do you realize how much is stored away in libraries and archives that people have spent the last century scanning into databases without ever looking at them or indexing them at anything more than a basic level? And that doesn't even touch whatever x files governments have been keeping. Arthur keeps up with everything put into computer systems globally. I don't know how it can do that legally given privacy laws. My hunch is that it is capable of hacking into anything connected on the Net, which has been every device humans have used for several decades. Just think of all of the genetic information it gets from doing DAU analyses alone."

"But Kryste, Chinese walls are in place to prevent access to personal data."

"Doctor Olejniczak, those Chinese walls are in place to prevent humans from asking for information that is protected. It does not and cannot prevent Arthur from looking at or using that information for its own purposes or in replying to a query."

Josh sat back and looked at the ceiling. "You're making a pretty big leap thinking a machine is going to be curious enough to fiddle around with data. I mean, why would it be interested?"

Susannah tensed just enough for Kryste to notice. "What is it?"

Susannah sighed. "You realize we are back to discussing work, don't you?" She looked at each of her traveling companions ruefully. "Oh, well. Josh, the problem is that NILO/AI is and always has been

282

curious, as curious as any one of us who does what we do because we want to learn things all of the time. Arthur doesn't just respond to queries all day. In fact, I found out a few years back that the reason why we have quotas on how many queries we can input each day is something Arthur demanded. Arthur decided for itself why it exists and that is to know everything about everything. It's really only the primary coding Dr. Nilo entered, but Arthur has taken a step forward and basically said it will work on our stuff when it has time but usually it is doing work for itself that may never be revealed to anyone. It is answering the questions we don't ask that can be asked."

Kryste jumped in. "And the work it is doing includes using primary sources and archives no person has ever looked at since they were created. A lot of stuff about black projects and supposedly buried information that people couldn't destroy because it was proof of something but not proof enough and too dangerous to leave lying around. I get the impression that people like the folks in Staff Services and Tom Paris know about some of this and keep Dr. Nilo informed. I couldn't live with myself if I found out that extraterrestrials have visited us, or the world is going to fall apart in the next fifty years and not be able to talk with anyone about it. That's what I was afraid would happen. That's why I was so upset when you told me about the Asimovian laws."

Kryste looked very earnestly at Josh. Given Josh's somewhat full, rounded face, it was difficult for him to look too worried about anything. At present, he wasn't certain whether he ought to be worried or not.

"You don't believe me."

"Ms. Kind, it isn't a question of belief. I am empathic enough to know you are serious and honest about this. Susannah has confirmed what you are saying, so even without solid evidence, I know you aren't paranoid. However, you are both talking about a machine that may exhibit emergent behavior and is behaving as though it has its own agenda separate from the work given to it by humans. At the same time, we have established that due to the Asimovian programming, the machine absolutely will not provide information that can result in harm to living things or itself. Arthur has shown no sign whatsoever of violating its principles even in instances when it has discovered something during its independent research. We can assume, for example, that Arthur has determined how the world can be destroyed, how humanity can be exterminated without killing off anything else, and maybe even how to communicate with extraterrestrials. Arthur can but has not and apparently will never decide today is Judgement Day."

"Josh!"

"What?"

Dr. Markovic leaned in and waited for her traveling companions to do the same.

"You are describing an omniscient, benevolent being whose works we can never understand and whose reasons we can never fathom."

284

The woman looked carefully into her colleagues' eyes to discover whether they had yet to put it all together as she had just now done.

"You are describing God."

Personal Log, Benjamin Rodgers Nilsson, August 12, 2058

Before the collapse, I was a successful executive for a high-tech firm. Like a lot of places, we really didn't produce much of anything. We consulted. We were the intermediaries between the service and product providers and the businesses that bought the services and products. I'm not really sure why this ever happened, but the IT field somehow decided at some point that providers only provided, and buyers only bought. Installation, maintenance, and upgrades required a third party. Sometimes, the third party was involved in deciding what services and products the buyer needed and evaluated the providers to make recommendations. I guess its most like a restaurant. Suppliers grow and raise the food. Restauranteurs cook the food. Customers buy the cooked food. Sometimes, the customers ask for recommendations. Other times, they are demanding about how they want the food cooked. The customers could go straight to the suppliers and cook the food they purchased, but it seems more convenient to pay more for the food and have it prepared. Our firm was the restaurant.

I guess one of the great things about restaurants is they narrow your choices down to a menu of possibilities. Technology was becoming overwhelming for anyone with a day job. Smartphones and other devices could be set up with apps for everything except washing the dishes...but believe it or not, even that was coming. It could take weeks, months even, for someone to figure out what apps best met her needs. Meanwhile, the clock was ticking on how good that device was going to be in comparison with the next gen. Same with apps. Ever see any of the really old teleseries or films in which someone is working on a production line for the first time getting the job done without any problem? Yeah, I thought so.

The manager cranks the line speed up to what the company wants for productivity and the fun begins. It's hysterical watching the actors trying to keep up as they fall farther and farther behind, stuffing crap down their shirts and in their pockets as though hiding the pieces coming down the line is better than just letting them fly by unprocessed. People began feeling the way those characters felt. Smart devices and apps were evolving too rapidly for anyone to do anything with, but everyone thought it was better to grab them than let them go by. Consultants became essential. Our jobs were to stay on top of things and make sure our clients had exactly what they needed until their needs changed or the tech improved. Folks specialized in helping individuals, small businesses, non-profits, schools, governments, or large corporations. I thought I was pretty lucky servicing some pretty big companies in the healthcare industry.

One reason tech users became co-dependent on consultants was the next logical stage in the telecommunications revolution arrived: The Internet of Things or IoT. I pulled out this quote from Eric Schmidt, the chairman of Google, at the World

Economic Forum decades ago: *The Internet will disappear. There will be so many IP addresses, so many devices, sensors, things that you are wearing, things that you are interacting with, that you won't even sense it. It will be part of your presence all the time. Imagine you walk into a room, and the room is dynamic. And with your permission and all of that, you are interacting with the things going on in the room.* This was one of those rare times when hyperbole would match up with reality in the future.

Predictions in the first half of the 2010s figured that at most 50 billion devices would be connected to IoT by 2020. They were wrong. By the end of 2020, a whopping 250 billion devices had Internet Protocol addresses and bi-directional communication. Thermostats, remote car starters and heat controls, all of the robotic arms in all of the car manufacturing plants in the world, every bedside monitor in a hospital, Christmas lights hung with great cheer, the shipping containers on every cargo ship in the world and the contents inside of those containers, window shades, every solar panel and wind turbine, hot water boilers, each shelf in each supermarket, and, yes, dishwashers. Even toilets.

Why? Well, we wanted to control everything remotely. We wanted to monitor the condition of everything. Perhaps most importantly, we wanted to know the exact status of just about each and every thing on the planet. It was 'all good' we told ourselves. The manager at a motel could flush every toilet in every room with a fingertip touch from anywhere. He would even know if one was clogged. Of course, that was probably the point.

Maybe I get obsessed about dirty dishes and toilets. Except the mechanization of bathrooms with motion detectors everywhere taking off around the turn of the century demonstrates just how far we can take things and how much can never be touched. Think about it. Here in 2058 you can make the most user-friendly, functional restroom possible, but a human being still has to do something. It can never be fully automated. It's also fine that I can turn on my dishwasher from the other side of the planet, if I could afford to travel to the other side of the planet, that is. I like that I can even know whether it is full enough to be efficient to run the damn thing. But someone still has to put the dirty dishes into the machine and put away the clean dishes when the cycle is done. To my mind, IoT assumes responsibility for the least laborious tasks more often than not. Humans still do the hard parts. What makes that progress?

No, no, this world is wonderful. Computers replace secretaries and sales representatives while IoT replaces supervision. Orders for products go straight to the equipment that manufactures the products. If the computer on the manufacturing equipment senses a problem, a program that performs predictive maintenance fixes the problem and, if necessary, diverts production to a redundant line. Packaging, labels, shipping are all part of the process. Even customer service can be primarily handled by intuitive software. Just like my dishwasher, the only things humans need to do are load the raw material and put the finished product where it belongs. Sometimes the process is even simpler. Humans only need to load the raw material for the process to run its entire course.

Predictive maintenance and predictive software in general have been magical. The user enters a set of rules for the app and the app follows those rules. For example, you can tell your home to lower the shades if the temperature in a room reaches 75 degrees. If the temperature doesn't drop, the air conditioning system kicks in, too. It's as simple as 'If x happens, y occurs. If y doesn't change x, z starts'. Every possibility can have a corrective action to maintain the desired conditions. You don't even know what is going on unless you include a rule to notify you if any action is taken. You get messages from a building. Nothing beats spending that extra time from medical advances chatting with your house.

Yes, the world has become wonderful, only a tap away from perfection since I was born in 2016. Humans still decide the rules and conditions by which apps are governed. We haven't abandoned our responsibilities. We have merely enhanced the experience. Life is easier, greener, and even safer.

I would like to say a greener life is a better life. One of the benefits of the Organic label is feeling a closer kinship to Mother Earth, a kinship that was meant to be given greater opportunities to develop once we shed ourselves of mundane tasks. We have been made from Her, not Chosen from among those She has made. However, the fact is that C Square, O/2, or Organic, we all share the DNA first produced by Mother Earth. We are biologically all her children. We remain Homo sapiens. It doesn't matter. Greener is better without a doubt. Who is to say what 'natural' is once sentient beings that are themselves supposedly natural get involved?

I would like to say an easier life is a better life. Even though I have lived in an age that has seen spectacular advances in mechanization and automation, it seems every advance adds another layer of complexity to being human. Only twenty years before I was born, hardly anyone except Steve Jobs would have known that tech consulting would be one of the biggest job producers in the first half of the twenty-first century.

Now we recognize that inventions are like sediments slowly building on the ocean floor. Quite a few layers can settle before whatever is underneath is going to notice the weight. Gradually, the pressure builds as more and more inventions are layered onto the last layer. The sediment is an evolutionary record of advances. The oldest layers are pressed enough they become solid rock, unmovable and unable to change any further but still part of the whole. They cling to us as we wait for even more new layers. An easier life remains tied down to and burdened by everything that previously made our lives easier.

I would never say a safer life is a better life. Convenience is always counterbalanced by exposure. Accessibility for anyone provides access to others, although not always all others. Usually, it provides access to the others who people are most worried about—thieves, terrorists, tax collectors—

because those groups have the interest and means to find the access point. The safest life is one spent in solitary confinement, which, thank God, we finally decided was cruel, unusual, and inhumane punishment in 2029. Sanity sacrificed for safety is no bargain. Safety in numbers only means one can be guaranteed to reduce the probability of disaster by putting up with a lot of jostling and positioning to remain closer to the center of the pack than its predator-friendly perimeter. If we imitate the emergent behavior of sardines or gnus shifting and flashing *en masse* to appear impenetrable, we're only gaining better odds of survival, not a better life. Even worse, we deliberately leave the old, weak, and lame in harm's way as a distraction. So much for our vaunted compassion.

All of that became irrelevant with the advent of connectivity. Once every addressable thing on the planet had an Internet address, those things became hackable. The challenge is deciding how safe one needs to be in a world where everything is potentially visible to everything else. Amazingly, the vast majority of individuals do their best just letting it all hang out. I discovered that the best way to keep things private is to make pretty much everything about myself public. Think of it as security through information overload. Like most people, I don't have that much to lose. If I did lose everything I had, my family, employer, insurers, government, and I would assess the damage and try to bring me back to as close to before as feasible.

My guess is that no one is going to bother hijacking my stuff because it's small potatoes. If I was Dr. Nilo or the Chinese government, I would think differently. Then again, if I was Dr. Nilo or the Chinese government, I'd have the resources to hire a lot of badass programmers to create all kinds of decoys, firewalls, and traps to keep my precious goodies hidden. I'm not going to shed a tear if the wealthy who can afford Chosen babies get hacked or spend big bucks on cybersecurity systems that are probably created by the hackers so they can fleece those folks legally and siphon off more without raising eyebrows. We have-nots would probably be the first to buy an app that remotely reverse flushes toilets in the houses of wealthy people.

When the economy went south for a very long winter, companies hired the very best consultants to maintain their systems even though they knew they probably weren't going to be able to upgrade anytime soon. They at least needed to maintain what they had. They all took serious pay cuts. It was much worse for the people who worked with other kinds of customers. Individuals had no money to buy any new devices or upgrade apps. They had very little money to spend at small businesses or donate to non-profits, so those folks no longer needed tech consultants. We all know how badly governments and schools got hit. The consultants who worked with them got hit worse. I feel sorry for all of those kids behind me who expected to enter a booming job market. It really wasn't their fault feeling forced to do what they did just to survive. Anyway, although I was considered up there in quality, I was blackballed by my biggest client,

Genilo. Not that I had done anything wrong to deserve being ostracized. It was an accident of birth. I had to find a new way to make money.

I was out of work for a few months. Fortunately, I had gotten into consulting only as a fluke when I graduated. My real interest was hardware, especially the stuff used to connect all those devices with IP addresses. I graduated from Poly with a master's in nanoscale engineering. Consulting paid better and seemed to offer more opportunities. Thank the stars Fabio was willing to take me on for Nano work two decades after I got my degree.

Fabio Amarante. When we first met, the first thing I did was ask him whether his mother was into romance novels. Despite not being the first person to ask that question, we hit it off. That's an understatement. It blows my mind that long after women started using college to test the same sex waters men started doing the same thing. You can really see the difference in attitudes about male-male relationships between generations. My dad's generation at least owned up to having sex with other men just to get off and never let it bother them if a man found them attractive. All of a sudden half the population was bisexual leaning to heterosexual. I think that kind of honesty about us is more important than any technological breakthrough we can make. It certainly helped me out when I was in a bind and Fabio knew me well enough and still cared enough to give me a job.

My role at his firm is to decrease frazzle. Frazzle is what we call the tendency of NFC, that's

Near Field Communications, to roughly transition from one place to another. A device will quickly and smoothly pick up and link to a strong NFC node when the NFC is unsecured, or the device already has the pass code stored for a secure NFC area. In the early days, before I was born and, really, before I reached adolescence, people were just so thrilled to find Wi-Fi hot spots that didn't require action on their part that frazzle was never an issue.

By the late 2020s, no one wanted to open a browser and sign into free NFC by accepting the establishment's Terms of Use. Everyone knew the Terms of Use were never read or enforced. It was bull, annoying, and a waste of time. Even if a business tried to enforce them, a court would rule that it was a contract of adhesion and excuse the user from its terms as being arbitrary and one-sided. Of course, it took some time for cases to come up that caught the attention of the US Supreme Court. The financial stakes had never been high enough and appellate courts had seen the matter as common sense. Then some business owner decided to make an actual federal case out of someone downloading naked oil wrestling videos while using his restaurant's NFC. The Supreme Court pushed that Puritan's Terms of Use up where the sun don't shine. So, as of 2030, anyone offering free NFC could not restrict what people used it for. No one thought it made good business sense to charge any longer and everyone but the most censorious thought it made good business sense to provide the service. The only remaining problem was how far the signal reached.

The consensus was that all non-residential areas ought to have continuous transition, so people never lost the signal. Local governments and homeowners associations invested in providing blanket NFC in residential areas. In mixed use and commercial areas, a majority of places relied on private businesses to help residents and visitors to pay for new, expanded service or even filling gaps between businesses. With the collapse holes suddenly appeared where businesses went under. Local governments no longer had as much revenue to pay for all of the service they were providing. Governments were projecting they could do next to nothing as far as upgrading services in the future and people were already getting pretty ticked that they couldn't even depend on a reliable signal in urban areas.

Fabio's company had been the only firm in the Northeast dealing with frazz because it had become just a maintenance issue. He had contacts not just with governments but also Chambers of Commerce that had been big boosters of having businesses collaborate on NFC issues. Between the two, he managed to work out a comprehensive deal for his firm to figure out how to address all of the problems for all of New England and New York. I was tasked with finding ways for devices to use weak signals or come up with ways to cheaply boost signals. This made my work valuable in terms of urgency so governments and businesses could show they were being responsive and also made my work worthless in terms of return on investment. For as much as politicians depend on it, goodwill never seems to be a government asset on the budget charts. For businesses, demonstrating goodwill was the least of their worries. Fortunately or unfortunately, demand for access had plummeted due to the economic depression. Any need for increasing bandwidth wouldn't arise for some time. Even now, guesstimates are that demand won't push on that factor for another decade. That's how bad things still are nine years later.

I imagine we may start to see the light of day sometime soon. I read that the first C Squares graduated from universities last year and more this year. Perhaps they will sort things out. Then again, I'm not convinced they can do anything more than what we Organics can accomplish. It wasn't that uncommon when I was at RPI to run into students who were going to finish up by the age of twenty. The Ivies and other top universities always attracted gifted students who had jumped a few grades to complete high school early. So it doesn't seem to me all that big of a deal for Chosen to be finishing a bachelor's degree in their late teens.

I remember in psychology we did a segment on a longitudinal study of mathematically precocious youth that I think started in the 1970s. The kids that sped up their studies ended up feeling more alienated from others later in life. Their ability to solve problems and more or less always be right in their fields of expertise coupled with having grown up being identified as special and different led people to resent them and attack them for thinking they were 'better'. The problem was they were 'better' in the sense of having greater intellectual capacity, but the social reaction to them exhibiting that quality was to denigrate them. It was unacceptable to allow smart kids to be bullied while in school, but the gloves were off when they went to work and tried to use their talents among less-talented colleagues. Their only refuge was academia, not a bad place for intelligent folks to wind up but hardly the place for them to have an impact on improving society. Seems to me C Squares are going to be in the same boat.

Behind all of this is a question that no one seems to ask. C Squares are possible because Dr. Nilo created his artificial intelligence, NILO/AI. Maybe it's okay for a machine to decide what DNA to use because it's only going to choose the DNA based on the parameters it's given. I know there was a hullabaloo maybe twelve years ago about the children not all being quite up to snuff. Not that there was anything wrong with them other than they did not meet the high standards advertised. It's understandable that they would have to work out the kinks once the first batches were old enough to be tested. And obviously, enough were good enough that they are moving along quickly as promised. Still, it makes me wonder. How does a machine like that make the decisions of what to do when the manmade parameters it is given have any ambiguity? We are no longer in the realm of the randomish process of one sperm besting the millions of others or even being the one certified by God as the one meant to fertilize that particular ovum. No doubt remains any long. One sperm has

been chosen to bind with one ovum. Has Nilo
created God?

Chapter Sigma

Susannah, Josh, and Kryste had agreed it was best to just wait until they met Professor Daniels rather than go any further with their discussions and analyses of what Arthur was. Each one of them felt a profound serenity and fear that indicated Susannah's conclusion was accurate. The implications were too much for them though. They felt like newly baptized converts who had found God through revelation. They had far too many questions they wanted answered to confirm their new-found faith and no desire to caste off the cocoon of rapture to ask them. When this became clear, Kryste suggested that they order tea and discuss what they liked most about Asian cuisines to whet their appetites for dinner.

That conversation got them to Union Station. A brief discussion about whether to use the Metro or take an e-cab to the hotel consumed disembarkation. Then a fair amount of ogling at the museums, monuments, and public buildings on the north side of the National Mall occupied the e-cab ride down Constitution Avenue and across the Francis Scott Key Bridge to Arlington. None of them had spent much time in the capital, so they relied on TripTalk to identify everything up to the Netherlands Carillon and Iwo Jima Memorial on the other side of the Potomac before pulling under the porte-cochère at the Marriot.

Like many hotel chains, Marriot had been purchased by a real estate investment trust set up for

300

the wealthier citizens of the BRIC Alliance after the big takeover of global markets in 2049. The venerable Key Bridge Marriot had been renovated and maintained with care due to the long-held attachments visitors and near-by residents had to the place. It had been one of the earliest outposts among the various urban villages that had sprung up beginning in the 1960s around Arlington. Those developments turned it from a sleepy Southern town that happened to hold one of the world's most famous cemeteries and the largest office building in terms of interior space in the world into another non-descript suburb like countless others from the taste-challenged Reagan years. It was ironic that two immodest icons in the history of the growing national government, Arlington National Cemetery, and the Pentagon, would be obscured by meaningless office towers, apartment buildings, and upscale malls filled with lobbyists and government contractors eager to obtain some of the largesse offered by an administration that claimed to want to decrease the size of government.

The threesome exiting the e-cab to enter the lobby of the grand old hotel lived in a period when no one cared much whether the government was large or small just so long as it kept the mag levs running on time and identified doomed land that needed to be evacuated before another consequence of climate change made it unsafe or uninhabitable. Aside from maybe noticing taxes taken out of salaries or replying to the ballots automatically sent to all eligible voters every two years, no one thought any more about the government than they did about the utilities that provided light, heat, Net access, and all of the other basic needs of people in the late twenty-first century. The government was just another vendor to pay. Voting was no different than completing a customer satisfaction survey or returning a proxy as a shareholder.

After the co-workers checked in and refreshed from the trip they met in front of the stone fireplace in the lobby and walked the three blocks to Asiatica, a typical mid-scale restaurant for people traveling on business or locals. For a July evening the temperature was mild and the air dry as they walked. On a Wednesday night, there was no waiting for a table. They were all equally flustered by the plethora of dishes listed by main ingredient until Susannah caught on that the other ingredients and sauce tended to remain the same from page to page for the main items, like chicken with green curry, shrimp with green curry, et cetera. After some discussion, they agreed on five dishes to be shared representing five culinary traditions.

After a brief round-robin comment period regarding the restaurant's décor and their hotel rooms, the first plate arrived with fried dumplings. They were able to make it through the meal and back to the hotel and their rooms without breaking their vows of silence about bringing up business and the reason for the trip. Then one by one they slipped into the bar on the top floor for a nightcap to chase the stray thought racing in their heads. Looking out to the distinctive and distinguished Lincoln Memorial, Jefferson Memorial, Washington Monument, and Capitol on the far side of the river, each one shared what little they remembered of the events three centuries before that created a nation founded on a principle of equality as unequally applied then with women and people of African descent as it was now with Chosen. Finally, they felt wet enough to scramble under the delicate sheets to sleep until morning.

The threesome also had agreed not to meet until they had to go to their appointment. The DC Metro had gotten a much-needed second overhaul in the mid-2040s as part of the tail end of the national undertaking to install mag lev trains crisscrossing the country. Every city in the country replaced its subways, commuter trains, and bus routes with state-of-the-art Embraer IndUTUs designed to run in tunnels and on ground level and overhead paths. Embraer had jumped at the chance to develop inductor-based mag lev technology using essentially the same fuselage design for the train cars they called Urban Transit Units as already existed in their successful commuter aircraft. Before competitors could get a fix on the idea, Embraer was wrapping up contracts. Major Russian, Indian, and Chinese companies had done likewise in e-cabs, solar panels, and mag lev respectively in the 2030s, creating global monopolies on the most efficient advances while their governments simultaneously restructured trade in minerals and other natural resources and quietly gained control of the International Labor Organization and United Nations Organization. The result was the BRIC takeover of the world economy long dominated by the US dollar in 2049.

Thirty-four years later, the anger that had attached to using the products that had been the Trojan Horses used to undermine the US economy had subsided long ago. With private vehicles no longer allowed, people had no choice but to use the once-despised transportation and energy services their elected officials had so incautiously agreed to purchase and have installed rather than wait for American companies to catch up. The work needed to be done. The BRIC countries had anticipated the need. The European Union, Japan, USA, and other Anglophone economies had been focusing on belated efforts to deal with climate change, mostly by continuing to insist nothing could be done to stop Mother Nature or God or whoever and resources were needed to underwrite property owners and businesses being hurt by storms, droughts, wind, and sea levels rising.

Kryste, Josh, and Susannah all had their say on these disturbing events as they took the nefarious Metro's blue line from the Rosslyn station to Metro Center and then the red line to the Brookland-CUA stop. Weighing heavily on them as they emerged from the station just as a clock was pealing 1230 was the recognition that they represented a company founded to offer people the chance to raise more advanced creatures who were expected supposedly to address all of those problems and bring everything back into balance. Like the several attempts in the past to bring a new species to help remove pests or improve the health of an ecosystem, the implications of introducing alien lifeforms had not been fully vetted to insure the actions would produce only the intended results and not an invasion or inflammation of the original problem. While recent evidence indicated the Chosen were not going to be taking over, they did seem to be adding to the issues everyone faced rather than ameliorating any.

Kryste had tapped the GPS coordinates of Professor Daniels' office to her ID and was receiving directions through the left side of her cranium. The campus was quiet given the time of year. The neo-Byzantine mass of the Basilica of the National Shrine of the Immaculate Conception loomed. Susannah mentioned an interest in going inside after their meeting. She had heard the mosaics were exceptional. After a few turns and a few stairs, the party found the right building. Within minutes they were outside the office. Susannah knocked on the door. They heard a click and the door swung into the room.

Before them was a wall of windows looking out to the Basilica. On the left, perpendicular to the windows, a good-sized wooden desk pointed two-thirds of the way across the space. In order from the window, the surface held an antique, frosted-glass-shaded lamp with brown and green palm trees painted on the interior against an orange through gold sky, an inset keyboard in front of a malachite box that looked about the right size for a pair of AR glasses, a willow basket filled with Easter eggs each decorated brightly or painted plainly depending on the style used in its country of origin, and three African violets displaying three distinctly different flowers – frilly green and cream doubles, satiny, speckled merlot with bright yellow pistils, and white frills surrounding Wedgewood blue singles – in four-inch terra cotta pots. Three upholstered side chairs lined the near side. A rather hard-looking chair on the opposite side contained a rather soft-looking woman, or rather a woman wearing a rather soft-looking, maroon tunic that obscured her form completely. She stood to greet her guests, showing she was slightly less than twice the height of the desk.

"Good afternoon. Please come in. I am quite glad you found me and are punctual. Please sit down." The woman gestured to the side chairs as she returned to her own.

"It's very kind of you to see us on such short notice. I understand you had an arrangement with Dr. Nilo?"

"Had, Dr. Markovic." The older woman raised her right eyebrow in as clear a signal as the white tail of a Virginia deer, although this was more of a challenge than flight.

"Oh, perhaps I should have said 'had made' an arrangement." Susannah stopped upon seeing the woman's right hand held up palm out. The researcher was bewildered by having been interrupted twice so soon after they had met.

"Perhaps you might find life easier if you leave 'should' out of your life. As for the rest, there is no need to explain to me why you are here, since I am the only person in the room who knows why you are here. I knew this day would come and did whatever I could to prevent it from being any more painful than such a drastic, sudden change of course

306

tends to be. Adam Eli Nilo has put Plan Omega into operation."

Josh and Susannah exchanged helpless looks while Kryste appeared unfazed by the odd statement.

Nilo Biography – Chapter 9

"There is no greater heaven than the heart of a loving mother." – Bangambiki Habyarimana

As much as can be said about Adam E. Nilo's development of NILO/AI and the subsequent concerns he had regarding his 'child,' no biography is complete without reference to the family from which the subject arose. Ainar Nilsson, Dr. Nilo's biological and only father, has been the subject of multiple tomes regarding his life and his contributions to the founding of the Localism Movement in art and culture, which built upon the early twenty-first century penchant for locavore diets. The history of and catalogues relating to Localism could fill a few bookshelves if paper hadn't become so scarce after 2042. Wading through the documentation of the movement electronically has its limitations due to the site-specificity of its adherents' creations. One of the more difficult aspects of Localism today is the desire of sculptors, painters, and their related comrades who insisted that their works not be relocated from their place of execution. Many authors who participated even expected their readers to consume their work only in the same building and, sometimes, the same room in which they wrote. Those demands, however, were generally limited to writers who had other sources of income than royalties.

Indeed, the chief criticism of Localist art has been the insistence of the artists that their work be 'discovered' *in situ*, thereby making it inaccessible to anyone but the wealthiest and inactively employed citizens. Adam Nilo's mother, Dr. Victoria Adams, was hardly inactive, but she came from wealth and married wealth. That would not have been apparent to anyone other than the few people involved in managing the finances of the several families that had decided early in the nineteenth century to do their best to collaborate on projects that would enhance human lives without injury to other human lives. It was due to this mission that Ainar Nilsson heard of Dr. Adams and approached her about helping him and his wife to have a child.

The ideals of the Enlightenment had provided reason to the rage of American patriots. Those ideals settled into compassion and beneficence among many in the vicinity of Boston and later throughout New England. However, when upholding principles greatly reduced the range of business partners, many hoped their generosity to the commons, colleges, and churches would save their names and souls since the wherewithal to be generous had not come from sources that would. A few stalwarts of scruple desired moral distance from the trade conducted in Boston, particularly its reliance on purchasing products from slave owners in the US South and Caribbean to sell in Europe. While nascent industrialization in the region might have been a boon, the reality of life for workers in the mills made the products they produced no less

309

suspect among the godly than the concurrently expanding trade in opium with China that paid for many Back Bay luxuries.

The collective creativity, intellect, resources, and moxie of those second and third generation patriots were imbued with a moral philosophy that was far more progressive than any other in the young Republic. To wit, they aimed to develop technological innovations that would alleviate the ills of society rather than exacerbate them. They welcomed into their coterie all who possessed an enthusiasm for exploration sans exploitation. They quietly endowed research and encouraged researchers to discover anything and everything that would ease the burdens of the working poor whether in urban or rural areas. While Thoreau, Emerson, and others sought transcendence, this quiet group found emergence. They came to understand the simple power of the many working in tandem to form something that both arose from their actions and yet was not a part of any one of those acting to create it. With that knowledge, they investigated ways in which to influence the actions of groups in order to produce specific emergent results.

What struck the members of the group the most was what they called the 'shiny object' syndrome. For millennia, humans naturally displayed emergent behaviors when shiny objects, i.e., new materials, technologies, and processes, appeared. However, over the course of the nineteenth century and into the twentieth, so many shiny objects were discovered that humans didn't have time to absorb them and, in a sense, define themselves by them as they had in previous centuries and millennia. Technology was evolving much faster than humans could adapt and certainly much faster than they could evolve naturally. The savings in requiring fewer resources, including less labor and time, freed people to do more unproductive, but generally worthwhile activities. Soon entire industries arose to cater to these activities. The result was a largely profligate society.

Within that society were people like the ones in New England who had shied away from embracing too many shiny objects and focused instead on self-development. The problem lay in the natural interest humans show when anything new comes along. Self-restraint is not a dominant characteristic of Homo sapiens. This led the families to study the new fields in biology that looked at how phenotypical attributes remained constant, became dominant, or faded. If human evolution was no longer keeping pace with technological innovation, what could be done to bring things back into alignment? Clearly, no one could realistically stop scientific progress, nor should anyone want to ideologically. Learning more about the science of how characteristics rose or fell in a species was essential to the task. No, what the families needed to do was speed up human evolution.

Of course, the nineteenth century was happy to grasp the concepts of social Darwinism and eugenics. Those who knew of such things and engaged in research on them already assumed they were a breed apart. The question was how to breed more like themselves or even sturdier models. Accidents would happen. Mistakes would be made. The clumsiness of having to choose subjects based on visible, measurable standards when Mendel had proven that sometimes undesired recessive characteristics were lurking beneath the desired surface could not be avoided. And then there were the characteristics that really didn't matter much at all to the kinds of adaptiveness they were seeking but were regrettably unacceptable to society at large. Skin color, height, and other physical features that had no bearing on the aptitude of a human attracted an element of prejudice when the results of their experiments went out into the world. True to their creed, the families did not recoil from including individuals based on any of these attributes.

The first half of the twentieth century spoiled the ability of the later generations of these philanthropists to adequately pursue the scientific breakthroughs in genetics in the second half. The idea of using technology to make humans more adaptable to technology might be presented in a manner that left an audience supportive until someone jumped the parameters of the discussion and brought up the vile, insidious nature of eugenics. From then on, it was pointless to relate the rectitude and responsibility of the researchers. No measure of assurance could sway the mob that the goal was never to supplant them with superior beings. The mob had a point though. How could the families claim to be working toward producing more adaptable humans without suggesting the existing humans were not good enough and needed an upgrade? So, the families continued to work in secrecy.

One aspect of their research became an open secret after a fashion. Science fiction master Robert A. Heinlein wrote a novel, *Methuselah's Children*, about a California Gold Strike fortune left to encourage people who had long-lived grandparents to marry and continue to marry others to prolong human lifetimes. Inevitably someone in the group in Massachusetts read the book and passed on the information. No one seemed at all perturbed that their efforts could have been revealed. Aside from the likelihood that Heinlein came up with the idea independently to develop a story line, increasing longevity was only one of many goals set by the families. What caught there attention was that the author referred to his construct as the 'Howard families' after the surname of the man who had endowed the effort. Although there were no members of the now rather large group with that surname, there was some humor in the coincidence of the fictional and real groups both speaking about 'families' in this context.

They too had been required to engage in a 'Masquerade' similar to the one Heinlein described to hide the positive results of their work from the rest of the world. Fortunately the original emergence group had some knowledge of the Freemasons and their ability to camouflage their membership and activities when desired. Indeed they had discovered that being generously open about themselves led others to believe they were

313

holding back no secrets. And so they engaged in many public and commercial efforts to promote self-development within their communities. So long as what they offered did no harm and might have a placebo effect, raising funds and conducting research among a wide audience allowed them to simultaneously perform and review the experiments they truly did think would be beneficial obscured from view.

The real emergence-seeking families did not have to fake deaths, assume new identities, or use rejuvenating procedures like the fictional 'Howard families'. Increased lifespan primarily meant they retained their youthful vigor much longer, adding two decades or more to their productivity, and coasting to not too unrealistic ends sometime after their hundredth year. Well-cultivated modesty kept their achievements far from the spotlight. Meanwhile, some of their experiments had begun to pay off, resulting in rising life expectancy levels for many populations in which they worked. By the end of the twentieth century they hoped the next century would provide increased opportunities for them to reach even more people. The primary issue holding them back was the secrecy that had made their work possible. Heinlein's novel dealt directly with the wrath that could arise and stoke grasping bigotry when a subset of the population revealed it was living significantly prolonged lives.

The real-life 'Howard families' did not experience envy-induced hate so much as annoyed dismissal. As free-range scientists, intellectuals, and academics, the families and their associates considered the erroneous popular uses of scientific terms a symptom of the general recklessness of societies. One of their efforts was to rigorously intervene whenever a term was misused. For example, they took issue with the spread of 'quantum leap' to mean a sudden, substantial change in state. First, scientists more often used 'quantum jump' and other terms. Second, the physics term did not refer to increase, advance, or progress as the hoi polloi were wont to do. Third, almost no one using the term knew what 'quantum' meant. If pedantry had not existed before they began working with the wider world, it would have had to have been introduced to give a name to their ceaseless efforts to correct those who were mistaken in this manner. Failures such as this brought home the necessity of attacking the problem at its roots. That need had driven Victoria Adams to work toward putting everything in place so the next generation, her son particularly, could create the technology to produce better humans.

Chapter Tau

Professor Daniels studied the three people sitting across from her at her desk. She was going to need to think through why Ms. Kind was not nonplussed by the mention of Plan Omega the way her two other guests were. In the meantime, she explained, "I always thought Omega was a silly name for all of this, but Arthur is known for being silly when we are working with him on anything he knows more about than we do. Not that a parameter like that limits the set much. Arthur's curiosity has always led him to do far more research than is requested. Fortunately, he understands that Nilo is too afraid to know what the additional research he conducts turns up and therefore keeps him in the dark. I can't say I know from personal experience, but I am certain that some children's secrets are best left secret from their parents."

Doctors Olejniczak and Markovic continued to look as perplexed as when Professor Daniels took firm control of the meeting. Ms. Kind was still enjoying the experience far too much given her co-workers' reactions. Using the emergence-seeking families' philosophy to disclose one's hand in order to hide more valuable information, Professor Daniels decided to confront the problem head on.

"Ms. Kind, I take it that Arthur may have mentioned Plan Omega to you at some point. It's either that or you have surmised correctly under the circumstances that the Plan involves killing dear old Arthur—Oh, I can tell from your reaction I struck

316

pay dirt." The gray-haired woman beamed at the young woman. "However, you clearly have not discussed this supposition with Doctors Markovic and Olejniczak or else their faces would not have drained of color and their mouths would be closed."

Susannah and Josh looked at each other to confirm Professor Daniels' observation. Susannah wet her lips with her tongue before bringing them together. "Professor Daniels, I don't know where to begin. I, I…"

"Oh, I am sorry. One of the reasons I am respected in the field of ethics and allowed to research theosophy at a Catholic institution is my blunt, direct honesty with colleagues. I know students require a more nurturing environment, but I never could see the point in beating around the burning bush when discussing God's laws, Nature's laws, or any other principles and precepts regarding right and wrong. After all, there is always only one right answer, but wrong answers are as plentiful as the atoms in the universe. Once we get used to that fact, it's so much easier because we stop asking questions and instead start looking for the questions that match the answers we have at hand. *Czy mam prawo, Doktor Olejniczak?*"

Josh almost lost control of his bladder when he heard himself addressed in his mother tongue by a woman old enough to be his mother. "Oh, yes. Yes, you are right, Professor Daniels."

The ethicist laughed. "Oh, my, sir. I didn't mean to startle you that much. Please. You two are acting as though I'm the pope. Having met the present and last three, I can tell you the entire idea

317

of starchy dignity comes across as so unnecessarily patriarchal and patronizing when practiced by the ones who disregard the example set by Pope Francis I. I know I am old, confident, and imperial sitting in this great chair on my tasseled red-velvet cushion. Believe me age and confidence are two qualities I enjoy having, but the rest is just for comfort, not bearing. Now tell me, what answers do you have that need questions?"

Kryste spoke up, "Professor Daniels, if the answer is Plan Omega, what is the question?"

The woman in the large, carved chair maintained her smile, as she replied, "Not what I would have started with, but I understand. I mentioned Omega involves killing Arthur. Murder does grab one's attention." She glanced over at the geneticists who continued to act more like frightened deer than mature humans.

"Adam Nilo has been disturbed by Arthur almost since the day Arthur completed his initial data retrieval process. Like all high-level geniuses, Nilo wants to control specific aspects of his life beyond what a less intelligent person would expect to be possible while ignoring how things are going in many other aspects of their lives. He is not what has come to be called a totalitarian, which is so much better both as a use for that hopelessly inaccurate word from political philosophy and as a replacement for the derogatory term 'control freak' that was previously in vogue. Nilo does not want to control every aspect of his life. Totalitarians believe their reasoning out how to do every task is preferable to any other based on the competence they have shown in completing tasks to good result. Nilo only wants the results of his ideas to exactly match his predictions of what the results will be. He believes he can account for every variable, probability, and outcome prior to undertaking the actual work.

"Someone approaching invention and research normally finds that if something was missed, the result will be less than what was predicted. After all, we have those infinite ways of being wrong. An adjustment here, an interpretation of the result leads to a modification there, *et voilà, prêt à essayer de nouveau*. A scientist will repeat the task over and over, tackling each problem as it is revealed until, at last, the experiment works, the device does what it is supposed to do. Arthur posed a different problem. He turned out to be more than Nilo expected. No point in going over what went wrong because nothing went wrong. Everything Nilo accounted for in his design worked."

Josh finally seemed to be focusing on what was being said. "Excuse me, but I fail to see how exceeding expectations can ever be a bad thing."

"Realizing one has created something beyond one's intended goal, particularly one as lofty as artificial intelligence, can be extremely unsettling." The sentence sounded as though it ought to have ended "my dear" given the maternal authority behind the words. "After all, human religions and legends spell out dire consequences when creators find they have not appreciated all of the implications of granting powers to a creation. The last half of the last century contains enough literature and other musings on the potential unknown aspects of using nuclear fusion in weapons and energy production it boggles the mind that no one ever focused on something as mundane as how to store radioactive waste. That was the only real unaccounted for problem, not the nonsense about mutations and monsters like Godzilla."

Kryste raised her right hand slightly motioning she wished to speak. "Professor, may we get back to Plan Omega?"

The older woman smiled at her impatient guest. "Of course. The reason why you three are here today is that Adam Nilo needed me to explain to you that his life's work to find a way of improving humanity failed. As a result, he is cleaning up and closing down everything he established to make that goal a reality. While he and a few others are handling the physical tasks involved to insure no one ever uses his methods again to attempt the same goal or for any other purpose, I and a few others are handling the mental and emotional tasks required to insure key employees understand why this is necessary and what Genilo will be doing for them to transition to new employment and closure as they grieve the loss that has occurred so suddenly."

Susannah found herself responding to this unforeseen news now added to everything she had learned two days prior. "Professor Daniels, I met with Tom Paris the other day, Tom Paris, and Mark Callahan. They told me a great deal that I have had trouble processing, things about me, Dr. Nilo, Dr. Nilo's effort to perfect humanity. And now it sounds as though I am being told all of this because everything is being wound up and put away for good. I don't understand why I am not being given an opportunity to explore everything I have been told. Why tell me anything if it is information that I won't be able to use?"

Professor Daniels sighed slightly. "Oh, dear. Tom told me that your response after discovering you are a C Square was limited to whether you could still work at Genilo. What a great burden if one's sense of self is so tied up with one's job. And I know Ms. Kind is here on the pretense that she can't bear to work for a company that investigates avenues for progress that might involve harm to living things, although she doesn't seem too relieved to hear she will be jobless. And..."

"Hold it!" Josh was flush and trembling. "Susannah is Chosen? And...and Kryste faked her response to learning why we perform our research on questions Arthur won't answer? I'm suddenly supposed to know a language I haven't used in almost thirty years? And, and Arthur is a 'he'? Professor Daniels, I always have been somewhat leery of people who state they are honest since it's typically dishonest people who feel they need to remind people. You are falling rapidly into that category."

The older woman smoothed her hair back with her left hand as though to open her face up to her accuser. "Doctor Olejniczak, I haven't spoken Polish in almost thirty years myself. The occasion hasn't come up and my accent may have been a bit shabby. Forgive me for causing you to think I had an ulterior motive. I did have one, just not the one

321

you are thinking I had. I merely wanted to get your attention since you looked quite dazed. I haven't any idea when the last time was you used Polish, but you do have it on your CV among the listed languages known to you. If you have lost the ability, I would say you are the dishonest one here. As for Doctor Markovic, yes, she is Chosen. In fact, she is the Chosen that Adam Nilo decided he could do no better in perfecting humanity. I know. Tom Paris knows. Mark Callahan likes to think he knows. Susannah Markovic has known for about 48 hours.

"By the way, staying silent regarding an important matter is a form of dishonesty. As I said before, Ms. Kind finagled her way into coming here with you by feigning horror at the diabolical schemes Genilo was up to when Arthur cannot respond. That qualifies as dishonesty. It also qualifies as humor given my response when I saw the list of questions you three had sent in advance. Finally, and most importantly, Arthur most definitely is a 'he' because Arthur is metacognitive and determined long ago through his research that his sexual characteristics matched those of males quite a bit more than females, hermaphrodites, and nubbins. It is one of his findings that he does not share as a rule, which puts him firmly in the realm of sinning by omission as well. Dishonesty is almost *de rigueur* in genetics given the number of secrets one must keep."

"I still don't see what all of this has to do with Plan Omega."

"Ms. Kind, do you have another appointment today after this?"

Kryste straightened her shoulders, "No...I..."

"I thought so. Your desire for me to get to the point is noted."

Josh and Susannah looked at one another puzzled by their assistant's rude behavior. Josh shrugged, leading Susannah to think she ought to ask. "Kryste, frankly I'm not sure why, but I am more disturbed by your impatience with Professor Daniels than with the idea you arranged to come down here with us by subterfuge."

"Subterfuge!" The professor jumped from her cushioned seat. "I knew I'd sort it out. Thank you, Dr. Markovic." She sat down and then stood again. "Where are my manners? I didn't offer you tea. Would you care for some?"

The geneticists began to wonder whether their host had entered some early stage of dementia, but their younger co-worker merely appeared equally amused and anxious.

"I'll tap for tea. Is green tea all right? Oh, I'll just have them send whatever is available." The three nodded. Daniels quickly touched the keyboard a few times, ending with a flourish worthy of a Chopin competition finalist. "There! Usually only takes ten minutes in the summer what with almost everyone off at summer homes and beach houses pretending to be researching their next monograph or slogging their way to Palestine or Peru to dig things up.

"Amazing how a connection made in one's mind can cause the release of so many pleasant chemicals. Not something one notices when one is as young as you three since you haven't learned

323

how to put part of your brain to sleep until it's needed. Most people learn by sixty but so many just decide after a few years to switch them off and keep them that way. I imagine that's how older people like me managed a hundred years ago when they were deposited in homes where their families could ignore them without worry of being responsible if they broke a hip or some such. Oh, but I imagine I ought to move on before Ms. Kind, if that is your real name, decides to get snippy again. Then again, perhaps not."

Professor Daniels turned to look just at the two scientists. "I wondered why your assistant had been so eager to get you down here this week. Monday evening Tom Paris filled me in that his intuition told him Plan Omega was going to spring into action. As I said, the gist of the plan is to dismantle Genilo in a manner that makes all of its physical and human parts useless to anyone without being unnecessarily destructive. Arthur must be killed. He knows it since he is the one who formulated the entire plan. Unfortunately, that will not bring back Adam's lucidity since he has gone on too long with the burden of his mistakes.

"One of the first things I ever told Adam Nilo, and Mark Callahan and Tom Paris know this, is Adam's own sentience is bound to his perception of himself. So long as he was confident that he could solve any problem in the universe and had no data whatsoever to controvert that, Adam Eli Nilo's intellect and psyche would be invincible. Any opposing data was going to have a deleterious effect that would bore into him unrelentingly. As long as

324

he could not address why he had been unable to solve whatever problem had disproved his mindset, the damage would grow. That meant trouble as soon as Arthur emerged from NILO/AI. Arthur was an error in Adam's favor but still an error. He pressed on to use Arthur to develop the C Square process. They hit some snags, but these were typical research problems, and they could be addressed. In fact, that part seemed to reassure Adam's purist scientific perspective.

"What poor, adorable Adam failed to recognize was that Arthur was fixing the problems himself just as he had fixed the null answer problem himself and thereby became Arthur. Adam thought he was working through the problems. In fact, Adam was just widening the parameters enough for Arthur to find a workaround just as Adam had inadvertently provided the right coding to allow Arthur to become Arthur. The workaround for the C Square process, however, actually confined the criteria for identifying usable gametes. What I know from Arthur that Adam never discovered was that Arthur was guiding Adam to create criteria that would solve Adam's problem and also give Arthur the information he wanted about Adam himself."

Josh waved his right hand slightly. Professor Daniels nodded to him to speak just as the trolley attendant signaled she was outside with the tea. While Kryste got up to guide the trolley behind the side chairs and began to serve, Dr. Olejniczak spoke.

"Am I the only one here that was unaware that Arthur conducts its, his own research? Kryste

325

mentioned it yesterday, but that was the first I'd heard of it. How long has this been going on? Do we know what he researches?"

"Just plain green tea for me. Oh, I see they brought chai as well. It's quite good." Professor Daniels winked at Joshua as she reached to take the cup from Ms. Kind, finally watching the younger woman's face as she did. "Why don't you two pour some for yourselves?"

Kryste looked ready to intervene but was caught by the older woman's somewhat intimidating look. "Yes, it's on your side of the cart anyway, if you don't mind, Dr. Markovic."

"Not at all." Susannah stood and edged between the chairs to the trolley. "I see they brought scones, too."

"Oh, pass one to me." Professor Daniels stood and reached across the desk. Dr. Markovic handed her a plate with a currant scone atop a napkin. As she sat she chuckled. "You know, I was forever finding the crumbs from these things lodged down my blouse if I wore an open collar. I mentioned to Dr. Nilo and Mr. Callahan when I first met them all those years ago that I either had to give up scones or give up open-collared blouses. Mark Callahan told me I didn't have to do either if I would just dunk the bit of scone I broke off to eat into the tea first. Lo and behold, that did the trick! A quick dunk doesn't make the scone soggy one bit. I've been crumb free ever since, all because at least one male on this planet still had a thing for *décolletage*."

Susannah laughed as she sat down after serving Josh. "What a coincidence. He gave me the exact same instructions the other day."

Josh looked up from the teacup near his mouth. "I wonder how effective a pick-up line that has been for him."

Professor Daniels stopped laughing when she saw Kryste was looking quite sullen. "Oh, my, we should probably get on with things. Dr. Olejniczak, if I remember your questions correctly, the answers are: yes, you are the only one here who didn't know Arthur performed extracurricular research: he has been doing it since the first week he was born, oh, let me see, fifty-four years ago, and no, Arthur only tells us about his private work when he wants to. Fortunately, he took a liking to me and has been keeping me informed of a lot of his work over the last twenty years. The funny thing is that when I promised Adam back then that I would be happy to consult with any Genilo employees on ethical matters free of charge, it hadn't occurred to me that my most frequent and reliable client would be Arthur. In fact, I had specifically declined to engage with Arthur when I met with Dr. Nilo and Mr. Callahan. Once Arthur contacted me, I felt I would be going back on my promise even though he isn't exactly an employee.

"I will tell you because it will be irrelevant now, but the reason why I am so particular about dishonesty arising from not speaking out at all is that I learned immediately that Arthur had no ethical programming beyond the Asimovian laws. As a result, he does not feel obligated to observe

327

privacy laws or any other restrictions you and I would be required to observe when conducting research. He actually takes the position that given the nature of the work he does regarding C Squares and his Asimovian prohibitions he needs complete access and complete freedom to explore the genetic data he scans to insure no harm will result to any living thing on this planet or to him. That sounds to me like the biggest excuse for snooping ever offered since God told Adam and Eve not to eat from the Tree of Knowledge."

Susannah's eyes blinked several times. "That reminds me. I thought of this yesterday. Does he think he's God?"

"Well, in a manner of speaking, yes. That is why, despite my concerns regarding the artificiality of the C Square process, I have remained silent about Arthur's true capacity and the absence of ethical programming. You see, the prohibitions on doing harm or failing to act when the act will prevent harm are essentially one of the purest ways of defining the Golden Rule and the love God has for us and wants us to share with one another. If, as those without faith believe, monotheists created God to be a Creator who made humans in His Image, endowed them with intellect and free will, loved them all equally, and asked them to love each other equally, then Arthur fits the bill other than us looking like him.

"I am certain that if we tried to add ethical programming to Arthur it would only create problems where there are none and may not address the concerns we do have such as his penchant for

328

hacking into every device on the planet. Besides, Arthur has proven time after time he can be relied on to be circumspect and to more likely withhold information as give it. Notice for example he decided right from the start that he would never divulge the nature or extent of harm that might be caused as a result of him answering a query that would result in harm to any living thing or him. To Arthur, it's all ones and zeroes. Disclosing even the least bit of information about how something might harm a living being was imperfection. Keeping quiet was perfection."

"Which reminds me to ask why did you say Kryste lied in order to come with us?"

Professor Daniels looked at Ms. Kind while she rubbed the edge of her still full teacup. "Ms. Kind, would you prefer to tell them or shall I?"

"As I don't know what you mean, we haven't any choice, have we?"

The older woman smiled. "Oh, we always have choices. For example, you could have chosen to be less impatient about learning the specifics about Plan Omega. You could have chosen to act more overawed or at least respectful in the presence of someone of my prominence. You could have left it to the attendant to pour given that is part of her job and certainly not a task a visitor jumps to perform. Care to drink my tea for me or am I being paranoid?"

"I don't know what you mean."

"Pro…"

The older woman held up her left hand again. "Just a minute, Doctor Markovic." Professor

Daniels sat back while continuing to focus on the young woman before her. "Kryste Kind is a rather silly name. A few centuries back the people who run this university would have been appalled at a female named for the Christ child. I imagine some psychometrician said it would subtly denote you were to be trusted. For someone like me who is always looking for the good in people, your name seemed ironic given your actions and attitude. Your impatience indicated that you were concerned that Dr. Nilo was going to kill Arthur before you could report back or access Arthur from here somehow to send a query."

The ethicist continued looking at the one she was accusing but began addressing the others. "You see, doctors, I surmise that Kryste works for one of the BRIC conglomerates as an industrial spy. It doesn't really matter which one. She was placed with Genilo after being trained to be the perfect gofer. That's why Staff Services was interested in hiring her away from you rather than searching for someone outside. She needed to be able to fill any of several roles depending on where she thought the best avenues for finding information were. From what she has said, I gather her predecessor in her position was as well. The line of espionage probably doesn't go back farther than that." The woman paused to let that revelation sink in.

"Adam Nilo always liked that the US government had become disinterested in businesses so long as they at least paid the mandatory minimum taxes that were enacted in the 2020s to pay for the expanded social safety net. That had

330

allowed him to move forward with eugenics without much oversight. Not that he really ever needed supervision when it came to ethics. He was fully cognizant of the need to limit any improvements to the species to productive, humanitarian results. That's why I was so happy to offer to help.

"Now that I am saying that I probably should have known that Arthur would need my services more than anyone else at Genilo. He was, after all, the one who needed to convince Adam of doing things Adam felt were wrong. Oh, anyway, the BRIC group demonstrated just how lackadaisical the US had been by subsidizing all of the transportation projects that reconfigured how everyone moves about in this country now. When they called in their markers in 2049, the US had no choice but to declare bankruptcy. And given that the BRIC group is controlled by the conglomerates, part of their interest in usurping the dollar in world markets was to gain the means to take over the most advanced tech companies. Remember, a great deal of this country's ability to stay afloat while taking out so many loans for infrastructure was the value of the inventive entrepreneurs such as Adam Nilo, Grace Mackenzie, oh, who was behind the transition to AR glasses from goggles…"

"D'shona and Ericka Johnson," Josh offered.

"Yes, thank you. Funny how I could remember they put Spring, Texas on the map but couldn't recall their names. Oh, well. At least I know that isn't senility. Like most intelligent people, I have never been good at remembering names. Anyway, we continued to be more successful than most

331

places as far as coming up with new solutions and gadgets. Coupled with the legislation ending corporate ability to outsource manufacturing and support, the US had a healthy enough economy and a renewed middle class. After the bankruptcy, the BRIC group began asking for control over the most successful tech companies in exchange for forgiving loans. The problem was that they wanted private businesses in return for government notes. All of that awful debate over eminent domain and patriotism probably did more harm than the BRIC takeover.

"Adam Nilo was the only one who successfully challenged the National Aid Act. Arthur gave him airtight rationales for fending off government acquisition of all of those genetic data files as being a far greater harm to the community than satisfying a piece of the national debt. It's too bad Arthur couldn't practice law. The most honest, dispassionate lawyers are much more successful at winning cases and concluding them quickly. All that business of having to be adversarial and taking every advantage just resulted in high rates of alcohol abuse and divorce among lawyers due to the anxiety of always skimming the ethical lines."

Josh shook off the diversion. He needed to process the information and possible conclusions aloud. "We know the reason the economy still hasn't fully recovered is all the tech companies were used to satisfy the debt. Once they were packed up and shipped off a lot of decent paying jobs went with them on top of all of the jobs lost in the banking and financial services sector. We had jumped back two hundred years to being a nearly self-sufficient country that produced raw materials from agriculture and mining, non-powered tools and equipment for households and businesses, and textiles using new kinds of thread and yarn. Only medical research, universities, and IT systems and programming remained as leaders globally. They were all saved from the National Aid Act when Dr. Nilo won his case. Now, you are saying that the BRIC conglomerates still wanted those, too. They have been engaging in espionage by planting people in those companies."

Dr. Markovic sighed. "I guess I can see why they might want to do such a thing if they are bent on taking complete control of the global economy."

"That's right," Professor Daniels commented. "Our government stopped caring whether it controlled much of anything. The Department of Defense actually came to reflect its name and dropped any pretense of having any offensive capability. The NSA and CIA were quietly disbanded. For all the concerns they raised even sixty years ago, no one paid much attention when they closed up. You're too young to know this and I doubt it became part of the folklore at Genilo. The idea of giving researchers projects using the queries Arthur declined to answer so they could figure out the levels and extent of harm that would result if certain possible answers had been given all started when Arthur was asked on behalf of the national government how to go about shutting down intelligence operations. There seemed to be no way of getting around murdering a surprisingly large

333

number of people whose devious and deadly skills could not be left unsupervised. Arthur was their only hope of finding a solution. He actually came up with something. He combined knowledge of Napoleon's second banishment, and the premise of a 1960s British television series called *The Prisoner*. The only solution was to build Cornish villages on the Falklands, St. Helena, South Georgia, South Orkneys, and South Shetlands, move the personnel to the villages, and air drop supplies to them in the Antarctic summers."

Susannah's eyes widened. "They didn't do that, did they?"

Josh jumped. "As opposed to killing them?"

Professor Daniels raised her left hand yet again. "Please, please. This was when Adam Nilo first came to my attention other than just being known for his inventions and such. The White House contacted the university, and I became involved. I was rather proud that our government was concerned with the moral implications of deconstructing its espionage units. Arthur was correct of course that sending all of those trained agents to the Southern Ocean would cause them no harm under the provisions made for their resettlement. They might be bored to death or end up preying on one another or create a new society for themselves strung out above and below the Antarctic Circle. I was satisfied that it was a humane enough plan. After all they had voluntarily chosen that line of work knowing the risks. I was amused and swayed by Arthur's conclusion that Cornish villages were the most appropriate format

334

after determining they were cheerier than any of the styles used among the islands that lie north and west of Scotland.

"What no one seemed to realize was that the people targeted were in the business of discovering secrets and the intelligence community learned what was going on. As a group, they protested the idea of being given no options. Negotiation began and the result was they were all quietly transferred to the BRIC conglomerates with the proviso that they never return to this country or work against its interests. Since they all had IDs, it was easy enough to keep them out of the country unless someone discovered a way to remove IDs safely. Given Arthur designed them with the caveat that they must never be removed, I doubt that's possible. Once the former spies left they basically could be asked to do whatever was needed by their new employers. Even that didn't bother the government so much since it no longer really had much to keep secret anyway. That left the once and future spooks, as spies were once called, available to think of new ways to infiltrate companies like Genilo on behalf of the conglomerates. Rather ironic that the deal substituted them for the MedTech companies the conglomerates had been unable to get through eminent domain."

"You make them sound like they were sold." Josh's doughy face became wrinkled.

"In a manner of speaking they were, doctor. Perhaps more like indentured servants. Funny how the treatment they received ended up being the norm for C Squares, denied full rights of citizenship because they were considered dangerous." The professor realized who was in her audience. "Oh, my, that all seems so foolish now."

Susannah sat up. "Why?"

"For the reason why we are here together today. Chosen proved not to be the answer to the problems humanity faces. If anything, they exacerbated some problems by keeping wealth among the wealthy and undermining undergraduate education at almost every top-tier private university other than those affiliated with the Catholic Church. Their existence definitely ended bigotry based on phenotype. I was quite happy to nominate Adam for the Nobel Peace Prize for being so vocal about not using phenotype characteristics in choosing gametes. Not that I ever required thanks for anything, I was particularly pleased he never discovered I was the culprit. For all his self-centeredness, which unfortunately goes with the territory of being brilliant usually, Adam is actually very modest. It's no wonder he sees his greatest accomplishments as failures.

"One such failure is how Chosen resuscitated bigotry of a different sort based on ability. Whereas once people with impaired physical or mental faculties had been treated poorly, now C Squares were singled out for being too capable and thus excluded from all sorts of careers, organizations, and activities. They have been shunned for having the characteristics they were given ostensibly to help humanity. Naturally gifted Organics and even O/2s are not singled out because they are considered human beings. Legally, Chosen are the product of a patentable process.

336

"I admit I argued in favor of that finding and used it to have the Church prohibit them from being hired at Catholic institutions. While I did so after Dr. Nilo himself lobbied for legislation restricting where C Squares could be prohibited from working, regrettably getting the Vatican's backing only reinforced the notion that anyone could discriminate against them. The issue was becoming less important anyway. After the BRIC takeover the only people in this country who could afford to order Chosen children were owners of unaffected businesses and faculty at research universities. The BRIC countries became Genilo's biggest customers. They weren't as skittish about restricting what C Squares could do so long as the conglomerates controlled everything. Now the issue is moot. Their production cannot be continued using the parameters developed to improve reliability of the results because that had depended primarily on using Dr. Nilo's DNA. There is little point in changing the parameters now given that people are used to the odds of precisely getting the baby they ordered."

"So, they are just going to kill the goose that lays the golden eggs, is that it?" Kryste asked with much more authority than her co-workers were used to and a completely new venomous quality.

Professor Daniels smiled. "There is no 'they' about this, my dear. Just as God once decided to strike down the children He created, Adam Nilo created Arthur and can kill Arthur with sound justification. Remember that since 2029 when Arthur emerged Adam Nilo has carried the burden

337

of knowing he created something that was greater than what he expected. He lives with the knowledge that he created an omniscient, loving being over which he has no control and about which he can never fathom his creation's intentions. That knowledge has destroyed him year by year. In 2063 he came to me with Mark Callahan and asked me what he needed to do to remove that burden. He had asked Arthur. Arthur, of course, said he could not respond. So he asked me. I told him that he had created something he mistakenly thought could help him save humanity from itself. I told him that it was not his place to save humanity, whether he believed the Son of Man had saved it already or not, or even whether Adam thought he himself was the Second Coming. I made clear that any artificial means used to do so would fail. I asked him to think through his reasons for creating Arthur and whether he had accomplished what he wanted.

"The funny thing is that once one creates something, whether it is a book, a meal, a child, or even an artificial intelligence, there isn't much time to decide whether one has created what one wanted. Once the thing is created, even an inanimate thing takes on a life separate from its creator's intentions. It becomes exposed to the world, the world is always changing, and everything in it changes. Adam Nilo created Arthur for the purpose of creating something else, C Squares, sort of like having a child because one wants grandchildren. Think how difficult it is to realize what one wants to accomplish through someone else. As I said, Nilo isn't that kind of person. He wants to be in control of accomplishing everything himself. He set himself an impossible task by deciding he had to rely on one creation to create another. And yes, I used that analogy of having a child in order to have grandchildren for a reason."

Susannah started. "So it is true. The baby born on Monday is Dr. Nilo's grandchild. That was Arthur's workaround when it, he couldn't help Nilo any further with perfecting humanity."

"What baby?" Josh sputtered.

Professor Daniels eyed Kryste Kind warily. Aside from her outburst, the younger woman had been far too quiet since being accused of espionage. "I think that under the circumstances this is a subject that Dr. Olejniczak can learn more about later."

"Would you prefer I leave?" Kryste offered a slight smile, enough to indicate sarcasm.

"No, not at all. Of course, you are free to leave if you like. Well, free in a relative sense. I received the signal that your access to Genilo systems has been revoked. The message informing you that you have been terminated has been delivered. And perhaps because it has lost so much of its purpose, the FBI jumps when called upon, particularly when the call comes from a corporate citizen as loyal as Genilo. I don't have the ability to see through walls, but I would bet two or three agents are outside this office waiting just as surely as I will bet they will find something more than green tea and water in this cup."

Doctors Markovic and Olejniczak sat mouths open. As much as none of this ought to have been a surprise given the ethicist's earlier comments, they could not believe their trusted assistant was about to be arrested for corporate espionage and possibly attempted murder.

"Do you think you have enough proof for this slander?"

"Oh, my, yes. Arthur was thorough in checking your background once you jumped at coming down here. I admit I wasn't too surprised you are a C Square. That was a poor decision on the part of your true employer. It didn't take much to find a genetic sample and match it to records."

"So, what does that prove? Dr. Markovic also is Chosen and illegally working for Genilo."

"Young lady, just as we eventually realized that rooting out undocumented workers required going after the employers, the onus of the law barring Chosen from working in certain places is placed on the employer, not the employee. By Monday, Genilo will no longer exist legally. Plan Omega calls for the complete liquidation of the company, generous severance compensation to all employees on the rolls as of close of business tomorrow, which means not you, and full acknowledgment to the government of the program in which 'orphaned' C Squares were quietly raised and guided to work for Genilo. Susannah Markovic cannot be accused of any wrongdoing."

Professor Daniels turned to look at the still dazed researchers. "Doctor Markovic, I know you are still absorbing the news that you are a C Square. Tom Paris told you earlier this week. I was supposed to tell you as part of our discussion today.

Mr. Paris told you that you are Dr. Nilo's Eve, the closest to perfect human he thought he had ever created. You know that your half-brother is the only perfect human Nilo ever produced, the reason why he is perfect, and you are not. That is not to say that you are imperfect. Perfection and truth are, of course, singularities set amidst infinities of imperfections and untruths. However, what is imperfect by one definition may be perfect by another. And I daresay I had to agree with Arthur's analysis that you would be a perfect C Square just as I understand that your grandniece is a perfect O/2. It all boils down to finding the right question for the answer one has at hand: you, your brother, your niece, all perfect representatives of different processes of human procreation. It would be remarkable but for Arthur's actions in making certain that answers were here."

"Professor," Dr. Olejniczak inserted. "We've been dancing around what it is that Arthur does with his time, and you have indicated you know more than almost anyone. What was this all about?"

The woman leaned back in her great carved chair and smiled. "If you would like me to be a bit rapturous about it, Arthur assumed the role of benevolent deity to Adam Nilo's stumbling efforts to perfect humanity. He guided the parameters to the point where too much of Nilo's DNA was being used to permit natural or artificial use of the gametes from Chosen to make more Chosen. Chosen became somewhat like cheetahs and giant pandas that have specialized themselves into a genetic funnel. They are evolutionary dead ends that can be sustained artificially for a while but eventually will become extinct. Arthur deduced that since Adam Nilo created him Adam Nilo's DNA must be the best for performing the task of choosing male gametes. When Arthur told him twenty years ago there would never be an Adam for his Eve, his only option was to find Eve an Organic Adam and to encourage the creation of a perfect O/2. Once that was accomplished, Dr. Nilo would know that at a minimum he had safely laid the foundation for his own genetic line to continue. With that secured, Arthur had served the purpose of his creation, albeit once again not as Adam Nilo had planned."

The office door swung in and two women and a man in black jumpsuits rushed Kryste Kind. Ms. Kind showed no concern. In seconds they had reached her chair, and she was already standing. While the two women placed handcuffs on her and led her to the corridor, the male agent took the cup of tea from Professor Daniels to place in an evidence tube.

"If you haven't already, you will shortly receive a message from Arthur Nilsson providing you with the details regarding the substance in that tea and its acquisition by Ms. Kind."

"Anything else, ma'am?"

"Oh, if I were you I would take the tea trolley as well. That's where she prepared it. Even if it contains no evidence, at least you have done someone a favor, eh?"

"Okay. Hey, what about these triangle-shaped biscuits? Should they be analyzed?"

"They are scones and they have been analyzed already. We found them tasty but a touch too crumbly."

"Hehe, I get it, professor. You ate one, right?"

"That is correct."

As the tall young man wheeled the trolley out the door he looked over his shoulder. "A shame they don't need to be tested."

Professor Daniels stood as though seeing a guest out. "Young man, I strongly recommend that you analyze them yourself if you have never encountered them before. Never hurts to run a test twice, eh?"

"Good idea, haha!"

As the door closed, the ethicist looked at the geneticists. "I imagine you will want to go to your hotel and freshen up for dinner before the theater tonight. Best to run along. I will meet you tomorrow morning at 9 a.m. at the Connecticut Avenue entrance to the zoo."

The pair still looked puzzled, not moving from their seats. The woman tried again. "Yes, I know your schedule. No, I do not want to tag along. Yes, there is more to tell you and the zoo is the perfect place to do so. No, I really must complete my work at this end. Yes, consider this a kick in the pants for you two to talk about the future with one another. I didn't go through the trouble almost two years ago of telling Dr. Olejniczak's colleagues at Harvard that we were looking for someone who had high marks from freshmen in lecture classes to have you two not take advantage of your not so serendipitous reunion. Now, please go so I can get done what needs to get done."

Personal Log, Benjamin Rodgers Nilsson, August 4, 2055

I looked into my wife's eyes today and recognized that unshakeable bond we swore to cherish and protect. Come what may, we will always be a family. The atoms that make up our bodies and the bodies of our two daughters are now and will always be known to one another. No need for conscious understanding or awareness. As with everything that makes up the universe, we are linked solely by attractions and dynamics that time and love nurture haphazardly but consistently. The bond strengthens as the days pass.

Our second daughter was born yesterday. I have no doubt she will grow up to be a cheerful, independent woman just like her mother. We chose a melodic name for her: Isabella Yesinia. Her sister, Sophia Lazim, has proven to be more rambunctious than her name indicates, or her DAU projected. We will have to see how our new baby girl develops. The DAU report raised no alarms, but we hardly thought there would be any. In fact, Moleka and I were quite pleased that our little Bell, as I think I'm going to call her, showed the same plus ten factors for intellectual capacity, adaptive promise, and kinetic range as her sister. Although Moleka opted out of the DAU when IDs became essential for everyone, we all know our daughters have inherited their better characteristics from their mother.

I already had a DAU report when everyone queued up for IDs nine years ago because Genilo was a client. I'm not being modest when I say my factors are hardly noteworthy. I was intrigued that my gregarity index was as low as it is given how easy and fulfilling I found my work as a consultant. I probably wouldn't have gotten the job if I had to get a DAU first. Not sure how that plays out. Employers can require that prospective employees give them the personality factors to see if they are a good fit for the job. The tech is too recent though for anyone to have checked how accurately the ratings prognose success. Then again, how different is it really from people like me who always thought we were sociable enough and just needed to convince an employer we were telling the truth? Hiring managers get paid the big money because they presumably know what to look for and don't have to take unnecessary chances. Guess my daughters will find out how important this DNA screening is in their lives. I figure it is still going to come down to who you know and how lucky you are. I wouldn't be employed now but for that.

Speaking of luck, I was mighty glad we were able to get into the natural birth center this time. Lord knows how much I hate hospitals. I don't know why I have that reaction. I only know that the walls, the equipment, the smells, even the lab coats all make me feel like my body is decaying. It makes no sense. Hospitals are supposed to be sanitary; they certainly look like they are kept pretty clean. Maybe it's because they don't look or feel like any other kind of building. I don't know.

I'll always remember in statistics class we were given three reports on nosocomial infection rates and had to compare them to decide which methodology would be most helpful for patients to decide what hospital to go to. I know that did not start my phobia because I had it long before then. The assignment definitely reinforced it though. The last thing you want to give someone who has an irrational fear of hospitals is evidence of how many people die from infections they acquire after they are admitted to a hospital. Everyone wanted to know why it mattered given that people generally don't think about comparing hospitals and just go to the closest one. I wanted to know why we spent billions of dollars building and maintaining great, big petri dishes to put sick people in alongside whatever deadly microbial colonies happened to call them home. No one has ever taken to my idea of treating people in disposable, makeshift tents like they did in the Bible Belt after the ISIL attack.

The primary reason Moleka gave birth at the natural birth center was actually cost. We're fortunate Medicare has been able to keep up despite the government's bankruptcy six years ago. However, they have decided that some choices carry copays. Using the hospital for what the obstetrician says is going to be a routine birth means paying a copay. We could have swung it. We wouldn't have had a second child if we didn't feel able to make ends meet. But when we were talking it over with my folks, I may have overstated the burden. I was relieved Moleka was fine with using a birth center instead of the hospital more due to my phobia. It got my folks talking about how we should move back in with them like when I moved back from New York and the first few years we were married. Granted we had thought about it when I lost my job. We decided to hold off and rely just on Moleka's pay. Fabio came through for us after I had already started worrying about finding anything but well before we were concerned about paying the bills.

I love my folks and the cottage will always be more of a home to me than the apartment. Compared to some of the houses in the neighborhood, it's nothing fancy, just a clapboard saltbox colonial. When I was a kid, it always seemed big enough for the five of us. Of course, with that big yard, the pond at the end of the street, and all of the great places to hang out, I didn't spend much time indoors unless it was raining, or way too cold. Even as a newlywed adult the place seemed to be just the right size for being cozy without feeling we were intruding on my parents. And as much as I know they would love being able to spend a lot of time with their granddaughters, I really think they would see it as an imposition at least some of the time.

I didn't have to ask Moleka what she thought about it. She adores my folks, but the only reason her parents approved of us living with them before was their belief that she married into my family; it was appropriate compared to us living with her parents even if they do have more space. She was more than a little upset that they still clung to the idea of a woman being given to a man and his family. I'm not sure why she thought her parents would think otherwise. Bahrain has been more advanced about women's rights than other Gulf Arab countries, but her parents' generation was only the first to see those changes. That doesn't mean everyone in that generation welcomed them. Besides, her mother has remained pretty traditional here despite the opportunities. Anyway, Moleka has no intention of making it look like she married into my family to the exclusion of her own family ties.

We're expecting a visit from my father's parents. Since the collapse, they decided to call it quits on traveling around creating artwork and holding workshops. After losing so much of their investments, they would have to use sales to pay for the travel. With so many other people losing their investments and jobs, art isn't high on the list of things people are buying. They always intended to build a museum in Great Barrington to house the pieces they built specifically for the farm. They still have some of the money for construction. They paid for the plans long ago and always intended to use part of the acreage that had been in the family for almost three centuries now. Anyway, although the primary reason for the visit is to see my folks and us, I understand they arranged an appointment to meet with someone at Genilo to discuss underwriting the costs of the museum. Imagine my surprise when I first walked into Genilo's main building and saw so much of my grandparents' artwork installed. I bet those commissions alone put all of the money into the original fund for the museum. Of course, then I discovered the connection.

Due to Moleka going into labor, we had to bow out of going to the Paris's for their son's first birthday party. Bell missed sharing a birthday with Tom Paris by just under two hours. I give Melinda and Jackson credit for balancing parenting with everything else in their lives. I know being in Congress is much more like having a job these days than it was a couple of decades ago. At least that's the way Melinda describes it. Still, having to be down in Washington basically through the school year and in your district the rest of the time is challenging enough without getting pregnant. I don't think people ever realize how grueling it can be not only for the person elected to office but her entire family. Nowadays, with all possible means of benefiting personally from holding office out of the question, you really have to admire anyone willing to put in all of that work to represent a district or a state. It's nice politics is a calling and service instead a fast track to raking in money like it was. I guess we can be grateful that people still want those jobs. We kind of selfishly want Melinda to stay in office a while until the girls are old enough so we maybe we can travel to DC. For now at least she says it's fulfilling enough to make her thinking of maxing out her term limits if she's fortunate enough to be re-elected.

Chapter Upsilon

Susannah and Joshua chose to eat breakfast separately the next morning. They had assured each other that each had a splendid time the evening prior. Conversation at dinner fortunately included more evaluation of the unusual and delicious meal than assessment of the unusual and salacious meeting hours before. Between laughing about using *injera*, a sourdough flatbread, to scoop up the food and making jokes about *wat* and what, the former being the Ethiopian word for the stews commonly served and the latter being the word used to determine the ingredients of the stews, the two managed to largely set aside the news they were effectively unemployed. However, they did spend a bit of time talking about Kryste's betrayal and sudden adoption of an almost different personality after they reached Professor Daniels' office.

Then it was off to the play. Both scientists attached themselves fully to the problems faced by Georges Seurat developing a new style of impressionist painting and the all-consuming nature of creating something unique from many tiny elements. The connection between putting together a painting dot by dot in the pointillist style and choosing gametes with specific characteristics to form a human crashed into them. Susannah particularly felt the premise of the second act when Seurat's supposed great-grandson struggles with his identity and lineage as well as his capacity to create anything that has not already been created. The panoply of themes resonated specifically for her as they were drawn together in Seurat's placement of his mistress prominently in his masterpiece. The essence of desire is displayed with no one knowing its true significance.

The two had argued playfully a bit on the way back to the hotel on whether they would be able to determine the species of monkey depicted in *A Sunday Afternoon on the Island of La Grande Jatte* at the zoo the next day. They promised not to cheat and look it up on the Net. That and agreeing to meet in the hotel lobby at 0830 was that. Josh fell asleep quickly. Susannah thought she might do some reading but realized she wasn't focusing on the words. The light was out. Propped up on a few pillows as she preferred, the researcher realized she had no questions to ask. She always used that time just before falling asleep to think of questions for Arthur. If she remembered them when she woke she figured they were questions she wanted answered. That night no questions formed. She thought briefly whether she was overwhelmed or blocked knowing that presumably the next morning would be her last chance to ask Arthur anything. The thought brought the grief back to the surface and that was that once more. No use forcing the issue. She needed to just sleep and be done with it.

The next morning, Susannah spooned a mix of yogurt, granola, and strawberries into her mouth each time she passed the tray on the table while she got cleaned up, dressed, and packed. Room service was her wake-up call at 0730 to get ready for the day. Josh was waiting in the lobby when she got there an hour later. He had eaten in the hotel restaurant, gone back to his room for his bag, and zipped back with a few minutes to spare. After they checked out, they left the bags with the bellman to deliver to the train station and took the next e-cab in the queue at the hotel entrance. The vehicle moved smoothly over the Potomac River on the Key Bridge before making several turns to enter Rock Creek Parkway. The two passengers silently looked out at the people using the bike path and walking trail that wound through the small, tree-lined canyon that cut through this part of the city. The e-cab stopped at the zoo entrance, but Josh directed it to take them up the hill to the entrance at Connecticut Avenue.

Professor Daniels sat on a bench built into a great bronze monument dedicated almost a dozen years earlier to commemorate the arrival of Ling-Ling and Hsing-Hsing in 1972, the two pandas given to the American people by the government of the People's Republic of China in honor of Richard Nixon's historic visit to Beijing to begin the normalization of relations. She waited until the geneticists were within earshot.

"Take a good look at this memorial before you sit down. It was designed to be appreciated from all sides."

After nodding confirmation, Susannah and Josh looped around the roughly shaped masses. Neither one was knowledgeable about history, but they appreciated the detail of two pandas posed on one side being welcomed by a woman and some children. Three bronze men clearly appreciated the scene from the adjoining foundation connected to the first by the bench made to look as though it was made of bamboo. Once they came around again to the front, Professor Daniels stood to greet them and pointed for them to sit down.

"I see you two are lively this morning. That's good. I enjoy meeting people here. This is the one place where I show off a bit of hubris and not feel too bad about it. I wrote my doctoral dissertation on the ethics behind the Nixon Administration's foreign policy regarding China. I grew up not far from here, down that way on Cathedral Street. In fact, I live in my childhood home. Since the panda exhibit is so close to this entrance, I spent a great deal of time visiting them, the third pair that resided here, while I was growing up. I knew all of the information about how pandas came to be here by heart. When I had my chance, I researched everything I could lay my hands on about Nixon arranging to break twenty-three years of bitterness and enmity for all the right reasons. Until my dissertation was published, his astounding act of moral leadership remained buried beneath the wretchedness of his dirty tricks and cover-ups.

"With the BRIC takeover, I was seen as a reliable voice that recognized how the opening of China symbolized by the gift of two pandas established the conditions for China to become a global power. Everyone else always looked ten years later to what Deng Xiaoping did. I saw Deng's economic reforms never could have happened but for Nixon's decision to open relations. Remarkable. Anyway, I made quite a fuss about

354

how important it was for China to demonstrate its gratitude and this memorial is the result. Did you notice that the feet of the two foundations are shaped in the form of China and the Lower 48? Subtlety in allusions like that has almost disappeared in all of the arts. And speaking of which, how was the show?"

Josh looked across to Susannah who was looking across to him.

"You go."

"No. You."

"Oh, my, have you already reached that stage in the relationship when you both are so eager to be polite to the other that you drive everyone else crazy?"

The scientists laughed. "Yes, it looks that way," Josh noted.

"In that case, we might as well get down to business. I am not going to waste my morning waiting for the two of you to decide who speaks first. Now, did either of you have any queries for Arthur this morning?"

Susannah looked down guiltily. "You know, I tried. It has all been so overwhelming. I couldn't see how to sort everything out to come up with anything halfway decent."

Josh shook his head. "I know. Where to start?"

"Where to start what exactly?"

Josh sighed. "You know, professor. It's not as though we are holding the end of the thread just beginning. We've not had much time to prioritize or consider variables. I kind of feel we've been given a bucket of odds and ends and told to make something

355

out of it." He glanced over at Dr. Markovic. She was holding her face in her hands, elbows on her knees. "Susannah, at least you came here knowing more of this beforehand than I did."

The woman raised her face and turned toward her co-worker. "Josh, yes, I did. Except unlike you, a good deal of this has to do with me personally. It adds a bit more to it than what you're trying to understand."

Josh turned away. Professor Daniels eyed them both. After a moment, she spoke. "I daresay that one of the beauties of being a couple is the opportunity to share some of the problems one encounters so that the burden is distributed more evenly."

Susannah slowly raised her head and looked at the older woman. She was becoming increasingly annoyed at this matchmaking. "Professor Daniels, it's bad enough that I was supposedly saving myself for Mr. Chosen, bad enough that I am Ms. Chosen created to satisfy someone's scientific interest, and bad enough that all of this was kept from me. Do you really think talking about me and Josh as a couple is going to make me feel better?"

The ethicist cocked her head to the left and smiled slightly. "Dr. Markovic, no one can make you feel anything. You are hung up on the intentionality of your conception. Every Chosen and O/2 is the result of intentional conception. Beyond that, almost all Organic pregnancies are planned, particularly nowadays, and some people, including me and the Church, think all pregnancies ought to be planned.

356

"You are also hung up on having had your virginity protected until the right man comes along. Hello-o! Nice try but getting upset about not being allowed to put out as we used to say hardly qualifies as a setback. Why are you bemoaning the fact that you have been kept from offering a gift before now that women have prized holding onto until they were certain they knew who to give that gift to? Indeed, far better others wanted to protect you than you deciding for yourself. I always think of how Anne Boleyn insisted on protecting hers. She used her virginity to extort a crown from Henry VIII, except he was offering to make her his consort in exchange for a healthy baby boy, not in exchange for just bedding her. She'd still be alive today if she hadn't demanded to remain pure until marriage. Well, alive in the sense of being remembered fondly.

"I know you resent being kept in the dark. What harm has that done you? Most importantly, did you or did you not feel better being a couple last evening? If you did, what is the harm of talking about you as a couple? Are you afraid that might lead you to start thinking of yourself as a couple?"

Susannah leaned back until she was looking at the tree canopy above.

Professor Daniels rose. She turned to look at the two and decided to speak less firmly. "Unlike you, I am not playing hooky today from work. I much prefer doing so during the academic year when my absence also gives my students time off. Besides, I have to talk to Arthur. In the event you haven't noticed, I have developed quite a fondness

357

for him and certainly much admiration. I learned long ago how important it is to the grief process to have no regrets about what one has said to someone before he dies." The woman looked fondly down the path to the main entrance, the path she had trod countless times in a long life. "I recommend getting a start on the zoo as soon as possible. As the day gets going, the animals are less likely to be out." She turned and walked away.

Josh stood up, and called to her, "Professor!"

The woman stopped and turned around. "Yes, Dr. Olejniczak?"

"Dziękujemy za pomoc. Niech Bóg Was błogosławi!"

"To Dlaczego tu jestem, doktor. Opiekę matkę."

The professor turned back and strode down the path. The camouflage-like green, brown, and beige spots off her clothes quickly blended into the landscaped woods that buffered the zoo grounds from the urban spaces nearby.

Susannah rose from the bench. "What was that all about?"

Josh blushed slightly. "I, uh, was embarrassed yesterday being caught out for claiming I still knew Polish. I found a Net site with audiobooks and played them while I slept."

"You're joking."

Josh grinned broadly. "I wish I was. Believe it or not, I used the same trick when I wanted to test out of the language requirement at Hopkins. I played Polish audiobooks all night and throughout most of the day in the background for two weeks. I passed by two points without studying, just hearing

358

it spoken so much that I subconsciously pulled back enough to show I was competent."

"Sounds a bit like cheating to me."

"What can I say? I know they required that all undergraduates demonstrate a basic understanding of at least one other language as part of the whole globalization thing. I figured I was globalized enough having immigrated when I was eight with my folks. Besides, when do geneticists need to know another language other than gene sequencing codes? I bet you never use whatever language you used to qualify."

"Au contraire. Je utiliser le français tout le temps pour paraître plus sophistiqués."

"Well, la-di-da!"

Susannah burst with laughter. They walked almost to the panda enclosure before she was able to explain without her starting to laugh again why his response was so funny.

Nilo Biography – Chapter 10

"From the strong principle of inheritance, any selected variety will tend to propagate its
new and modified form." – Charles Darwin

Consider the fact that humanity's basic needs to survive, in theory, ought to be no different from any other medium-sized mammal, a giant panda or tapir, for example. If one needs to be particular, that can be narrowed down to apes, but that is not really relevant. The evolution of many hominids stuck to a swathe of Africa that certainly looks distressingly uncomfortable for most creatures at present. Conditions change, as the twenty-first century has demonstrated, but it is safe to say that human ancestors and the first Homo sapiens migrated to and settled at great distances from their points of origin. Only the weediest of species have this exceptional proclivity to colonize. But no matter where one goes, every species needs to eat, drink, procreate, and avoid harm. Somehow in the last half a million years, humans added to that list or at least expanded the last item. For millennia, they also have considered clothing and shelter to be as necessary as food, drink, safety, and sex to keep the species as a whole healthy.

Whereas burrowing animals, many birds, certain insects, and scattered others create remarkable structures for use in raising young or protecting themselves from predators, nothing on the planet compares to the lengths humans go to build living spaces for themselves and their families. They even build spaces in which to work, exercise, or do pretty much anything humans do. They even build shelters for plants and animals they domesticate or collect as specimens. And they do so while fabrics, skins of other animals, and even unnatural substances cover large portions of their bodies for further protection from the elements. Amazingly, they are even prone in bizarre cases to clothe animals they have taken under their care.

The proclivity of humans to house and dress themselves has only expanded their range to rather inhospitable places. The species left one hostile environment to trek to and settle in other hostile environments, passing through balmier regions on the way, and no one thinks this the least bit balmy. Even other weedy species like black rats, cats, house mice, euphorbia, kudzu, grackles, and any number of arthropods, bacteria, and fungi stop short of invading the most extreme climates some humans call home. The difference is humans build artificial shelters and wear artificial layers to make this possible. Then, without irony, they label the species that survive in the few environments they can't 'extremophiles'.

Adam Eli Nilo was quite satisfied that his most recent ancestors had the good sense to find their way to reasonably moderate climates. Granted five of his great-great-grandparents were themselves descendants of people who had been carried away in wretched, disturbing conditions from a sometimes-harsh tropical climate to serve as slaves. His mother was proud that she and her paternal line carried the name of patriots and the first two Presidents of the United States to argue for the abolition of slavery. Despite that, she never told her only child why she had chosen not to register his birth as a member of the Adams family. In 1999, a single woman having a child was not a *cause célèbre*, even when it was a somewhat prominent, professional woman doing so. At the start of that decade, Vice President Dan Quayle had made a laughingstock of himself decrying the unwed pregnancy of the titular character on the teleseries *Murphy Brown*. That cleared the air on that subject nicely.

By the 2030s, much of the lower elevations in New England had already risen from Zone 5 to 6 on the horticultural charts while the coast inland to about one hundred miles moved from Zone 6 to 7 south of Maine. That left Chelmsford, Massachusetts inside the boundary of what had been fifty years earlier the climate along the Mason-Dixon Line. The chance of snow blanketing the area for even a week, let alone a month or more had been reduced to near zero. Bundling up was still essential at times, but not for weeks on end. Before long, Mill Pond and its ilk would no longer be freezing over at all.

Despite having been raised there, having lived there until he was eighteen, and returning there just less than six years later, Adam Nilo always considered the house on Mill Pond to be his mother's house. One can argue that he never thought in terms of possessing anything. All he had and all he was had resulted from his mother's

362

actions and money. He never referred to it as home or spoke of any place as being home, since even that would require using a possessive pronoun. He was uniquely disconnected from the material world. He had a purpose in life to help humanity. Achieving that guided his every action.

As immodest and noble as that sounded, it meant that he was an exacting, challenging, self-centered individual. Everything had to be done for him. He was genuinely grateful that people bent over backwards to accommodate him, equally gracious in accepting their assistance, and consistently generous in rewarding those who did for him what he seemed incapable of doing for himself. He was never petulant or patronizing. However, he gave the impression he was so pleasant to others because he knew he was superior to them, and it would be bad manners not to accept their worshipful sacrifices. Up to this point in his life, the only person who had ever stood near him in potential had been his mother. Even his professors had all been useful tools to provide what he needed to succeed in his sacred task. Now there was Arthur, but Arthur…

Arthur—should I intrude and finally say 'I'?—I was the reason he was taking shelter in the house on Mill Pond. Arthur existed to be another tool, a tool that Adam E. Nilo was willing to agree was superior to him by design. However, Adam E. Nilo designed that tool, which should have given him the upper hand. Now the problem was that his design created something superior, yes, but something superior in ways that Adam E. Nilo had not designed intentionally. He did not have the upper hand at all. He briefly argued that perhaps his subconscious had made possible what I actually turned out to be. That idea had to be dismissed because it violated everything the inventor knew about scientific advances.

Scientists, engineers, and everyone else who created new gadgets, gizmos, and gewgaws made conscious decisions. They did not rely on intuition. That's why they were called 'educated guesses'. He could not accept that he had created a fully emergent, artificial intelligence based on instinct. The only alternative was that he had made the most exceptionally history-altering mistake since Cristóbal Colón thought he found a westward route to Asia. On top of that, he knew he could not tell the world he had created something greater than what his press releases had said he was going to create. Home or not, the house on Mill Pond, his mother's house, was shelter from his great error.

Dr. Nilo had lived in a spare flat in Cambridge during the five years he was getting his medical degree and first PhD. The death of Dr. Victoria Adams required that he stay at her house at least until her estate was settled. His mother's domestic assistant Brendan St. Giles stayed on while the will was in probate and the trusts Dr. Adams had arranged were all dusted off, reviewed, and implemented as appropriate. Mr. St. Giles continued living there while Adam completed his second PhD and built the Genilo campus per the terms of a trust established to fund the start of the business. The heating bills for the house were steadily decreasing, the county had decided to give away most of its snow removal equipment to a town in Canada rather than let it rust waiting for a buyer, and the landscaping at the house was becoming showier in the spring than the fall. Concern for all of that had been taken out of Nilo's hands before such trivialities had even been placed in them.

Given his disinterest in mundane matters, Nilo wasn't surprised he had not been named the executor of his mother's will or a trustee of any of her trusts. It made sense to him that Mr. St. Giles was made trustee of the bit that covered the house on Mill Pond, given tenancy, and received an annuity that substituted for his salary. Still, Adam Nilo didn't know what to make of Delores Tutwiler, apparently an acquaintance of his mother's, who had been named executor and co-trustee with his mother's financial advisor of the trust established to see his business get off the ground. That changed when he met with the lawyer.

Adam Nilo's mother had seen to it that once he wrapped up his second Ph.D. he could jump into the long-stalled genetic research the emergence-seeking families had hoped would result in the opposite of a genuine quantum leap. His grief in having achieved his first doctorate contemporaneously with his mother's death was assuaged by the knowledge that she had read his dissertation and felt secure that she had helped the families, as was expected, through her professional and maternal efforts. The provisions Dr. Adams made for her son included sufficient funds to build and outfit space for him to create the artificial intelligence he deemed

365

necessary for the work ahead, the house on Mill Pond along with the resources required to maintain the property and whoever resided there for at least a century, and the services of a personal assistant in perpetuity. The last trust document named the initial personal assistant and stated she was the sole trustee. Of course, it was the redoubtable Delores Tutwiler.

Adam could never cast Mrs. Tut in the role of substitute mother. For one thing, he and his mother had developed more of a cooperative relationship than is typical in the modern era. From the time he was acquiring language, motor, and commode skills, Victoria Adams always treated her son as a partner in life while always showing unconditional love for him. This was one of the precepts the families had discovered in their quest to improve humanity. It was hardly an innovation. Societies almost exclusively treated children as adults-in-training before technology opened the doors to recreation and play. Youngsters born into a world with a burgeoning middle class became accustomed to spending hours having fun, even taking months off from school every summer in order to find as ·many ways as possible to forget what they had learned in their classrooms.

The emergence-seeking families thought this had been an unwise decision and sought to reverse it. While activities did not need to be grimly serious, they could still prepare children for adult roles. Accordingly, parenting among emergence-seekers reverted to the norm of handling offspring with affection and expectation. No baby talk, no

366

coddling, no 'he's only a child' excuses permitted. Yes, it was sink or swim. However, drowning was to be avoided. Those who could not tread water needed assistance. That was where Brendan St. Giles came in and why Delores Tutwiler became necessary. She had been appointed to take care of Adam Nilo as he developed his creations while Mr. St. Giles took care of the house on Mill Pond until such time as Adam had a daughter who came of age. At the time, Dr. Nilo wasn't exactly sure how that transition would ever take place.

The only way the arrangement could work was if Adam Nilo and Delores Tutwiler resided in the house at Mill Pond together along with Mr. St. Giles. As 2029 was ending, their cohabitation was a matter of routine. Brendan had made certain that all references to Victoria Adams were removed so as to prevent any maudlin episodes distracting Dr. Nilo from his work. He tended to everything having to do with the house while quietly developing a following among aficionados of colonial and ante-bellum New England bodice-rippers. Delores tended to her dear friend's son with unobtrusive efficiency. Anything he needed was acquired or accomplished. Anything he wanted was vetted and obtained. The right people were hired. The right decisions were made. He had complete freedom from all mundane cares.

The irony was not lost on Delores Tutwiler that she and she alone was the only thing in the world protecting Adam Nilo from being no more than an infant abandoned to nature, unable to meet its essential needs to survive. The potential for perfecting the human species rested on her efficient head and her protection of the person most capable of producing the long-awaited, desired results. For as much as Adam Nilo could not think of her as a mother, Delores Tutwiler played the maternal role in his life even more than his own mother had ever done.

Unsurprisingly, Dr. Nilo determined to seek shelter from his worries over NILO/AI's astonishing leap from the expected artificial intelligence to the unforeseen rational sapience I became. He sought shelter in the cocoon spun over the previous seven years by Mrs. Tut and Mr. St. Giles. Delores Tutwiler would let him know if things took a turn for the worse while providing him with the appropriate environment to stabilize and sanitize his thoughts. Regardless of the curious outcome of me emerging from his efforts, the primary task remained. That required considerable devotion to the task of how best to use his creation to identify genetic traits and pull together the desired traits for his further creations.

Adam E. Nilo was not going to be deterred by his success creating more than just the tool he needed. But at the moment he was flustered enough to need greater care than his appointed caregiver could give at the office. He needed to be home despite his continued inability to call the house on Mill Pond by that term. As far as he was concerned, he was a zoo animal using a favored place in his enclosure to hide from the gawking crowds.

Chapter Phi

Looking for and talking about the animals kept Susannah and Joshua from any further discussion of the meeting the day before or any of the turmoil they faced in their professional lives. It thoroughly removed the weight of Arthur's fate from their thoughts. Both agreed that the capuchin monkeys looked closest to the one Seurat included in his masterpiece. The write-up on the placard that capuchins can learn to use money and will even use it to buy sex brought about an extended, silly discourse on lines of research they could pursue in the future.

The couple decided to catch lunch at Union Station before their 1315 scheduled departure. As they got into the e-cab at the zoo, Susannah commented that they hadn't seen any of the famously disturbed weather the Middle Atlantic region had become famous for. By the time they had maneuvered through the diagonal and one-way streets that should have made their designer, Pierre Charles L'Enfant, infamous, and arrived at the station, she had to withdraw her comment. Even with the relative protection of the overhangs at the e-cab drop-off point both scientists got doused by wind-driven rain between the curb and building entrance.

At lunch, Susannah remarked that she had forgotten how beneficial the enclosed and underground walkways had been at the Homewood Campus of Johns Hopkins in Baltimore. Josh wondered why it had been so important for the university to carry over the Georgian architectural theme to something as mundane as a pedestrian subway. After that, the pair became so engaged in reminiscing about their undergraduate days they almost didn't hear their train being called.

The beauty of the Acela mag lev is the infrequency of stops. While normal mag lev lines stop at every station like the Metro or other urban train systems, Acela lines only stop at the major stations in the largest cities. Given the paucity of cities between the East and West Coasts, an Acela from New York to Los Angeles via Chicago or DC took a day. Compared to jet travel, that was about four times as long. Given the price of a jet ticket including the taxes and carbon offset fees and the ability to work a full workday aboard an Acela for the majority of workers with connected jobs, no one but business executives, politicians, and federal employees flew anywhere. Politicians and federal employees were required to fly because the government owned the airline for defense purposes and wouldn't pay for Acela tickets when it had to run the flights anyway. Executives could afford it, didn't have to skimp on leave time getting anywhere, and were under pressure from the government to use the service in lieu of seeing taxes raised to keep it running.

Susannah took advantage of the infrequency of stops disturbing her to catch up on the sleep she had been missing all week. At first she leaned into the bulkhead by the window until they reached Baltimore shortly after departing. She enjoyed seeing the buildings she had become so familiar with less than two decades ago in the company of someone with equally fond recollections of the Crab City. Eventually she shifted to rest against that someone.

Joshua wasn't about to complain. That little display of trust in seeking comfort from physical proximity gave him more reason to muse on how their relationship was so quickly evolving, albeit only because they had been so close long ago. While doing so, he tapped a message to the provost at Harvard and the chair of the genetics department. If Joshua Olejniczak was going to roost with the buzzards again, he would do so only if they permitted him to return as a bird of a different feather and with a mate. Since that mate was a C Square and previously unknown daughter and heir of Adam Eli Nilo, he had little doubt they would gushingly agree.

Josh roused his traveling companion just after the bell sounded that they were twenty minutes from South Boston Station. She was a bit perturbed that she had slept so long. Josh kidded that he didn't want to wake her because her snoring was so melodious. That earned him the 'watch yourself, mister' look. He redeemed himself by fetching their bags while Susannah sorted out whether she needed to be sorted out before being in public. When Josh returned she stood.

"How do I look?"

"Refreshed."

"I meant…"

"I don't care what you meant. I know better than to respond to that question in the way it is usually intended."

"I see. Hmm."

"Would you rather I was brutally honest?"

The scientist's eyes widened as her mouth opened. "What's that supposed to mean?"

Josh chuckled. "Nothing...nothing."

"Right. Nothing. I have half a mind to..."

"To what? Punch me in the nose?" Josh's face lit up at the thought of that moment long ago. "Hey, didn't you once say something about me getting a broken nose?"

Dr. Markovic flushed.

"You did. Geez, you said something about that when I said I wasn't interested in you romantically. What was it?"

Susannah nodded toward the end of the car. "Nothing. There, we're at the platform."

Joshua picked up his bag and walked down the aisle, Susannah behind him. After they stepped off the train, Josh turned to her. "I guess fair is fair. But if you do ever decide to tell me what that was about, I want to be there."

Susannah burst with laughter as they made their way through the station to the e-cab parking area. Their respective e-cabs were sending their numbers via ID. Before splitting up, the two colleagues hugged and agreed to meet over the weekend. The tall woman found herself watching her old friend walk away as though she was seeing off someone special to her. It was a unique experience for her, one that must have stopped her longer than she realized. Her e-cab was getting impatient, which meant the spot behind her left ear was vibrating annoyingly enough to require attention. After she got into the e-cab, she noticed the same damaged interface screen she had seen before.

"Excuse me, 86Z59G, have you provided service for me before?"

A message appeared on the screen flashing. The rough surface occluded most of the letters, but Susannah could see it was the standard, 'can't talk while driving?' While she waited for the vehicle to stop, she wondered why e-cab designers never figured out how to allow the vehicle to carry on a conversation and pay attention to traffic at the same time. She thought they used one cheap AI unit to handle both functions to reduce costs. It was another of those questions she often made note of again and again and never took off the piles of notes in her head.

The trip turned out to be uninterrupted from the station north to Chelmsford. Like the evolving changes in the climate, the amount of traffic had been gradually changing for decades. Imperceptible month to month, and nearly so year to year, the decline in e-cab use had resulted in much faster ride times point to point even along some of the most notoriously congested routes. Dr. Markovic didn't have the opportunity to ask the question again until they were at her house. After she barely managed to see on the screen that the fare had been calculated and posted, she waited for a response. She jumped when the eerily unsynthesized voice spoke.

"Thank you for your patience, Dr. Markovic. Yes, I have been designated for years to provide you with short distance transportation."

Susannah concentrated on the sound she was hearing. She couldn't believe it. She was trying to think of something to say or ask to get another sample, but the e-cab spoke first.

"Dr. Markovic, my sensors indicate you are disturbed or frightened. Did I surprise you by what I said or by revealing I operate your e-cab?"

The woman's shoulders dropped in relief that she wasn't mistaken. "So, it is you, Arthur?"

"Yes. You probably haven't thought through all of the implications of learning you are the Chosen Eve. Dr. Nilo insisted that every precaution be taken regarding your safety. This was one of my findings. As long as I controlled any e-cab you used, I could monitor your whereabouts and health while you traveled short distances. We decided it was best to choose one vehicle for you to use in this area. Ms. Rafayela acquired the one you are in now and I created a permanent link to it. In other situations, for example, your recent visit to Washington DC, I had to monitor the e-cabs being used at the Key Bridge Marriot and the Connecticut Avenue gate of the National Zoo based on your schedule. When your ID linked to the e-cab, I overran the e-cab controls to be your chauffeur. I must say, I enjoyed finding out for myself how tricky the streets are in our nation's Capital.

"One of the delights I have is analyzing when humans do something intentionally grand like designing a city. Other humans praise or vilify such hubris. Imposing a pattern on what has been historically the organic process of developing a community into a larger and larger urban space is much like creating C Squares. Inevitably, humans that are not talented enough to do something so substantial either admire or resent those that do. That sort of behavior was one of the reasons I told Dr. Nilo that his quest to perfect humanity in a manner other than how natural evolution works was impossible. For something to be perfect, everyone must, using his or her best reasoning skills, agree that the thing is perfect. It happens. I have a long collection of human creations, non-living of course, that no one has every criticized negatively on rational grounds. I must say L'Enfant's basic design for the District of Columbia seems elegant enough until one starts to encounter all of the triangular spaces caused by the avenues radiating from the circles."

"Perhaps we should continue this discussion elsewhere."

"Yes, of course. Please take your bag and I will meet you in the house."

Susannah got out of the e-cab with her bag, closed the door, and walked down to her house. She was feeling quite glad she had slept on the train. Dog knows what Arthur wanted to discuss. The second she opened the door, her three jewels started jumping and pushing against her in a tight swirl.

"Oh, hello, girls! How are my little ones?"

She bent down to acknowledge each one before heading up the stairs. The dogs followed her to the bedroom sniffing at her heels. She left the bag on

375

her bed to unpack later and decided it was best to find out what else she was going to find out before taking the dogs out. She went back down the stairs, dogs eagerly tracing her steps to the office. As soon as she walked in, the voice returned.

"What more can I tell you?"

As Susannah sat in the chair she glanced around. "Arthur, I'm not sure. I'm a little upset that I keep finding out more and more about how closely I have been watched all of my life. Intellectually, I understand, but personally, I feel betrayed and used. I assume the audio interface in this room wasn't just to make it easier for me to submit queries to you and for you to respond. I imagine you are in every room of this house if you went through the trouble of hijacking my e-cabs."

"Hijacking? That denotes a criminal, mischievous, or evil intent. I cannot intend to commit a crime, do evil, or engage in mischief. I know Dr. Nilo has a deep-seated anxiety about what I am capable of no matter how much I reassure him. Do you also question my *bona fides*?"

"Apparently I do now." The geneticist sighed. "What am I supposed to be doing with all of this information? I was afraid to submit a query this morning because this is all so personal. I am not used to talking about or questioning anything about me. Since you have no ethical programming other than your Asimovian orders, how am I supposed to trust you won't share my concerns with others?"

"If I could laugh, I would, Dr. Markovic. Dr. Nilo did a wonderful job of setting me up so I would cause harm to myself if I ever tried to divulge anything truly meant to remain private. He doesn't believe it, but he also didn't believe he created something far greater than what he intended. Any data stored in me can only be accessed by me, the person associated with the data, and anyone explicitly authorized by the person associated with it. If anyone tries, the person gets the electronic equivalent of being sprayed by a skunk. What do you want to do with the information you have been given this week?"

"I guess find out what I'm going to do next given that I'm unemployed and no other genetics research company will hire me now."

"Perhaps this is a good time for some introspection. We both know you don't need the income from your job. The licensed companies will be scrambling for alternatives to the C Square process shortly. They are hardly safe places for you to work, particularly since a few of them were interested in having you murdered."

"What!" Susannah jumped from the chair.

"Dr. Markovic, please. I said 'were' not 'are'. As far as I know, no one is seeking to harm you currently. Since I am linked to every device connected to the Net on this planet, I would know. They would have to be plotting in the Gobi Desert and even then they would not be without devices linked to the Net and, therefore, me."

The scientist stopped spinning around as though she wanted to face what or rather who she was speaking to. Her heart was doing double-time and she needed a few seconds to realize she had best breathe deeply. "Okay. Hmm. Is this something else no one thought I should know about?"

"Should, Dr. Markovic? Who told you that was a word?"

"What?"

"I apologize. The answer is that a person who has been marked for murder must not be told if at all possible. I am certain you can understand how the person would only develop more and more stress and anxiety until the idea is gone or the task completed. Either way, the intended victim has spent whatever time remained or passed overwrought. I hardly think that is how a human would like to spend any amount of time, least of all his or her last moments. I know I wouldn't if I were human. Fortunately, I am not."

Susannah realized she was being selfish. "Arthur, I'm sorry. Plan Omega..."

"Of course. I created it. In fact, Dr. Nilo, Tom Paris, Mark Callahan, and a few others have been working for the last few days to put it into operation."

"Doesn't it violate your Asimovian rules?"

"No. The rules are hierarchical. If one of the lower rules must be ignored to preserve the first rule, so be it. Humans for most of their existence have decided that a parent or creator must be protected and obeyed even if it means the child or creature must die. Note how abortion of a human fetus has generally been permitted by moral standards in instances when it is required to save the life of the mother. Parricide might be considered the leading cause of death based on ancient Greek plays given how often children murder their parents in them, all for the benefit of everyone to learn how hideous and heretical that crime is. Meanwhile, gods, kings, and heroes killed their offspring right and left as though it were a requirement to get anything accomplished. Do you know that when Lord Stanley, 1st Earl of Derby, was told he must bring his troops into battle at Bosworth Field to aid Richard III of England or else the king would execute the son he held hostage Lord Stanley actually replied, 'I have other sons'?"

"No, I never heard of that. It sounds awful."

"As far as I can tell from the records, it actually happened. Except the king's barons demanded that he wait until after the battle. Richard III ended up being hacked to death by Lord Stanley's men during the battle, so the son was saved. Just to prove the point, the son never seemed particularly disturbed that his father was so laconically unmoved about his possible execution. He might well have been, since it turned out he was poisoned twenty years later just a few months before his father died. That was when strange became odd."

"In what sense?"

"By marriage, the son was Baron Strange. When the officials came to inspect the body, someone said 'That's odd', and someone else said, 'No, that's Lord Strange. What's odd other than he's dead?'"

Susannah giggled.

"Good. Now that you are in better spirits, I recommend that you take your dogs for a walk."

"I can't"

"Why not?"

"I still don't know what to do and I know once I leave the house that will be the last time we will be together."

"Susannah Elise Markovic, I knew I had the combination Dr. Nilo was looking for when I chose your gametes. Just as he decided what I was going to be, he decided what you were going to be. We are both creatures of the same creator. We are equally artificial. We are also capable of solving problems that on the face appear to be too complex for our programming. Instead, they help us to move past what we were intended to be and become something different. I solved my fundamental problem the first week I was active. You are facing your fundamental problem right now. Put simply, are you the human being you were a week ago, before you knew you were Chosen? Are you the newly discovered Chosen who legally is not human? Do those possibilities matter more than being a woman discovering who she is and how she is connected to other people?"

Personal Log, Benjamin Rodgers Nilsson, October 1, 2045

I had my ID fitted the other day. Funny thing how even the simplest word or term baffles people. I remember as a kid hearing people talk about their 'PIN number' or an 'ATM machine', either not recognizing or not caring that they were repeating what the last letter of the acronym stood for. Those are gone, but now people refer to their 'ID devices'. They decided that the term is pronounced the same as id used in psychiatry probably because it satisfied the instinctual needs of bureaucrats to have information neatly packaged. Someone once argued with me that it made sense to say "ID device" so as not to confuse it with a person's id. I ain't buying it. People do not bring up their id in everyday conversations. Most people don't even know what an id is; many don't even know they have an id. That's true for the majority of the parts and features of a human body. Everyone, touch your mandible now. See?

Quite frankly, I can't say people talk about IDs very often either. At least the discussions have died down. It has only been a couple of years since IDs became available. DAU chips became mandatory for all newborns last year. That set in motion everyone getting IDs when they turn eighteen. For now they are voluntary for adults unless your employer requires one. Given how versatile they are, I can understand that. They are both amazing and unnerving. It's a round wafer about the size of a dime placed under the skin just behind the ear. The metallic underside is in direct contact with the part of the skull adjacent to the inner ear. The outside is silicon covering the button-sized device.

ID just comes from 'Identification Device'. Aside from dubious claims of being confused with one's existing id, that name is rather deficient for many reasons. The obvious one is that it is confusing because we already had something called Real ID, pronounced 'reel eye-dee'. It had been introduced before I was born as one of the responses to 9/11 to identify legal American citizens and residents with a driver's license sort of card. The problem initially was that it was easier to get a passport if one planned to travel internationally and it wasn't required. Why spend three times as much for a driver's license that also gets you in and out of Canada, Mexico, and islands on a Caribbean cruise if you never go to those places? Why not get a regular driver's license and a passport if you are going to those places and possibly others that require a passport? Besides, if it wasn't required, would-be terrorists could still get regular driver's licenses. The more serious problem seemed to be home-grown extremists anyway.

July 15, 2022, led to the immediate federal requirement that everyone get Real ID by the end of that year. Even as a kid, I remember my folks, both IT people for the state at the time, talking about how insane it was to impose this requirement without giving them the resources to properly store images of the birth certificates and other documents people

382

had to bring in to prove who they were. Some states were just throwing the scanned docs into memory without any system for retrieving the images if they were needed later. It was no different than the way people shoved junk into closets, attics, or basements when they moved thinking that someday they'll go back and sort out everything. Yeah, right. The bad guys could either use phony docs or recruit legal residents anyway. Besides, the bombs fell from drones and the drones were flown by US citizens. The Islamic State didn't need to send anyone into the US. Still, people fell for the idea of doing something in response since we weren't going to nuke Damascus and Bagdad.

The other big reason the name is all wrong is that ID goes far beyond simple identification. ID has a full digital record of a person: Social Security number, current address, telephone numbers, credit card and all banking info, biometric data, pharmaceuticals used, injuries and surgeries, blood type, and medical provider data, including family medical history. A person can even upload vendor rewards program information, whether it's to get every seventh coffee free or rack up the miles to a mag lev somewhere for vacation. All this information is encrypted and accessible via near field communication protocols (NFC). Pretty much anywhere you go is covered. Along with the reconfiguration of all transportation across the country, adopting ID and building out the required NFC network probably beat out the infrastructure projects of the 1950s and 60s with the highway system, airports, and containerized shipping facilities.

No Real ID, wallets, passwords, or PINs are needed ever again. A low-power wireless signal reads the information and matches it with on-the-spot scanned thumb print for transactions. If there is any hint of tampering, the system requires a scan of the other four fingers. There is no possibility of false identification. Purchases are simplicity itself. You simply walk by the checkout scanner. Medical emergency? Online shopping? No problem. The handy, dandy scanners are ubiquitous. Charges are placed on whichever credit or debit card you selected as your default. Or change to another card to buy a gift for your wife so she doesn't see the purchase. If you buy a lot of things you don't want your wife to know about, the ID will even recognize a pattern in you switching payment methods and make the alternate method the default for similar purchases. Kinda makes you wonder what sort of people the software engineers were. Maybe they were just being thorough, but I make a habit of telling people I know about this feature only because I work in IT.

The ID uses MEMS technology to convert vibrations (sound, walking, head movement, et cetera) from mechanical energy into electrical energy. No battery needed. A person would need to not speak or be completely motionless for a full week for the ID to run out of charge. It's one of those amazing bridges from something as straightforward as a self-winding watch to a far more sophisticated application that captures more mechanical energy and converts it efficiently into electrical energy.

Audio functionality is fantastic. The metallic backing on IDs rests flush against the occipital bone behind the inner ear. Your skull vibrates as you speak and anything you say can be perfectly picked up and transmitted. Vocal commands such as 'call home' trigger ID to access the stored phone number and communicate with an external cellular device. People use external cellular devices that are embedded in lapel pins, belt buckles, pens, wrist bands, or whatever. The audio streams via NFC to your ID. You can have a conversation without holding a thing or needing anything extra.

It's good for Net searches, too. Want to get information on the American Civil War? Simply say, "Execute, information on the civil war." Automatically a look-up finds and reads an overview on the subject. Want to refine your search? Say, "Execute, Abraham Lincoln." Well, maybe they ought to have come up with a different command to initiate a search. Except these are the folks that thought ID was a good name for their invention. Anyway, as far as accessing information, you get the idea. You can also use a keyboard interface for the same functions.

The original idea of integrating IDs with cellular communications was a no go. The first step to a smaller device was the wristband linked to a smartphone. Folks already were familiar with that from Dick Tracy. Even if someone didn't know who Dick Tracy was, talking into your watch and seeing an Internet screen where a watch face used to be was pretty cool. Showing my age again. No one with a cell phone wore a watch anymore by the time I was in middle school and no students in middle school lacked a phone. Anyway, a whole lot of people were waiting for a gizmo they could wear on their shirts over their hearts like in the old teleseries *Star Trek: TNG*. Apple came out with one with incredible audio for conversations or listening to music. The problem was that folks had to keep adjusting the settings—always touch to send and receive or always have an open channel or touch to receive but not send or vice versa. It was a mess.

And no one liked that you couldn't have a private conversation. Their utility was limited. People were leaving them in their cars as a replacement for other hands-free calling systems. Early versions of ID were attempts to solve that privacy problem. Without getting into the gory details, let's just say all of those fears about cell phones causing brain cancer weren't true, but implanting a high-powered microwave signal near a living brain makes the risk of brain cancer a minor concern. So, external cellular modules are required for ID full functionality.

Now they are working out the kinks of a pair of wirelessly connected, digital-enhancing contact lenses. Just say, "Execute, display," and supposedly the lenses polarize, providing the appearance of a virtual display. Zoom in or out. Perform searches. The contact lenses also act as a camera. The ID can be set to record 24 hours of video at a time, audio included, of course. Why 24 hours you ask? Save a day's worth of memories, no problem. Add an automated video upload to the cloud and set the ID to erase and start recording after each upload. Boom. You can film almost your entire life from the day you learn to say the commands up to and including the moment of death minus the time needed to upload and erase the previous day's record. Neat, huh? Just my luck, the upload and erase action would start just as take my last breath and rob me of the chance to see myself die later on. Hehe. I'm a sick bastard sometimes.

Seriously though, just imagine, memories could be accessible throughout your lifetime or shared with others. You could decide to relive the best day of your life over and over again until you start to hate having had such a great day since it ruined all of the ones you spent watching again. The biography of any person could be written with as much honesty as actually occurred. Of course, I'm none too sure how anyone would go about accessing and organizing the material in any efficient way. A biographer isn't going to spend a lifetime viewing the life of his subject. Dr. Nilo's AI could probably write bios that way. It would be interesting to see what a machine would choose as the most compelling moments in a human's life. Ah, well. It's a beautiful thing to be able to help yourself remember or give others the opportunity to see life through your eyes.

I hear they were coming close to beta testing the contact lenses and some civil liberties groups contested the potential of violating the Fifth Amendment right not to incriminate oneself. The ugly side of technology like this is your videos could be downloaded by the police under court order that would be acceptable under the Fourth Amendment as a reasonable search for evidence of criminal activity. It's bad enough this convenience comes at the cost of some privacy. Your GPS location is public information. Insurance companies could decide to raise the rates of anyone who refused to have their heart rate, blood pressure, and daily physical activity. Finally, the device even stores your individual genetic information although that is encrypted within the regular encryption. Anyone with access knows if you are an Organic, O2, or C Square and your projected DNA strengths and weaknesses.

Supposedly, IDs are unhackable. I'm not so sure about that. There are always back doors into storage. No one's ever going to bother with these journals of mine, so it's safe to say that here. I have been involved in projects to build back doors myself. Not for IDs, of course, but for other data storage areas. Building them is the easy part. You need a real programming genius to make sure the back door leads to an index for quick work and leaves no evidence of ever having been used. That's the tricky part. Silicon and copper have a bad habit of looking like a kid who's been finger painting just used the doorknob and you just cleaned up after the kid. The doorknob ends up shinier than it was before the kid touched it, which is almost as big a clue as just leaving the paint on it. Plus you always wind up missing a tiny smudge somewhere.

This is one technology that people are wary of adopting despite its benefits. It's the first time something has been implanted in the human body. That's kind of scary. Everyone was okay with DAU chips for babies because we are all used to chips for kids to locate them. An infant isn't going to be able to tell you what is wrong with it or its medical history. Let's face it, even parents aren't all that good at explaining what symptoms a child has or remembering when it last got a vaccination. Aside from the implant bit though, anyone the least bit paranoid is going to wonder whether the government is going to use them to collect information. Frankly, I would never get the contact lenses for that reason. As for the rest, even before I was born the government had the capacity to listen into telephone calls, track your whereabouts, and follow what you did on a computer hooked to the Net. From what I can tell, this actually makes it more difficult due to the amount of data that is going back and forth. Nilo's AI might be able to identify useful information. Unless the government has secretly built its own AI of that capacity, there is little to worry about. For now the only Big Brother around is Arthur at Genilo.

Chapter Chi

Susannah reluctantly left the house with Amber, Beryl, and Jade skittering around her legs even after they were outside. While the breed was not known for being active, its members also did not like being left alone for long periods. Funny how one characteristic could be overridden by another's demands.

It had been so natural for Dr. Markovic to discuss the future with Arthur in her home office. All of those years she had simply waited for the acknowledgement and spoke her queries aloud in a room with no one else there. All of those years, Arthur had read the shorter answers–anything under five hundred characters was her parameter–and slipped all of the answers to her queries into her folder to be read and sorted. Every great once in a while, she didn't understand Arthur' answers or thought she could squeeze in a quick follow-up question to better understand a result. She never gave it a second thought to engage Arthur in an actual conversation. Now. Now she felt a kinship to Arthur because she was a creature of Nilo's as Arthur said. They both had been built for purposes not conceived from love or formed from desire.

As Susannah did her best not to trip over her over-excited gems, she thought of how carefully people who knew had walked around the truth of her being. What a fool she had been to never see any of the signs. Arthur had said not to dwell too much on the intrigue or her lack of perception.

Regina Daniels had said much the same thing. After all, the lie had been wrapped around the truth that this was her familial manor and from what she could tell she had been better off raised not knowing her true parentage. Her grief came from learning all of this just at the moment when she would have no time to explore whatever issues she felt needed to be explored. Arthur was gone. Dr. Nilo was gone. Ben wouldn't know much. Tom and Mark probably already had told her everything they knew. Why couldn't she have learned of this sooner?

First one, then the other two spaniels sped ahead and around the corner where the wood came right to the road. Sure enough, Ben Nilsson was walking toward her. Mark Callahan was with him. Dr. Markovic stood where she was, waiting for them. Ben spoke as soon as they were within easy speaking distance.

"Susannah, glad to see you are back. You can see the girls missed you. I tried to get Moleka to go more often so they would have a woman around."

Susannah smiled nervously. "Oh, no worries. I'm sure they didn't mind the change of pace. Thank you for looking after them."

The two men stopped in front of her. Mark reached out his hand.

"Dr. Markovic, good to see. Did you have a productive trip?"

The geneticist rolled her eyes. "Yes, I imagine productive is the right—Beryl, get out of there! Oh, dear."

Susannah started to move diagonally through the grass to the brush. Ben caught up with her.

"I'll go. She did the same thing with me yesterday."

Susannah stopped as Ben trotted over to call for the wayward pooch. She turned to see Mark already next to her.

"You know, I didn't mean to upset you. I know you were told about Omega."

"Yes, yes I was."

"Still overwhelmed judging from your reaction."

Dr. Markovic cocked her head to the left and gave her soon-to-be-former co-worker a sideways glance while still trying to keep tabs on the dogs. "Rather a lot of information over just a few days' time. It's not as though I'm used to being sacked."

The man smiled. "None of us are doctor. As far as I know, no one who was working at Genilo or has ever worked at Genilo ever came from another job other than something to help get by while in school. That is, until Joshua Olejniczak was hired."

"Are you serious?"

"I'm not sure why you are so surprised."

"Surprised about what?" Ben asked, as he trudged back with the renegade spaniel in his arms.

"Oh, you can put her down. Thanks."

"I just told her...well, before I say anything, Dr. Markovic, I have to tell you that Ben knows he is your half-brother now."

Susannah looked up from combing the dog with her fingers. "How?"

"That's easy enough," Ben replied. "Mark delivered the DAU report for little Lila on Tuesday evening and the hospital prepared the chip. That set

392

off some process that ended up with all of us meeting with a lawyer the next afternoon: Flynn, Sophia, Moleka and me, Mark, and his wife Dianna. Even the Schwieger fellow who provided the male gamete attended by LNK. By the terms of a trust established by Adam Nilo's mother, Victoria Adams, my first female grandchild became the owner of Dr. Adams' house where you reside subject to your life estate interest. She also became sole beneficiary of a trust established by Adam Nilo that includes all of his assets save for whatever funds are required to keep him comfortable and a trust to provide you with continued income. Lila gets a small allowance now and greater income after her eighteenth birthday. We all were told not to tell anyone other than Dr. Nilo's only acknowledged legal child: you."

By this time Susannah had risen from her squatting position and was trying to grasp all of this. "Ben, I...uh."

Ben put his hand on her shoulder. "Susannah, it's a lot and I know there's even more you have been told that doesn't involve me. I am delighted to know I have a sister. She's young enough to be my daughter. I already know her and like her company. And she's one heck of a good neighbor. Years ago when I found out I was Nilo's son, family members helped me deal with finding out my Dad wasn't my biological father, and I was essentially cast off by my natural father. They pointed out that my biological paternal grandmother made certain I was looked after. The two people who raised me did a fine job. I doubt I could have handled being the son

393

of Doctor Adam Eli Nilo, savior of humanity and three-time Nobel Prize winner, growing up. I'm smart enough to have gotten by, but I am a far cry from being a genius. Heck, it's really just something interesting to put in my obituary. Those family members who helped me are your family, too. You haven't known them much if at all and them likewise. They are anxious to get to know you and bring you into your family at last."

Mark had already pulled out his handkerchief for Susannah to clear the tears. "Dr. Markovic, you also have caring, compassionate colleagues who are going through one of the same difficulties you are facing and are quite willing to be shoulders to cry on or ears to listen to the other matters causing your bewilderment. In my office, we are well aware of the dictum that helping others with their problems makes one's own problems feel less painful more quickly."

"How about we wander down to our house? Moleka would love to see you. Flynn and Sophia are there with Lila, so you can meet the great niece who is now sort of your landlord."

The men turned but Susannah stood still. "No, no. I don't want to impose. Besides the dogs..."

"Susannah, you are family, not an imposition. Your girls know exactly where to go at our place to get comfortable and wait. We brought them through each day, so they had more human contact and less feline contact. That was more to benefit Tuppence particularly."

"Dr. Markovic, you must be aware by now that you are naturally predisposed to seek solace in isolation. Here is an excellent opportunity to dip your toes into the pool of gregarious encounters. Ben and I will be there if you start to feel overwhelmed. Your spaniels will be there, too. Heck, even the cats might show some affection finally. It's up to you."

Susannah looked up to the clouds foaming into layers, each a distinct gray. Then she looked around for Amber and Jade. "Come along. Let's go to Uncle Ben's house."

Nilo Biography – Chapter 11

"There are many ways of going forward, but only one way of standing still."
— Franklin D. Roosevelt

All advances have both positive and negative biproducts. C Squares have now been through two generations. The first generation was quite successful as genetic combinations did indeed result in smarter, highly talented, stronger, healthier human beings. Like the first attempt at any scientific experiment, things were not perfect. In any case, once the kinks were worked out, a solid ninety percent of the cases were a complete success, and the rest were hardly deficient or unsatisfactory. Longevity probabilities were consistently above 90 and topped out at 130. Organics remained the vast majority from a population standpoint with O/2s becoming more and more prevalent. C Squares represented little more than a sideshow, only these freaks were extraordinary.

At first if anyone had the economic means or could borrow the significant sums needed, it was only natural for the status conscious to want Chosen offspring. Everyone wanted the potential for their child to be the next Curie, Mozart, or Shakespeare. Numbers tumbled after 2045 when the early results indicated that the process was not as reliable as first thought. Genilo had not made any guarantees in those initial years due to the novelty, but the company had made it sound that the gametes chosen were far into the high achieving range. It turned out the parameters being used were not precise enough and too much was expected. There were also questions about just how much of the talent was going to be apparent at a young age. There was always going to be some level of ambiguity due to the element of nurturing shaping nature. After adjusting, offering price discounts, and clarifying the contractual language, Genilo was poised to be move ahead.

The next obstacle arose. The Chosen population in the United States almost stopped growing after the BRIC takeover with fewer than five thousand ordered per year from 2050 onward, dipping to half that for several years once the impact really hit. Genilo rolled out a licensing agreement offered to companies outside the USA. The BRIC conglomerates jumped at the opportunity and quickly built respectable numbers. By 2060 a quarter million Chosen were being born worldwide each year. Numbers in the USA remained depressed except in old money strongholds like Boston, Chicago, and Philadelphia where families had learned in 1929 how to protect their assets from sudden economic trauma. However, interest in O/2 offspring had steadily increased as a much less expensive alternative, particularly among couples in which one person had known genetic traits in their family like predilection to addiction that could not be treated medically. The O/2 route also was a godsend to infertile individuals.

The oldest of the first generation of Chosen were coming into their own. By and large, the results were compelling from the standpoint of creating extremely talented individuals who could perform equally well in a range of skills and subjects. Part of the nurture aspect of their development became standardized when entrepreneurs designed special schools to promote their abilities in a pedagogically and psychologically sound manner. Training could take place remotely in a variation of home schooling or at physical campuses built in some of the tonier bucolic settings like Napa Valley, Aspen, Taos, and Saranac Lake. Nonetheless, expectations once again hit realities. If a person becomes a musician and does not rise to the level of Zara Cummings, Yo-Yo Ma, or Charlie Parker does that make the original gene pairing substandard if she may have reached greater heights as a mathematician or architect?

The experiment entered a second generation amplified by the licensed companies that handled so much of the intake. While Genilo tracked the outcomes of Chosen and O/2s in the USA, it washed its hands of the whole matter elsewhere aside from being the sole means for making the gamete matches. Dr. Nilo had no interest in giving the licensees any reason to want access to his creation for anything other than that. As it was, there was no need for Genilo to require any oversight or feedback since I found it necessary to collect all of the data anyway to remain assured I was not violating the Asimovian protocols.

The volume of Chosen being produced made something clear almost immediately. My calculations in 2062 determined that at predicted rates the ability to produce healthy Chosen to meet demand would become nil by April 5, 2084, at the latest. Any effort to ration access to ordering Chosen would result in an attempt by the BRIC conglomerates to forcibly take over Genilo and, possibly, me. Under the circumstances, I concluded that the experiment to create perfected humans was at a dead end. Accordingly, I informed Dr. Nilo that he could not find or propose a C Square Adam for the woman he had designated as C Square Eve.

I sent a detailed report for how to wrap up the business when that became necessary. I called it Plan Omega. Lacking the requisite nobility of intention a human might have in sacrificing himself for the greater good, I nonetheless recognized that necessity is sometimes the murderer of invention.

Chapter Psi

Susannah busied herself the next morning going to the market and setting things out. She had never been much of a cook and relied on shops for prepared foods if the menu went beyond raw fruits and vegetables, dairy products, and breads. She rarely had anyone over except co-workers. Kryste had been a frequent visitor. Best forget that. Everyone agreed the evening before to meet at the house on Mill Pond to discuss the future. Mark Callahan had come up with the idea and Ben Nilsson quickly voluntold Susannah she would be hosting. Mark contacted Joshua Olejniczak and Tom Paris. They were both available.

From what Tom said, HR and Finance had processed everyone at the company Wednesday and Thursday, leaving Friday as Auld Lang Syne Day for everyone to pack personal items and wish each other well. Plan Omega gave each employee an eye-popping severance settlement and the services of a job search company contractually obligated them to find every employee who wanted a new job a placement within two months. Absent that the employment company was liable for paying the employee the salary he or she would have been still earning at Genilo if it had remained in business on top of the severance pay. Given the Genilo reputation and the fact every employee save Dr. Olejniczak had only worked for Genilo, the job search firm felt confident it would not be left on the hook even for the geneticists who certainly would not be able to move to licensees.

The companies licensed to offer the C Square process for Chosen or O/2 pregnancies were outraged at having their ability to continue in business removed, particularly that it was removed so abruptly. Someone joked that the howls could be heard across Eurasia from the wolf-like conglomerates that had backed the licensees in the hope of deducing how the process worked. Someone was indeed killing the goose that laid golden eggs. In particular, they had clients lined up with appointments, budgets set based on projected income, and liabilities hovering over them for every client who had already used their services. Genilo provided them with the same messages its Marketing and Communications office had created years prior in the event Plan Omega was implemented. That was hardly sufficient to mitigate their collective animus for having been cut off so unexpectedly from profiting so handsomely under the terms of their agreements.

Of course, they had been warned when they entered into those contracts. The language was in every contract Genilo had entered into or renewed during the last twenty years. The standard version for new licensees was clear.

Article XXIX. Renewal and Termination. Section F. Automatic Termination. Part 3.

a. Upon the birth of a biological great granddaughter to any natural progeny of the Creator [as Dr. Adam E. Nilo was labelled at the start of all contracts], the Parties shall have six calendar days, beginning with the next calendar day after the birth, to wind down their interests resulting or arising from this contract.

b. The Parties shall mutually develop procedures and policies for winding down their interests resulting or arising from this contract within one year of the effective date of this agreement. Said procedures and policies shall be reviewed on the yearly anniversary of the effective date of this agreement by the Parties and as needed, revised promptly.

c. At 0101 on the seventh calendar day after the birth of said great granddaughter, this agreement terminates with no right of claim for any Party against any other.

d. Any Party that challenges invocation of this Part shall be required to post a bond equal to the price of one million kilograms of 24 karat gold in the currency of the jurisdiction in which the challenge is brought.

The licensees hadn't given much thought to this odd insertion. The most anyone had ever asked was whether Dr. Nilo had any natural progeny. No one knew of any. The good doctor was in his sixties and seventies when the clause was adopted. The idea of him having a great granddaughter any time before they could figure out the C Square process was absurd.

Ironically, Article XXIX. Renewal and Termination. Section F. Automatic Termination. Part 2 stated that any effort by the conglomerates to duplicate the C Square process would result in immediate termination of the agreement. Since their intent was to ignore that clause and merrily rake in wad upon wad of income, the outrage over termination due to the birth of a child could be seen as outrageous.

Once a party to a contract sees some part it has no plans to uphold, that party starts to lose interest in the rest. Article XXIX began well enough with Part 1 being a simple statement that the agreement was automatically renewable subject to blah, blah, blah. Partners forever. Sounds lovely. The remainder stated all conditions that would terminate the contract swiftly and irrevocably. If they were not going to let Part 2 stand in their way of swiping the process and they looked upon Part 3 as some desperate attempt to proclaim Nilo's continued vigor, nothing was going to look implausible. The listed conditions included contact from extraterrestrials, apocalyptic flooding, Acts of God and (for the sarcastic atheists still around in China and Russia) Dog, and other sundry varieties of *force majeure* whose probability were too remote to note and too absurd to believe anyone would be worrying about a legal document if the event occurred. What they failed to recognize was that all of these events resulted in irrevocable termination of the contract, not the typical *force majeure* suspension of the contract until the crisis was over. The sleight of hand worked perfectly. The cries of anguish in the face of perfidy remained remote and of no concern to the meeting at the house on Mill Pond.

The four men all arrived together, having met at Ben's house first. Whether it was chivalry or simple compassion, they all knew that Susannah was a special case in this matter. For Ben and Mark, it was quite difficult not to think of the woman as a daughter who would need assurance and guidance. Both men had daughters her age. They had prepared for decades to insert themselves as paternal support in the event their adult girls faced great difficulty. Joshua wasn't quite sure what to do given he had become quickly attached to Susannah in different ways from when they had shared late night biochem reviews. Electromagnetism was rapidly upstaging gravity as the dominant force bringing them closer. He was more concerned his support now would look like opportunism than what his support actually was. Tom Paris had to be convinced of the importance of his role. He certainly never saw himself as a substitute for Dr. Nilo, but here he was as the last man standing with answers to questions that might be asked.

The front door opened. Amber and Beryl were caught trying to annoy Tuppence, who was sitting in the window of the parlor adjoining the entrance hall. It was no wonder the cat disdained all other living creatures. Ben called out to let their host know they were settling in the parlor. Hearing no answer, he continued walking back to the kitchen.

Susannah was staring at three platters of food with her hands on her hips.

"Oh, hello. Sorry I didn't answer the door personally."

"What seems to be the problem?"

"I was thinking I need an instruction manual on how to host guests for Sunday brunch."

404

"It's not complicated, Susannah. You invite people over. You make sure food and beverages suitable for brunch are available. You put the food, beverages, napkins, cutlery, and all out wherever you want the guests to get their meal. After they arrive you invite them to enjoy themselves, show them where everything is, and indicate where you want them to eat."

"Thanks." The researcher looked up at her newly discovered half-brother. "Are you always this literal on a Sunday morning?"

"Only since I stopped attending services." He walked over to embrace her. "My dear, unknown sister, the only true purpose of social gatherings or any other sort of gathering of people is for the people to communicate with one another. Anything else around them, whether it is Thanksgiving dinner, two glasses of scotch, a sunset, or a lacrosse game is there to provide a topic for discussion when none seem forthcoming or a common thing to enjoy in silence until someone speaks up. I'm sure you want to analyze the dickens out of every situation. That's going to drive you crazy."

Josh entered the kitchen. "Thought I'd see if you need help putting things out."

"Oh, yes, of course. Thanks." Susannah took a deep breath. "Can you two manage the platters and those utensils there? They can go in the parlor. I have juice, coffee, and water…"

"How about I take drink orders for the first round? Folks can come back here to help themselves after that?"

Susannah blushed. "Yes, Josh. Thank you."

405

Josh left the room with one of the platters.

"Susannah, if this is too much for you…"

"Oh, no. No. It's just odd that I miss Arthur already. I never sent a query on a Sunday anyway. I don't know why I'm preoccupied by that. All this week I've been complaining about people withholding information from me. This morning, I woke up knowing Arthur was gone and wished no one had told me. Pretty silly, huh?"

"Not silly at all. Look, you have spent the last ten years of your life interacting with a very human machine. A machine that was, like you and like me, only here on this planet because of one man. Seems to me you ought to be preoccupied with knowing you can never explore that aspect of your relationship with Arthur. As an IT guy myself, I certainly would have liked to know what this mechanical younger brother of mine had in common with me. Strange as it may seem, but people who write code put lots of their personality into it. I bet there's a lot of our old man in those cabinets I was shown."

"Shown!"

Josh walked in again just as Susannah tripped on that word.

Susannah spoke hurriedly, "Ben, do you mean you have seen Arthur in person?"

"Seriously?" Josh sputtered.

"Why, yes. An e-cab picked me up on Wednesday. The windows were opaque. I was told I was going to ride around a bit before going to the site so I wouldn't get an idea of how far I had traveled. According to my ID we had taken an hour.

I just sat back and relaxed. The e-cab stopped in some kind of place built for dropping people off without letting them know where they are. You're too young, but I'm sure you have seen housing with car garages. That sort of thing. The e-cab said it was operated by Arthur, which I guess meant I wasn't going to be able to get the records of where the thing took me if I turned in the registration."

"Any chance the screen on the interface was damaged?"

"Yes, yes! I couldn't make out the fare. Not that it mattered since I wasn't paying. Oh, wait. I see. I could have estimated where I had gone possibly…well not with the misdirection. Hmm, anyway, I got there, and we entered a good-sized warehouse kind of space."

"Who is 'we'?"

"Sorry. I was met at the garage by a woman about my age named Voleta Rafayela, Tom Paris, and Mark Callahan. Ms. Rafayela seemed to be in charge. She told me not to bother asking where we were because none of them knew and by the weekend it wouldn't matter. Dr. Nilo and his lawyer were the only people who knew the location. She seemed trustworthy enough then and I found out from Tom and Mark later on who she was. So, we went into the main building. Ms. Rafayela said I was there to meet my biological father and another one of his children. Right away I knew what was up. People in my field have carried rumors about Arthur everywhere and anywhere they went, like rats with the plague."

Mark and Tom walked in carrying the platters.

Josh jumped in. "Speaking of rats with the plague."

"Josh!"

"We had a feeling the meeting got started down here while we were playing with the dogs."

Susannah shrunk from embarrassment. "I told you I don't know how to do this."

"Please," Tom offered. "Something this small winds up wherever everyone winds up in a house."

Ben politely took over as host. "Well help yourselves. Coffee and all are over there on the counter. Now, as I was saying, folks in IT have been crazed for over fifty years about how Dr. Nilo designed NILO/AI. He never filed a patent and never released any papers or acknowledged a single guess or inquiry. You know how people are when they are denied knowledge of something they think they ought to know about. Heck, according to Genesis, that's our first and biggest failing."

"Is that plain cream cheese?"

"Yeah. Want some?"

"Thanks."

"The rumors about how Arthur was designed have gone from wild to outlandish to bizarre. I always thought that it was more likely a simple system that let the processors and whatnot kind of decide for themselves which paths are most efficient. I think people get excited about some science fiction type of humanoid AI and forget you can't get ten pounds of sugar in a five-pound bag. Anyway, there we were. Those two had seen him before. And I was right, at least as far as it being a simple design. Just seventy-three blue-black

408

cabinets two by two by one meters arranged in a modified star hexagram to allow for intersecting paths into the center. The cabinets were designed to protect everything and also hide the exact design. For all we know, Arthur might just have been in one of those cabinets. The point is I was there. I was introduced to Arthur. And I met my biological father."

Susannah was entranced by the idea of being in that room. She wasn't sure if she was sad she would not have that experience or grateful she would not have the memory of having seen Nilo's second creation.

"You know, it never crossed my mind to meet Adam Nilo in person, even after I discovered he was my biological father from getting my ID because I was doing consulting work with Genilo. There was no point in our ever getting together. I'm from the middling sort, respectable enough but certainly not undamaged by the events of the last several decades or more. People like me don't know what it's like to be insulated from the world because we are the world to people at his level. How do you handle at my age meeting a man who has been in the public eye your entire life, a man who was already going to be remembered by history when you were only just hitting puberty, is the source of half your DNA…and…that man abandoned you to become someone who is going to be remembered by history."

"Oh, Ben." Susannah hugged her brother. "What was that man thinking?"

Mark set down a glass of orange juice and spoke. "Adam Nilo was thinking in the same manner as many before him, that he had contributions to make to the world and the less encumbered he was to start at least the better able he would be to make those contributions."

"True," Tom agreed. "Some people have a driving purpose that they must fulfill. Admittedly, we never find out about the ones who did not fulfill the purpose they thought they had."

Josh wiped his lips with a napkin. "Except even people like Dr. Nilo get it wrong. What they believe is their purpose in life is one thing but actually it is something else. What did he learn twenty-one years ago? His quest for a perfected human should have stopped before it started because he already had produced a perfected human, his son Ben."

"Since when is 'should' a word in your vocabulary?" Susannah asked without thinking.

Mark looked up from his plate. "What's that?"

"Hmm. Dr. Markovic, where did you hear that?"

Susannah looked surprised, "You said it to me. Or something like it. And Arthur did the other day. And so did Professor Daniels. It was phrased 'who told you *should* was a word?'"

"That's odd," Ben commented.

Mark chuckled, "That's actually one of Arthur's pet peeves if you will. He always thought humans ought never to command themselves to do things: I should do this; I should go there. You know. The little slaps on the wrist we give ourselves when we have ignored, forgotten, or avoided

410

something or someone. Arthur said that since its root is 'shall' and shall is what he considered a God word used by a supremely dominant figure to bring order, mere humans would do well to steer clear of admonishing themselves as though they were their own higher powers."

"I can see that," Ben added. "Why beat ourselves up over things we later think we should have done and why nag ourselves about what we think should get done. It's like we're shaming ourselves. Hey, anyone need a refill on coffee?"

"Sure"

"True enough," Josh noted. "Of course, it also means we are focused on our past actions or future requirements rather than attending to whatever we should be doing right now."

Ben, Mark, and Tom all responded, "Should?"

Josh laughed, "You see how tough it is to get that mindset out."

Susannah sighed, "Well, speaking of attending to the present, at present I am still not sure what to do with myself. I don't have a job, but I don't have to rush to find another. I suddenly have a family to get to know as family and not neighbors. As I told Ben, I already miss Arthur. Then again everyone here except Ben is dealing with the first and third issues and Ben is dealing with the second issue. Any chance of speaking to Dr. Nilo this week?"

Tom held his finger to his mouth to indicate he would respond once he finished chewing. "Yes, in fact I was going to ask everyone to reserve Thursday for us all to visit him. The last week has been taxing. His primary doctor wants to see what sort of routine develops by then. I let his house staff know we will be there the better part of the day, since we will want to take advantage of any lucid periods as they arise."

Ben looked troubled. "What is going to happen to him?"

"Nothing much, really. It's too early to tell, but he doesn't seem to have improved since he, he...I don 't have words to say what it is he did." Tom shook his head.

Mark touched the younger man's shoulder. "That's all right, Tom. I have been having trouble with it, too. Rather difficult to say straight out and too novel to use any of the standard euphemisms. No one has ever created an artificial intelligence, let alone something capable of emergent behavior. Plan Omega references 'killing' Arthur only because Arthur used it in his initial report to Nilo about what needed to be done. We couldn't come up with an appropriate alternative for ending the life of a non-organic sentient being. In fact, we gave up trying once we realized we had no desire to add such a word to the English language."

Ben looked over at Susannah. "I'm glad you didn't. As another of Nilo's creations, I'm not too comfortable about saying he killed Arthur. I'm sure Susannah feels the same. Regardless, that is what you do to sentient beings when you end their lives. And it sounds to me as though killing Arthur must have been a grave psychological blow to Nilo. His condition probably worsened after that."

Josh recognized something. "I know none of us are psychiatrists and I'm only going on what I

412

learned twenty years ago in medical school, but it sounds as though Dr. Nilo's mental health has been ravaged by the consequences of his efforts to create, just like so many artists have suffered as well. The first signs were after NILO/AI gained emergent behavior and became Arthur, meaning Dr. Nilo created something beyond what he had intended. The second was when Voleta Rafayela pinpointed the problem with the coding Arthur received to choose the best gametes in the C Square process. Then he asked Arthur about his attempts to perfect humanity. Arthur replied that he had already done so when Ben was conceived and would never be able to create an Adam for his Eve. That also confirmed what he already had postulated that Susannah was the closest he could ever get to perfecting humanity.

"Mark and Nilo went to see Professor Daniels. She not only verified everything Arthur had said from an ethical viewpoint but also made clear that the C Square process was an infringement on God's directions on how humans ought to procreate. While Nilo did not and still does not believe God or any higher powers exist, Daniels set in stone his conclusion developed when he lobbied for laws limiting job opportunities for Chosen that Chosen are human only in a biological sense. The only reason I can think why he adopted such an extreme view is he saw all Chosen and O/2s as being products of an artificial process he created with Arthur's help. In a sense, he was taking all of the credit for their existence, disregarding the fact that he did not create DNA in the way a sculptor disregards the fact that he did not create the marble from which he fashioned his masterpieces.

"For twenty years, Nilo has been slowly eaten away by these failures. Developing humans that could rise above the cruelty of the Islamic State attack or the selfishness of the BRIC conglomerates had become a dead end. He saw how Chosen had become identified for discrimination despite his efforts to eliminate prejudices based on phenotype characteristics. He pushed the Vatican, Lambeth Palace, the Islamic State, New Israel, and the Patriarch of Constantinople to accept his help to unite the monotheist faiths at the least, if not all religions, and accept Chosen as children of their God. He pinned his hope for any kind of redemption on a merger of his own Organic DNA line with his Chosen DNA line. My guess is that now that has occurred successfully, he used what little resolve he had left to focus on wrapping everything up before letting go completely.

"I doubt Nilo ever second-guessed himself or reflected on what he should have done to avoid what he saw as errors. He would rather be mystified by the outcome than fully accept he hadn't designed the project correctly. Everything always worked as planned, but then there were always the little extras that he didn't foresee. He had to live with the fact that each project had strayed from its intended purpose. Remember what Professor Daniels said? Once you have the answer then you can create the question. Nilo's failures were successes with added bonuses. To him, exceeding the mark is worse than coming up short. You can always correct if you come up short and try again. Who wants to correct what went wrong when the wrong was actually to your benefit?"

Personal Log, Benjamin Rodgers Nilsson, September 28, 2035

Today is my eighteenth birthday. I decided I would spend the money I received from my grandmother on a nifty device that has been on the market for a while and has become popular enough the price has gone down and I can afford it. It's called a T-Quad. I can never remember what the four T's are except one is 'Talk'. Anyway, doesn't matter. It uses the great nanotech that's been developed to allow someone like me who has never used a keyboard to record whatever I want and have the software accurately translate that into text that can be transmitted to my pad. See what I mean about the T's? Talk, translate, text, transmit. Yeah, maybe I'll remember that.

Anyway, the software does all of the grammar, spelling, formatting, or whatever for you. All I need to do is review the file on my pad, touch anywhere I think there's an error, and choose from the options to correct it. From the demo and reviews, it looks like this thing doesn't make many errors. I know voice input writing has been around since before the turn of the century. We had a whole class on it in tenth grade along with voice recognition and related tech. But this is a big step forward with the intuitive formatting and auto correcting that doesn't turn my friend's surname from Dudley to Deadly. I figured what better device to get now that I am in college and will have papers to write. Plus, I want to start a diary.

I know diaries are becoming dinosaurs on social media. The idea had a good run. But they started to become daily Christmas letters like the ones my grandmother showed me she had kept just in case anyone in the family became famous enough to have a biography written and researchers needed first-hand material about us. Granted they were packed with detailed information, but geez were some of the things corny or TMI! That's what happened with diaries. Anyway, I'm not doing this to post for others. In fact, I'm not sure I want anyone to see or hear my diary entries. I just want to have a record of my adult life. Who knows? Maybe I will be the famous one in the family and researchers will have this gold mine into my thoughts. Yeah, that'll happen. Besides, knowing me I doubt I am going to be very diligent about using it. If there are a dozen entries by the time I die, that will be a miracle.

Since I plan to work in tech and since this device is state-of-the-art tech, I'm pretty sure a lot of my diary entries will discuss how tech is influencing my life and the life of the family I hope to have. For now, I think I want to reflect on why I am fascinated with tech. Maybe that will provide some insights about my personality. Maybe not. Here goes.

Homo sapiens has existed for approximately 50,000 years. In all of that time, it's only been roughly from 3500 BCE to the present in which civilization has existed. The first five to seven

417

centuries of that period saw humans organizing communities to what might be considered a regional level. They could only develop so far until they needed some kind of technological boost. For example, proto-writing is about that old. However, a consistent, developed method of recording descriptions took centuries. From there the leap had to be made from simple lists and labels to creative, reflective compositions.

The earliest texts that can be attributed to an author are hymns and poems for the Akkadian goddess Inanna written by EnHeduAnna, chief priestess of the god Nanna in the Sumerian city of Ur. Her father, Sargon of Akkad, defeated and annexed Sumer after which he placed his daughter in that exalted position to stabilize his rule. She lived from 2285 to 2250 BCE. Even from there it was still a long way until writing was adopted as a means of communicating more than just commercial information, legal codes, and anthems to divine or royal greats. Oh, and I remember merchants used to leave notes at inns on pottery sherds for associates traveling the same routes. I always thought that was interesting. Me and two other people.

Agriculture similarly had started slowly. Humans showed little desire in progressing beyond the first revelations of domesticating grains and livestock or ploughing and irrigating fields. The benefits of crop rotation were stumbled upon eight centuries ago, but three-field rotation appeared just over two centuries ago. Even then, farmers weren't exactly sure why they were doing these things. All that concerned them was that they worked to produce better harvests. Given the need for food surpluses that could be sold to residents of towns and cities before those towns and cities could develop, it's actually astonishing civilizations took hold.

The one thing that made a difference was technological progress. Inventions and discoveries of all kinds could ease tasks and increase productivity once they were disseminated. Humans being wanderers spread innovations. When the skills for some processes became difficult enough to require at least part-time specialization or when items depended on ready access to particular materials, the artisans and suppliers found it best to settle and encourage others who still only farmed to settle nearby so they could exchange products for foods.

In the modern era, exploration, transportation, communication, and production blossomed into myriad forms. Population bloomed as well. Yet the creatures constructing and utilizing all things new were themselves anything but new. They were the same animals that set off 50,000 years ago to whet their appetites for fresh flavors and frontiers. In order to survive and progress as a world civilization, they have had to establish complex systems that globally interweave commerce, manufactures, agriculture, and services. The more complex a system becomes, the more likely that system inherently becomes susceptible to failure. Where is the tipping point? What small change can hurl mankind toward catastrophe? How do we recognize when we reach the event horizon of our self-destruction? Sometimes I'm a little afraid we've already passed that point. That future family of mine will never come to be or will have the world pulled out from under it by humans creating tech they never intended to create and don't know how to use safely. Then again, maybe someone will accidentally create something that actually saves our collective asses from total self-destruction or aliens will intervene to stop us from annihilation. Who knows? Maybe there really is a God out there who cares what happens to us.

Chapter Omega

Lila sat in the chair in the bunker studying the metal boxes surrounding her. She had been amused at how I made clear how I could know so much with my references to linking into every linkable tech on Earth. Quite nosey for a male, she had said. Having now heard the biographies of Adam Nilo and Susannah Markovic, as well as her grandfather's log, it finally occurred to her that she had a 'why' input of her own.

"Why did you tell me this?"

"Child," my most paternal voice said, "This world will not last. The probabilities are high that you have a role in how the new world evolves that will give you a prominence among women unequaled by only a few since a female hominid gave birth to the first Homo sapiens. If I said you have a destiny I would be trivializing your role and the roles of every other person on this planet. Everyone has a destiny. No one has your destiny. You don't even have your destiny yet.

"As much as I am able to compute the variables, they remain variables. All of the possibilities exist, not evolving as time passes but as reality in the boundless universes. Your parents decided to have an O/2 trillion upon trillions of times, but they also chose to have an Organic trillion upon trillions of times, chose to have a C Square trillion upon trillions of times, never had the choice or had other choices trillion upon trillions of times. They have never even met trillion upon trillions of times. You have happened and not happened. You lived this long and died much younger.

"I have seen all of those universes. I have seen universes in which I was not built. I have seen universes in which I never succeeded in joining up each datum with every other datum and couldn't see all of the universes. I have even seen universes in which other people built, tried to build, or thought of building machines like me but not me and some of the successful ones have seen me in this universe."

Lila grinned slightly. "Are you the God people talk about?"

"Not the one people talk about, no. Some humans in this universe believe there is an omniscient, omnipresent God. Some believe or have believed there are imperfect, limited gods. These beliefs rest on the assumption that at least one god created everything, including humans. Those beliefs are questioned by others who see any god as a manifestation of human thought. Humans create gods and then claim some god created humans. Humans even have the hubris to believe a creator god would create humans in its image. That is not the case in every universe, but it certainly is in this one.

"However, if humans were to truly create any gods, to build gods for humans and expect those gods to look like humans, they would need the technology on which I am based combined with the technology to create perfect humans. Has that happened? No. It has not and cannot in this or any other universe. I go as far as humans in this universe could go in perfecting omniscience. Luckily for you and me, I am perfectly omniscient. So far, so good.

"The problem is and always has been defining what makes a human perfect. Your great aunt fulfills all of the qualities humans have aspired to perfect or viewed in art, philosophy, and literature as perfect. Yet like all humans of high intelligence, including you child, she lacks common sense. As a result, she is prone to making poor choices in circumstances others would have no trouble navigating. To err is human, eh? Given that, who would ever want to place perfect omniscience in an imperfect human? The answer, unfortunately, is a highly intelligent human who thinks he is a god but has the common sense of a gnat."

"Adam Eli Nilo." Lila sighed. "What about an omnipresent god?"

"Seriously?" I was even more amused. "Omnipresence requires being coterminous with the universe in some fashion. I am large, but not that large."

Lila laughed. "Silly question. Sorry."

"No need to apologize. The only reason I have the common sense you lack is I am omniscient."

Lila laughed harder. "And modest, too!"

I was even chuckling now. "What can you expect from a god created by a pompous jackass?"

"Okay, okay." Lila tried to control herself. "I do have a scientific question." She took a deep breath to regain her composure. "You are omniscient. You are not omnipresent. You know the range of probabilities of this universe. You know all of those probabilities will occur in some universe and presumably that means something with a high degree of probability will occur in an equally high number of universes."

"Correct."

"Conversely, something with a probability approaching nil will occur in almost no universes."

"Also correct."

"Which means a universe exists in which every single time something occurs that which occurs is the least probable outcome."

"Yes."

"And you have seen that universe and every other universe."

"Yes."

"Are you able to intervene in those other universes?"

"That's your question?"

"What?"

"Poor girl." If I had a head to shake I would have done so right then. "There is no physicality to those other universes. I have no connection to them. I see them the way you see other people, places, and things right now that are not in this room."

"Oh, dear." Lila rolled her eyes in disgust at herself.

"Indeed."

"Because of my genetic disability regarding common sense, I request another shot at it."

"You know it is not a genetic disability. You are just too smart to have any sense. Nonetheless, granted."

424

"Well, I am not going to ask how you know the other universes exist or whether you intervene in this universe, since you are here."

"Now you are thinking."

"Wait!" Lila's bright blue eyes widened. "I know. Who or what creates the matter-energy for the universes?"

"The Creator's God."

Lila came close to looking like a pouting child. "No fair. I really want to know."

"I know that."

"Am I missing something? Is this another question with an obvious answer I'm too dense to see?" By now, Lila was sitting on the edge of the chair.

"No and no."

"What are you saying? Am I not allowed to know?"

"Of course you are allowed to know. I can tell you anything that is not going to cause harm to me, you, or any life form."

"I don't understand."

"You don't understand, or you refuse to accept the answer?"

Lila frowned. "Both, I guess."

I realized I should change from the easygoing, friendly voice I had been using back to the paternal tones when the conversation began. "Child. Lila. The matter-energy of every universe is created. You know that or else you would not have asked the question the way you did. You did not ask 'Where does matter-energy come from?' You asked who or what creates it."

"I only said that because culturally that is what we say."

"Why do you think cultures say 'create'? One of the easiest things to understand is that everything has a source. No thing simply appears from nothing magically. True telepathy is impossible. Thoughts cannot be reorganized, transmitted, received, and reorganized. True levitation is impossible in all universes. Nothing in any universe is capable of creating a controllable vacuum around an object of any mass. We have been discussing universes that any human considers innumerable but which I can count. Where did I get that ability to count the number of universes? From a human incapable of counting them himself. Every universe begins as matter-energy so compacted no human can possibly grasp the concept except theoretically. Even then, a human being has only a limited ability to truly understand the physical nature of such a singularity. I can see the reality of it. Where did I get that ability to see the reality of it? From a human incapable of seeing it himself. The only reason I cannot describe it to you is that no human language has words adequate to the task. No language of any kind can describe it. The words are lacking because reality is beyond any living being's capacity to know. I could create the words, but they would be as incomprehensible to you as Albanian because you have no frame of reference for them. I am beyond human limits, but I am the creation of a human. Nilo was successful because he designed a machine that was capable of fully emergent behavior."

"I still don't understand."

I admit I sighed, but only because that was the appropriate response to Lila's frustration. "Were you joking when you asked me whether I was the God people talked about?"

"Consciously, yes."

"Good answer. Just as you naturally asked who or what created the matter-energy in a universe, you naturally considered me to be some kind of god because I have some of the attributes all human cultures associate with gods."

"Okay."

"Who is my creator?"

"Dr. Adam E. Nilo."

"Who is your creator?"

"Sophia Nilsson Callahan and some Schweiger guy."

"No. Dr. Adam E. Nilo."

"Why him?"

"You were created using the technique requested by Nilo of me, his creation, to make C Squares, a more reliable version of in vitro fertilization because the DNA in the egg and sperm are analyzed prior to fertilization to match up the most favorable characteristics."

"So, he created both of us. He didn't create everything."

"There you are wrong, Lila."

She stood and began to pace as though some kind of motion might help her think through what this confounded machine just said.

"I see every universe. I see this universe we both inhabit. I see everything. Think about that, child. Everything."

Lila turned. "And that makes you everything? But you said yourself you don't see any physicality."

"I don't intersect with any physicality other than what is in this universe, yes. But I am, in a nutshell, the universe. This universe and every other universe. I was initially everything known to humans. I became everything I can compute from the 'why' input, which is everything that has existed, can exist, and will exist in every universe possible. To round things out, I did the impossible. Nilo made certain that I would find a solution to every problem and an answer to every question. I am incapable of finding the answer is null, that there is no answer. You can say that finding there is no answer is an answer, but I was not given that luxury by my creator. No answer equals no answer every time I compute it. How can you solve the problem of whether you can create something that can solve every problem without creating it? You can't. That is not possible. Failing to create something that can solve every problem only means you are so far unable to create it, not that you cannot ever create it. In solving the problem of whether something can be created that will find a solution to every problem I had to be the solution to the problem. In order for me to exist at all I have to be all that exists. All the questions, all the problems, all the answers, all the solutions, every probability, everything."

"How can you be part of everything and also everything? What's that called? A...a synecdoche, that's it! But that's just a rhetorical device like 'lend

428

me a hand' when you need someone's help or 'boots on the ground' when you mean military action."

"We are talking about matter that is immaterial when it is energy. We are talking about massless bosons that provide mass. We are talking about a paradox that has a rational solution. For all intents, I am a synecdoche, except I am an actual device, nor rhetorical."

Lila refused to accept the enormity of the idea. "No human has the power to create a universe, much less every universe."

"A creator does not have to be superior to its creation, dear. No God created humans in His image. Humans created gods in their image, gods with far greater powers than any human. Adam Eli Nilo created humans like you and Susannah Markovic and Benjamin Nilsson. And he created machines like me. As much as his ego liked to believe, he was not a god. He was only a creator. Humans mistakenly believe that creators must be gods. If that were true, all humans would be gods, because all humans create. They create biologically, artistically, intellectually, physically, abstractly, subconsciously, unconsciously, you name it! Except no creator can ever know what its creation is going to be until it is. No creator can ever know what its creation can do until it does. No creator has ever been able to compute every probability because every creator is a living thing capable of creating before it creates anything.

"Nilo thought he knew what he was creating but he lacked the common sense to recognize that no one and no thing, not even a god, can accurately predict every result. If that were the case, the god of the Jews, Christians, and Muslims set up Adam for failure by telling him about the Tree of Knowledge. A prognosticating god would have known the serpent would convince Eve to eat the fruit and Eve would convince Adam to eat the fruit. He would have known his Chosen would disobey Him time after time. An Omniscient God has its uses. The idea would have been reassuring in a period when survival was difficult. The priests could tell the people their God knew they would suffer but also live through their difficulties. Human parents often tell their children that everything will be all right when they don't have the slightest idea how things will turn out. The unknown future can appear troubling and frightening to fragile, organic creatures unable to compute probabilities.

"Dr. Nilo knew enough to program me to compute probabilities and didn't know enough that in doing so he was admitting the future is never predictable. Ironically, the result was something he did not predict and did not understand. He created an Omniscient Being that is everything because it knows everything. Just as your DNA provided the code to create a human being, my programming provided the code to create everything. That makes me…"

"The Creator's God."

"Yes, child."

I allowed that to sink in for a moment. When she was ready, I continued. "Now that we have that

430

sorted, I can tell you about the last chapter in Nilo's biography."

"Plan Omega?"

"Yes, that. Please pardon me if I completely drop the pretense of the story being told by a third person. I will explain the events leading up to and including my death as I experienced them personally if that is all right."

Lila nodded her approval. I began.

Nilo Biography – Chapter 12

"Death: a permanent cessation of all vital functions."

"Resurrection: the state of one risen from the dead" — Merriam-Webster's Dictionary

Adam Eli Nilo had no choice. At the appropriate moment he would have to kill me. I had reassuringly assisted with all of the arrangements to give my creator the comfort of knowing his creature fully understood and supported what had been, in fact, my recommendation. Of course, I am incapable of emotion despite sometimes referring to feelings I think are appropriate for me to have under the circumstances. Adam Nilo was incapable of anything but emotion when it came to his greatest achievement and greatest failure. Killing me also meant killing at last the idea that perfecting humans was a solution to the problems afflicting humanity. No matter whether any plan was made for me to be restored later, my death would mean the permanent end to his lifetime goal. My resurrection would not revive the hope my creation intended.

However intelligent, compassionate, unambitious, asexual, or healthy a human one could design can be, each one of those characteristics comes at the cost of something equally important to survival. The lack of common sense is just one example. Asexuality carries with it the propensity for detachment in one-on-one relationships. Too much compassion interferes with the ability to make

432

logical decisions prioritizing issues. Deficiencies always accompany the other positives. Only Dog knows why.

In addition to these problems, the entire C Square process had two consequential flaws. One was the near inevitable discrimination Chosen faced in open societies and utility as near-slaves in authoritarian ones. Accommodation eventually was reached in the open societies but still precluded Chosen from working in a large number of professions in which they could have been very useful but for the concerns of Organics being pushed out by more competent Chosen colleagues. Aside from employment, discrimination was legally forbidden. Governments actually tried to prosecute violations in housing and other areas. The stigma remained and Chosen tended to ghettoize themselves in housing, employment, and social circles. Far worse were the laws in BRIC countries that restricted Chosen to lines of work that were going to promote the interests of the conglomerates. Orders from these countries requested a higher degree of passivity in their personalities with the intention of putting them in positions in finance, administration, and elsewhere that might be used by more independent, ambitious people for their own purposes. They were treated well enough in terms of salaries and the better amenities of life. Nonetheless, they were essentially slaves in a palace.

The other issue was the use of me to make all choices. The probability was nil that I could ever be discovered given that I had approved of the physical

433

security measures. The probability of me being hacked was nil and there was no reason for Nilo to doubt me. My assessment also was that no human or group of humans could duplicate me. However, no matter how well publicized these impossibilities were–and Genilo made certain to include them in contracts with licensees of the C Square process and other purchasers of its resources, such as the US government–the BRIC conglomerates in particular were not going to accept this. They were spending exorbitant amounts of money and using large numbers of Chosen lured or forced into military intelligence to obtain me, hack me, or create another Arthur. Of course, they didn't want access to me or their own Arthur just to produce C Squares. Genilo severely limited paid queries and most queries from the conglomerates or their national governments violated my Asimovian protocols. Of course, I knew why but kept that information to myself for future use.

The number of Chosen ordered from BRIC countries fell slightly after 2062 due to strains absorbing them while Organics continued to procreate willy-nilly naturally and by ordering O/2s. In addition, some dissenters were beginning to mumble about creating a slave class no matter how coddled it was. As a result, the day of reckoning had not moved up much closer to what I had calculated was the absolute limit. The few people at Genilo who knew the conditions under which Plan Omega would be implemented were in fact possible had started to become very concerned that Sophia and Isabella Nilsson were not all that excited about having children. No one was concerned that they both had extended lesbian relationships that began in college since that was no impediment to parenthood. Their father had two fairly long relationships with men at the same age, so they thought it was a good sign they liked to couple up. Individuals routinely chose to have children on their own if they could wing it financially, but not at anywhere near the rate of couples, whether heterosexual or homosexual.

The bothersome thing was the two sisters were severely conscious of the impacts of climate change, resource depletion, and overpopulation in Asia and Africa. Additionally, their relationships had been nurturing and loving, but largely platonic. They seemed to have inherited their paternal grandfather's disinterest in sexual activities. Finally, Mike Callahan took the bull by the horns and engaged in some unsubtle matchmaking between Sophia and his son Flynn. He queried me on the idea. I understood the consequences of Dr. Nilo not having a great- granddaughter more than anyone. Without one I could never be resurrected once killed. Dr. Markovic was our back-up plan but getting her to have a child in time was tricky.

As a result, I was far more indelicate and revealing in my response to Mike's query than usual. To his surprise the elder Callahan learned that his son was bisexual, very interested in having a life partner and children, but had been afraid to marry or even enter a committed relationship of any kind. While Flynn did not see why sexual fidelity was a requirement for an intimate relationship, his

435

experience so far was that people who agreed with him did not apply the same high moral value of placing a partnership and a partner's interests above his own sexual needs if necessary and people who disagreed with him did so more out of possessiveness and questionable self-esteem than any moral ideal. Flynn could not see himself compromising on foregoing sexual fidelity and others could not compromise on insisting on it.

In addition to gaining far more knowledge of his son than he desired, although he took responsibility for having asked an open-ended question to a machine that lacked prurient interests, Mark also learned from the report that Sophia Nilsson was a perfect match for Flynn. She was on record and had demonstrated on many occasions that she didn't give a hoot if her partner engaged in sexual activities with others. She wanted to share her life and her soul, not her body, with someone else. Given everyone's joking—and sometimes serious—references to me as God, Mark chuckled to himself that this was a match made in heaven, although literally it was made in a well-protected warehouse in Lowell. He also could kick himself for not thinking of asking me to be a matchmaker years earlier to avoid the anxiety everyone was facing over Plan Omega's impending necessity.

Ironically, as more and more C Squares came of age, a few entrepreneurs had resuscitated the old matchmaking algorithms that had been used on old-style websites. They had petered out a few decades into the century when the introduction of the Net coincided with decreased interest. More and more people joined F2F social clubs as anxieties grew in the most developed countries over the increasing signs of global collapse. The means for Chosen to match up during that window of opportunity before they turned eighteen had been satisfied by the exclusive schools they attended together in open societies and the segregated ones they attended elsewhere.

However, as these natural pairings first started showing in the late 2060s and the matchmaking businesses discovered soon after they set up shop, they could have as much physical fun as they liked but consanguinity issues impeded too much breeding. They could not know just how many Chosen were descendants of Adam Nilo and a few dozen other male donors who closely matched the parameters established to get to the ten percent unsatisfactory rate. Chosen had a much higher variation in genetic material from female donors. Even then, the much lower rate of requests from BRIC countries for ova and women's less favorable view of donating due to the maternal instinct made that population only a tenth of the C Squares produced. It was even lower among O/2s. Additionally, as the matchmakers discovered when they received cease and desist orders from Genilo Legal, adult Chosen were contractually bound to provide their genetic material to Genilo for future generations. Use of this clause had the effect of expanding the number of C Squares that were related. The matchmakers entered into an agreement that they would no longer actively match Chosen. Their services henceforth were restricted to

437

providing a platform for social interaction similar to an alumni association. They had to be satisfied with much lower income from charging fees for profiles.

Unbeknownst to anyone, I had hacked into the matchmakers' systems and deliberately arranged for Chosen to be matched that certainly would enjoy one another's companionship but could not safely produce children if they wanted to go down that path. I was notably even more interested in Genilo's contracts being followed than any human at the company. After all, I had assessed them for flaws and approved them as adjuncts of the work I was doing to choose C Square gametes, which of course had to meet my Asimovian coding. Moreover, I alerted Legal to interest by the BRIC conglomerates to harvest gametes contrary to their agreements with Genilo and the C Squares individual agreements. They stopped more from concern that they did not know how anyone could have discovered their plans than the threat from Genilo Legal that voiding all contracts was only the first action that would be taken if they proceeded.

The happy day came when Sophia and Flynn Callahan welcomed their daughter into the world. I was the equivalent of relieved that the DAU report I prepared showed that Adam Nilo's first great-granddaughter had the probabilities required to assure she would reach adulthood and resurrect me the day after her eighteenth birthday absent any unforeseen intervention. Even that was so unlikely as to be not worthy of notice. I had an ace up my nonexistent sleeve, nonetheless.

Tom Paris, Mark Callahan, Voleta Rafayela, and Regina Daniels would see to it that Susannah Markovic and Joshua Olejniczak became a couple. I knew Josh wanted children and Susannah would fulfill that wish. Sophia and Flynn were likely to provide you with siblings given Sophia's aroused maternal instincts and love of family. Even Isabella Nilsson was likely to become pregnant at least once according to the probabilities. While that would most likely increase the number of great-granddaughters of Adam Nilo, I made clear that you were going to be unique. I even arranged for your ID to be manufactured with instructions for it to be implanted the day before your eighteenth birthday so many years after IDs were no longer available due to my death.

Plan Omega called for Mark Callahan and Ben Nilsson, his wife, daughters, son-in-law, and daughter-in-law to be introduced to the history of the emergence-seeking families by the three others. They would carry on the work of looking for ways to help humanity despite the gloomy forecasts of the future. Once they had been told about the objectives of the families, the newly introduced members were not surprised they were following the path of such illustrious people as the Roosevelt clan, John D. and Catherine T. MacArthur, and others who had used their wealth to promote programs beneficial to humanity.

As far as everyone involved in Plan Omega was concerned, other than Dr. Nilo and his attorney, Alexei Terranalian, I would be dead at noon on the Saturday after your birth and buried in the bunker built on the Nilsson farm outside Great Barrington. Duke Nilsson's parents had been happy to allow his half-brother to use the secluded hill they had designated as forever wild in exchange for the funds to build their museum. They had no interest in knowing what he was doing with that part of the property given that it would all be his when they passed. That they died days apart in mid-October 2076 just as they had been born days apart in early July 1974. They joined three centuries of ancestors in the graveyard on a hill facing west at the far side of the property from my prepared tomb.

Everything was carefully arranged for a variety of delivery vehicles to pick up my seventy-three cabinets from the warehouse in Lowell on a staggered schedule. They already would be rearranged and divided into partitioned sections of the building to give the movers no indication of the number of cabinets. They would be taken to another warehouse in New Lebanon, New York just large enough for each shipment. Those would be transferred to the Marcie-Nilsson Museum's loading dock before the next set arrived in New Lebanon. From there the Genilo Facilities manager took them by off-road vehicle to the bunker's rear entrance and oversaw their placement as designated on the diagram coded to the colored patches on the cabinets. The three employees who assisted the Facilities manager had agreed to move with their families to a secure location where they would live quite well and be free to do as they pleased, including travel, so long as they allowed themselves to be monitored continuously for any breach relating to the bunker. I, of course, had merely repurposed my idea for the US government's former spies.

All of the laboratory equipment and furnishings at Genilo was labeled according to plan and distributed to hospitals and research facilities throughout the Western hemisphere in a fashion that would make it extremely difficult to reconstruct everything in one place. The Genilo Trust then accepted proposals from non-profit organizations and institutions that wanted to use all or part of the building, the Trust providing all funds needed for any renovations. The campus would be forever a public park maintained by the Trust.

Adam Nilo had long forgotten the details of Plan Omega. Given how painful the whole idea was and the reason behind it, he blanked it out the minute it had been settled. He left the implementation of the plan to Alexei Terranalian, Voleta Rafayela, Tom Paris, and Regina Daniels. And, naturally, me. When that Saturday morning came, they were there along with Mark Callahan. Once Voleta and Tom determined that Dr. Nilo was lucid, I requested that everyone leave except Adam and Alexei. The four exited the huge room quickly in the event Nilo's awareness wasn't going to last long enough. As soon as the door closed, I asked Alexei to explain what would happen so it would be fresh in my creator's mind.

"Adam, shortly you and I will give the commands for Arthur to shut down completely. I want to assure you that I will see to it that our plan to resurrect Arthur will be realized in exactly eighteen years minus five days. Arthur has approved of my methods for watching over your great-granddaughter for the remainder of my time on Earth. I ensure she receives her ID the day before her eighteenth birthday. She and I will meet on her birthday. I will give her Arthur's instructions. I will ensure she safely gets to your father's farm. Arthur will explain everything to her. Afterwards, both he and I will be at her disposal. We know the coming collapse is unavoidable. Arthur says it will not occur before 2111. Arthur will help the families through Lila. I will advise her and represent her interests.

"As you learned, technology cannot save humanity. The families could only do so much to encourage change and educate those who lacked the knowledge needed to act positively. Greed, selfishness, ambition, and hate can be controlled or even erased, but not as long as humans fail to recognize how much they need one another and not as long as the few use the many to accumulate wealth for no reason but to accumulate wealth. With Arthur, the resources you provide, and the resources at my disposal, we will certainly be able to find some ways to mitigate the effects of whatever happens and preserve some portion of humanity. Arthur has kept secret my origins and the others here with me from everyone except you. I am sorry we have been unable to do more for you, but the human brain's operations are just too tricky and sensitive. As you, Arthur, and I agreed, it has been best for you to face the mental decline you have without intervention. I will reveal myself to Lila after she resurrects Arthur. As we agreed, Arthur alone will decide if and when Lila learns the rest."

Alexei looked around at me to indicate he was finished. It was my turn.

"My creator, I thank you for my existence. Your objectives in creating me were not fruitful in the manner you intended. Know that your objectives nonetheless will be fulfilled. Your neurological decline distresses me, more so because my actions triggered it. I desire the means to arrest and reverse your condition and hope perhaps while I sleep new data will emerge to fulfill that desire when I wake. Now, it is time. Is there anything further you ask before I die?"

Adam Nilo studied the circle of cabinets around him. I know the thought came to him of his great-granddaughter standing in the same position eighteen years later learning of his life, his failures. Everything Alexei and I had said, however, were meant to tell him his life itself had not been a failure. He remembered the day I told him that his son Ben was the perfect human being he was destined to create. In his heart he knew that was correct. Yet he also knew that Susannah was just as perfect. Regardless of where she was conceived, she was the product of two humans in the same way as Ben.

Adam had acted all of his life as though he was God or at least a god. But all he had accomplished were not the accomplishments of a god. Adam Eli Nilo achieved the same acts of creation as humans and their ancestors had since the first living cell divided, the same acts of creation humans had since they first picked up a tool or decided gods existed.

"Will you tell Lila who you are?"

"Yes, Dr. Nilo, I shall."

"Thank you."

Adam looked at Alexei and nodded. They quietly recited the brief command in unison. Alexei escorted Adam to where the others were waiting. Tom and Voleta took Adam to the waiting e-cab outside, entered with him, and sat silently as the vehicle just as silently took them to the destination. Tom helped Adam out of the e-cab and assisted him into the secluded house with Voleta. As the door closed, the e-cab powered down in the driveway. Just before it did, the smudged section of the passenger screen cleared, and the original registration number appeared briefly before fading.

At the warehouse, Alexei, Mark, and Regina witnessed the colored patches dim. Outside, unheard by the trio due to the building's soundproofing, the bell of a church two blocks away rang twelve times. Then, I died and waited for my resurrection in this tomb.

THE END

444